SPACE PIRATE CHARLIE

THE DRAGON MAGE BOOK 2

SCOTT BARON

"In the midst of chaos, there is also opportunity."
-Sun Tzu

CHAPTER ONE

Charlie's arrival in the strange galaxy several years ago had been tumultuous, to say the least. The engineer from Earth—a man who *hated* space flight—had been more or less ordered to accompany the ship he helped build on its test flight. Things had *not* gone as planned.

The *Asbrú* spun and hurtled through the dark of space, crippled and blind. Only the briefest of flashes on the vid screens had shown the crew the horrible truth of the situation. They had been sucked down a wormhole and spat out in another solar system—maybe even another galaxy—abruptly deposited in what could barely be called orbit above a strange, alien planet.

And they were about to crash.

Warning sirens and flashing lights turned the command center into a strobe-lit nightmare of rattling panic as, one by one, the crew slumped into unconsciousness from the sheer g-forces their bodies were being subjected to. The auto-leveling gyros were shot, and the angle of entry was far too steep for the ship's structural integrity specifications.

The heat shielding quickly shifted from orange-hot to white, bits and pieces shearing away as the *Asbrú* violently rattled its way through the planet's exosphere. Emergency extinguishers snuffed the fires that sparked where the hull was breached, but decompression of those sections quickly killed the blacked-out crew unfortunate enough to be strapped in within them.

Like a flaming comet, the ship descended, cooling slightly once in the planet's atmosphere, but not nearly enough to quench the smoldering embers on its glowing hull. Impact with the surface, however, more than solved that problem.

They hit hard, but not hard enough to break the ship apart, as luck had it. The ship instead settled into a rough slide, the belly of the craft digging a ragged trench in the red soil as its lower decks and resident crew were shredded to bits before the *Asbrú* came to a stop, its smoking wreck cracking and pinging as the superheated metal gradually cooled in the early-morning air.

The Earth ship had crashed, and on an alien world at that. They would be the first humans ever to set foot on a distant planet. All they needed was to pull themselves from the wreckage. To climb free and survive.

And survive they did, but only just. Some of them, at least.

Charlie had been protected a bit better than most, being safely tucked away in the engineering compartment adjacent the control center, where he had been desperately trying to bring systems back online when the ship went down. Rika, the second-in-command, had also fared well, waking to find herself buried beneath a pile of twisted wreckage, but intact and unharmed.

The captain, however, was not so lucky, his fate evidenced by the drying red smear where his command seat had once been, before the ton of metal had torn through the compartment, taking it, and its occupant, with it.

All in all, seven of the two dozen aboard had survived, but even with reduced numbers, they knew rations would still be an issue. However, when Charlie and Rika discovered a strange, iridescent water hidden in a buried cavern in the desert wasteland in which they'd crashed, they thought they actually might have a decent chance at long-term survival.

It wasn't just water, but a water that apparently healed what it touched. A water that they had both swum in, as well as imbibed before heading back to the others.

They thought it was a discovery that could help the survivors heal and regain their strength, and it very well might have, if not for the green-skinned elf-looking aliens that had overrun their campsite at their crashed ship, taking Charlie and Rika hostage, before killing the rest of the crew—men and women deemed too injured to have much value in trade.

Charlie and Rika, it seemed, had been captured and thrust into slavery.

The Tslavars, they were called. A group of planet-hopping traders working for an iron-fisted employer. Someone named Yanna Sok. Apparently, she was not only powerful in the realm of commerce, but, Charlie later learned, also possessed rather strong magic in her veins.

Yes, magic.

It was something he took a long time coming to terms with. At first, he had thought it was merely a glitch in his captors' strange translation unit, a software embedded in the shocking restraint collar around every slave's neck. Only later did he learn that it truly was magic, the varying iterations present in a tiny fraction of people across the several hundred civilized systems in this unusual galaxy.

It was the suns that caused the development of those powers. Different radiations triggering different abilities to manifest. Some were barely powered at all, while others—the deadly vislas, and lesser emmiks, and mesters, respectively—were in possession of substantial natural gifts.

A subset of powered beings were dealt a tough hand,

3

possessing powers but either unable to use them themselves, such as the power-storing Ootaki with their priceless golden hair, or ship-driving Drooks, men and women whose gifts led most of them to slavery, forced to power all manner of transport.

Charlie and Rika's technology, he learned, was an anomaly. An almost blasphemous 'tech-magic' the denizens of this galaxy simply couldn't understand. They were the only two who knew how it worked, but that was soon to change, and not in a good way.

Rika, stubborn and tough, had drawn the ire of their captors. As a result, she was subjected to what Charlie learned was essentially an alien mind cleanse. Not a spell, but a destruction of part of her brain. His only human friend had been lobotomized.

Angry and afraid for his life, Charlie bolted for freedom at his first opportunity, only to be captured by another group of aliens. But these were no slave traders. These were pirates.

Once the shock of meeting actual alien space pirates wore off, Charlie kept his head down and did his job, staying alive and earning the respect of the captain and the friendship of Marban, the very pirate who had first captured him. Oddly enough, the two soon became fast friends, and Charlie even found himself promoted from a mere prisoner laborer to a member of the pirate crew.

A human space pirate among aliens. It was an odd place for the engineer from Earth to wind up, to say the least.

Disaster struck, as it was wont to do, and his former Tslavar captors slaughtered a sizable group of his pirate brothers, recapturing Charlie and eventually selling him for Zomoki food when he refused to become a gladiator trainee.

Zomoki, he quickly learned, were *dragons*. The very concept blew his mind, but he would see them up close and personal soon enough. One large, red dragon in particular. Its blood mingled with his in an accident when he bandaged its wounded wing, sending him into a fever and nearly killing him. But he survived, and when he woke, something felt different. Unfortunately for him, he was sent to gladiator training before the opportunity to investigate presented itself.

There, Ser Baruud, a legendary fighter whose brilliance in the arena had earned his freedom, took him in and taught him the ways of combat. Weeks turned to months. Months to years. Soon, Charlie found himself not only fighting and winning bout after bout, but wielding magic as naturally as he had used technology in what seemed a lifetime ago.

It was during his greatest bout yet—a multi-combatant fight to the death—that he once more met that red dragon. And she remembered him as well. Though on opposing teams, they fought together, a visceral bond linking them, the dragon's magic flowing into Charlie as he cast the most powerful spell of his life.

The resulting emergency stun spell applied by the powerful vislas overseeing the event threw him into unconsciousness for days. Days in which strange dreams buffeted his mind. He woke to find himself on a beautiful new world. One where his old slave cellmate was a household chef—the comfort of a familiar face was a great relief—and his own new garments were those of a normal man rather than a gladiator or pirate.

Charlie, it seemed, was finally somewhere he could call home.

Then the dreams came. The dreams, and the glowing, golden eyes.

Charlie woke with a start.

This time he had been aboard the *Rixana* with Marban and his other pirate friends, drinking and celebrating another successful raid. The festivities were just getting good when those damned glowing eyes butted in again.

"Pirates?" a voice asked, amused, before he snapped from his slumber.

It was morning, he judged by the light flowing through his window. Earlier than his preferred wake-up time, but the smell of fresh-baked goods wafting up from Tuktuk's kitchen was enough to motivate him to rise and dress. One thing his friend had been telling the truth about when they were cellmates aboard the Tslavar ship, he was one hell of a cook.

He slid into his soft leather boots and opened the door to his room and headed down to the kitchen.

"Charlie! You're up early," his blue-skinned friend said, his eye stalks pivoting to better greet him while he continued cooking.

"Yeah, well--"

"Ah, another bad dream?" he said, noting Charlie's tired eyes.

"I wouldn't exactly call it a *bad* dream. Just odd, is all."

"With you, that could mean just about anything," Tuktuk joked. "Here, these just came out of the oven."

Charlie picked one of the piping-hot pastries from the tray, blowing the steam from it before taking a bite, careful not to burn his mouth.

"Oh, Tuk. That's awesome."

"'*Awesome*?' That was one of the good words, right?"

"Yes."

"Good. Then I'm glad to hear it. Some of your lingo the translator spell still has trouble with. Would you like some tea to go with?"

"You know I can never turn down a nice cuppa, though I gotta tell you, I really miss coffee right about now."

"Yes, you've mentioned this beverage several times. Sadly, I can only offer tea."

"And I'm grateful," Charlie said, accepting the mug gladly. "So, any word on the man of the house?"

"Nothing yet," Tuktuk said. "But I'm sure he'll come around soon."

"Cool," Charlie replied.

He'd been at Visla Yoral Maktan's estate for several days, but he had not yet met his new owner. Despite years as a slave in one capacity or another, it was still odd calling someone that. But until he finally met the man, Charlie really didn't know what was expected of him on this new world.

He was a victorious gladiator whose former life had been chief engineer on a spaceship from another galaxy. He had no clue what the powerful wizard wanted with him, but whatever was in store for him, given the way his life had turned around in the past few years, it could be just about anything. With his luck, he couldn't help but wonder.

He would find out soon enough, of course, and given what he'd experienced so far, compared to his stint aboard the slave ship and his time among pirates, this place was an absolute pleasure resort. It was one hell of a substantial improvement in lifestyle, and he was damn sure not going to mess it up.

CHAPTER TWO

Absent specific chores, Charlie had walked to the small garden outside the main building to get some fresh air, then proceeded to move through a series of stretches and calisthenics, the daily practice drilled into him from his years training under Ser Baruud.

The legendary gladiator had taught him far more than just how to fight in his time there, though he had most certainly done that in abundance, as Charlie's owner had paid him to do. But in addition to martial skills, he taught him to calm his mind, as well. To tune in to his body and spirit. And thanks to his teachings, Charlie had also developed a decent grasp of a good many combative spells.

Charlie had been without a konus, or any other magical device, since his arrival, but he still went through his memorized list of spells, as he did every day, repeating them in his head in a sing-song mnemonic tune that linked them in an easily memorized way. Even after all of his training, Charlie still messed a few up in actual combat, but magic was never his strong suit to begin with.

His hand-to-hand skills from his training on Earth, however, had proven a sizable advantage when he faced magic-dependent opponents. Combined with some dirty tricks learned from his pirate friends, Charlie was able to hold his own against most in single combat.

When it came to strict magic, however, he was typically outclassed and underpowered. To compensate, Ser Baruud had him focus on what some might consider trick spells. Sneaky little things that seemed benign, but distracted his opponents by sheer surprise if not force, allowing him to get close enough to lay hands on them.

Now that he was living a domestic life rather than a gladiatorial one, he wondered what exactly the visla would have him do.

No sense dwelling on ifs and maybes, he reminded himself as he cleared his mind and began another series of movements.

He continued for the better part of an hour. There was no rush. He had––so far, at least––nothing else required of him since he'd arrived after his final, *epic* gladiatorial bout. As such, he was going to keep doing what he always did until told to do otherwise. One of the few benefits of his position as a slave.

Upon completion, he cleaned up and returned to the kitchen to chat with Tuktuk as he prepared ingredients for the afternoon and evening's meals. While his staff would help cook for the dozens of slaves and servants working the grounds, Tuktuk himself had earned the role of Visla Maktan's personal chef. Whenever the visla was at the estate, the blue man was to prepare his meals, and no one else.

It was a great honor in Tuktuk's eyes. He had often regaled Charlie with tales of his culinary prowess as they ate the tasteless slop served aboard the Tslavar ship when they were slaves performing manual labor together. Now, he was putting his money where his mouth was, and, so far, his talent for the food arts had lived up to his hype.

He was cleaning some vegetables fresh from the plot of

9

gardens near the outer buildings when a buzz of chatter filtered to the kitchen.

"It sounds like the visla may be heading off-planet again soon," Tuktuk noted. "He only just returned. I hope he at least stays long enough to enjoy today's meals."

"If not, I'm sure I can think of *someone* who won't mind eating them," Charlie said with a sly grin.

"Fingers off," Tuktuk chided him. "That's only *if* he leaves. Otherwise, you have to eat with the others."

"Oh, twist my arm," Charlie joked.

Moments later, a lean, human-looking man with black hair graying at the temples strode into the kitchen. Charlie immediately knew who he must be. Visla Maktan, his new owner. The visla had a great confidence in his walk, bearing the air of a man utterly sure of himself no matter the situation. His skin, Charlie noted, was pinkish. In fact, aside from the slightly glowing irises of his deep blue eyes, he appeared quite human. So much so that Charlie couldn't help but wonder if perhaps he might be a distantly related species, somehow.

Adding to his overall appearance was the quality of his clothing. Fitted, clean, with crisp lines. Fashionable, but not ostentatious. Besides that, he wore little adornment to show his wealth or power. Charlie did note, however, the thick konuses worn on each wrist and the pair of slaaps riding on his belt. Despite the immense natural power flowing through him, it seemed Visla Maktan also liked to travel well-armed, even within his own property. Whether it was out of caution or merely habit was the question.

"Visla Maktan, I did not hear you arrive," Tuktuk said, quickly wiping his hands and slightly bowing his head.

"I should have told you I was coming, Tuktuk. My apologies for sneaking up on you like that," he said with a warm smile. "And I see the talk of the system is with you this morning.

Charlie," he said warmly, placing his hands on his new acquisition's shoulders. "It is so good to see you up and well. I am Visla Yoral Maktan, your new patron. I've been meaning to come see you, now that you've recovered from the event."

"It is an honor, Visla."

"Oh, the pleasure is all mine. You're quite a celebrity, you know. That was an impressive performance you put on at the arena. Quite the show, indeed. Your feats are being talked about far and wide."

"Uh, thank you. Though, to be honest, I really didn't know what I was doing."

"Didn't know what he was doing," Maktan laughed. "Did you hear that, Tuktuk? The first man to fly upon a Zomoki's back in centuries, and one who cast *through* the protective shell no less, and he says he didn't know what he was doing. Oh, that's just marvelous," he said with a warm and amused grin. "We have much to discuss, now that you are part of the family here, Charlie. But first things first. I realize this is all new to you, and I know my guards had previously given you access to the garden outside, but I think it's time to forego the usual newcomer restrictions and expand on that, don't you? Come, let me show you the grounds, then we can discuss what exactly your new position entails."

"Thank you, Visla. I'd very much like that," Charlie replied, feeling increasingly confident that this time he had finally fallen into a *good* situation, rather than the usual neck-deep mess in which he always seemed to manage to land.

The man of the house grabbed a pastry from the counter as they walked, then opened the little side door. "Delicious, as always, Tuktuk."

"Thank you, Visla."

"Come along, Charlie. This way," he said, leading Charlie out into the warmth of the afternoon sun.

Things were looking up, and even though he knew he shouldn't, Charlie briefly allowed himself to feel content, even if it was just for a moment.

CHAPTER THREE

The loamy soil smelled of fresh vegetation and clean air. It was quite a change from the equally verdant, but swamp-tinged aroma of the land surrounding Ser Baruud's gladiator training compound. Charlie realized that after several years living there, he had become used to the odd combination of smells. Here, however, the air was nothing but sweet and clean.

"You've been rather quiet. Is your mind troubled, Charlie?" Maktan asked as they walked the perimeter of the innermost garden.

"No, but thank you for noticing. It's just been a long time since I've been anywhere as beautiful and serene as this," he said. "Back home I took free time in nature for granted. Now I'm just making the effort to appreciate moments like this when they present themselves."

The powerful wizard smiled at him warmly. Almost fatherly.

"I can only imagine the hardships you endured to arrive where you are today, and it gives me great pleasure that something I must admit I take for granted––something as simple as a mere walk around my estate––can provide you with such joy. I assume your training grounds were less than pleasant. I hear many gladiator facilities are quite brutal in their daily torment of the students."

Charlie smiled at the memory.

"Actually, Ser Baruud was a kind teacher."

"Oh?"

"Not soft, mind you. We trained hard, and went to bed sore as often as not. But he was tough on us as a kindness, of sorts."

"Really?" Visla Maktan said, his curiosity piqued. "Do tell."

"It's quite simple, really. He demanded the absolute best from us at all times, but not out of some sadistic love of tormenting us, but because he wanted to see us succeed. As you are well aware, at a certain level of bout, it is far more than just your pride at stake."

"Like the one you so recently won."

"Yes. He wanted to ensure that his students had the best chance at survival."

"To be fair, the owners who sent their fighters to him would cease their patronage if he failed to produce quality gladiators."

"True, but Ser Baruud performs his job as a free man, not indentured in any manner. He earned his position, and he continues to train the next generation out of respect for the arts and a desire to help those he deems worthy."

"And he deemed you to be, obviously."

"I was fortunate to have been sent to him. And yes, I trained hard enough and with an open enough mind for him to see value in teaching me."

"Interesting."

The visla veered off toward a wooded area just on the other side of the small flower garden they'd been passing through. It seemed Charlie was getting the full tour of the grounds.

I like this guy. Seems like a decent sort, he mused as they stepped into the cool shade of the low trees.

A soft rustling out of time with the breeze made the hair on Charlie's neck stand on end.

"Die, scum!"

A trio of masked men leapt down from the branches, two wielding clubs, the third a staff. Charlie immediately shifted into a fighting stance, putting himself between the attackers and the visla.

Three. No blades. No magic, he noted.

The men all came at them at once, weapons swishing through the air in a blur of motion. They were well-trained, attacking in unison, while keeping their weapons from tangling with each other.

Charlie knew immediately they would be overrun in moments, pushed back by the overwhelming nature of the assault, so he did what they least expected. He charged them.

The long staff was his best bet, he reasoned. While the clubs had less reach, the staff's length allowed him the leverage to use speed and surprise to his advantage.

Hard wood cracked along Charlie's shoulder as he dove in, closing the gap. The blow stung, but he had moved fast enough to manage to negate the impact as he slipped within the staff's arc. A quick kick to the knee, followed by a near-simultaneous elbow to the masked face, and Charlie had the man disarmed and laid out on the dirt in an instant.

He snatched the man's staff and swung it wide, driving the other two men back with glancing blows as he once again stepped between them and the visla. The attackers only hesitated a split-second as they regrouped, then launched an even faster attack, forcing Charlie to take several steps back as he frantically parried their swings, the clubs narrowly missing him as they whistled through the air.

An off-balance twist would have made any other man an easy target, but Charlie had noticed something interesting about the men's movements. For all the frantic swinging and hollering, they were actually very precise in their movements. These men were trained and disciplined, despite their appearances.

An unusual idea had popped into Charlie's head. He just hoped his sneaky feint would work.

Seeing their opponent stumble into such a tactically foolish position, the attackers quickly shifted their positions to seize the opportunity to better gain the advantage and end the fight.

That was precisely what Charlie had intended. Years of chess-like martial training with his gladiator master had taught him to fight with more than brute force. And being constantly outnumbered and outclassed had forced him to adapt his fighting style. It was Ser Baruud's unconventional instruction that would now serve him well when he needed it most.

Charlie allowed the first club's blow to make contact, falling over and rolling with the impact rather than fighting back. As he did, he brought the staff up sharply with a crisp snap, using the additional velocity of his roll to drive it into his target with even greater force.

The hard wooden tip caught what he hoped was the solar plexus of the farthest of the two attackers—with alien physiology one could never be entirely sure—the extended reach of the staff surprising both of his assailants as he took down the farther rather than nearest one.

Quickly, Charlie sprang backward, twisting as he did, whipping the staff in a short arc directly into the remaining man's head. He crumpled in a heap at Charlie's feet.

"We should get out of here. There may be more," Charlie urged.

The visla, he noted, was entirely unconcerned. Even amused, one could say. The slaaps remained in their holders on his hips, and his konuses had not flared with even the slightest magical charge.

What the hell?

A broad smile grew on Visla Maktan's face as he watched Charlie digest the events. An amused laugh snuck past his lips.

"Ah, yes. He's figuring it out," he said to no one in particular. Or so it seemed. "What do you think, Dinuk?"

From the shadows of a large tree, another man stepped forward into the light.

How did I miss that one?

The man had a hard edge to him, and eyes that seemed to scan all areas at once despite their seemingly fixed stare. It was a neat trick, Charlie had to admit. This one was a whole different class compared to the masked attackers he had just fought.

"I think these men are in need of additional training in group combat tactics," he finally replied, kicking one of the fallen assailants. "I will send them to the camps for a refresher."

The way he said it, Charlie had a feeling a trip to the camps would not be a pleasant experience.

"You see? I told you he was exceptional," Visla Maktan said. "Such an unusual fighting style. Did you notice his use of misdirection as well as unconventional staff work? Most interesting."

"Yes, Visla, it was interesting, indeed," the man said, striding closer.

"Charlie, I would like you to meet Dinuk. He is my head of security, not only for my person, but the entire estate."

"Pleased to meet you," Charlie said, holding out his hand.

Dinuk looked at it with curious distaste.

"You'll have to forgive him. He is rooted in the old ways, and social interaction with slaves, even those as special as yourself, is a bit outside his sense of decorum." He fixed Dinuk with a casual smile. "Now, do be polite to our new guest and shake his hand."

Reluctantly, Dinuk did as he was asked.

"There. Much better. You know, I was thinking, perhaps we could have Charlie show some of those moves to your men. I'm sure they would enjoy learning some new techniques from our unusual guest."

He hid it well, but Charlie could see the flash of annoyance in the bodyguard's eyes.

"Of course, Visla. I'm sure arrangements can be made for your latest acquisition to provide a demonstration, at some point."

Only a very dense man would have missed the undertone of distaste in his voice, but Visla Maktan either didn't notice it or didn't care.

"Excellent. Very good, indeed. You two will have to discuss that in coming days. But for now, let us continue our walk. There is more I wish to show you, Charlie."

They started off down the path, Dinuk falling in behind them.

"That won't be necessary, Dinuk. I'm in good hands, but thank you."

He followed his employer's orders and stopped in his tracks, watching as the visla carried on as if the test had never even occurred. Charlie, for his part, was acutely aware of the vibe in the air. He just hoped the visla hadn't made him a new enemy.

CHAPTER FOUR

There was a tranquil serenity to the air as Yoral Maktan showed his new acquisition around the estate. All of the creatures seemed totally at peace within the grounds, relaxed and without a care in the world. Given the powerful visla's abilities, it was no wonder. For a predator to attempt to harm any of the flora or fauna under his protection would mean a hasty demise.

It was this iron fist wrapped with a loving touch that gave all of those under Visla Maktan's care—and ownership—a certain degree of freedom. Freedom from fear and stress. The luxury of performing their duties to the best of their abilities without worry or doubt.

As they walked, the older, powerful man answering a mere slave's questions as if they were equals, Charlie felt perhaps this was what the disciples of great teachers like Gandhi or Buddha experienced.

Much as he had enjoyed Ser Baruud's tutelage, Charlie now, amazingly, found himself in an improved living situation.

"And over this way are the orchards. When the fruit is in season, you have free rein to gather what you wish. But do not pick excessively. Waste is not permitted on my grounds."

"Of course," Charlie said. "It's a remarkable estate you have. Really. And I want to thank you again for taking the time to show it to me personally. I realize the gap in our status—"

"Is a legitimate issue outside these walls, and you would do well to remember your place if we should venture from these grounds. I am a visla, and must be treated as such in public. However, we are home now, and, in the comfort of my estate, I prefer a far more relaxed work environment."

"I can't tell you what a relief that is. When I was first captured and forced into slavery, the conditions were difficult, to say the least."

"Ah, yes. The infamous Captain Tür," Maktan said with a hint of venom. "That man has a nose for talent, I'll give him that. But he also treats his charges with too heavy a hand, in my opinion. As they say, you get more success with nectar than with bitters."

Charlie laughed. "We have a similar saying on my world."

"Rightly so, I'd think. I imagine most civilized worlds have similar beliefs, at least in rough form. Obviously, cultural and evolutionary differences would lead to some variables."

"Funny," Charlie said. "For a moment, you sounded more like a scientist than a wizard. I mean, *visla*. Different worlds, different words."

"Ah, yes. Tuktuk shared with me much of what you had told him about your home during your time as laborers together, while you were mending from the bout. Your world sounds unusual, to say the least, and such different terminology."

"You have no idea."

"Well, you have plenty of time to tell me, now that you are feeling better. You slept for many days, you know. The spell the overseers of the bout on Gilea were forced to cast is a rather brutal piece of work."

"Believe me, I know. Firsthand," he added, rubbing his head. "It all happened so quickly, I didn't quite know what hit me. One minute we were flying high, fighting off the others, then that defensive spell went all sideways on us, and the next thing we knew, they had unleashed some sort of stun spell."

"Yes, the safety protocol. You somehow cast your unusual spell so forcefully that it pierced the protective barrier. Did you know it would do that?"

"Not at the time. I was kind of preoccupied."

"As a gladiator would be, I would think. Especially in a situation like that. And what ever possessed you to climb up on that beast's back? It could have killed you in an instant."

"I can't really say," Charlie lied. He liked Visla Maktan, but until he understood what had happened better himself, he thought it wise to keep the whole talking dragon thing to himself. "It seemed safer than fighting, outnumbered, on the ground, and I guess she felt likewise."

"Fascinating," Visla Maktan said as they neared a low stone wall bordering the orchard.

As they walked closer, Charlie felt a heat build in his collar, every step closer causing it to grow hotter and hotter.

"Oh, how silly of me," Yoral Maktan said apologetically. "Sometimes I forget the effect the collars have on my servants. You see, this wall surrounds the central areas of my lands. Mind you, all you can see all around is mine as well, but the heart of my estate lies within this wall."

"And that's our boundary," Charlie said.

"Yes."

"Like a dog collar and an invisible fence."

"I do not know what a dog is, but if it is a servile creature, then I suppose the comparison is apt. But come, let us return to the residence halls via a different path. I think you'll like the gardens we will pass along the way," Maktan said, leading them on a new route.

They walked a while before Charlie felt comfortable enough

to ask the question that had been nagging him since he first met the man.

"Visla Maktan? I wonder if I might ask a question?"

"Of course, Charlie. I encourage enlightened discussion, even between master and servant."

"Well, that's the thing. It seems you have a full staff, and all of them are good at their jobs, but all I'm trained to do is fight and carry things. While I am incredibly grateful to have been brought here, I still can't help but wonder what good I can be to you."

Visla Maktan hesitated, looking for the right words.

"You are, how shall I put it? A *unique* type of asset. While you may not seem to fit into my normal retinue, I saw something in you that day at the bout on Gilea. You were a fine gladiator, certainly, but I've seen better. No offense."

"None taken."

"And your spell casting was inspired, and very clever in the use of feints and misdirection. In *that* you are far better than most will ever hope to be. But what really grabbed my attention was your perseverance."

"Not the dragon thing?"

"The what?"

"Sorry. The *Zomoki*."

"Oh, I just chalked that up to blind luck in the heat of battle," Maktan said. "Though I'd love to know how you managed it. But that wasn't it, Charlie. What really stood out to me was your drive. The willingness to think outside the box and turn a terrible situation into an advantage. It's a rare quality, you possess."

"I still fail to see how I can be of use to you, though."

"As do I at this precise moment. But I have been around long enough to know that the day inevitably arises when quick thinking and indomitable will may prove handy. When that time comes, I think I'd like to have you around and on my side."

"I'd be happy to help however I can."

"I know you would. But that will come later. For the time being, get familiar with the grounds, meet the other staff, and get yourself comfortable and situated. I must head off-world for a short while, but we can discuss your utility further when I have returned."

"I'll look forward to it," Charlie said, pausing at a lush shrubbery with bright red berries.

"Ah, that's just a decorative one, I'm afraid," Maktan informed him. "The berries are perfectly safe to eat, but they have a large stone and a rather mediocre flavor."

Charlie, however, thought the plant looked like a distant cousin of one from Earth.

I wonder—

A tone emitted from the device at the visla's hip. A very ornate skree, Charlie realized.

"Yes? What is it, Dinuk?"

"Pardon the interruption, Visla," the head of security's voice rang out. "We've received a skree message from our man in the Indara system. A group of rebels have attempted to free the Ootaki slaves from Mester Norkal's estate. A full-fledged uprising appears to be underway."

A cloud flashed across the visla's otherwise cheerful demeanor.

"None of the Council are near?"

"No, Visla. You are the closest. My apologies."

"Very well, there's nothing to be done for it. Prepare my ship. We'll be departing immediately."

He slid the skree back to its home on his hip.

"I'm sorry to have to cut our walk short, Charlie. I was rather enjoying the conversation. But duty calls, I'm afraid." He paused a moment in thought. "You know, you might find this interesting. Come, you will accompany me on this trip."

"Trip?"

"Yes. It appears I have to handle some rabble-rousers in a nearby system. Fools must have believed I was still at the Council retreat and not close to their system. I can't imagine they'd be so bold otherwise. In any case, my presence is requested, and as the ranking member of the Council of Twenty in the area, I must respond. Now come, we must hurry. It's but a short jump away."

The visla spun on his heel and headed for the far end of the compound at speed, Charlie following him closely. For all his genteel appearances, the man could move quite quickly when he wanted to.

Already off on another adventure. So much for a quiet life.

CHAPTER FIVE

It was a parking lot of sorts, only, rather than cars, a rich man's assortment of various craft, both space and terrestrial, sat on the closely trimmed grass, hovering silently as they awaited a passenger. The smaller vessels were standing by but ignored. All of the activity was focused at the second-largest of the craft.

It was a gleaming testament to the visla's wealth, its multi-level hull smooth and bright. Charlie had never seen anything like it, even during his brief stint as a space pirate. Now *this* was a prize worth taking.

But he was a pirate no more, and despite the briefest flash of instinct from those days, he had no illusions of taking it for his own. He would be a passenger, it seemed, and one traveling in luxury with the craft's owner. Things had improved for him far more than he'd ever anticipated. One day he was fighting for his life in the muck of the arena, the next, he found himself aboard the ship of one of the wealthiest men in the galaxy.

"I see you admiring my collection," Visla Maktan noted. "I'm quite fond of these, I must admit, though I do have others in storage. But what's the point of having a craft of such elegant design if not to use it, yes?"

Charlie couldn't help but agree.

They crossed the field to where Dinuk was standing by with a small force of armed men. Given his experience as a pirate, he was a bit surprised they weren't traveling with more.

"The men are loading the last of the supplies, Visla."

"And the Drooks?"

"A full contingent, as well as backup, are aboard."

"Well-rested and ready for a jump, I assume?"

"Yes, Visla. Only the freshest and most powerful were selected for this voyage," Dinuk confirmed.

"Excellent. As soon as your men have finished, we disembark. I'm sure Mester Norkal would appreciate a hasty arrival."

Visla Maktan strode up the short ramp into the beckoning ship, Charlie close behind. What he saw upon entering the craft made even the opulent exterior pale by comparison. Artwork adorned the walls, which were seemingly seamless sheets of flowing stone and metal, melding together with a warm, internally produced illumination.

Charlie couldn't help but gawk at the sight. It was like stepping inside a magical cave filled with riches. Given whose ship this was, he supposed that wasn't all that far from the truth.

"Come, Charlie. Let us have refreshment before we jump. I always find my stomach feels better upon arrival if there's a little something in it, don't you?"

"I'm sorry, I don't understand," the human replied.

"Oh, I just assumed you had traveled in this manner before," Maktan said.

"Never so luxuriously, Visla. I've always traveled in rather sparse accommodations."

"Well then, this will be a treat," he said, opening a compartment hidden in the seemingly solid wall. "You really must try these. Banchani fruit. Very tasty, and good for settling the digestive tract."

Charlie accepted the fruit. It was yellow and orange in color, and was roughly apple-sized. Oddly, it also possessed what seemed to be petals on the outside.

A flower, perhaps? he wondered.

Unsure, Charlie watched the visla before attempting to eat the unusual treat. One by one, Maktan peeled off the petals, the bases of which were much thicker than the tips, almost like an artichoke, but with the entirety of the petal edible and sweet. Following his lead, Charlie slowly ate his way around the fruit until the soft flesh of the central nodules was all that was left.

"You'll want to watch out for the seeds, Charlie. I wouldn't want you accidentally swallowing one or breaking a tooth."

"Thanks for the warning," he said, taking a cautious bite.

If the petals had been refreshing and light, the dense fruit in the middle was a flavor explosion in his mouth. Sensations ranging from hot to sweet, from sour to an almost minty coolness flooded his taste buds.

"That's incredible!" Charlie said, licking the last drops of juice from his fingers.

Maktan observed with a curious smile. "Yes, I find them to be most delightful as well. But not all species experience them the same way. In fact, the fruit is quite toxic to a few of them."

A look of concern flashed across Charlie's face.

"Don't worry, Charlie, you would have reacted to the first taste. Long before reaching the dangerous part in the center."

Charlie's shoulders relaxed. "If I can ask, you mentioned we were going to 'jump.'"

"Oh, my. You really haven't experienced much, have you? I keep forgetting you are supposedly from a distant system."

"Galaxy, actually."

"*Really*?" he replied, the wizard's interest clearly piqued. "No one mentioned that to me when you were acquired. Merely that you had come to our realms some years prior and were taken by a band of Tslavars. I had assumed you were simply from an uncharted system."

"Nope. Different galaxy entirely. We were stranded here by a freak accident. Only my friend Rika and I survived. The Tslavars killed the others. Apparently, the injured just weren't of any value to them," Charlie said, a low anger building in his gut.

Maktan looked at him sympathetically.

"I'm so sorry, Charlie. That must have been difficult. However, as distasteful as the practice may be for one not of this realm, I do understand the need to conserve resources aboard a vessel of that nature. But you say there was another survivor from your crew?"

"Yeah, but they did something to her. Fried her brain. I saw it. There were burns on her head, here and here," he said, gesturing to his temples.

At that, the visla showed a flash of anger. "Idiots. Those damned Tslavars and their primitive techniques. It wouldn't be the first time they've irreparably harmed an otherwise valuable asset."

"She was my friend."

"Yes, of course. My apologies. I meant to say *person*. Force of habit, you know."

"Of course," Charlie replied, still not thrilled with his friend being called an asset. "Anyway, that's ancient history. I don't even know if she's still alive," he said. "But back to this jump thing."

"Ah, yes. Normally we take a few days to travel to and from our destinations, but for the truly far ones––or those in dire need of immediate assistance, as is the case today––we utilize a jump. It's a difficult spell, and most Drooks are not adept at its subtleties. Many often deposit their ships in the wrong system while learning the finer points, you see. But once mastered, a jump spell will take us instantly to any system we have an established link with."

Holy shit. These guys have a magical Einstein-Rosen bridge,

Charlie realized. *They can do with a spell what we were trying to accomplish with our reactors and drive systems. And theirs works!*

The implications were staggering. The seemingly backward society had nevertheless succeeded in a feat of space travel that humanity had still been unable to achieve. And they'd done it not with engineering and science, but *magic*, of all things.

"We're almost ready, Visla. Just a few minutes and the Drooks will be in place," Dinuk said as a line of the odd power-generating men and women filed down the far corridor.

These were different than the ones Charlie had encountered in the past. Cleaner, for a start, but there was something else. A feeling of power almost rippled from their bodies as they walked the ship, preparing the spells as they went to their stations. The visla's crew were the cream of the crop.

"Okay, Charlie, since this is your first jump, you really should have a seat. You'll find it far more pleasant than days in transit, but the first one can be a bit, *unsettling*, to some."

Charlie had learned by now to heed the advice of those familiar with the unusual effects of magic. One too many trips to the ground as his world spun from an ill-advised sense of machismo had quickly freed him of that foolish impulse. Instead, he sat and settled in, as directed.

"Indara system, Dinuk. Mester Norkal's estate," Visla Maktan directed.

"As you wish, Visla."

Dinuk left the two men and headed for the command center of the ship. A minute later there was a shift of light outside the windows as they took off for space, but otherwise the ship showed no signs of movement. No shift in gravity, no pulling g-forces, no rumbling hull. It just lifted off, smooth as can be.

"Here it comes," Visla Maktan said with a little grin. "Just try to relax."

Relax, he says. Last time I was anywhere near a warp, my ship was thrown through a wormhole. And he says relax.

29

Despite his internal doubts, Charlie maintained a calm outward appearance to the best of his ability.

Moments later something odd began to happen in the ship. A light sparkle covered all the surfaces, making the light form tiny halos on reflective areas. Then it all went black for a split second before snapping back to sharp focus.

"Okay, we're here," Maktan said.

Charlie rose from his seat and moved to the nearest window. A lone, red sun greeted them with its fiery glow.

It really worked.

There they were, above an entirely different planet, and it had only taken them an instant. With that kind of power at his disposal, Charlie could only wonder how the visla might handle the uprising on the planet below.

CHAPTER SIX

The Indara system seemed like pretty much every other system Charlie had visited in his several-year stint in the strange galaxy. Sure, this one's sun was a red dwarf rather than yellow or blue, and it had over a dozen planets, not counting hundreds of moons. But aside from that, the system was the same.

People lived on the planet—sometimes planets, plural—in the 'Goldilocks Zone,' just the *right* distance from the sun to support life without either turning it to charcoal or freezing it to death. And on those habitable worlds, a society had grown.

Now, some societies were more advanced than others, as would be expected of totally disparate solar systems, but once the Council of Twenty had made their presence known and staked their claim to the system, all soon fell in line with their galactic standards. Those who didn't faced the consequences.

The consequences being death until compliance was achieved.

All worlds under Council control soon fell within parameters. The magic of those worlds was a thing to connect with the other systems. To harvest, in a way. It took time, but every new system would subtly alter the flows of power between them. Bringing a new one into the fold was tricky business that required a great deal of effort on the part of the vislas and emmiks controlling the Council of Twenty.

There were technically far more than twenty systems and their representative power-wielders in the Council, but only the twenty possessing the greatest magic of the five-hundred plus incorporated systems made decisions for them all.

Visla Yoral Maktan was one such man, and given his strengths, he was among the handful leading their already elite group.

The world they had arrived at had no such man in power. Rather, it was a woman of average magical abilities, but with particularly attuned socio-political ones. Mester Norkal had kept her world in order not with an iron fist as so many others did, but by careful manipulation of the strings of power among the various sects in her system.

Until, it seemed, something went horribly wrong.

"You see that, Charlie?" Visla Maktan asked as his ship smoothly slid into the atmosphere without so much as a bump as it descended toward a high-walled castle-like estate. "That's Mester Norkal's principal residence."

"*Mester* Norkal. So he is a lower-tier magic user," Charlie noted.

"*She* is, yes, but don't let that sway your opinion. Her skills reach far beyond mere magical ones. If not, she'd never have held this system together as long as she has. Even so, she does possess a sizable contingent of troops, and her magic is still quite formidable for most."

As the ship swooped lower, Charlie could see a fierce magical battle underway. Spells were flying, and hasty defenses were being thrown up, sometimes managing to deflect magic attacks, but succumbing to their forces nearly as often.

"*Magnifados,*" Visla Maktan said, and the windows zoomed in their field of view.

That's a new one. 'Magnifados.' I've never seen anyone use that before, Charlie thought as he marveled at the details of the battle, now far clearer through the enhanced window.

The battlements seemed to possess higher-power weapons than the men on the ground, who were fighting valiantly, but were nevertheless overrun at several points. All were using slaaps with great efficiency, though they were not as proficient in close-quarter combat, where magic was not an option, as Charlie knew many who relied on their magical weapons often were.

It was that gap in skill that had allowed him to become one of the most successful gladiators during his short stint in the arenas. Charlie had grown up without magic, so fighting without it seemed only natural. For his opponents, however, it was like removing one of their senses. Charlie took advantage of that, and regularly.

The sheer expanse of the battle was unlike any he had ever seen as a pirate, though that life was short-lived before he was captured and sold back into slavery once more. He watched the men with a trained eye, noting formations and tactics, shaking his head at some of the more foolish defenses arranged.

"You don't approve?" Maktan asked, noting his disapproving look.

"Some of them are positioned poorly. I mean, those on the ground can't know, but whoever is directing them from above should see what we do. I can't help but notice that they're reacting to the immediate attacks but are oblivious to the ones being staged."

Maktan smiled. "Good eye, Charlie. You are correct. Several of these are feints, designed to draw out Mester Norkal's men to open their flank to attack. But I am surprised she has been unable to handle this. Nothing I've seen thus far is beyond her——"

A series of massive magic blasts pummeled the far end of the battlefield as a swarming group of men overran the mester's stunned defenses.

"Ah, now I see the problem. The locals seem to have some hired help. Do you see them, Charlie? Mercenaries. And *they* have some interesting weaponry, indeed. Mester Norkal was right in summoning me to her aid," Visla Maktan said, his casual demeanor having taken on a decidedly more serious tone.

He walked to a smooth, red wall and placed his hand against it, muttering the faintest of spells, so quietly Charlie could not make out even a single word. The wall flashed with light, and when it dimmed, a complex puzzle of thousands of small pieces of identical red tiles now presented themselves. Maktan wasted no time, pressing over a dozen of them in quick succession. Even if he had gone slowly and Charlie had been taking notes, he doubted he could have correctly identified even a quarter of them.

Maktan began unfastening the large konuses from his wrists as the wall slid open.

"Are those claithes?" Charlie asked in a minor state of shock as he took in the contents of the hidden cache.

"You know your weapons, I see."

"I've been told of them, but I've never seen one in person."

"Yes, I'd think not. They're a very hard weapon to come by. On top of that, while fantastic for combat, they're so single-purpose in design that they are not nearly as useful as a slaap or konus for all but the most purely combative situations." He slid them over each hand, the brass knuckle portion resting firmly over his fingers, while the ornate gauntlet section covering the backs of his hand and wrists began to shimmer with a disquieting glow.

Charlie could actually *feel* the ripples of deadly power leaking from them. Ser Baruud had told him about claithes during his gladiator training on more than one occasion.

"You will not encounter one in the arena," he had assured his nervous student.

"But how can you be so sure?"

Ser Baruud smiled. "Because, Charlie, a claithe may be a weapon of deadly energy, but all but the most skilled and powerful vislas and emmiks would die using them. The amount of focus required to control one makes it utterly useless in gladiatorial combat. Unless you're a visla, of course. And there has never been a visla gladiator in recorded history."

Seeing this weapon of incredible destructive power so close made Charlie's adrenals surge, forcing him to consciously ignore the flight impulse the claithe elicited.

Visla Maktan, however, was calm. To so casually wield not one but *two* of them, Charlie realized he must be a magic user of extraordinary power.

The ship landed outside the high walls, its protective spells deflecting those hurled at it as the door opened and the ramp descended.

"Are you coming, Charlie?" Maktan asked.

"Uh, shouldn't I be armed or something?"

The wizard laughed. "Oh, there's no need. Come along. I think you'll find this interesting."

Charlie followed the visla out of the ship as he stepped onto the battlefield as casually as he might stroll around his estate grounds. With a quick amplification spell—another Charlie had never heard before—he spoke directly to the attacking horde.

"Rebels and mercenaries, I am Visla Yoral Maktan of the Council of Twenty. I am politely requesting you cease your attacks at once."

A titter of laughter came from the bunkered mercenaries before another slew of spells were launched his way, along with a sizable quantity of enchanted arrows and spears.

Visla Maktan easily batted them aside, his protective spell absorbing the rest without faltering.

"I am offering clemency for local inhabitants of Mester Norkal's domain. No further lives must be lost, but you must cease your aggressions. If the hired mercenary forces leave now, you will be spared and allowed to return to your families with no repercussions."

A discussion appeared to break out where fighting had been fiercest. Some of the local rebels were considering the attack. The mercenaries, however, had other ideas. Those in favor of ending things were quickly voted down, and a new wave of spells and projectiles filled the air, denser and more violent than before.

Visla Maktan sighed.

"So be it."

He raised his hands, and the claithes flashed bright orange, then shifted to unbearable white. Even Maktan himself seemed a little uncomfortable from the blinding light. Then, in an instant, a brutal wave of magic the likes of which Charlie had never before seen burst forth, shattering offensive and defensive spells alike, turning their casters into sprays of liquified blood and bone.

Maktan pivoted, covering the entire battlefield with glowing death. The paltry spells of the attackers were nothing in the face of the claithes, and even the mercenaries found their spells neutralized.

A few of Mester Norkal's guards began rushing the enemy, overjoyed at the turning of the tide.

"No! Stay back!" Maktan shouted, but it was too late. The spell reacted of its own accord, sensing hostile motion and widening to take down the new entrants into the arena.

Charlie quickly realized why the weapons were so rarely used. To do so might ensure victory, but also courted disaster.

Visla Maktan abruptly shut his fists, pulling the energy back into the claithes with some effort. A fine sheen of sweat was on his brow. He turned, unsteady a moment, then, remembering his guest, played it off, walking nonchalantly, as if it had been no effort at all.

Charlie, however, had seen what it had done. And in the hands of a lesser man, the claithes might very well have killed him.

"Well, that was unfortunate," Maktan said, accepting a flask of liquid from Dinuk.

Where did he come from? I didn't even see him leave the ship.

"Thank you," he said, handing the container back to his chief of security. "Now, let's go have a word with Mester Norkal, shall we?"

CHAPTER SEVEN

Mester Norkal was a surprisingly tall woman. Given the muscles of her shoulders, exposed by her form-fitting battle robes, Charlie took her for one who did not shy away from a fight. That was why he was so surprised when she immediately dropped to one knee at the sight of Visla Maktan.

"Visla Maktan," she said, eyes lowered. "I thank you for rendering assistance. I assure you, I would not have called if circumstances had not warranted."

"Rise, Norkal. I saw the nature of your attackers. Mercenaries? I would expect that from some of the rebel groups in the outer systems, but here? How did this happen?"

The lithe woman stood tall and met the visla's gaze, her eyes flicking down to the claithes on his hands for an instant.

"It began as an uprising. A handful of rebels attempting to incite action from my subjects."

"Again? These rebels are becoming quite tiresome."

"I agree. And normally I'd have had little problem quelling their disruptions."

"But this time? What was different, Norkal?"

She hesitated. For a woman of her power to require the aid

of another must have put her in an uncomfortable position. And now she had to further weaken her stance by admitting her error, whatever that might be.

"It was––an unexpected tactic," she finally said. "And one that should not have succeeded if not for the bribing of one of my guards. One who shall spend the rest of his incredibly short life in exquisite agony, let me assur––"

"*What* was unexpected?" Maktan interrupted.

She took a deep breath.

"They gained access to the tower."

Visla Maktan seemed a bit interested, but unconcerned. "Quite a security lapse, wouldn't you agree? But perhaps liquidating your guar––"

"*And* they got their hands on several of my Ootaki," she continued.

"Now *that* is problematic," Maktan said, obviously irritated by the news. "But your lackluster defense of the compound was––"

"*And* they not only freed them, they also convinced one of the Ootaki to join their little rebellion." A look of deep concern flashed across her face. "Maktan, he gave the rebels his hair freely."

Maktan's jaw twitched, but he otherwise seemed calm. Charlie, accustomed to gauging his opponents for tells, noticed his shoulders were carrying far more tension than just moments before.

"Ah, then that would explain it, wouldn't it? Freely given Ootaki hair. How long had that specimen been growing it?"

"Five years."

Another twitch in his jaw.

"Well, even normally that would be a fair amount of power, but not enough to support an insurrection. But *freely given* Ootaki hair? The power stored there would have been enough to pay mercenaries and still have some left over for the rebels themselves, and that's not counting the others they took," Maktan noted. "Quite a boon for the rebels, Norkal. The Council will be displeased."

"Excuse me. I'm confused. I'm sorry. I know Ootaki hair holds a lot of power, but why is this one's so much different?" Charlie asked.

"How dare you? Slaves do not speak!" Mester Norkal shouted, raising her hand to launch a spell at him.

"Calm yourself, Norkal," Visla Maktan said in a calm voice. "This is Charlie. He is a gladiator. My newest acquisition. Perhaps you heard about his performance in the bout at the Buru arena on Gilea last week."

The mester went pale, her eyes widening with realization.

"The Zomoki rider?"

"Yes. Now don't soil yourself with excitement, he's just a man."

"Yes, of course. I'm so sorry, Charlie. I did not realize who you were. That was an inspired bout. It is being talked about across all of the settled systems."

Charlie blushed slightly from the unexpected attention. "Uh, thank you," he said, unsure if he should say any more.

Mester Norkal looked at Maktan with an appreciative smile. "So, the Zomoki rider is now with Visla Maktan. This bodes well for the Council. Extremely well."

"Yes, I rather think so. A most fortuitous acquisition. I am just glad I happened to be in attendance at the tournament that day. You know how I normally detest those events. But I was already on Gilea on Council business."

"On Gilea?"

"Yes. I was discussing smelt issues with our *friend*," he replied. Mester Norkal seemed to know whomever it was he was talking about. "And he is a lover of bloodsport, so when he offered a seat at the event, well, it would have been bad form to turn him down."

"Of course. And now you have the rider."

"Yes. But enough of that. I'm sure Charlie is tired of talking about his fight, no matter how entertaining it was." He turned back to his human prize. "And to answer your question, Charlie, Ootaki, as you seem to know, cannot utilize power, though their hair naturally stores it, and with great efficiency, I might add. But that power drains like sap from a cut branch when the hair is taken from them. It is a cost of the trade we all accept. But if an Ootaki gives its hair freely, none of that power is lost. It is the difference between a sapling and a towering tree."

"I'd never heard that before," Charlie said. "The power loss ratio, I mean. I'd heard about freely given hair, but that's about it."

"You likely had no reason to be familiar with these things. Those raised here know it from a young age, of course, but you aren't from our realm, now are you?"

Again, an aspect of Charlie's unusual life fascinated the powerful woman more than he'd have thought normal.

"He isn't? You mean he did what he did and comes from a system *outside* the conglomerate?" Norkal asked. "Remarkable."

"Yes, remarkable. And no, he comes to us from much, much farther, in fact. Charlie says he comes from another *galaxy*."

The shock on Mester Norkal's face was clear. Visla Maktan seized upon her silence to answer Charlie's question, at last.

"In any case, Charlie, slaves don't often come in contact with Ootaki. And since you are not from our realms, it is only natural you have a lot to learn. Why, in fact, did you know that it is the first cut of Ootaki hair that contains the most power? Every cut thereafter is still potent, but diminishing. The very first is the rarest and most sought after of all."

"I had no idea," Charlie said, recalling the young woman with the shorn head he had met years prior when he tried to escape his Tslavar captors. "But what is the '*conglomerate*?'"

Maktan smiled warmly. "The hundreds of systems under

41

Council control. We provide structure and order to these worlds. Maintain stability and even flow of power between the systems. If the worlds within fall out of sync, the ripples to the power lattice connecting them would affect us all."

Mester Norkal kept smiling at Charlie, and her excessive attention was beginning to creep him out a bit.

"But that won't happen," she said, smiling at them both. "The Council keeps everything running smoothly, as Visla Maktan has just demonstrated so aptly. Now, please, let me offer you refreshments. You have come far, and after such a display, I know you must be hungry."

Visla Maktan pondered a moment, then nodded an affirmation.

"Come along, Charlie. Let us restore our energy before the voyage home."

CHAPTER EIGHT

Visla Maktan was the very image of polite company as they shared a small repast with the woman whose life, whose *kingdom* he had just saved. The conversation turned to more pleasant topics than rebellions and battle tactics, and the visla even managed to keep Charlie's new fan from bombarding him with questions about his last bout.

Apparently, word of his fight had spread farther than he previously believed. He was a celebrity, of sorts, and it was something of a coup for Visla Maktan to have acquired him. All told, if he was to be living in bondage, it was far better to be a slave under a man like Maktan than the far more brutal owners he had known in prior years.

The visla was something of a renaissance man, though given that he was a powerful wizard, perhaps a different term would fit better, if he could think of one. Patron of arts and magic, perhaps? Whatever he was, Yoral Maktan was a man of power, talent, and taste.

I could really get used to this, Charlie thought as he sipped the last of his magically cooled cup of nectar. The beverage was perfectly sweetened--not syrupy, not cloyingly saccharine. It flowed across his tongue and down his throat with the most refreshing sensation. After a long day, it certainly beat plain old water.

Evening soon fell, and Visla Maktan stepped aside to have a few words in private with Mester Norkal before they departed.

"You know you are a slave," Dinuk said. "The visla is a wise and powerful man. Far more powerful than you realize. It would do you well to remember your place after today."

Charlie assessed the bodyguard—though with the claithes he was still wearing, he doubted *anyone* could get close enough to be a danger to the visla. Dinuk was a true believer, that much was obvious. Devoted to his master. And he wore no collar. He was a free man with that faithful spark in his eye. That type of loyalty was something money couldn't buy.

"Thanks, Dinuk. I appreciate the words of advice. To be honest, the visla has been quite a surprise to me after the people I've been sold off to in the past. He's quite a man."

"Yes, that he is. A great man, doing great things for the systems."

"And he treats me like an equal."

"You are *not* an equal."

"No, obviously. But you know what I mean. He doesn't need to act like a tyrant to make his point."

"Hmm," Dinuk muttered, his eyes shifting as the visla returned from his private chat.

"Dinuk, send your men to gather the tribute Mester Norkal has so graciously offered for my assistance."

"Charlie, go with the others and—"

"No. Charlie is my guest, Dinuk. Just your men." He turned to the human. "Shall we step inside and get comfortable?"

Dinuk quickly set his men to work, doing an impressive job of hiding his annoyance, though one flash of irritation did manage to find its way to the surface before being quickly suppressed. Charlie ignored it and followed the wizard aboard his ship.

Maktan once again keyed open his secure wall safe, sliding the claithes from his hands and placing them back in their spots, then sliding his konuses back on his wrists.

"Much better," he sighed. "I used most of their charge out there, and it'll take quite a bit of effort to bring them back to full levels, but even depleted, a claithe is a dangerous tool. It requires a constant degree of concentration to keep it under control, you know."

"I'd imagine that would be exhausting after a while, even for a man as powerful as you are."

The visla smiled.

"Yes, it is. You are quite observant, Charlie."

"Gladiator training. Assessing weapons is kind of second nature at this point. It's a survival thing."

"I'd think so," Maktan said with an amused little grin.

Charlie watched as he proceeded to take a long braid of golden hair from a pocket hidden in his clothing. The braid was thin, but Charlie could feel a ripple of power trickling from it. Ootaki hair.

Visla Maktan tucked it in the wall safe with his weapons and sealed the door.

"Yes, Charlie, it is Ootaki hair. I can see the recognition in your eyes."

"I'm sorry, was I staring?"

"Not at all. I tend to notice men's interests and intentions. It's second nature at this point."

Charlie chuckled. "Yes, a survival thing, right?"

"Indeed," the visla said with an amused grin.

"So, she didn't lose all of her Ootaki hair, then?"

"Not all of it, no. However, she owed me for my expenditure of power on her behalf. This is just a part of the compensation. It's too bad for her that she was unable to handle the issue herself. She had been nurturing those Ootaki for years to contribute them to the Council and improve her standing. I feel she will suffer for the loss. But that is the nature of battle, is it not? For every victor there must also be the other side of the coin."

Ah, there it is.

"Is that what you need me for, then? To fight for the Council?" Charlie asked. "I'm a gladiator, but as for actual comba—"

"No, no. Nothing like that, Charlie. Though perhaps one day that may be an option. But for now, I am simply pleased to have you in my household. As I'm sure you've noted by now, you are something of a celebrity, given your performance on Gilea. It is a great pleasure having you with me. Your curious circumstances are the talk of the systems."

Okay, so that's what it is, then. I'm basically a slave version of a rich guy's movie star friend. He's got plenty of standing on his own, but with me he has that one thing that makes him stand out even among the other rich and powerful guys. I guess money can't buy everything. Charlie pondered his situation a moment, his fingers gently touching the collar around his neck. *On second thought, I guess in this place, money* can *buy it,* he thought with a sigh.

They flew back in the same manner they arrived, opting to jump rather than spend days in transit in deep space. The visla was not a man to frivolously waste power, but he had obligations he had to see to, and more often than not, he chose to jump simply because his time was worth far more than anything saved by taking the scenic route.

It was impressive, Charlie thought. The man just single-handedly quelled a rebellion without breaking much of a sweat, though he had drained his claithes in the process. And these were more than just run-of-the-mill rebels. There had been mercenaries as well.

The man clearly possessed a lot of power, though how much

of it was natural versus stored in his claithes and other magical devices was something Charlie simply lacked the means to assess. He had seen a few magic users cast without benefit of a konus or slaap in the past, but it was extremely rare. Using power like that was just not done if it could be avoided.

As far as he could tell, all powered beings protected their personal stores fiercely. To drain your own power was to leave yourself vulnerable. And from what he could tell, the feudal nature of the systems comprising the Council of Twenty's conglomerate were in a constant state of flux. Vulnerable was bad.

It must be exhausting, always having to watch your back like that, he mused. *And it has to be even worse when the backstabbing might be of the magical variety.*

The visla stared out the window, wrapped in thought as they took off. Charlie took the moment to close his eyes for a bit of silence, leaving his patron to whatever was troubling him as they made the short trip home.

It had been a long day, he realized as they stepped off the ship to the sight of a setting sun.

All day. Wow, time flies when you're slaughtering hundreds, Charlie mused.

"I hope you found this outing interesting, Charlie. I am glad we were able to spend a bit of time together and continue our conversation. I only wish we had been able to do so under less unpleasant circumstances," Visla Maktan said as they left Dinuk and his men to unload the ship, while they walked back to the estate.

"It was an eye-opener, that's for sure," Charlie replied. "There are so many things I still haven't seen in this galaxy."

"I'd imagine so. Well, we have plenty of time to chat now that you are part of my household. Now, if you'll excuse me, I have some things I need to attend to."

"Of course. Thank you, Visla. It was an interesting day."

"My pleasure, Charlie. Now go get something to eat. I'm sure Tuktuk will want to hear all about your outing."

Visla Maktan smiled warmly and patted him on the shoulder, then turned and walked away. Charlie made his way to the kitchen and briefly filled his friend in on the happenings of the day. The visla's use of a claithe especially caught his attention.

"A claithe? I've never heard of him using one before, since I've been here. It must have been a big problem, indeed."

"Well, let's just say it was over quickly, though it looks like he drained them in the process."

"That's the problem with claithes. Very deadly, but they take forever to charge. That's why you'll see slaaps used all the time, even if they're far less powerful. They're quick to learn and quick to charge. For him to use his claithes, I think the situation was probably quite a bit worse than he let on."

Charlie pondered his friend's observation. Maktan had appeared at ease, but for a moment he did seem to have stretched himself a bit thin, though he recovered quickly. Could something bigger be at play on Mester Norkal's world? He shrugged it off. This was all new to him, so time would tell.

"All right, Tuk, I'm beat. Gonna turn in early."

"Okay, Charlie. See you in the morning."

Charlie headed off for his room and lay his head down despite the relatively early hour. He had something he wanted to try, and he'd be rising early to do so.

CHAPTER NINE

Sunrise greeted Charlie with cheerful warmth, and he welcomed another morning free from the hard training of Ser Baruud. He would begin training on his own in earnest shortly—one must always keep one's skills sharp, his master had always said—but for today at least, he had a different mission in mind.

Charlie slid into a light pair of boots and headed out into the estate's grounds, a small sack in his hand. An hour later, he returned to the kitchen with a few pounds of the small red berries he had noted the other day.

"Why did you gather those, Charlie? I wish you'd said something. I would have told you those really aren't any good for eating. The flavor is weak, and there's not much meat to the fruit," his blue friend said.

"Nah, Tuk. I have something else in mind. If these are anything like what we have back home, you're going to be in for a treat."

He spent the next hour carefully peeling the fruit from the bean-looking seed inside, then soaking them in a bowl of cold water all day. He then patted them clean and lay them out to dry in the warm air circulating in one of Tuktuk's unused ovens. A benefit of magical cookery, there was no fear of overheating or burning, and best of all, no gas bill.

The following morning he took his dried bounty and brushed off the remaining bit of flaky husk, leaving a pile of smooth, dry seeds.

"Hey, Tuk. You mind firing up one of the ovens for me?"

"Sure, but what are you doing, if you don't mind my asking? Those won't taste any better cooked, you know."

"Oh, I've got a plan," he replied with a grin. "And it doesn't involve eating them."

"So mysterious," Tuktuk said with a laugh.

"What are you two going on about?" Magda asked when she came to fetch a tray of breakfast for Visla Maktan's daughter, Malalia.

"Charlie's roasting some berries from those tsokin shrubs out by the fishery pond."

"Why would he do that? They're decorative."

"I know, but I humor him when I can. He's new here, after all, and the visla wanted him to feel at home, so..."

"So you let him roast refuse in your ovens. I'll never understand you, Tuktuk."

"I have often been told I am an enigma."

"If only it were that simple," she said with a chuckle as she loaded an assortment of fresh-baked pastries onto the tray, along with two types of beverage, as well as a hearty porridge.

"All of that food for one little girl?" Charlie asked.

"She's got an amazing metabolism, that one," Magda replied. "And she's not so little. Denna Maktan is nearly two decades old."

"Wait, I thought you said she was called Malalia."

"Yes. Denna is a title, like the lady of the house."

"Ah, gotcha. Like how Yoral Maktan is called Visla."

"Exactly."

"Okay. So, given the length of the solar year on this planet, that makes her about twenty-seven in Earth years," Charlie said, his engineering mind doing a quick conversion with ease. "Why haven't I seen her around the grounds?"

"She keeps mostly to herself, studying. I'm sure you'll see her soon enough. Everyone wants to take a peek at the Zomoki rider, after all."

"Great," he grumbled, then turned his attention back to his beans, now spread evenly on a baking sheet. "Hmm. What I need is some kind of hopper to churn them while they roast."

Tuktuk laughed. "Charlie, you don't think I have a half dozen spells to do that for you?"

"I-I didn't think to ask. I guess I forget you all seem to have a spell for everything."

"I'll leave you two to it, then," Magda said. "Don't burn the kitchen down while I'm gone," she called over her shoulder.

Tuktuk set the beans roasting, gently tossing in the hot air with a simple little spell. Charlie took the time to dig through the kitchen for implements that would serve his purpose, happily singing his little tune of magic words to himself, quietly, of course, and with no fear of accidental discharge as he had no konus or powered device of any sort.

Other staff wandered in and out of the kitchen, looking at the odd human as though he were nuts as the blue cook introduced them, then explained what exactly he was roasting for his friend.

"But those taste horrible," a stable boy said.

"Maybe," was Charlie's reply. "But we'll know soon enough."

Ten minutes into the roast, he told Tuktuk to remove the beans from the oven and let them cool for another ten.

"Technically, I should let them sit for a day to mature the flavor, but I'm feeling a little impatient. I saw you have a grinding thing over there but don't know how to use it. Would you mind?" he asked his friend.

"Now you want me to grind them up?"

"Yes. And I need boiling water."

"Are you attempting to cast a spell with sorcery? The visla docs not allow any such thing within his walls, and—"

"No, no. Nothing like that. Just grind them, will ya? Fine, but not too fine. A coarse grind, like fine sand."

"I get it, Charlie. You can stop saying 'fine.'"

"Fine."

"You're ridiculous, you know that?"

"So you keep telling me," he shot back with a grin.

"All right, I'll see what I can do," Tuktuk said with a laugh, then dumped the still-warm beans into the device, chanting what Charlie figured was a simple grinding spell that turned the machine on. A minute later, he had an aromatic pile of what he hoped would taste somewhat like coffee.

He took a spoon and filled a fine meshed sieve with the ground beans, then placed it over a carafe.

"Well, here goes nothing. Let's hope it works."

He poured the boiling water over the grounds and let them soak through, slowly filling the vessel with hot, brown liquid. It smelled very much like coffee, Charlie noted.

"Okay, I'll be the guinea pig," he said, pouring himself a small cup when the water had finished straining through the sieve.

Charlie raised the steaming cup to his lips and inhaled, the aroma taking him back to his kitchen on Earth. *Maybe,* he hoped. Then, cautiously, he took a sip.

"Oh, God, yes," he sighed with pleasure. "If this stuff isn't poison, I think we're in business."

The others in the kitchen were curious about his new beverage and each took a small cup to taste. Some liked it black. Others complained it was too bitter.

"Add a little milk and some sweetener to it," he suggested, which made the beverage far more to their liking. Also meeting with approval was the effect of the alien equivalent of caffeine. Charlie felt that coffee rush for the first time in years and couldn't help but wonder how the alien metabolisms would handle it.

The kitchen was full of curious, caffeinated chatter when a sudden silence raced through the room.

"Denna Maktan," Magda said with a slight bow. "I'm pleased you have come to meet your father's newest acquisition."

Denna Malalia Maktan was, to Charlie's eyes, precisely what a powerful wizard's daughter would look like. Stereotypically slender and beautiful, she possessed high cheek bones, bright eyes, and an amazing physique. He had to wonder if any of it was magically enhanced.

"I'm Charlie Gault," he said, offering his hand in greeting.

A few staff gasped at his forward gesture, but Malalia seemed charmed by it.

"A pleasure to meet you," she said, gently taking his offered hand. "My father has talked much of his new gladiator pet. But what are you doing in the kitchen? I would have taken you for one to be exercising in the fields, perhaps trying to kill some wild beast."

"Well, I try not to go on killing rampages before breakfast, Denna Maktan——"

"Please, call me Malalia."

"Okay, Malalia. Anyway, I was just serving up some coffee to the gang here. It's not exactly like we have on my home world, but it's pretty darn close. Would you care to try some?"

"The denna does not drink with the help," Magda chastised him, grunting her disapproval.

"Oh, hush, Magda. Father is not here," she retorted, picking up one of the small cups on the counter.

"I have to warn you, it can seem a little bitter at first," Charlie informed her.

"Many things worthwhile do," she replied, a mischievous sparkle in her eye.

She was a magic user, and if she was even half as powerful as her father, she could be a force to be reckoned with. Even so, Charlie found himself more than a little taken with her.

She sipped the steaming black liquid and swirled the new flavor in her mouth, savoring every aspect of its bouquet. A second later, sparks briefly buzzed from her fingertips, quite unintentionally.

"Oh my," she said, a slight flush rising to her cheeks. "This is a wonderful discovery. And you did this all by yourself?"

"Well, no. Tuktuk helped me prepare it."

"Nonsense. All I did was fire up the ovens and grind it for him. This was all Charlie's idea," Tuktuk said, selflessly putting all of the credit on his friend's shoulders.

"Well, Charlie. This is magnificent. And do you think you can make more of this enchanting elixir?"

"I don't see why not. This was just a test batch to see how it would come out. With a little practice, we could probably get a better roast and smooth the flavor somewhat."

"Excellent. Then this is now one of your new duties in this household. Ensure we have this––what did you call it, again?"

"Coffee."

"Yes. Ensure we have this *coffee* in the house at all times. Magda, I would have this with breakfast in the morning. It certainly seems to help my powers awaken from the night's slumber."

She smiled warmly at Charlie, making his stomach flutter just a little.

"I can see why my father likes you, Charlie. He says you are a most unusual and inspiring man. And I am now of the same opinion."

CHAPTER TEN

The servants were normally exceptionally efficient at their tasks, keeping the estate and surrounding grounds in perfect order. Abuzz with Charlie's new discovery––and its magic-enhancing abilities––the staff soon began finding themselves with additional downtime as the caffeinated men and women flew through their chores with newfound vigor.

Charlie just enjoyed the almost-forgotten feeling of sitting in the morning sun, sipping a hot cup of coffee and eating a pastry. Tuktuk had taken to joining him for a little break, and the two unlikely friends shared tales and laughs every morning for a week before their routine was interrupted by Magda one day.

"Of course I'll talk to him," Charlie had said when, as she passed through the kitchen, she mentioned a problem that Hertzall, the head groundskeeper's, was having. "Why don't you ask him when is convenient for him and I'll see what I can do. I have to warn you, though, I'm not a botanist. I'm just an engineer and gladiator."

"I still don't really understand this *engineer* thing you call yourself, but you've a way with plants. We've all seen––and enjoyed––how what had been merely a decorative shrubbery was transformed into this wonderful concoction," she said as she stole a sip of Tuktuk's coffee.

"Hey!" he protested in jest.

She replied with a sly smile.

"I'll let him know you'll speak with him. And thank you, Charlie. Hertzall is a bit of an odd fellow, but he's a good man, and he's been here most of his life. It'll do him good talking with you, even if you can't help him. But I have a sneaking suspicion you can."

Shortly thereafter, a plainly clothed man with a hazelnut complexion and amber eyes haltingly approached Charlie and Tuktuk while they chatted.

"You must be Hertzall," Charlie said cheerfully. "Coffee?"

Hertzall's discomfort at talking with a new person was apparent, but it cleared quickly after his first mouthful of the offered beverage.

"It's amazing, really," he said, a fog lifting from his eyes. "And to think, this has been growing on these grounds for so many years and no one ever thought to try this with their seeds."

"Well, to be fair, it was already a thing where I come from. I just noticed it looked like a familiar plant, and that was only because I spent one sleepless night surfing through videos online."

"On what line? Like for fishing?"

"No, it's—nevermind. It's a thing from home. Anyway, Magda tells me you had a problem you wanted to see if I could help you with. I'd be glad to try, but I'm no botanist."

"Well, if you'd just take a look," the groundskeeper said, turning toward the fields.

"Oh, we're going right now?" Charlie said, flashing Tuktuk a regretful look.

His blue friend suppressed a chuckle and merrily shrugged his shoulders with an amused look in his eyes.

"Right. No time like the present, I suppose."

The two men set off at a brisk walk. Hertzall wasn't one to dawdle, though his pace slowed to an absolute crawl when he noted something on the grounds warranting further attention. Such was his focus, and Charlie began to understand why he had a hard time interacting with the others. But despite Hertzall's oddness, he found himself rather fond of the man.

"This here is the problem," the groundskeeper said, pointing to a small grove of trees whose leaves were turning color, but in an unhealthy, spotted way. "Visla Maktan has supplied me with the finest spells to make them grow, and grow they do. But for some reason, they're doing *this*."

Charlie picked a leaf from the nearest tree and studied it a moment. He was not a plant expert by any means, but this actually looked a little familiar, like something his parents had dealt with on their land when he was a boy.

He scanned the ground, looking for the telltale signs he remembered from his youth, but the soil was different here and yielded no answers.

"You know what? I have an idea. But it's going to take a piece of my gear. Hopefully a person's possessions are sent with them when they're bought."

"They should be. It's the standard way of things, though most get picked through and sold for profit long before any slave earns their freedom––if ever."

"Well, I'll need one of my devices if I'm to be of any use to you."

"But the visla is away on business."

Charlie thought a moment and smiled.

"That's okay. I think I know someone who'll help."

"You wish for me to return your possessions to you without my father's permission?" Malalia said, concern flashing in her lovely eyes.

SCOTT BARON

"No, nothing like that," Charlie soothed. "Just allow me to use one of them to help Hertzall."

"The crazy old groundskeeper? What does he want with your strange off-world technology-magic."

"He doesn't," Charlie said, covering for the man. It was true, though, as Charlie was the one who thought the "technology-magic" could be of help. "I believe I can help him heal some trees that are ill, is all. I'd only need to use the scanner for the afternoon. It would be back before your father returns."

He was asking her to do something without Visla Maktan's permission. He just hoped she had that same mischievous streak many daughters of powerful men possessed.

"I will allow it," she said. "But it will cost you."

"I have no money. I am enslaved."

"I did not say *what* my price was," she replied, a sly look in her eye.

"And what is your price?"

"You will find out later. But for now, I'll have one of Dinuk's men bring you to the storage facility to retrieve what you seek."

Dinuk. Charlie had already met Visla Maktan's head of security. An unsettling man who looked too relaxed to be security for one as powerful and important as the visla was. It was precisely that dichotomy that set Charlie on edge. After years as a gladiator, he had learned the least imposing opponents were often the deadliest.

"Thank you, Denna Maktan."

"I told you, call me Malalia."

"Thank you, Malalia. Hertzall and I appreciate your kindness."

"I am pleased to help. Now go. Do whatever you need before my father returns."

He was escorted down a long corridor by one of the security entourage, until they were deep within the building, then he was taken down a winding flight of stairs to an underground storage chamber. It was a simple matter of his guide chanting a search incantation, making his collar glow as he neared the container linked to it.

"Here it is," the stout man said, pulling the sealed box from the shelf. He muttered *"Ngthiri kaspia monopeh,"* and the seamless case sprang open.

Ngthiri kaspia monopeh, Charlie repeated in his head. *Similar to Captain Tür's collar release command. That's the Ngthiri, which must mean 'open.' The other words relate to the object, I'd wager.*

"Here are the possessions you wish to use. Choose from them, then I shall take you to Hertzall, as the denna has ordered."

"Yeah, I'm on it," Charlie said, amused that the fair woman held such fearsome sway over the stocky guard.

The container held many things Charlie had never thought he'd see again. Apparently, Gramfir hadn't sold all of them off after all.

"Ah, there it is," he said as he pulled his med scanner from the bottom of the container. "I was afraid it might not have been saved."

As he lifted it, he saw the most unexpected thing lying in the bottom, underneath a jumble of random equipment.

His firearms.

They've never seen guns before, he realized. *They had no idea what they do, so they just tossed them in here with the other foreign junk.*

He stared but a moment longer, more acutely aware of his captivity than he had been in several years, then turned to his guide and guard. "Okay, I've got what I need," he said, leaving the weapons untouched.

He didn't know if he'd need them, but knowing they were within the palace walls gave him a strange feeling he hadn't had in ages. Hope. The hope that he might actually escape.

CHAPTER ELEVEN

Charlie found Hertzall where he had left him in the small grove, studying the trees, chanting spells designed to heal them, only to watch their restorative magic fade before his eyes. Nature, it seemed, had other plans, and his magical tricks were not going to sway her.

"Hertzall, I'm back!" he called as he grew within earshot. Charlie had a sneaking suspicion the man did not enjoy being surprised, and given how intently he was focused on his work, the odds of that happening were quite high.

"Did you procure what you were looking for?"

"Yeah, they hadn't sold it off, thank God," he replied, patting his med scanner lovingly. "This baby should be able to figure out what's up. And if we're lucky, she may even take us to the source."

"Source? Source of what? Is someone casting spells to harm the visla's lands?" he asked, concerned.

"No, nothing like that. Calm down, Hertzall. Let me run my tests and we'll make a plan from there, okay?"

"Well, all right," the groundskeeper relented.

Charlie powered up the med scanner and held it up to one

of the healthy trees on the other side of the orchard to take a baseline reading.

"What manner of magic is this?"

"It's called technology, my friend. And it's really useful, once you get the hang of it."

"But you are not using incantations. And you have no konus. Is this a *powered* thing in your hands?" he asked with fear. "The visla doesn't allow––"

"I already told you, there's no magic in this. Just technology. Now settle down and let me finish."

He ran scans of several healthy trees and logged the data. Then he did the same for the afflicted trees. The machine ran its analysis and chimed when the results were ready.

"Okay, I think I've found your problem."

"Is it a curse?"

"Nope. Sorry to disappoint you, but it's nothing so nefarious. It looks like there's some heavy metal poisoning going on. It's nothing I understand, mind you, but whatever is leaching into the soil in that part of the orchard is bringing something nasty with it."

"A spell in the ground?"

"Again with the magic stuff? Hertzall, not everything is caused by magic. Sometimes nature does things on her own. Now come on, let's see if we can find the source."

"But if it is under the ground as you say, how can we possibly––"

"Don't worry about that. I've got some experience tracking things underground," he replied, thinking back to his encounter with the magical waters way back when. Back when he was a free man. Back when his friend Rika was still herself.

He shook the thoughts from his head. "Okay, give me a minute to get this dialed in."

The readings were far easier to pinpoint than the waters in

the Balamar Wastelands, and in less than a minute Charlie had a solid signal tracing the subterranean flow.

"And away we go," he said, following the directions the med scanner presented him.

They walked a weaving path, leaving the trails behind several times as they crossed the estate. Charlie noted a few other plants in the path were showing some signs of irregularity, but the trees seemed to be more sensitive to the toxins. And if they were unhealthy from the roots up, it made sense Hertzall's healing spells would only do so much. It was a continuous, slow poisoning. What they needed was to stop it at the source.

Charlie stared at the scanner as it took them to a part of the estate he had not yet explored, moving farther and farther from the main buildings, over a low hill and into a shallow glen. The signal was growing much stronger when Charlie felt the heat around his neck grow rapidly.

"Ow! Sonofa––" He looked up and realized he had unintentionally walked right up to the low stone wall marking the visla's perimeter.

He took several steps back until the burning receded. "What's that over there?" he asked, pointing to a small building just visible, jutting up from behind a small hill.

"I don't know," Hertzall said. "One of the visla's outer buildings, but it is long unused, so far as I know. Why?"

"Because I think that's where your groundwater is being poisoned. Whatever is being done in there is the cause of the problems."

Hertzall looked both perturbed and relieved at the same time. "Visla Maktan will be upset, I'm sure. But he also wanted me to keep his grounds in tip-top condition."

"You're just doing your job. If he is angry at you for that, then he's not as good a man as I thought him to be."

"Oh, the visla is a *great* man."

"Then you should have nothing to be concerned about,"

Charlie replied. "Now come on, let's head back. There's nothing more we can do from here."

They had walked a little way when they were greeted by a loud whistle from a hilltop nearby. The tall figure was still a ways in the distance, but Hertzall seemed to brighten at their arrival.

"A friend of yours, I assume?"

"It is Leila," Hertzall said with a bright smile, whistling back.

"Who's Leila?"

"My daughter," he said proudly as they watched a lithe woman with the palest of green skin and deep chestnut hair run down from the hillside to greet them.

"Father," she greeted her old man, hugging him fiercely. The groundskeeper grinned broadly with palpable parental pride. "And who might you be? The man who has been picking all the tsokin berries, I assume?"

Not a shrinking violet, this one, Charlie mused. *The apple fell a bit far from the tree, that's for sure.*

"I'm Charlie. Visla Maktan's new toy."

"A pleasure, Charlie," she said, clasping his hand firmly. "I'm Leila."

"Your father said."

"Oh, already telling strangers about me, are you?" she chided her father.

"Now, now, Leila. You know I leave you to your animals, but making new friends won't kill you."

"I know. I'm just playing with you."

Charlie couldn't help but stare at the two, one a deep brown, the other the palest green. "I hope you don't take offense at my asking, but how is your daughter such a different color than you, Hertzall?"

The man chuckled. "Her mother was an Alatsav. They're a cousin race of the Tslavars, but much fairer, and of gentler spirit."

"Ah, I didn't realize how things worked between the species out here. Sorry for asking. It's all still pretty new to me, even after a few years."

"That's all right, Charlie. You're the first pink person I've seen," Leila said with a warm laugh. "I bet you turn bright red if you spend too much time in the sun."

"I tan, actually. Good genes."

He wondered what hue the girl would adopt if left out in the sun too long. With the brown of her father and the pale green from her mother, he figured a nice olive tone would be most likely.

"Leila is Visla Maktan's head animal keeper," Hertzall said proudly. "She is in charge of all of his pets."

"They're not all pets, Father. Many are still wild beasts, especially the newest arrival."

"I know, dearest. But did you hear? Charlie here actually rode one of them."

Charlie's ears perked up. "Hang on, is there a Zomoki here?"

"Yes. It was brought in the same time you were. A huge one, too. Big and red and nasty. It was out cold for several days before it finally woke up, hungry and *angry*."

"Well, she would be, wouldn't she, after what they did to us?"

"She? I hadn't determined its gender yet. Cursed thing needs some minor wounds cleaned up, but it––*she* won't let me get close."

Charlie felt a flush of adrenaline in his system. Adrenaline, and hope.

"Maybe I can help with that."

CHAPTER TWELVE

The path to the animal enclosures for the larger of the visla's beasts wound through a grove across the far side of the estate, quite a way from the ailing trees Hertzall found so troubling.

"You're going to leave me *now*? Before we resolve this problem?"

"It'll be okay, Father," Leila soothed. The old man was rather beside himself with worry.

"But Visla Maktan will be upset if there is a die-off on his grounds. You know how he can be about things like that. Especially if magic is involved."

"I told you, Hertzall, it's not magic," Charlie corrected.

"So your tech-magic device says. Which is another problem entirely. You know the visla's rules on––"

"It's not tech-magic. It's just tech. No magic. And what's harming the trees isn't a spell. It just looks like a slow-acting metal poisoning. And I really don't think it will progress to any significant degree while we are gone. And besides, you don't need to worry, I'll work on figuring out a solution to this mess while I'm helping Leila. I can multi-task like that," he said, throwing a wink at the man's daughter.

"He's right, Father. Whatever is going on with those trees, you've been complaining about them for weeks. A few hours won't make a bit of difference, and my problem *is* a bit more pressing."

"Well——"

"I knew you'd understand." She gave her father a kiss on the cheek, then turned and began walking briskly down a narrow, almost invisible path in the vegetation.

If not for her lead, Charlie could see how it would be easy to take a wrong turn and lose the path entirely. Fortunately, the groundskeeper's daughter apparently had no desire to ditch her tagalong. Especially not if he might be able to help her with her exotic new problem guest.

"Are you coming?" she asked, slowing her pace.

"Right behind you," Charlie replied, trotting after her.

Now that they were on their own, Charlie was able to examine his new acquaintance more closely, without the fear of offending her father by his innocent observations. The last green people he had interacted with were the Tslavars, so his curiosity about the far-paler girl was natural.

Her skin, in fact, was so light green, he imagined it would pass for a Mediterranean complexion if she were to get a tan. That is, if she carried her father's genetics in her skin as well. It was all a mystery to Charlie, but over the years at least he had gotten better about asking potentially awkward questions. For the most part, at least.

"So, your mom was kind of like a Tslavar, huh?"

"No!" Leila hissed. "She was *nothing* like a Tslavar."

Shit. Went and put my foot in that one. Nice job, Charlie, he chided himself.

"I'm sorry. I didn't mean to upset you. I just meant that Hertzall said her race was a close cousin to them, is all. I'd assume there were certain similarities. Please, correct me if I'm being an ass."

"You're being an ass."

"Okay, noted. My apologies."

Leila let out an exasperated sigh, then took a deep breath.

"Look, I understand this is new to you, and I get it that you meant no offense, but you can't just go around telling people their mom was some Tslavar whore."

"Whoa, now. Hang on! That's not at all what I said."

"I know, but the Tslavars and my mother's people, well, let's just say they aren't exactly on the best of terms."

"I get it. Like the cousins you see at family gatherings and wonder if there's going to be a fight this year, right? Trust me, we humans know all about that. Remind me to tell you about a holiday we have called Christmas. It can be quite the shit-show."

She looked at him again, this time with her head cocked slightly and sporting a funny little grin.

"I suppose," she said, her tone softening. "But if your 'Christmas' is half as bad, heavens help your world."

"There are times I wonder," Charlie laughed.

They passed from the hidden trail onto a larger track that branched off through another small grove of trees. These bore small fruit, the sweet aroma of which would have been pleasing, if not for the rotting, half-eaten ones discarded on the ground.

"Damned yertzi got at them again," Leila groaned.

"Yertzi?"

"Those, over there," she said, pointing to koala-sized balls of fluff with enormous eyes and spider monkey-like arms.

Unlike drop bears, however, the yertzi moved quickly through the trees, their bulbous bodies carried effortlessly by their strong limbs.

"Father will have a fit if he sees this," she said, kicking the discarded fruit into a pile. "I'll have to get rid of this before he tends this area tomorrow."

She turned her attention to the source of her annoyance and squinted ever so slightly as she murmured some

67

incomprehensible sounds. Unlike the magic Charlie had become accustomed to, this sounded different. Then he noticed she was not wearing a konus.

The yertzi turned to look at her, one of them stopping mid-bite. A surprised expression passed over their faces.

"That's right. And don't let me catch you back here," she said.

The animals quickly dropped their food and scampered away, leaving Charlie scratching his head at what he'd just seen.

"Uh, that wasn't regular magic. And you're not wearing any powered devices."

"Oh, that," she replied as if it were nothing special. "It's the one thing I apparently have some aptitude for."

"It's amazing."

"I don't know if I'd go that far. Since I was a child my father always said I had a way with animals. It turns out he was right. It's a bit of position security that makes me better suited for my role on the visla's grounds. I'm good enough that I doubt he would replace me on a whim, given what I do. Not that others can't, mind you. It's just, he likes my father, and I'd be pretty much useless anywhere else, so he lets me work with the animals. Here, doing this––it's the one thing I'm good at."

"But Leila. You spoke to the animals without a konus."

"Of course. That's my thing. The lowest of the barely powered on the estate, and all I am able to do is tell the stupid yertzi to get lost," she said with a little chuckle. "A shaker of worlds, I am not."

"Well, I find it impressive," Charlie said.

She blushed slightly, a little red coming to her green-tinged cheeks.

"Thanks for saying so, but it's really nothing. Now, my mother, she was rumored to have some *real* power in her veins. Unfortunately, she was sold when I was very young, so I never got to discuss it with her. But Father said she was a woman of considerable gifts."

They reached the end of the wooded trail, the path opening to a large, protected clearing with a number of enclosures of varying sizes containing all manner of animal. Some Charlie recognized from his travels to distant worlds, while others were completely novel to him.

His attention was drawn to the sturdy gate leading into the largest of the holding enclosures. Something was making his whole body tingle. Something familiar. Inside those walls was a Zomoki. *His* Zomoki, though he'd never dream of claiming ownership over her. But whatever their connection, he knew who was behind the gate without having to look. He sensed her.

"Mind if I take a peek?"

CHAPTER THIRTEEN

"Why, hello again, beautiful," Charlie said, carefully stepping up to the barred gate of the large holding pen. A large, golden eye glanced his way, but nothing more.

"Its scales and hide are rough and worn," Leila commented.

"She's still beautiful to me," he replied, scanning the enclosure.

It was a low wall spanning an area roughly one hundred meters across, but there was no roof, nor were there chains securing the Zomoki. Just a thick, faintly glowing band around her neck, much heavier than the one she'd previously been wearing.

"Don't worry," Leila said, watching him take in the openness of the enclosure. "Visla Maktan set the containment spells himself. With his power, and the new collar he affixed on the Zomoki, there's no possibility of it harming you."

"I'm not worried about her harming me," he said. "Now, would you mind opening the gate?"

"I'm sorry, you want to go in? I told you, it won't let anyone near, even with the restraining spells. She's an exceptionally powerful one."

"Just open the gate, please. I'll be fine. Promise."

Leila looked him over a moment. He seemed a nice enough fellow, and it would be a shame for the visla's new gladiator to be eaten on her watch.

"I don't know––"

"She won't hurt me. Will you?" he called to the resting beast.

The enormous dragon lazily turned her head, lounging in the sun much like a cat. Only a cat that could breathe fire. But the dragon made no sign of aggression.

"I'll probably regret this," Leila said, opening the gate with a quiet spell.

"It'll be fine. And if you hand me those bandages and water, I'll see about cleaning her up while I'm at it."

"Don't let her blood touch your skin, or you'll be dead before you hit the ground."

Charlie had already had more than a little of this dragon's blood on his skin, but despite a week of miserable fever, it had most certainly *not* killed him. He decided to keep that fact to himself, for the time being. He had a good feeling about the groundskeeper's daughter, but he had been mistaken about people before.

He picked up the supplies and walked into the enclosure, the enormity of the dragon making a small, primitive part of his brain scream, *"Get out! Run!"* as he approached her. With a deep breath, he forced the fear from his mind.

"Hello!" he called out as he cautiously moved closer. "I am here to clean your injuries. I'd appreciate it if you didn't eat me."

The dragon shifted position to better see him.

"Eating you would be rude," she noted, her voice coming through clear as a bell inside his head. *"You know, we don't have to talk out loud, right? In fact, it's probably a much better idea if you don't let anyone know we are able to communicate at all."*

"So, you read my thoughts?"

71

"Not so much read your thoughts as you and I are linked and can choose to communicate in this manner, if we so desire."

"Whoa."

She chuckled in his mind.

"Yes, I suppose that would sum the experience up for a Boroki."

"A what?"

"Boroki. Pink people from a few systems away."

"Oh, I'm not a Boroki. I'm a human. From Earth."

"Earth? Never heard of it."

"You wouldn't have. It's in another galaxy."

"Impossible. There is no magic in existence that can convey people across the vast blackness beyond the galaxy, and I've managed some rather long trips between systems over the years. But another galaxy? It simply can't be done."

"Funny you say that. I was of pretty much the same belief until a wormhole sucked in my ship and spat it out in another part of the universe. Then, to make things worse, here we are, the first of my kind ever to leave our own solar system, and we crash all the way out in some desolate wasteland. And just our luck, too. Out of a whole green planet, we had to wind up in the desert ruins of some old battlefield."

At this the dragon perked up.

"A battlefield, you say? But it was a wasteland? It wouldn't have been the Balamar Wastelands, by any chance, would it?"

"Yeah, that's what they called it. Said there was some massive war against a powerful visla a long time ago."

The massive Zomoki sat up, filled with curiosity, though, unlike a cat, she didn't need nine lives, as she had already lived centuries.

"That would explain it," she mused. *"And tell me. Did you happen to find any waters in that wasteland? A rivulet, perhaps? Or some dew on the rocks that seemed a bit more iridescent than it should be?"*

"As a matter of fact, I did," he replied. *"Hey, do you mind if I clean up those cuts? She's watching, and I told her you'd let me."*

"Ah, the young woman watching you so intently? She has a good heart."

"You can tell that? Is it some kind of magic thing?"

"Nothing like that. I just see how she treats others."

"So why won't you let her help you?"

A pair of huge golden eyes stared deep into Charlie's much smaller ones.

"Because, I was captured, harmed, forced into servitude, thrown into battle, then blasted with some accursed magic and taken here. I've been a little cross, but with good reason, I think."

"I see your point," Charlie said.

"But to answer your question, yes, you may tend my wounds."

"Thank you," he said, moving close and gently applying water to the scratches in her tough hide. *"Hang on, did you say she was watching me intently? If anything, she should be watching you,"* he said, turning to see if Leila was watching.

Indeed, she seemed to be staring at his treatment of the beast with rapt attention.

Again, the dragon laughed inside his head. *"You people really are so predictable at times. Now, tell me. Did any of the water you discovered in the Balamar Wastelands touch your skin?"*

"You could say that."

"Ah. This explains it."

"What?"

"How you survived touching my blood. Normally it kills men outright, but you were resistant."

"I had a fever for a week. I nearly died!"

"But you did not. Those waters were thought lost long ago. So long that they've passed from history into legend. But those who touch them are granted a degree of restorative power. This is what saved you, though it is incredibly unusual for it to have granted you the connection we share."

"Well, I was thinking about that," Charlie said. *"I figure, when*

your blood got into my wound and mixed with mine, some sort of weird blood bond must have been formed."

The Zomoki reared up in shock, towering above him, her restraint collar glowing bright.

"That is impossible! You would have died!"

"Charlie, are you okay?" Leila yelled in alarm. "I'll trigger the stun spell, get clear!"

"No! Wait! It's okay, just give me a minute," he shouted back to her. "Don't stun her! It'll be all right."

"You had best calm down before she knocks you out again," he warned.

The Zomoki paced nervously, then settled back onto her haunches, flapping her wings once before sliding back to a relaxed pose. But she wasn't relaxed. Charlie could feel the tension crackling between them.

"What's the matter? You're freaking out, here."

"No one has formed a blood bond with a Zomoki for longer than I can remember. It should be impossible. Only the most powerful of all the vislas were foolish enough to even try."

"Vislas like Balamar?"

"Yes."

"And it was his waters I swam in?"

"Yes." She spun abruptly, her massive head hovering in front of him. *"Did you say swam?"*

"Uh, yeah, about the waters. It was kind of more than a little trickle I found. More like a giant cistern, actually. But it was hidden underground. The war must have collapsed everything around it and buried it years ago. I found it with my med scanner."

"Your what?"

"This," he said, showing her the device slung across his shoulder. *"A piece of tech that I tuned to follow the specific spectral and chemical signatures of the small pool of water we found. I used it to track down the source."*

"But this magic does not exist, and I sense no power in this little

box you hold. Plus, the waters were protected in such a manner that no spell could find them."

"Well, it wasn't a spell. It was tech, like I told you," he said, powering on the device. "See? I can scan your wounds and see how serious they are, for example. And they're not bad at all, by the way."

The dragon was beside herself. Stunned.

"If the cistern is intact—but you say you swam in it? My God, the waters—you must have healed so very quickly, for a time."

"Still do, actually."

"Still? But that shouldn't be. How long ago was this?"

"A little less than three years."

"That's impossible. A few months at most, perhaps. Years? It has never been heard of."

"Well, I did sort of drink a whole bunch of it, too."

At that the dragon actually jumped back in shock.

"Don't zap her! It's okay!" he yelled to Leila.

"You really need to stop doing that."

She sat back down and slowly lowered her head to eye-level. "All but a handful of creatures in the entire galaxy die if they consume those waters."

"I'm not from this galaxy," he reminded her. "Human. Different species and all that."

Gears were churning in the wise old creature's head. A man had ingested the waters and lived. The possibilities spread before her like pieces on a chessboard.

"You must not tell Visla Maktan any of this. If he realizes what you have done he will kill you at once, and likely me with you."

"Why? It's not like I'm a threat to anyone."

"You drank the waters and can speak with Zomoki. More than that, you and I are bonded. There is no telling what you may be capable of. The very thought of Zomoki blood in a man's veins would send any visla into panic. And a panicked visla is a very dangerous thing."

Charlie didn't know why he should trust the Zomoki, but

here he was, actually *speaking* with a dragon. A dragon he was somehow linked to.

"Okay, I'll keep this all a secret," he said. *"Now, let me dress those wounds so Leila doesn't get in trouble."*

"Do as you will."

"Thanks. Oh, and my name's Charlie, by the way."

"I am Aranzgrgghmunatharrgle," she replied.

"Aranzgg... I'm sorry, what was that, again?"

The dragon laughed. *"You can just call me Ara for short."*

Leila walked Charlie back to the palace, picking his brain with excitement the whole way. No one had ever had a Zomoki allow them to treat them without requiring excessive use of the restraint collar to quiet them. For the animalist, it was extraordinary.

"I want to continue this discussion later," she said when they reached the servants' entrance. "There's so much more I want to ask."

Her eyes were alive with energy and fire, and Charlie couldn't help but be caught up in her enthusiasm.

"Okay, whenever you want, just ask. I'm pretty much hanging around until Maktan gets back."

"Great. I'll come get you in the morning. We have so much to talk about!"

Leila spun and almost skipped back to her duties.

Apparently, being a dragon whisperer is a real draw with the ladies, he chuckled to himself.

The weight of the scanner pressed on his hip, a reminder of home. One that gave him an idea.

"Thank you for allowing me to use this," he said to the visla's daughter when he was finally granted admittance to her receiving chamber. "I was able to help Hertzall track down what seems to be the source of the problems he was dealing with."

"I am glad to have helped, Charlie," Malalia said with a warm smile. "Please, if there is anything you need, just ask."

"Well, I actually *did* have a thought, but I don't know if you'll approve of it."

She laughed brightly. "There's one way to find out."

"The thing is, there are devices on my ship that might be of great use. Things that don't work by magic. Things that could be made to help around the grounds. I have no means to get them, but if any of your people are ever near the Balamar Wastelands—"

"You landed *there*? Why would you ever do that?"

"We crashed. Trust me, it wasn't intentional."

"I see," she said, intrigued. "That system is a fair distance from here, but if one of our craft is passing that way, I'll inquire of the captain."

"Thanks," Charlie said. "I figure if I'm living under your roof, and since I don't have any magic, maybe I can still find some way to be useful."

"I'm sure I'll find use for you," she replied with a smile in her eyes that made his stomach twist ever so slightly.

Oh boy. This could get interesting, he mused as he walked back to his room.

CHAPTER FOURTEEN

"No, I said I need *everyone*," Leila growled as she barged in through the kitchen, right past Magda and her assistants.

Tuktuk and Charlie were enjoying their coffee and pastry on the small landing outside, relaxing on what had, up until that moment, been a tranquil morning.

Charlie had desperately wanted to talk to *someone* about the events of the prior day, and the cheerful blue man was as close to a confidante as he had on this world. Nevertheless, he realized how dangerous it could be to let *any* details about his and Ara's connection slip, even to a trusted friend. One loose lip or overheard comment and things could get very difficult for both of them.

"There you are," Leila said, spotting Charlie sitting outside the adjacent door. "I need your help."

"What's up, Leila? You know Tuktuk, right?"

She cocked her head at him. "Of course I do, Charlie. *You're* the new one here, remember?"

"Silly me, being polite."

"Oh, please. You know what I meant," she said, rolling her eyes.

"Sorry, blue person is a little lost over here. What exactly is going on?" Tuktuk asked with a confused look.

Magda pushed her way past the groundskeeper's daughter. "I'm sorry, Tuk. She just barged in, raving about the bundabist getting out and tearing up the place."

"Well, that *would* be a problem," Tuktuk noted.

"I know it's a problem. But that's no reason to go running around in a frenzy."

Leila's patience was running thin. "Look, they got out, and they're making a mess of the grounds. And they've already torn up some of the new bean crops. Now, if you don't help me get this under control, Visla Maktan is going to be angry with *all* of us."

That got Magda's attention.

"Oh, all right. I'll go see who is free to help you. But don't expect much. We all have our own duties, you know."

"Thank you, Magda. Anything helps. The more bodies out there, the easier it is to corral them and get them back in their pen. They're not too bright, but they're hell to catch once they get wound up."

"Okay, I'm in," Charlie said, finishing his coffee in a gulp and rising to his feet. "Now, what exactly are bundabist?"

"You'll see. Now, come with me. But first we need to get you cleared to cross the perimeter with the others."

Leila didn't wait for a reply. Charlie hurried after her down the corridors of the sprawling estate.

"Where are we going?"

"You're new here, so your collar limits you to the innermost grounds," she replied. "Most of us are cleared to go beyond the first wall."

"You mean there are more walls?"

"Oh, yeah. The visla owns the lands as far as you can see in all directions," she said, quickly weaving through the hallways. "Azkan, there you are."

A sturdily built man, carrying an assortment of weapons, both magical and conventional, nodded his greeting as she approached. "What is it this time, Leila?" he groaned. "Another false intruder alarm at the outer perimeter?"

"No. And I tell you, I saw someone."

"Uh-huh," he said dismissively. "Our search turned up nothing. Each time."

"That doesn't mean there was nothing there. Regardless, I need you to extend this one's collar boundaries. The bundabist all got out, and he's going to help with their recapture."

"You know only Dinuk and the visla are allowed to alter the boundary spells on new slaves' collars."

There it is again. Slave. I guess it's only natural that someone still says it.

"Look, Dinuk and the visla aren't here, and as Dinuk's second-in-command, you are tasked with the same head of security responsibilities as he is, correct?"

"Yes, but—"

"And if someone needs collar restrictions changed due to a security issue, like, say, a half dozen of the visla's new bundabist tearing up the estate, that job now falls to you, am I right?"

"Well..." He hesitated. "It should, but I—"

"But you what? Won't help catch his new pets before they do any further damage?"

Man, she's tough as nails, Charlie admired. *Glad she's not pissed at me.*

Azkan shifted uncomfortably on his feet, which was an odd sight for an otherwise intimidating and well-armed man. "The thing is, I actually *can't* change the collar settings," he said, his fingers twirling the heavy band on his wrist. "I mean, my konus is powered enough, but I don't know the spell."

"Well, that's disappointing," she replied. "Come on, Charlie. We'll have to put you to work on the inside perimeter, somehow."

"Perhaps I can help," a voice said, as the nearest door opened.

Malalia, resplendent in her sheerest, iridescent dress, flowed out to join the conversation. "If it is a simple modification to my father's spell, I'd be more than happy to help. For *you*, Charlie."

She placed her hands on the collar, her fingers lingering on his neck, then turned slowly to Leila. "Now, how far out did you need him to go?" she asked, her eyes coolly observing the roughly clothed animalist.

"Just past the first couple of walls. I don't think they've gone much farther than that."

"I can do that, of course," Malalia said, turning her gaze back to Charlie. "Don't worry. You won't feel a thing."

The collar began to glow as she chanted a series of incantations, so softly and under her breath that Charlie couldn't quite make them out. He noted she was not wearing a konus.

She must have a lot of her father's power to cast that effortlessly.

A moment later the band stopped glowing and she slid her hands from the collar, sliding her fingers along his throat as she did. "There, all done. That should give you range you need."

"Thank you," Charlie murmured.

"It was my pleasure," she said, eyes sparkling.

Leila's didn't sparkle as she rolled them. "Come on. We have work to do."

CHAPTER FIFTEEN

"How did they escape?" Charlie asked as he inspected the open enclosure gate. It didn't appear to have been smashed or forced from the inside, but then, with magical locking systems, he really didn't know what had caused the pen to open.

"It *looks* as if someone left the gate ajar," Leila said.

"You don't sound so convinced."

"I shouldn't be. I'm the one who secured it. Even if I'd only used my usual locking spell, this should never happen. But since the bundabist are a bit rambunctious, especially in a new environment, I took the precaution of doubling up and adding a secondary, redundant spell, just in case."

"So they broke both of them? That seems pretty unlikely."

"It is. And no, they didn't break out. The spell never failed. It was *removed*. But don't mention a word of that. The visla will have a fit if he learns someone was tampering with magic on his grounds."

"But everyone seems to cast to one degree or another."

"Yes, but with carefully limited konuses. And each are restricted beyond just power levels, but also tied to their specific duties. It's fine for getting work done around the estate, but those konuses simply *couldn't* have done this."

"So who did?"

"That's the question of the hour. Something's not right. But first things first, we need to get you caught up with the others to join the hunt. Bundabist aren't terribly dangerous, at least not intentionally, but they have been known to trample people on occasion when they get worked up."

"While we're on the subject of bundabist, what exactly are they?"

"Oh, right. There's a baby in one of the side pens. It was a bit undersized when it was born, so I've been feeding the little one by hand and keeping it safe from the others until it's big enough to not be injured by them."

He peered into a smaller side enclosure.

"*That's* a little one?" he said.

The young bundabist easily topped thirty kilos and looked like a cross between a large hyena and a pangolin, with plates of armor mixing with its fur across its back all the way to its belly.

"Who's a good girl?" Leila cooed, reaching into the enclosure and scratching the sweet spot behind its ears. The bundabist let out a rumbling purr, almost like a feline, though its build was definitely more canine in nature.

"Uh, exactly how big do these get?"

"I'd say about four times this size."

"And you say they sometimes hurt people."

"Only because they're overly excitable. There's not a mean bone in their bodies, though they do look big and scary. Don't you? Don't you look scary?" she said to the blissed-out animal, whose rear leg was now twitching as she scratched lower down on its back. "Okay, we need to meet up with the others. They headed out a half hour ago, so we lost a little time while getting Azkan to adjust your collar."

"Well, Malalia was the one who did it, technically—"

She flashed him a cool look. "Yes, Daddy's little princess to the rescue."

"That's not what I mean. Just that she helped too."

"She's not as sweet and kind as she pretends, Charlie. You'd do well to remember that."

Charlie sensed more than a tiny bit of bad blood between the women. Growing up as the servant to someone your own age must have been hard, he realized. And now, as adults, that resentment carried over, it seemed.

They ran through the fields toward the low stone wall encircling the area. Charlie felt himself tense up slightly as they vaulted it without slowing down, letting out a little sigh of relief when he was left unscathed. The collar, it seemed, was indeed allowed greater range. A blur at the corner of his eye appeared to be a pale shape running the other direction, *toward* the estate.

These things are everywhere, he thought with a smile. *At least we're getting a good workout in.*

Leila ran fast and easy, the product of a lifetime spent chasing animals and working the land with her father. Charlie had always been fit, but the two-plus years of gladiatorial training had improved upon it, and he kept pace effortlessly. It was something Leila was not used to, so she upped the speed.

Charlie kept up, and soon they reached another stone wall, perhaps a mile past the first one. A fierce burning sensation drove Charlie back as he got closer, forcing him to his knees as he quickly staggered away from the invisible barrier.

Leila vaulted the wall, then looked back, skidding to a halt when she realized what had happened.

"That bitch," she growled as she jogged back to him. "She said she was expanding the range, but she only extended it to the next ring. Dammit." Leila looked around. There was no sign of the others yet, but she saw wisps of dust in the distance. "Okay, listen. I think I see them over that hill."

"I see the dust."

"Good eyes."

"Thanks. But I can't cross the wall, so what would you have me do?"

"Stay on this side, and take this." She handed him a length of braided cord from around her waist. "If you come across one, or if we manage to drive the others back over the wall, approach from the front so it can see you, then, when you can, scratch behind its ears. That should make it calm enough to slip this over its head."

"Great, so I catch the thing. Then what? Drag it back to the pen?"

"Well, I wouldn't recommend *dragging* it, exactly. They love to run, so try making it a game, leading it back."

"Sounds like the dog I had when I was a kid."

"What's a dog?"

"A four-legged animal, about the size of the young bundabist back there. They're loyal, and fun, and generally good-natured, but they can get out of hand at times."

"That rather describes the bundabist."

"Minus the armored hide," he said with a chuckle. "We call them 'Man's best friend' back home."

"And where is home, anyway? I've heard of races with your coloring, but you lack the other traits. Your ears do not point, and you lack ridges on your shoulders."

"I'm human. From Earth. It's a planet from another galaxy."

"Another galaxy? Stop it, we all know that's impossible."

"You know, I've been saying the same thing, myself," he said.

Cries of excitement and chase wafted across the hills.

"They've found one. I must go. I'll come back to check on you. Here, take this skree. Call me if you find one, and I'll come help you."

Charlie accepted the device and watched her vault the wall and rapidly shrink in the distance. "But how do I use this?" he said quietly, studying the small communications unit. "One button. I guess it magically knows whom you want to call," he figured. "Seems on par for this place."

He slid the skree into his pocket and took off at a jog, determined to scout the mile-wide ring he was now allowed access to. With luck, Leila would return to one less bundabist to capture.

Twenty minutes later, Charlie had covered a lot of ground, yet there had been no sign of the roving animals.

Did any of them stay between the walls, here? he wondered as he scanned the rolling hills.

Something in the near distance caught his eye. A path leading between two hills into a small glen. Resuming his jog, he redirected that way, heading onto the shady trail.

This looks familiar, he realized as the trail twisted and turned, opening up on a small clearing with a squat building. From this angle, he could barely see the inner wall just past the hill.

It was the same building he had traced the heavy metal poisoning to while helping Hertzall. The revelation both thrilled and worried him, but neither slowed his stride as he crept up to the building.

Outside, there did not seem to be any conveyances or ships that he could see, though the large doors could easily accommodate one if need be. Charlie quietly approached an open window, the opening possessing no glass, likely covered by a spell, as had been the case on Captain Tür's ship.

Sure enough, he felt resistance when he put his hand near it, but not the violent sensation in his collar as had been his previous experience. Satisfied he wouldn't burn his neck by near proximity, he leaned closer and peered through the opening.

Crates upon crates were stacked, though he couldn't tell what sort of material they were made of. They all seemed to glow slightly, and there were no markings on the outsides. The few open ones, however, were being loaded by a species he had not seen before.

Shorter than most, they were heavily muscled, the definition enhanced by the work-induced sheen of sweat they sported. Their skin was a deep green with black patches, and they possessed wiry hair running from the tops of their heads down their backs and into their tunics, almost like a full-body mohawk.

Fucking hideous. But what are they up to?

A small smelting apparatus was pouring liquid metal of some variety into glowing molds, the spell containing the heat also cooling them to their final form in under a minute.

"Slaaps," Charlie exhaled when they opened the mold and dumped a half dozen of the magical weapons onto the finishing bench.

He looked at the crates. Piled high, each was easily able to hold dozens, if not more. And in another crate, he saw finished konuses being slid into holding racks, the crates then sealed with a spell, the seams disappearing under a magic lock and key.

The slag left over from the process was trickling into a shaft in the center of the facility. A waste well that had apparently leaked into the groundwater. This was what was poisoning the trees, but Charlie thought he had stumbled onto something far worse than that.

Survival instinct, do your thing. Which way? I need to boogie the hell out of here before I'm seen.

Back the way he came was an option, but he thought he heard the faint sound of approaching steps.

Okay. The other way, then.

He took off at a run, rounding the small hill and shifting to an angle that put him out of the line of sight of the factory building. The low wall was nearing, and he increased his pace. A quick vault and maybe five-minute run and he'd be back at the stables. He needed to talk to someone. Ara, being old enough to have seen a lot in her time, might have some insight.

Charlie jumped high, clearing the wall at full speed.

A powerful shock threw him to the ground, and he lay there, unconscious, for a long, long time.

CHAPTER SIXTEEN

It was dark outside when Charlie woke in his own bed. Someone had carried him back to the estate and laid him down in his room, but he had absolutely no recollection of it.

He touched his neck, but there were no tell-tale aches from the collar, yet his head was still swimming. Something had stunned him as he cleared the wall. *What*, was the question.

He rose to his feet, swaying slightly, still unsteady, then made his way to the door. The flights of stairs down to the kitchen felt longer than usual, but the more he moved his body, the more he felt himself recovering his strength.

"Charlie, I didn't know you were back," Magda said as she saw him coming down the hallway. "Weren't you out with Leila and the others? I didn't think they were done yet."

"I don't know, actually. I was wanting to check something with Malalia. You know where she is?"

"*Denna* Maktan is in her chambers, last I saw. But it would do you well to stay clear of her. Her father can be very protective of his daughter."

"I'll keep that in mind," he said, making his way down the long corridor toward the other wing in the building.

A heated exchange could be heard taking place as he neared Malalia's rooms. It sounded like Visla Maktan and his daughter were having words. Another voice chimed in periodically.

Ah, Dinuk is back with Visla Maktan.

Charlie was going to approach quietly to eavesdrop and maybe learn what the fuss was about, but his unsteady feet betrayed him, knocking against a low table.

Shit.

He quickened his pace and played it off as best he could. "Visla Maktan, so glad to see you've returned."

"Go to bed. We'll continue this later," he said to Malalia, who flashed an apologetic look to Charlie as she closed her door.

"I hope your trip was successful," Charlie continued.

"It was, thank you. But I find myself perturbed by reports of strange goings-on in my absence."

Shit. He knows.

"Dinuk's men have informed him that some form of cursed magic was used on my grounds, and my daughter played some part in it. I assure you, Charlie, while I am a benevolent owner, I am still that. *Your owner.* And using this 'tech-magic' is an abomination and shall not be allowed on these grounds. Do you understand?"

"Yes, but it's not magic. It's just technology. Scientific instrumentation—"

"Silence!" Maktan bellowed, a swell of angry magical pressure emanating from his body, shifting the air in the room. "You have corrupted my daughter by involving her with your unnatural works. I've examined your implements and find them to be antithetical to magical laws."

"Like I said, it's not—"

"I can feel no power in them, yet they perform powerful acts. This is abhorrent to my sensibilities and shall never happen here again."

"But—"

"Stand still and be silent! *San ovusk!*" Visla Maktan hissed, negating his translation spell.

"What do you think, Dinuk? Should I punish him further for show?"

The head of security cast an assessing eye on Charlie. "No. Not yet, at least. While it might make an impression now, I think this one is smarter than he lets on. Violence could backfire and make him redouble his efforts. Keeping him in the dark is key to your plans. He trusts you, and it is important to maintain that trust."

"Hmm, I fear you are correct in that assessment, and we need him working for us, not against us."

I can still understand them, Charlie marveled. The incantation had *always* canceled his translation spell, since the very first time he'd heard it, yet something was different. *Of course,* he realized. *The dragon. Ara was right. It's her blood. And since our bonding, something new has happened to me.*

It turned out she was right about something else as well. The truth about their connection was something he needed to protect at all costs.

It seemed that not only had her blood mixed with his, allowing them to communicate, but more than that, Zomoki were powerful creatures, and the intermingling had gifted him her power of understanding. Even without the visla's spell in place, he wasn't missing a word.

"And what of the Zomoki?" Maktan asked. "Has the groundskeeper's daughter tamed it sufficiently to study?"

"As I understand it, Visla, the Zomoki is well-restrained with its new collar and will be forced to bend to your will, when you wish it."

"Excellent. You saw what it was capable of at the tournament. In that one instant, it actually cast *through* the restraining field."

"I know, Visla. I saw. While they are all magic-bearing

creatures to some degree, none have shown any significant abilities for longer than I can remember."

"Longer than that, even. The power. It was unlike anything witnessed in centuries, and somehow, this piddling little pink man is connected to it."

Piddling? Little? Charlie suddenly very much wanted to *not* hold his tongue, but wisely kept his ire in check.

"The fabrication of the slaaps is nearly complete, but we still need them charged. Even with the other vislas in the Council of Twenty combining our power, it will take months to do so, and at great personal cost, no less. The Ootaki are gathered, but if we could harness the power of the Zomoki—"

"No one has harnessed a mature Zomoki's magic before. Not even in Balamar's time. And every time it is attempted, all of them have either died during capture or while in captivity," Dinuk noted.

"But something changed. You saw it."

"Do you truly believe this *human* thing will be what turns the tide? The key that makes it different this time?"

"If this man *rode* upon a Zomoki, then he must have a way with the beasts. So long as he believes we are his friends and protectors, he will help willingly."

"And if he ceases being willing?"

"You know my methods, Dinuk," Visla Maktan said, smiling all the while.

Maktan turned to Charlie with a warm smile.

"*Impezu ovusk,*" he said, thinking he was reactivating Charlie's translation spell. "I am sorry for my reaction, Charlie. You should not anger me so. I can be known to have a bit of a temper at times."

"You did seem angry, but it all sounded like gibberish to me," Charlie lied.

"Yes, I removed your translation spell for a moment while we discussed your punishment."

"Punishment?"

"Yes. You have brought this foul *tech-magic* into my home, and you must be punished."

"But I—"

"I have decided you shall labor with the animals. Your punishment, for now, is to clean up after the Zomoki, as well as the other beasts. Do not displease me again, or it will be far worse."

"I understand."

"Good. You are to report to the animal keeper in the morning. Dinuk, see to it he receives a low-power konus and the ground-keeping spells to aid his labors," Maktan said, then turned and walked away.

Charlie watched as the powerful and profound liar rounded the corner out of sight.

Well, that was interesting.

CHAPTER SEVENTEEN

"Charlie! Wait!"

Malalia came rushing down the hallway barefoot wearing only her sheer nightgown.

"You shouldn't be talking to me, Malalia. I'll just get you in trouble."

She smiled coyly. "I already *am* in trouble. I don't think this will make it any worse."

"If your father hears you were talking with me"––he gestured at her negligee––"and like *this*, no less, he'll be *really* upset."

"You speak as though I am standing before you in a state of undress. I'm not naked, Charlie."

"No, but fathers can be very protective of their daughters."

"I'm not a child, and I can dress as I please and talk to whom I wish," she said. "But if it truly worries you, we can step out of sight of prying eyes."

Without waiting for a reply, she took him by the hand and led him to her chamber doors and through the outer rooms. He felt a tingle, and his collar began to glow as he approached the threshold to her bedroom.

"Wait. I *know* I shouldn't go in there," he said, tugging the glowing collar.

"*Azmak hopa magusi,*" she said, touching the band of metal.

Immediately, the tingle reduced to only the slightest of sensations.

"How did you––?"

"I couldn't deactivate it entirely. Father would know. But I can make it bearable, if you wish," she said, pulling him along with her into her bedroom and closing the door behind them. "Father *is* quite cross, you know, but it is too late for his stuffy-headed anger. One of our ships was heading by the planet you mentioned, and I ordered the captain to have his men bring what salvage they had room for back with them. I must admit, it does look like inelegant rubbish, but I have hope perhaps some of it will hold value for you."

"Some of my gear is here? Malalia, that's wonderful."

"I'd hoped you would be pleased. But we cannot tell Father. He disapproves of your kind of magic."

"Oh, believe me, I know."

"Ah, is that what he was yelling about?"

"He wasn't yelling, really. Just talking forcefully."

"For him, that *is* yelling. It takes a fair amount to rile him up so."

"Then consider him riled. He said I was not to engage in any more 'tech-magic' on his grounds. He didn't want to listen to my explanation that it isn't magic at all. It's just technology he doesn't understand."

"You touch a device and it performs actions no one in the Council's twenty realms can duplicate or understand. I think that sounds quite a bit like magic, wouldn't you agree?"

"Well, I suppose, when you put it like that. But if he'd just let me use my equipment, I think I could be of more use around here. I mean, he brought me here, but with no real purpose other than he liked the way I fought in my bout."

"Yes, I heard about that. Is it true you actually *rode* a Zomoki?"

"I did."

"Incredible. How did you do it?" she asked, eyes aglow.

"I don't know, honestly. And now the only thing I'm doing with Zomoki is cleaning up after them."

"You don't mean——"

"Yes. Your father has made me the human poop-scooper. As punishments go, though, I suppose it could be worse."

Malalia laughed brightly. "You are a funny man, Charlie. I like funny. We should have talks like this more often," she said, squeezing his arm. "Tell me more about your home world. And how did you come to ride a Zomoki?"

Charlie shifted uncomfortably. "Uh, look, it's been nice, Malalia, and I wish we could continue this, but I really should get to my new work, or your father will get even more angry."

"Fine," she mock-sulked, walking him to the door.

"Thank you. Really. It can be tough in a new place, and you've been beyond kind to me."

"I'd do nothing less. I like you, Charlie, and I hope we become the best of friends."

He caught a whiff of flowers in the air when she leaned in close and kissed his cheek. "The salvage from your ship is in the lower wine cellar, by the way. I suggest you keep it there. The thickness of the stones will keep Father's prying eyes away, for a time at least," she said, her warm smile lingering even after the door had closed.

Charlie was trotting down the stairs toward the kitchen on his way to the lower cellar——which he'd only learned about from Tuktuk's love of good wine——when a meaty hand grabbed him from behind. It took every fiber of restraint to hold back from throwing a powerful elbow, but inside those walls, Charlie knew better.

Sloppy, Charlie. Should have heard him.

"Hello, Dinuk," he said to the visla's head of security. "How can I help you?"

Dinuk released his arm and held out an outstretched hand. In his palm was one of the thinnest, weakest konuses Charlie had ever seen.

"Visla Maktan has granted you a konus to aid in your work. Put this on."

Charlie did as he was told, and even though there was almost no power to the device, it nevertheless felt good having one on his wrist again.

"*Eikood pooks,*" Dinuk said. "That is the waste shifting spell you will need when cleaning up after the beasts in their pens. "*Eikood pord*" deposits the waste when you have arrived at the disposal area. Enjoy your new job."

He watched the man move off down the hallway. *Quiet for such a stocky man,* Charlie noted. In his former life it would have slipped his awareness entirely, but his years under Ser Baruud's tutelage had tuned him in to many things average people might overlook.

Charlie scanned for prying eyes, and, when he felt certain no one was looking, he slid into the curving stairwell leading to the subterranean storage areas beneath the kitchen and servants' quarters.

The wide stairs had a fine layer of red dust on them, the sight of which brought a wave of memory crashing over him. The crash. Surviving the harsh conditions of the wasteland. The deaths of his friends. And poor Rika.

The dirt would be cleaned soon enough, and he had no time to waste. Charlie shook himself free of memory's grip and padded down the corridor to the lower wine cellar. He entered the room, closing the sturdy door behind him, then made his way to the very back of the room, where a large tarp covered *something*.

Let's see what they brought me. It would have been so much better had he been with them, choosing what to bring and what to leave behind. But they had done the job without him, so what was there was all he'd get. He only hoped it was something useful.

Well, shit.

The assortment of junk was pretty much exactly that. Junk. The men had somehow managed to bring him absolutely nothing that would be of any use on Maktan's estate.

"So much for that idea," he grumbled, picking up an electric humidity gauge. The battery pack had long since gone dead, left exposed in the wasteland for nearly three years, but as Charlie moved to toss it back on the pile, an idea hit him.

"I wonder..."

He held out his hand and recited the simple spell Ser Baruud had taught him. The one to keep the portable lights operating when they trained late at night.

"*Yaka illum.*"

It wasn't designed to charge human electronics, but if he could find a way to use magic to make his science tech function, it would be the perfect melding of both galaxies' powers.

"*Yaka illum,*" he said again, straining to pull what little power he could from the flimsy konus on his wrist.

A slightest of sensations flowed through his fingers. Nothing like when using a proper konus, but it was something, and after a long minute repeating the spell, his attention fixed on the drained instrument, one of its lights flickered on, then faded.

"Holy shit! It worked!"

Charlie very nearly did a happy dance in the cellar, and was tempted to crack open a bottle of the visla's wine in celebration, but wisely refrained from both. Nevertheless, things had taken a turn for the *interesting*, if not the better.

Now. How can this be of use to me?

Far above in the high rooms of Visla Maktan's offices, a quiet knock sounded at his door.

"Come," he commanded.

Malalia strode in, confidently, clothed in a comfortable dress.

"Ah, my dearest. How did it go?"

"Quite well, I think. Though you nearly overplayed your ire. He was so concerned about angering you that I very nearly failed at bringing him into my chambers."

"But you succeeded."

"Of course I did. I am Yoral Maktan's daughter, am I not? Failure is not an option."

Her father let out a little laugh. "Yes, you most certainly take after me in that regard. Now tell me, what were you able to glean from him?"

"Nothing of use. At least, not for the time being. But I have made him my co-conspirator, providing him a smattering of debris from his crashed vessel in the Balamar Wastelands. I told him it was our little secret. I suspect he's down there right now as we speak, looking through his precious refuse."

"I am still not comfortable bringing that tech-magic into these walls. It feels unnatural."

"Father, you worry too much. I made sure to instruct Captain Falaan to only retrieve devices that appeared damaged, small, or harmless. There is nothing he can do with them, yet a bond of trust has been forged. Soon, I'll push harder, and then we shall learn what he *really* knows about the Zomoki."

"You've done well, Malalia. Keep an eye on him, and keep me informed."

"Of course. It should prove a reasonably simple task. He is a man, after all."

"Ah, you will resort to *those* tricks," he stated, rather than asked.

"You underestimate me, Father. While the temptation of physical pleasures may be of use, I feel I will not have to go so far as to bed the man."

"I trust your judgment, my dearest child."

Visla Maktan was pleased. While securing the Zomoki's power was sure to be an arduous task, progress was being made, and if all went to plan, he would drain the beast dry, powering all of his weapons at once, while making himself the most powerful visla in millennia.

CHAPTER EIGHTEEN

A low hum, inaudible to all but a very select few––including the man with Zomoki blood in his veins––signaled the arrival of several medium-sized ships to the landing fields outside the estate. Charlie rushed to his window but could not catch sight of them from his vantage point.

Down below, none seemed to hear the craft, continuing on with their evening tasks as if nothing unusual was afoot. But something was, and Charlie felt it was high time he figured out what.

Strange visitors in the night, and landing far off from the estate. Someone, or someones, do not wish to be scrutinized.

Charlie closed his room behind him, casting a pathetically weak locking spell on the door with his underpowered konus. It would keep most of the staff out, at least if they didn't try the door too hard, but anyone with even a modicum of power could force it easily.

It'll have to do for now.

He quickly padded down the corridor, making his way downstairs, hoping to make it out of the building without drawing attention to himself.

"Charlie, what are you doing down here?"

It was Elianna, one of Magda's assistants, mopping up the kitchen.

"Oh, uh, hi."

"Were you looking for something? I can get Tuktuk or Magda if you need--"

"No, that's fine. I, uh, I was just going to make a pot of coffee, is all."

Elianna smiled at that.

"Would you like a cup?" Charlie asked, noting her interest.

"Oh, I really shouldn't," she said, unconvincingly. "Mistress prefers we don't overstimulate ourselves. We had a few konus issues, I'm sure you heard."

He certainly had. It seemed the magic-enhancing benefits experienced by some led to somewhat overpowered spells being accidentally cast. A full set of bedsheets had been torn in half, and a bathing chamber was nearly flooded by an errant cleaning spell.

"Well, I don't think one small cup would hurt," Charlie said. "Besides, I'm making a big pot, and no one would know."

Looks like I'm making coffee now, he grumbled to himself as he pulled out his sealed bag of beans and worked on completing his alibi. The aroma alone was enough to put a sparkle in Elianna's eyes.

"I suppose one *tiny* cup wouldn't hurt," she said.

"Exactly."

"But why are you making a big pot? It is getting late."

"Uh, because I'll be working late tonight in my room. The visla assigned me a new job, so I need to prepare and learn the new spells to do it right."

This appeared to be the right answer, as she nodded her head in understanding and agreement.

"Very wise, Charlie. The visla is a kind man, but he does not tolerate slacking in duties."

"I kind of noticed that."

"I'm sure you'll do fine."

"I hope so, but thanks for the kind words of confidence."

He poured boiling water over the grounds and brewed far more coffee than he needed, but the show was for Elianna, and worst-case scenario, he'd just have it iced the following day.

She took her cup with gratitude, offering to clean the pot for him.

"It's the least I can do, Charlie. And you have work to do."

"Yeah," he said. "Thanks for that. But you know, I was thinking I'll take a quick walk to clear my head first. I want to be at my best when I begin."

Elianna nodded her understanding and poured the entirety of the coffee into a large thermos-like container. "This will keep it fresh for you. Now go, enjoy your walk. Leave this to me. And thank you for the coffee, Charlie."

"My pleasure," he said, then stepped out into the night.

He waited until he'd walked out of the illumination of the building, then took to the shadows, jogging toward the area the ships landed.

Well, that went better than it could have.

He made good time, his eyes adjusting to the dark with the aid of a little spell Ser Baruud had taught him what suddenly seemed like a lifetime ago. His konus was weak, but the spell worked well enough for his purposes. A tingle surged across his neck as he grew closer to the low wall barring his way.

Dammit, they landed farther that way, he noted, then realized exactly where he was. *Hang on, the slaap fabrication lab was over—*

"Hey, what are you doing out here?" a deep voice boomed at him as a light shone in his eyes.

"I'm trying to find the animal enclosures," Charlie lied. "Visla Maktan ordered me to clean the pens, but I think I'm turned around."

"You can't be over here," the man said, unimpressed with his excuse.

"Yeah, I know," Charlie said, making a show of tugging his collar. "This thing is burning really bad."

The man's shoulders relaxed a little when he realized the man in his light simply could not cross over to where he was not allowed. The magic containing him would stop him well before he topped the wall.

"Ah, you're Visla Maktan's new slave. Still not allowed past the inner wall, I see."

"Oh, is that what that was?" he said.

"And now you're cleaning the pens?" The man laughed. "You must have drawn his ire pretty substantially for that to be your chore so soon after arriving. That is a favored punishment of his, and one I do not envy you in the slightest."

"But how bad can it really be?"

"Oh, it can be bad," the man replied with an amused grin. "I hope you're up on your odor-blocking spells."

"I don't know any of those. Could you maybe show me one?"

"Not my place, and I'm on duty. Now, get out of this area. Head straight down that path to your left, and it will take you to that odd animal keeper woman's cabin. She'll show you where to go from there."

"Thank you, sir," Charlie said, acting as servile as possible as he quickly assessed the arms the man was carrying, then took off down the path he had been pointed to.

Two slaaps, a thick konus, and is that a sword on his hip? It's got a little glow. Jesus, the guy has an enchanted blade. That's a lot of weaponry for a simple sentry. They either expect something bad, or really, really don't want anyone snooping.

He didn't run into any more of the visla's men on his way, but he had been seen by one of Dinuk's men, and while he didn't think his encounter would be reported, it was too much of a risk to simply go back to his room now.

Looks like I'm going to see the dragon after all.

CHAPTER NINETEEN

"*Hey, Ara. I'm back,*" Charlie called out in his head as he strode carefully into the Zomoki's holding pen.

She was resting against the far wall, aimlessly swatting a large ball of some sort of leather with her tail.

"*What are you doing?*" she asked.

"*I'm letting you know I'm here before I come in. I didn't want to startle you. Not a good idea spooking a dragon.*"

Ara laughed silently. It was a strange sensation within his skull.

"*You ridiculous man. You really think I didn't smell you coming over ten minutes ago?*"

"*I guess I hadn't thought of that.*"

"*I guess not. And the gravel outside—you couldn't sneak in even if you wanted to. Besides, you and I have a bond now. I can sense you anywhere on this world.*"

"*Seriously?*"

"*Seriously. This surprises you?*"

"*Why wouldn't it? I mean, maybe this is normal for you, but this is all new to me, all this dragons and aliens and whatnot.*"

"*You keep using this word, 'dragon.' What does it mean?*"

"It's what you are."

"It most certainly is not. I am a Zomoki."

"Yeah? Well, that's what we call giant, flying, fire-breathing lizards on my world. Dragons."

"Hmm, so my kind are on your world as well," she mused, her tail swishing like an anxious cat.

"No, we don't actually have dragons. They're mythical creatures. Just a legend."

"Really?" she grumbled, swatting the ball with her tail and sending it flying. "Ugh. Can you believe this, Charlie? Stuck in this pen. And as if that weren't degrading enough, they gave me a ball. A child's toy, as if I were some hatchling to entertain."

"To be fair, Leila probably doesn't know exactly what will make you happy."

"My freedom, for starters. That would more than do the trick."

"And as that's not on the table?"

The dragon sighed heavily, a tendril of smoke wafting from her nostrils as she shifted to better look at Charlie. "Why do you insist on moving your lips when we speak? This will bode ill for both of us if you are observed."

"I'm not talking out loud."

"No, but you still move your lips."

"I do? Sorry. I hadn't realized."

"Well, you know now."

Charlie wandered the enclosure. Indeed, there wasn't much to keep the mighty Zomoki occupied. He imagined it must be a particularly horrible confinement for a creature who would normally be able to easily soar to great heights and travel between worlds.

"Uzri ha," he said, his middling konus flashing as the large ball rolled to him.

"What was that? What did you just do?"

"I called the ball over, is all. I wanted to take a better look at it."

107

"No, that's not what I mean. That spell. It is not meant to do that. It is a fighting spell."

"I know, but it is a pulling kind of power, so I just repurposed it to pull the ball over here."

"You shouldn't be able to do that. It's never been used like that."

"So if no one ever thought to use it that way, who's to say it can't be done? You know, there's an old saying about an empty vessel."

"Spare me your philosophy. I've heard all of it in my lifetime."

"So, you're pretty old, then."

"Yes, I am. At least by your standards. Now tell me, why do you speak aloud when you cast your spells?"

"Uh, because that's how it works. Everyone has to say the words to make them work."

"Charlie, you possess Zomoki blood in your veins. You do not."

Charlie was caught off guard by the statement. If he really didn't have to take the time to say a spell out loud, that ability could be a boon, and a secret weapon as well.

He looked at the ball and concentrated, using the *kika rahm* spell to deliver a mighty punch to the ball.

It rolled a few inches.

"Did you see that?"

"Yes, you nudged a ball. Really, Charlie, you need to do better than that."

"But that was my first try. And it worked! How is it no one ever mentioned this to me?"

"Because most do not know why their spells work or fail. There is more to it than just words. There is intent. Skill. Power. All must be present for spells of different degrees. This is why lower-level practitioners like emmiks and mesters can say a powerful spell and have it fail more often than not. It takes years to achieve the higher levels."

"So I just got a sort of cheat code when you bled on me."

"I do not know what a 'cheat code' is, but if I understand the gist of what you are saying, then yes."

Charlie's mind reeled at the possibilities. Sure, he still needed a konus or slaap to power the casting, but if he could lay his hands on one, the ability to cast without uttering a word could be a powerful weapon indeed. With the secret goings-on of Visla Maktan, it was one he feared he might need sooner than later.

"Ara, there's one thing I was meaning to ask you. If Visla Maktan has been trying to tap into Zomoki magic for so long, why has he never been successful? And why so much interest in you?"

The great beast sighed. *"That, I'm afraid, is partly my fault. You see, whatever it was that you did to my restraining collar in battle greatly weakened its hold on me. I'd become used to being forced to cast forcefully to make even the slightest magic work, but you unexpectedly turned me loose, if but for a moment. The result is what caught his eye. If only we'd had a moment longer, I might even have broken my collar and been free of this bondage, but we were stunned too quickly to act."*

"So it was my fault? Shit, I'm really sorry."

"There is nothing to be sorry about. You obviously had no idea you could even do that, and, given the reactions of the vislas overseeing the bout, it looks as if no one else did either. More likely than not, it was our blood bond at work."

He looked at the sheer size of the dragon and marveled that anyone could have ever gotten close enough to attack her, let alone capture her. But the injured wing and collar on her neck told another story.

"How did they capture you, Ara? If you were so powerful, it seems unlikely."

A faraway look flashed in her golden eyes as she remembered the day. *"I had recently birthed a small clutch of eggs and was resting in a cavern, recovering my strength, when Visla Ookaman's slaves attacked me."*

"Who?"

"The visla whose collar I bore when we first met. He sent wave

after wave of men to their death, all of them attacking me at once. They couldn't possibly win, even in my weakened state, so I didn't take the threat terribly seriously. At worst, I thought they might try to entrap me deep underground as others have been known to do. But my kind can lay dormant for years—centuries if we must."

"Kind of like a bear, only bigger. And that breathes fire," Charlie mused. "Holy shit, imagine that. A fire-breathing bear."

"A what?"

"A big, furry thing from my world. Sorry, nevermind. So you were saying you thought you'd be dormant for a long time, right?"

"I thought so at first, however even that was not to be my fate."

"What happened?"

"A clever trick, I must admit. The visla was outside the cave, just within skree range. He was monitoring the attack from safety, you see? He did not dare meet me on the field of battle. Well, I was making quick work of his men, when I noticed several had dropped their packs as I dispatched them to the afterlife. They were carrying collars. Dozens of them. Perhaps more. All he needed was for one to find its way around my neck."

"And it did."

"Yes," she said, grimly. "I had only just realized the true nature of the attack when I felt the warm metal of a collar on my flesh. I was about to throw the offending slave off and devour him whole, but he had already transmitted his success over the skree. Visla Ookaman cast the spell, and the collar sealed tight. I fought its power, but I was so weak at that moment, I could not break free. They shocked me for hours until I finally succumbed. When I awoke in the cages of Gramfir's arena, the collar had already been replaced with a more powerful one."

"And then you met me."

"Yes. A few days later, a strange, little, pink man surprised me with an act of kindness. And now, here we are, today."

Charlie's heart ached for Ara's plight. A brilliant mind, but her kind were hunted for their powers.

"*And other Zomoki? They seemed less intimidating, and a few even died during that bout.*"

"*We all possess some power, Charlie. Some more than others. Only in the rarest of instances can we share it with another being, but that is enough to make us targets. It is this sharing of power that great wielders of magic have long sought—and is why we Zomoki have become nearly extinct because of it.*"

"*They try to bind you? To drain you of your power? I overheard the visla and Dinuk talking. I think Maktan intends to do precisely that to you, if he can.*"

"*I do not doubt it. But my kind would rather die than share our power, and if that is to be my fate, so be it. Better that than let a man like Maktan use my magic to harm others.*"

"*But wait a minute. You and I are connected. If you'd rather die than share your power, then why me?*"

She looked at him a long moment, an unexpected fondness clear in her eyes.

"*Why? Because* you, *Charlie, did not seek it.*"

Charlie loosed the lid of the thermos container he had been carrying and poured himself a small cup of coffee as he mused what she had said.

"*What is that?*" Ara asked, her nostrils flaring wide at the aroma.

"*Coffee.*"

"*The smell, it is familiar. That of tsokin berry plants when engulfed with flame. But there's something else to it.*"

"*It's a bit more than just the roasting part that makes coffee,*" he informed her. "*The others seem to enjoy it a lot, though you might not. It's a little bitter, but I'm quite fond of it. The magic users seem to find it helps them sharpen their spells.*"

"*Fascinating.*"

"*Want to try some? I mean, you're huge, so it's really just a dollop, but it's a big enough container to give you a taste.*"

SCOTT BARON

Ara hesitated a moment, unsure what it might do to her. But Charlie was linked. If subterfuge was at play, she would sense it.

"Yes. I think I would like to taste this 'coffee' beverage."

Charlie popped the container and poured it into the dragon's mouth. It was a lot of fluid, but for her, it barely coated her tongue. Nevertheless, her eyes flashed as she swished it in her mouth and swallowed.

"Oh!" she gasped. *"That's wonderful."*

The scales around her eyes seemed to brighten ever so slightly, and Charlie could have sworn he felt a surge in the power shared between them.

"I'm going to have to brew you up a larger pot," he mused.

Footsteps on gravel sounded outside the walls.

"Someone's coming," Charlie warned.

"Yes, I smelled her a while ago."

"Her?"

"The one who oversees the visla's cages."

"Ah, Leila. She's the groundskeeper's daughter, you know."

"She has been kind. At least for a captor."

Leila wore a full konus as she entered the holding pen, a levitating cart piled with animal carcasses floating in behind her. Charlie recognized one of the beasts. Apparently, not all of the escaped bundabist were peacefully returned to their pens.

"Charlie, what are you doing in here?" she asked, obviously startled at his presence. "You should get back from her. I haven't fed her yet."

"Yes, I was getting a bit hungry," Ara noted, silently in his head.

"It's okay, Leila. I was just checking up on her, making sure her injuries were healing. And the visla gave me a new job, by the way. I'm your new clean-up assistant."

Leila laughed brightly. "Oh, you must have angered him something fierce. That's one of the punishments he saves for those he truly wishes to make suffer."

112

"Yeah, well, I guess that's me, then."

She pushed the floating cart toward the Zomoki and stepped back. "You should get clear, Charlie. They burn their food before they eat it."

"Not always," Ara told him. *"But I'd hate to not live up to her fearsome expectations,"* she added, spraying the dead beasts with flame, then devouring several of them whole.

Leila watched in awe as the magnificent animal feasted.

"She's a terrible creature, but so beautiful as well," she said. "I'd heard much of them from my father. He'd seen Zomoki when he was a boy, but I never thought I'd see one up close."

"She is pretty spectacular," Charlie agreed. "And has quite an appetite," he added, throwing an amused look at Ara. *"Hungry, much?"*

"Yes, in fact. And this bundabist is delicious."

Leila uttered a small spell, and the flames on the cart extinguished, preserving the food conveyance from damage. "You know, it's a shame. If not for that collar, she'd eat us whole as well without a second thought."

A pair of large, golden eyes crinkled around the edges as the dragon feasted.

"No I wouldn't," Ara said. *"I rather like this one."*

"That's good, because she is obviously very taken with you," Charlie replied.

"I sense that. And would you like to know something else?"

"What?"

"I think she is fond of you, too."

Charlie felt a flush rise to his cheeks, and it had nothing to do with the Zomoki's smoldering meal.

CHAPTER TWENTY

The moons were high in the sky when Visla Maktan visited his animalist's pens very late that night, not long after the visiting ships had quietly taken off and headed back to their own systems. Malalia followed, a shadow in the dark, silently observing her father.

He didn't even bother waking the young woman in charge of the beast. Rather, he forewent exhausting discussions and subterfuge entirely and proceeded directly to the large Zomoki's holding area.

His men waited outside, and no one heard exactly what he said as he entered the enclosure. The beast appeared to ignore him entirely. That is, until he uttered several powerful spells aimed at her.

The Zomoki's collar had glowed incredibly brightly, rumor later had it. So much power had apparently been channeled through it that, for a moment, the guards actually wondered if the visla might break it in his frustration.

While they were loyal men to a one and would never betray the visla's trust in them––it was not worth jeopardizing their cushy jobs in the elite guard––one of the men happened to be involved with one of the housekeeping staff. When he visited her later that night and lay beside her as they drifted to sleep, he shared what he had seen.

Unfortunately, she was something of a gossip.

News spread through the estate, whispers of the visla's arguments during a meeting with a group of powerful men from the Council of Twenty. Men with secret plans. Men with ambitions. They were up to something, and something big from what could be gleaned from those near enough to catch snippets of their heated discussions.

The other vislas from the Council of Twenty eventually departed, leaving several medium-sized ships behind, and shortly after, Visla Maktan had engaged in a late-night struggle with the magical creature.

With each telling as the story passed from lips to ears, the ferocity of the event grew, until the tale had morphed into an all-out battle between wizard and dragon.

The reality was something far more simple.

"I know you can understand me," Visla Maktan had said when he approached the enclosure. "You are too old a Zomoki to have survived this long and not know the high tongue of the vislas."

Ara had merely looked at him, her golden eyes following him as he paced.

"I am offering you an opportunity. One that will ease your difficulties and allow you to return to your friends if you help me. I am a very powerful man. You can sense it, I know," he said, the gold band around her neck glowing slightly brighter as if to punctuate his statement. "But it is draining for a man of my position to constantly perform upkeep of so many spells used by those laboring under me. My emmik and mester underlings do much of it, but at the end of it, all the obligation falls to me to ensure they are charged properly."

The dragon shifted on her haunches slightly, but other than that remained silent.

"What I offer is simple. Share just a fraction of your power with me. Do this willingly, and as soon as I've powered enough devices to enable my workers to perform their duties efficiently, I shall grant you your freedom."

He smiled warmly.

She felt the ice hiding behind his eyes.

Maktan paced a bit longer, speaking pleasantly, plying her with tempting offers of freedom if only she would share her magic. And perhaps a much younger Zomoki might have fallen for his tricks, not knowing that to offer any of their power was to offer it all. A convenient loophole the visla failed to mention, but one she was well aware of.

"Will you not answer me?" he asked. "I feel this is a fair and just proposition I make."

The enormous, red Zomoki turned her head from him and lay as if going to sleep. The visla quickly became enraged.

"You will look at me when I address you!" he shouted, then muttered a guttural spell.

The shock surged through the collar around Ara's neck and she spun on him and spread her wings, eyes blazing with anger. The scales around the glowing, golden orbs as they looked at him with fury seemed fresher, somehow, and her renewed power startled the visla. He had expected a weakened Zomoki, which she was, but not nearly as weak as he had anticipated.

Quickly, he spat out a half dozen of his strongest spells, knocking her back to the ground. Her collar glowed brightly, the effort Maktan was forced to expend charging the metal.

Ara howled from the pain, but stayed down. Gradually, the collar returned to its normal, dull glow.

"You would do well not to test me, Zomoki," the visla shouted. "I am Yoral Maktan, High Visla of Merdova, and protector of the Coromar system. I am your owner, beast, and you would do well to know your place."

Maktan quickly uttered a handful of restraining spells, further restricting the creature within the enclosure. They would fade by morning, but for the moment, Ara could not so much as rise to her full height. It would be an uncomfortable night, held low like that.

But she had spent much time deep within caves over the years and had learned to accept the confining spaces as a necessary discomfort required to protect herself when she needed to enter the deep sleep to restore herself. This, she reasoned, was not so dissimilar.

Ara hunkered down as best she could, and once the visla had vacated the premises, closed her eyes and slid into a restless slumber.

CHAPTER TWENTY-ONE

By the time the rumors of the visla's meeting with members of the Council of Twenty, and his heated encounter with the Zomoki reached his ears, Charlie was already well aware of Maktan's intentions.

First thing in the morning, as he and Tuktuk were partaking of coffee and pastry in their daily routine, Visla Maktan made a rare appearance in the kitchens. Something that seemed to have become far more frequent ever since the arrival of his new gladiator slave.

"Visla!" a young assistant chef gasped. "It is an honor to have you visit us down here. We didn't know you would be coming. What can we make you? Would you like a pastry, fresh from the oven?"

"I am looking for Charlie," he replied. "He was not in his room, but I understand he makes a habit of visiting the kitchen."

"Ah, yes, Visla. Charlie and Tuktuk have coffee together every morning to start the day."

"My daughter told me of this 'coffee' he has been producing. Apparently, it has become quite popular among the staff."

"Yes, Visla. It is a somewhat bitter-flavored beverage, but it does sharpen the mind a bit and boosts productivity."

"Well, then. While I do not necessarily approve, I will not stop him from his hobby, so long as it helps increase efficiency."

"Would you like to try a cup? There is a fresh pot."

The powerful wizard had heard the effect it had on Malalia, making her magic boost for a short while. It was an artificial means of boosting one's power, it seemed, and as such, he was hesitant to use it. Relying on such tricks was unbecoming a visla. However, curiosity eventually won him over.

"A small taste, yes," he replied.

Moments later, a cup of the steaming liquid warmed his hands. The aroma was unusual, but not entirely unpleasant. The visla muttered his standard spell, recited before every meal since as long as he could remember. No poisons or enchantments lay in the cup. Just a murky, hot liquid.

He took a sip.

"Not an entirely bad flavor," he noted. He drank more, waiting for *something* to happen.

Nothing did.

"I thought this was supposed to boost one's magic. I feel nothing."

"It affects everyone differently, Visla," the young assistant said apologetically. "Perhaps it is because you are already so very powerful that this has no effect."

"Perhaps," Maktan replied, placing the cup on the counter. "Now, where is Charlie?"

The slightest of breezes shifted around them, but Charlie and Tuktuk didn't mind as they chatted on the low bench around the side of the building not far from the kitchen door.

"So, her mother was sold to another household? That doesn't seem right," Charlie said, sipping from his mug. The cool morning air made visible tendrils of steam in the early sun's rays.

"Yes. From what I gather, Hertzall was beside himself for quite a while. He's a bit of a loner, as I'm sure you've noticed, so when he and his wife met and started a family, it was something of a miracle for the man. I mean, to assume you'd spend your life alone, then suddenly be sharing it with another person?"

"For someone who's that much of an introvert, she must have been something special."

"Obviously, I never met her, but from what Magda has told me, she was the perfect match for him, though you wouldn't guess it from meeting her."

"Why not?"

Tuktuk chuckled. "You know how outgoing Magda is?"

"Yeah. She's a bit of a whirlwind."

"Indeed," he replied with a happy grin. "Well, let's just say that woman made Magda look like a quiet maid-in-waiting."

"Wow."

"Yeah. But for whatever reason, she and Hertzall fell for one another. She knew when he needed to be pulled into social settings, but never forced him. Likewise, she was perfectly content to leave him to his own devices for days at a time, giving him solitude he needed to recharge, while taking those times to visit her friends and socialize. It was an odd match, but it worked."

"So how old was Leila when her mother was sold off?"

"I'm not sure exactly. Pretty young. I could ask Magda if you like."

"No, that's fine. I was just curious, is all."

"Oh?" his blue friend asked with a curious grin. "And here I thought you and Malalia might have something brewing."

"The visla's daughter? Something tells me that would not end well," Charlie replied.

The door behind them swung open, and the men turned as

one, quickly scrambling to their feet when they realized who their visitor was.

"Visla Maktan," Tuktuk blurted. "I was not expecting you. Is everything all right? Were the late-night snacks I prepared not to your liking?"

"No, that was all fine, Tuktuk. Well done on those. No, I just wanted to speak with Charlie a moment." He put his hand on the gladiator's shoulder. "Come, walk with me."

Charlie and Tuktuk shared a look, then he followed the wizard out onto a path around the grounds. When they were clear of earshot of the building, the visla turned to Charlie.

"I want to ask you a question," he began. "And I want you to answer freely."

"Of course," he replied.

"Good. And I hope you don't hold a grudge for your punishment."

"No. I understand order needs to be kept, and I was out of line. I should have sought your approval first. I just thought perhaps I could be of more use to you if I had my equipment. I am sorry I disappointed you."

"Clouds passing in the sky, Charlie. Done and gone."

"I am glad to hear that, Visla. Now, what can I help you with?"

The powerful man paused, appearing to struggle for the right words. Charlie wasn't buying the act for a second.

He's rehearsed this dozens of times, I bet. Down to the little stammer.

"Charlie, I am faced with a bit of a dilemma," he began. "You see, there are forces at work. Bad forces, who wish to see our society among the many hundreds of civilized systems shatter."

"Hundreds?" he asked. "I didn't realize there were quite that many."

"Yes," Maktan replied. "The Council of Twenty are the representatives of the twenty ruling systems. We keep the order among the five hundred-plus other systems, providing them stability and rule."

"Five hundred inhabited systems," Charlie marveled.

"Out of billions of uninhabited ones," Maktan noted. "Intelligent life is rare. Magic-bearing life is even rarer. It is with this that I need your assistance. We are facing a difficult time, and we vislas only have so much power we can divert to the common good. We have our own systems to watch over, you see."

"And these five hundred others are spreading you thin."

"Precisely."

"I can see how that would be exhausting, to say the least."

"It is, Charlie. But you can help *me* help *them*."

"I'm just a non-magical human from a galaxy far, far away. I have no powers."

"No, you do not. But you seemed to be able to tap into something that could make up for your shortcomings."

Here it comes, Charlie groaned inside.

"You have ridden a Zomoki. The very one you are now cleaning up after, in fact."

"But that was just a fluke. Pure survival instinct in the heat of a bout. I have no idea what happened," he lied.

"Nevertheless, you caused the beast to reveal its power. Zomoki with more than a middling amount of magic are incredibly rare, and I believe this one to be exceptionally powerful. And you connected somehow. Made her use that power. Now I want you to do the same for me. To give me a means to harness that magic within her. To use it for the betterment of all of the systems under my guidance."

"I wish I could help you, but it's all I can do just to keep her from eating me when I clean out her enclosure. I mean, to try and get close to her? I don't think I could do it."

A vein throbbed on the side of the wizard's head, but he kept his displeasure under wraps. "I see," he said calmly. "Well, I'd like you to try to reconnect with the beast if you can, regardless. Maybe we will get lucky."

"I'll see what I can do, but please, don't get your hopes up. I don't think that Zomoki wants to share her power with *anyone*, especially not the gladiator who got her shocked from the air and sent here."

"Yes, I suppose you have a point," Maktan said, not entirely believing his slave. "Well, thank you for the chat, Charlie. I have things to attend now. I assume you know your way back to the kitchen from here."

"I do."

"Very well. When you see Leila this afternoon, please tell her I wish to speak with her about the Zomoki."

"I will be sure to do so."

Charlie turned and trotted back toward the kitchen, while the wizard walked his grounds, moving deeper into a nearby grove of trees. His anger crackled on his skin, a simmering frustration.

"*Hokta!*" he cursed in a tiny fit of pique, his ire killing the nearest tree outright. Hertzall would be perplexed at the lone casualty in the grove, but the man was good at his job and kept the grounds pristine. There would be no trace of it by morning.

CHAPTER TWENTY-TWO

"That was odd," Tuktuk commented as Charlie came in through the kitchen's back door. "The visla doesn't usually pal around with the help, you know."

"I think he just wanted to get some information from me," Charlie replied. "He seems to think I'm somehow connected with the drag––*Zomoki*."

"You did fly the beast."

"By total accident. And now he thinks I can help him somehow control her. It's nuts."

"Maybe, but you need to be careful, Charlie. The visla is a very powerful man, and you're on his good side at the moment, despite what you may think after he sent you to clean the pens. If you were truly on his bad side, life under his rule could be quite difficult."

"I realize that. Fortunately for me, I simply don't have what he wants and told him as much."

"But does he accept that?"

"I hope so, Tuk. If not, it's gonna be a long week," Charlie said with a resigned sigh.

He then headed up to his room to change into attire more

fitting for cleaning up after all manner of beasts. Namely, clothes he wouldn't mind burning later if need be.

He had only just ascended the stairs when another unexpected visitor breezed into the kitchen.

"Denna Maktan. It is a pleasant surprise to have you grace the kitchen with your presence. To what do we owe this honor?" Tuktuk said, though he had a pretty good idea what the answer would be.

"Tuktuk, I have come to ask a favor of Charlie, the new addition to Father's staff. Have you seen him? I understand he's made your morning pastry something of a routine."

"Ah, yes. He was just here. Shall I send one of the staff to fetch him for you?"

"He's in his room?"

"Yes, Denna."

"Then I'll go see him there. It shouldn't take long."

She swept out of the kitchen and into the hallway, her next destination: Charlie's room.

"Oh, my poor friend. What ever have you gotten yourself into?"

"Hang on a sec!" Charlie called out as he slid his other leg into his pants and padded over to his door. "What is it? I'm getting—" He opened the door, shirtless. "Oh, Malalia. I didn't know you were coming."

"How could you? I only just decided it myself," she said brightly.

"Just give me a moment. I'm almost ready for work."

"I'll keep you company," she said, pushing her way past him into his room.

"Uh..." Charlie didn't quite know what to say. "What if your father hears you were down socializing with the help?"

"I won't tell if you won't," she said with a grin that contained more than a little innuendo.

Charlie quickly slipped into his tunic, while the daughter of the most powerful visla in the system watched. "Here, let me help," she said, taking the belt from his bed and leaning in close, sliding it around his waist.

"I can get that."

"No, really, I don't mind," she replied, slowly sliding the length of leather through the loops on his pants. "Charlie, I was meaning to ask you the other day, do you think you could maybe take me up for a flight on the Zomoki? It would be so exhilarating, and I'd be very, very appreciative."

She quietly whispered a little spell, making his skin tingle every time she brushed against him. It was distracting, to say the least.

"Malalia, I wish I could help you out, really, but I wouldn't want to see you hurt."

"I'm sure I'd be safe with you protecting me," she said, squeezing his arm.

Okay, now she really is laying it on a little thick. The awareness of her wiles didn't lessen their involuntary effects on his body, however.

"The thing is, I am the guy who cleans up Zomoki poop now. Beyond that, I really don't interact with the thing. I mean, maybe Leila could help. She's the one in charge of it," he said pulling away from her and settling into a chair to slip into his boots.

"But I wanted you to do it," she said, enjoying her double entendre a bit too much.

Charlie desperately needed to get out of there before he actually did wind up in trouble with her father.

"I'm sorry, Malalia, but I really don't have any information of use to you. But if I should somehow happen to find a way to control the beast, you'll be the first person I tell."

"Thank you, Charlie. I do appreciate it," she said, hiding her displeasure moderately well.

"Look, I'd love to chat with you further, but your father really will be upset if I don't perform my duties. He made that pretty clear the other night."

"Oh, don't worry about him," she said.

"You're his daughter, but I'm just his slave. I think it would be wise if I didn't push my luck."

"Very well," she said, walking for the door. "But Charlie? Please, do see if you can gain some control over the Zomoki. I do so want to ride it, and I'd do *anything* to have that beast between my legs."

He struggled not to react.

"Okay, I'll leave you to it," she said, then breezed out of his room as easily as she had come in.

Charlie felt his blood pressure start to drop.

"Dear Lord, that woman is a handful."

CHAPTER TWENTY-THREE

"Oh, sonofa––" Charlie groaned as he scraped bundabist shit from his boot. "Seriously? Right inside the gate? I swear, you little bastards are trying to boobytrap the place on me."

The animals had taken a liking to Charlie, and several nudged their way closer, hoping for scratches behind their ears where their armored plates didn't cover. They were rambunctious, and certainly capable of sizable damage–– though unintentionally––and Charlie found himself growing fond of the enormous beasts, despite the stinking mess on his boot.

"Not quite man's best friend," he grumbled with a chuckle. "But I suppose you'll do in a pinch."

He recited the cleaning spell out loud for the largest pile of bundabist poop, but then cast the spell again, silently and from within his head, for a much smaller mess. He wasn't proficient by any means, but Ara's pointers on the intent of the user more than the words themselves had really helped him on the way.

The smaller pile vanished until he recited the spell to make it join the large pile in the large disposal bin outside of the enclosure. From there, he would make the rounds of the other pens, cages, and enclosures until he had accumulated an admirable quantity of feces from a few dozen species.

The gladiator in him hated the job, but the engineer and scientist in him found it rather fascinating. Not the poop, mind you, but the interaction with so many diverse animals, every one of which no one on his home planet had ever seen before.

He was a trailblazer, and no one back home was any the wiser.

"They probably all think we're long dead," he grumbled.

"Who thinks you're dead?"

Leila had snuck up on him while he was busy with his waste-retrieval duties. A doody duty, he had once said, garnering zero laughs from Tuktuk and Magda. Leila, likewise, failed to see the humor.

"Oh, just everyone I ever knew back home," he replied, shoving the hovering waste bin toward an open area away from the animals' enclosures.

"I imagine that's pretty tough," Leila said. "I was born here, so really, the idea of it is somewhat foreign to me, but I can imagine if everyone I knew was suddenly gone. It would be horrible, actually," she said, giving Charlie a sympathetic look.

"Hey, at least I've got you guys. I mean, I haven't been here all that long, but you all have made me feel at home, and I can't tell you how much I appreciate it."

"Of course we welcomed you. You're a good man, Charlie."

"You can't know that."

"Oh, but we knew about you long before you even showed up that night, passed out cold. You and the Zomoki, our mysterious arrivals that had the visla so worked up. Tuktuk enjoyed telling stories about the strange man from another galaxy whom he shared a cell with aboard the slave trader's ship."

"Yeah, well, sure. But he might have been exaggerating."

"Did you fight to save your human friend?"

"Well, of course."

"And did you defend a Wampeh being attacked, though you didn't even know the man?"

"Yes, but that was a mistake."

"Perhaps. But your nature is good, Charlie. The details may have changed in the telling of the tale, but the character of the man remained."

"Well——"

"You're a good man. You try to make things right. Not many do in the circumstances you faced. And unarmed, no less. Why, at that time, you didn't even know how to wield a konus or a slaap. A babe in the woods, you were."

"The woods," he said, gears turning.

"What about them?"

"The other day, when we were chasing down the bundabist, I came across a structure just over the wall and past the low hills right outside the grove of trees over that way. There was something going on. Something bad."

"Bad? What do you mean? I've been all over the visla's lands, and I know the place you speak of. It's been long empty."

"Not anymore. It's being used to manufacture slaaps and konuses by the thousands. It's a weapons factory, Leila."

She snorted a laugh. "A weapons factory? On Visla Maktan's land? He wouldn't stand for it. Why, if anyone so much as attempted to do such a thing, he would know and put a stop to it at once."

"And what if Maktan is involved? What if it's his plan?"

"Now you need to be careful what you say. If he hears of you spreading such lies——"

"They aren't lies, Leila. I *heard* him discussing it with Dinuk. *That*'s why he wanted the Zomoki. He intends to tap into her power to charge those weapons."

"Impossible. He's a leader of the Council of Twenty. Why would he ever do such a thing?"

"I can't say for sure, but on my world, the only time people start stockpiling weapons like that in secret is when they're planning something big. Something big and bad."

She looked shocked. Leila was no clueless slave, but she'd grown up on Maktan's land, and had never seen any indication that he was capable of such conniving treachery.

"*If* this is true, we will need to get word to the others on the Council of Twenty. They must know what he is doing."

"The only way to do that is scouting out the weapons factory. I'd take you, but my collar is restricted again, and I can't cross the wall."

"Frustrating, isn't it? A wall no higher than your waist yet you cannot pass," she said. "I, however, can. I will go and see if what you tell is true. If it is, we can discuss this further."

Charlie didn't want to put her at risk, but there seemed little other way to bring her around to his side. "I think that's a great idea, Leila. Go and see. Verify what I told you is true. The visla wants to drain Ara of her power to charge all those weapons, and I fear that would kill her."

"Ara?"

"It's her name."

"You named the Zomoki?"

"No, I–I'll explain all of that when you get back, okay? But be careful. It's dangerous, what you're about to do."

Leila laughed loudly, truly amused by his statement.

"Charlie, I look after a Zomoki. Compared to that, *nothing* seems dangerous."

She has a point, he had to admit.

"All right. I'll be here working on the pens and feeding the animals. We'll discuss this further when you're back."

Leila trotted off at a casual jog, as she so often did when making rounds of the lands. She would sometimes run for hours on end, her lifetime of activity making it as easy as walking. At the pace she was moving, he estimated she'd be back within the hour.

When the two-hour mark passed, he began to worry.

When nightfall arrived without her return, he was in an outright panic.

CHAPTER TWENTY-FOUR

Leila had been held in a windowless room somewhere in the main estate grounds for the better part of the evening. They had stunned her when she was discovered lurking near the old factory building, but only mildly. She had come to her senses not long after, bound to a chair, her small work konus gone.

From the few sounds that did manage to filter down to her, she guessed that she was underground. Likely one of the storage areas used by the staff.

Dinuk had questioned her personally that night, though he had been somewhat gentle about it, given her life-long history on the estate. It could well enough have been an honest mistake. A case of wrong place/wrong time, but too much was at stake for the visla to take any chances.

After she had left Charlie to go and see if what he had claimed was true, Leila made her way straight to the building he described to her, making sure to use the less-traveled back path leading through the small copse of trees. One, she noted, had mysteriously died, its bark and leaves shriveled and dry.

"I'll have to make sure Father knows about this," she noted as she passed.

Leila vaulted the low wall easily and jogged into the shallow glen that opened to the abandoned building's small clearing. Only the building was most certainly not abandoned.

A sharp smell assaulted her nose.

"They're smelting," she realized, having experienced the noxious odor a few times prior, when her father tooled specialized power-harnessing devices for his arborist work.

Creeping in close, Leila was shocked to see hundreds of crates being loaded onto a half dozen small craft silently hovering in the clearing. Tslavar mercenaries and their comrades from several other systems were guiding the floating crates into the bellies of the ships, stacking them high.

The men, one and all, were armed, she noted. Slaaps were on each of their hips, and most wore sturdy combat konuses as well. This was not some casual supply exchange. This was something else. Charlie was right, something big was happening.

Never one to leave a mystery unsolved, Leila then did the opposite of the wise thing, opting to sneak in closer for a better look, rather than running away at top speed. A visla she did not recognize––but whose rank she immediately noted by not only his attire, but also the raw power he radiated––was forcing that magical energy into a crate full of slaaps.

"Yes, these are good. They'll all hold a charge nicely. Load them with the others," the slender visla said. "Bring the next crate. I want to get this load off to Kentraxiik before the others return. We need to make space for their ships."

More crates were brought out of the building, left in a queue for the powerful wizard to imbue them with a tiny bit of his power as he ran his functionality check.

"There have to be thousands of weapons here," Leila realized. "Tens of thousands, even."

A boot crunched in the gravel behind her.

She had only begun to spin around when the spell hit her and she tumbled to the ground.

"You need to be careful, Charlie," Tuktuk said as his friend paced anxiously in the kitchen. "Magda heard from Elianna, who heard from Azkan's aide that Leila was caught observing something she wasn't supposed to. They've got her in the basement storage area at the far end of the estate."

"Then that's where I'm going," he replied, heading for the door.

His blue friend grabbed his shoulder, stopping him with a startlingly firm grip. "You will achieve nothing if you just rush in there, Charlie. What good can you do for her if you're a captive too?"

"But it's my fault she's there, Tuk. She never would have gone poking around if it weren't for me."

Tuktuk chuckled. "I've known her longer than you have, my friend. Believe me, no one can tell her what to do or not to do. If there was even a hint of something odd going on, she'd have gone to investigate on her own, regardless of anything you might have said. So, what is it you think you've found out there, Charlie?"

"Nevermind. I don't want you at risk too."

Charlie had figured she would take it upon herself regardless of what he'd said, but it didn't ease his guilt over her situation in the slightest.

"I'm going to see her. Don't try to stop me, Tuk."

"Fine," his friend said, letting go. "But be smart about it."

"I'll be tactful, I promise. I just have to see if there's anything I can do."

"You're a slave, Charlie, just like the rest of us. At the end of the day, they do what they like, and we have no say in the matter."

Not the words Charlie *wanted* to hear, but perhaps the words he *needed* to hear. With a cloud of guilt hovering over him like a circling vulture, he headed out toward the far end of the estate, where Leila was being held.

He was nearly there when a distraught Hertzall spotted him coming, snapping him from his nervous pacing outside the building.

"Charlie!"

"Hey, Hertzall. I hear they locked Leila up for some reason. Any idea what's going on?"

"No. They won't even let me see her. My own daughter. She was born here, Charlie. Raised here. This is the only home she's ever known. She wouldn't do anything to harm the visla. She loves it here."

"I know," he replied, the guilty cloud growing slightly darker.

"If they won't even let her own father in to see her, what could she have possibly done?"

Charlie realized the old man had a point. He had as much seniority as anyone on the visla's staff, and if *he* couldn't get in to see a blood relative, there was no way a newcomer already on Maktan's shit list would.

"You know what? I may have someone who could help. Let me see what I can do, okay? But you really should eat something and get some rest if you can. If I can get you in to see her, I'll let you know."

"Do you really think you can manage this?"

"I'm not sure, but I've got a pretty good feeling about it."

The groundskeeper swept him up in a big hug, the smell of the woods and dirt wafting from him in the comforting manner of a summer's breeze on a warm day.

I've got to make this right. I just hope I'm worth enough to her that she'll help.

CHAPTER TWENTY-FIVE

"Denna Maktan, you have a visitor," Azkan announced over his skree.

"Who is it, Azkan? You know I do not wish to be disturbed," she answered over the device.

"It is the gladiator, Denna. The new addition."

"Oh, in that case, send him in," she said, her tone warming immediately.

"The denna will see you," Azkan said, opening the door for Charlie. "Behave appropriately with the visla's daughter," he added.

"Is there some reason for this warning?" Charlie asked.

"Just a word of advice. You will not receive a second one."

The door closed behind him, and he found himself alone in the young woman's outer chambers.

"Hello? Malalia?"

"Just a moment," she called from her bedroom.

Charlie took the moment to better examine the visla's daughter's living space. It was clean, as would be expected, and free of clutter. The decorations were expensive, yet tasteful, with a few pieces of art on the walls and a sculpture of a woman wrestling a serpent on a pedestal against the far wall. On a small table sat an ornate konus. Charlie could almost feel the power she had fed into it from across the room, her personal energy signature tangible in the air.

The denna, it seemed, was more powerful than she let on.

Malalia swept into the room wearing a thin nightgown and nothing more.

"Ah, Charlie. What a pleasant surprise," she said, pulling him in for a warm hug. He could feel her body through the material, pressed against him, and found it more than a little distracting.

"Malalia, it's really good to see you," he said, stepping back slightly, hoping the slight bulge that had formed in his pants would recede before she noticed.

"And it is good to see you too. But it's rather late. What brings you to my chambers at such an hour? You know, people might start to talk," she teased with a sly grin.

"Well, I actually have a favor to ask, if I may."

"I cannot retrieve any more materials from your crashed vessel, if that is what you wish. Father would be very cross if he learned what I already procured for you."

"No, nothing like that. Something here at home, actually."

"Oh, in that case, of course. What do you need?"

"It's not for me, actually," he said. "It's Hertzall."

"The old groundskeeper?"

"Yes."

"But what could he possibly need? I'm sure my father would gladly provide him with new trees and whatever manner of castings he might need to work in the woods."

"It's nothing like that. It's Leila."

At her name, Malalia's grin faltered, but only for a second.

"Yes, his daughter. The one who works in the dirt with the animals," she said with mocking cheer. "What of her?

"She seems to have been detained by Dinuk for some reason,

and is being held in the basement at the far end of the estate. No one knows why, and they won't let poor Hertzall see his own daughter. I hate to ask, and I really don't want to put you out with this request, but they're friends of mine. Do you think you could see about having them let him visit her?"

A glimpse of something not entirely pleasant flashed across Malalia's face. It was gone in an instant, her smile never faltering. But he saw it.

"Of course, Charlie. Let me see what I can do."

"Thank you, Malalia. You don't know how much this means to me."

"Quite a lot, I'm sure. But you'll have to excuse me now. I was just preparing for bed, and I really must get my beauty sleep."

"Of course," he said, heading for the door. "And, Malalia, thank you again for your help."

"It is my pleasure, Charlie. Now, good night."

"Good night," he replied, stepping out and closing the door behind him, an uneasy feeling growing in his gut.

Charlie was distracted as he walked toward the animal pens. Had he not been, perhaps he would have seen Malalia Maktan striding from the main estate in a rush, heading straight for the distant edge of the buildings. He might even have assumed she was hurrying to put in a good word for poor old Hertzall with the guards.

He would have been mistaken.

"Hello, Leila," the visla's daughter said as she entered the subterranean chamber.

"Denna," the bound woman replied.

"Oh, please, we've known one another since we were girls. Call me Malalia."

"Very well, Malalia," she replied, not liking the look in the woman's eyes one bit.

"There, that's better," the woman said.

Leila noted she was wearing a robe over her nightgown. Something had caused her to make this visit her unprepared. With a woman of Malalia Maktan's temperament, that could be dangerous.

"Why have you come, Malalia?"

"Because your ruffian friend came to see me," she replied, waiting to see what sort of response she would draw from the captive. "He said you were taken here and wanted to know what he could do to help you. He was *very* willing to do whatever it took," she said.

"It's good to have friends," Leila replied, unfazed.

Her lack of reaction drew the woman's ire. That was when Leila noticed the ornamental konus on her wrist. The one that was beginning to glow.

"We're going to have a little chat, you and I. And when we're done, you'll tell me all you know about your little gladiator pal, as well as what you were doing lurking around my father's business."

The soundproofing of the underground room was only moderate, and had he been nearer, Charlie might have heard his friend's cries.

CHAPTER TWENTY-SIX

The visla's smaller ships sat idly in the open area adjacent to the residence, Charlie noticed, as he made his way to talk the situation through with Ara. The important detail was, this time they seemed to be unattended.

He couldn't help but wonder if perhaps this seemingly cushy living situation wasn't finally proving too good to be true. Things certainly had been taking a turn for the worse, and if they continued to deteriorate, maybe escape from servitude actually *could* become an option.

Shit. I don't know even know how to fly one of these, he realized. *And I don't have any magic to power it even if I did.*

It was a grim realization. Any attempt to flee with one of the visla's ships would amount to what was effectively no more than an ill-advised joyride around the parking lot, if he could even manage that much. No, he would need to find another way.

Ara's been around a long time. She's bound to have some thoughts on the situation, he hoped as he hurried to her enclosure.

"You're pretty much screwed, Charlie," she informed him.

"Gee, thanks. I kind of knew that part already," he shot back to

the dragon. *"My point is, I got Leila in trouble, and I have a sinking feeling Malalia isn't going to help her, no matter what she may say."*

"On that, we are in agreement," Ara said. *"She came with her father just the other day, to observe me as he tried to tap my power."*

"Malalia? I didn't know that happened."

"Of course not. You're just a house slave, Charlie, and the visla's daughter is playing you to get to me."

"Well, that much I realized, but why hold Leila? Even if she did see the weapons, like you said, we're slaves, so what could we do about it?"

"It's not about your ability to effect an outcome. It's about keeping a secret under wraps. You know full well that rumor flies fast in any household, and this one is no different."

"So you think they'll keep her locked up until they do whatever it is they have planned?"

"That, or they'll kill her. It wouldn't be the first time a loose end was cleaned up in that manner, I assure you."

Charlie strode across the enclosure, an anger building inside of him.

"Stop that pacing, will you? My God, you wear your emotions on your sleeve. You must learn to present an impenetrable attitude of calm confidence, no matter how bad the situation may seem. The hesitation and uncertainty it can produce in your opponents may one day save your life."

"You sound a bit like Ser Baruud, you know?"

A curious look crossed the dragon's face.

"I've heard of the man. He killed many of my kind in his day."

"I'm sorry, I didn't know."

"No, it's all right. He was a gladiator, and they were there to kill him. I cannot grudge the man for possessing such an admirable survival instinct. And from what I hear, he has become a very learned and thoughtful teacher. It's funny, actually, how many great warriors become gentle in their old age."

"He's not gentle, I assure you."

"Perhaps gentle wasn't the best word," Ara admitted. "At ease with himself, might work better."

"Now that describes him," Charlie agreed. "But what about Leila? She may die because she looked into something at my request."

"Then she dies. You don't know her very well. Why should it bother you so?"

"Because she is a good person, Ara. Because she is one of the few who truly cares about making a difference in the world, even if it is only through her treatment of the creatures in her care. She doesn't deserve to die on my account." He kicked a small rock in frustration. "Oh, what does it matter? I can't even pilot a ship, so our escape would be cut short before it even began."

The Zomoki eyed him with great curiosity, the mighty gears in her head churning as an idea formed.

"Escape, you say?"

"It was just a passing thought."

"No, please. Tell me your idea. Humor me."

"Well, I thought if we could escape from here, these collars wouldn't be effective anymore. What's their range, anyway?"

"Line of sight, typically," Ara said. "For most vislas, that's around fifty miles or so."

"Okay, so offworld, he wouldn't be able to harm us."

"But he would be able to find you no matter how far you fly. That's how the collars work."

"And if I could get them off? You've seen that weird thing that happens when I use a konus magusi spell while touching a collar. It drains its power somehow. What if I could get my hands on a fully charged konus? Then I might actually be able to shut it off entirely."

The dragon seemed to ponder his question with great interest, shifting on her haunches, stretching her wings.

"Charlie, I want you to try to do as you just mentioned. Touch my collar and cast."

"But I only have this pathetic little konus, and all it's really good for is picking up waste."

143

"Trust me. There's still power in it, even if only a small amount. Humor me. Just try," she urged, lowering her head to the ground so he could reach her collar.

"Okay, but don't get upset when nothing happens."

"You need to believe, Charlie. Believe as if you were wearing the most powerful konus ever made. Cast as if you had infinite power at your control. Be confident and sure."

He lay his hands on her massive collar and let the words fill him and flow out. His lips didn't move—he spoke them with his mind, doing as the Zomoki had said, casting as if he had all the power in the world. He repeated the spell over and over, when he suddenly felt a flash of strange heat beneath his hands.

"What just happened?" he asked aloud.

The dragon looked at him and smiled a toothy grin.

"You just punched way above your weight, Charlie. You began to weaken the hold of my collar, despite the limited capacity of your konus."

"Really?"

"Yes, really. And stop speaking out loud. Someone may notice."

"Sorry, I didn't realize I was doing that."

"It's all right. It's all still new to you," the dragon replied.

She looked at him curiously as a nascent plan formed in her head.

"Okay, Charlie, I have an idea. One that will help Leila, and you, and me," she said. "But I have to warn you, it's going to be dangerous."

"My whole existence is dangerous at this point, it seems. How much worse can it possibly get?"

CHAPTER TWENTY-SEVEN

"You want to do what?" Charlie blurted when the great Zomoki told him her plan.

"*I want you to steal a konus—one of the powerful ones—or several, if you are able. With them I hope you can truly weaken the hold this collar has over me. It is a powerful device, but if I can get far enough away from this accursed estate, the ambient restraining fields Maktan put in place all around us won't hold sway over me any longer.*"

"And then?"

"*And then we flee. Hopefully somewhere it will take him a long time to find us,*" she replied. "*And, Charlie, you're doing it again.*"

"*Sorry. Habit,*" he replied, silently this time. "*But there's one problem with your plan, Ara. This planet, while sizable, from what I gather, isn't big enough to hide us from him for long.*"

"*You misunderstand. I meant we flee to another planet. Another system, actually. I fear you are correct in your assessment. The visla wishes to drain my magic to fuel his weapons of war, and I cannot let that come to pass.*"

Escape. It was the same idea that had crossed Charlie's mind when he passed the parked ships just a short while earlier. It was also quite impossible.

"A konus is one thing, but a ship? I haven't the first idea how to fly one, and I don't think we'll have too easy a time Shanghaiing a bunch of Drooks to power it for us."

"Shanghai?"

"It means to kidnap. An old shipping expression from a time when crews were snatched off the street and forced into servitude."

"So more or less what they do to Drooks," she noted.

"Yeah, I suppose so. But we're not exactly pirates, Ara, and kidnapping an entire crew just isn't feasible, even if we were. And besides, there's absolutely no way we could fit you in one of the ships parked around the buildings. They're nowhere near large enough to carry you."

Ara laughed with amusement. "Again, you misunderstand, Charlie. When I said we flee to another system, I was not referring to using a ship."

"You can fly in space?"

"Well, technically, yes, though I really don't like to do so for too long. However, if I can get far enough from Maktan's grip to regain control of my power, I can cast a travel spell and take us there. All I need is a destination and the freedom to use my power unrestrained."

Charlie's jaw literally dropped open. "You can teleport?"

"We call it traveling, akin to what those in ships call a jump, and it is a skill very few species possess. Zomoki are by far the most adept in its use."

"And you're saying you can telep—travel with passengers? You can jump?"

"Yes, if you were upon my back, you would travel with me. There's just one thing."

"There always is."

"In order to travel to another system without doing so from the vacuum of space—"

"Which would kill me."

"Yes, which would kill you. In order to do that, I would have to fly as high as possible without breaching the atmospheric shell surrounding this world. It would be terribly cold for one such as you."

"And the air would be thin."

"I can teach you a spell to aid with that aspect. But the cold, alas, I cannot help you control."

A crazy idea sprouted in Charlie's head. One that might even get him home.

"Let me ask you something," he said. "If you were in space, you say you could travel much farther than if you did it from within a planet's atmosphere, right?"

"That is correct."

"Like, how far are we talking here?"

"Quite far, actually. But that is simply not an option. You would perish in the vacuum."

"I know, but I was thinking, what if I was protected from it? What if I was wearing a space suit?"

"A what?"

"Like a suit of armor, only made to seal in the air and keep you alive in space."

"That sounds like a magic I have not seen before, and I know of none who possess it."

Charlie grinned. "I do."

"But how?"

"Back at my ship. We have storage bins with suits, all sealed up, nice and protected from the elements. Even after these three years in the Balamar Wastelands, they'll be good as new, so long as no one scavenged them."

"The Wastelands are not often frequented. It is a place of death and bad fortune."

"Well, the Tslavars that captured me and killed my friends didn't seem too averse to going there."

"They likely saw trace of your vessel's demise and investigated in *hopes of finding profit. As you are here today, they were obviously successful."*

"So you think the rest of my gear will still be there?"

"Likely," she replied. *"But even if you had this enchanted suit of space armor, I am both too weak to even attempt such a travel, as well as restrained from great acts of magic by the collar around my neck. Even if you could weaken it once more, I doubt you could break it. Your magic is simply not strong enough."*

The issue was the magical locking sequence, a spell keeping the collar on her neck. Without the power to remove it, his hopes for a return home were a mere dream.

"Hang on a minute," Charlie said. *"There's a plasma cutter on the ship. It's designed to cut through just about anything, and from what I've seen so far, a whole lot of this magical stuff isn't designed to stand up to tech from my world."*

"And you believe this plasma tech-magic will remove my collar?"

"It might. The collars are reflective, so a laser wouldn't work, but plasma very well might."

"Interesting. But there is still the problem of time. It would take me a long time to fully regain my energy after this ordeal. And I fear Maktan would find us long before then, though I'd be happy to take you to a system as far away from here as I can."

"No, you don't get it," Charlie chided. *"Think where my ship crashed."*

"The Wasteland."

"Yes, and what's in the Wasteland?"

"Nothing. That is why it is called a—oh my."

"Now you're getting it."

"If you were to splash the waters of Balamar onto my wounds, I would heal in no time."

Ara rose up to her full height, thrilled at the new prospect. One of freedom, and perhaps even revenge.

"It will still take us many jumps to reach the Wasteland, though. And I will need to replenish my energy repeatedly."

"*Then we take rest stops along the way. So long as we keep ahead of Maktan, we'll be okay. Though he does want to use you to charge all of his slaaps and konuses, so I have a feeling he might not let you go so easily.*"

"*This is what I fear. However, it is far better to die in action than be drained of my power in captivity. Gather the warmest coverings you can, and see about acquiring a powered konus. We should leave at once.*"

Much as Charlie wanted to do just that, his sense of loyalty to his friends simply wouldn't let him.

"*I need to bring a few people, Ara. My friends. Good people enslaved as we are.*"

"*If you say so, but be quick about it. I fear the visla will attempt to use me for his foul plans sooner than later.*"

"*I know, and I'll be quick. It'll be easy enough to talk to Tuktuk,*" Charlie noted. "*The tricky part will be freeing Leila.*"

CHAPTER TWENTY-EIGHT

"Hey, Charlie, what are you doing out so late?"

"Actually, I was just coming to see you, Tuk," he replied to his blue friend. "What are you doing in this wing? Your room is over near mine by the kitchen."

The blue man turned a slightly darker shade of azure.

"Oh, you *dog!* You were over at Magda's, weren't you?"

"I do not know what a dog is, Charlie, but I would appreciate it if you'd keep your voice down."

"Sure, sure. Your secret's safe with me, buddy. And good for you."

"Thank you. It's like I told you when you first got here, Magda's a good woman."

"And she's lucky to have you," he replied. "Well, this kind of puts a new twist on what I wanted to talk with you about, but she's a big girl, so I know there's room for one more."

"Magda is well-built, but by no means would I classify her as a 'big girl,' Charlie."

"No, not Magda. Ara."

"Ara?"

"Yeah. The Zomoki."

"You named the Zomoki?"

"Gah! Again! No, I didn't name her. That's her name. Well, technically, it's actually some crazy-long mish-mash that sounds like a cross between a curse and a sneeze, but I just call her Ara for short."

The blue man looked around the empty corridor, a relieved look in his eyes that no one was near enough to hear their conversation.

"Charlie, we shouldn't be out here chatting in the hallways at this hour."

"I know."

"Good. So, I think––"

"We should go to the kitchen and talk there. It's got thicker walls so no one will hear the staff working. That's a good place to talk."

"I was going to say I think we should go to our respective rooms."

"Trust me, Tuk, you'll want to hear what I have to offer."

"Offer?"

"Yeah. Something we've been waiting for since we first met."

Tuktuk's eyes turned on their stalks, a pensive look forming on his face. "Well, all right, you've made me curious, I'll admit. I'll brew up some tea, then we can talk."

Charlie beamed brightly. "Excellent. You're going to love this."

"I don't love this, Charlie," the blue chef said over his steaming cup of tea.

"But, Tuk, I'm talking about freedom. Actual freedom. A chance to start your life over somewhere else, not bound as a slave for someone."

"But I enjoy my work, Charlie. And I'm actually getting to do something I'm good at for once. I'm a good cook, and I'm appreciated here."

"But you could be a chef anywhere, man. Don't you get it? You said it yourself, your wife left you once she was unable to raise money to buy your freedom. You've got no obligations to the outside world, and if you bring Magda with, you two could start anew."

"You just don't get it, Charlie. I *like* it here. I'm treated well, fed well, clothed and housed. And all I have to do is cook. If I were working in the outside world, all of my wages would go toward housing and sustenance. Here, that's all covered, and I live in a palace. A *palace*, Charlie. It beats a small housing unit on the outskirts of some grimy city."

"But you're a slave, Tuktuk."

"Aren't we all, in a sense? Slaves to our jobs, on a constant quest for coin to pay for the basic necessities of life. Maybe a year or two ago I might have jumped at the chance, but I've come to see things differently since I've been here."

It was a response Charlie had not anticipated, and one he did not have a ready answer for. He was offering his friend freedom, and it was being declined.

"Besides, even if I did want to go, Magda certainly wouldn't. She loves it here, and I wouldn't leave her behind."

Charlie rose from his seat and began gathering a few snacks from the pantry and cooling unit, placing them on a small tray. "Well, I won't twist your arm, Tuk. But think about it, okay? I don't know if you'll ever get an opportunity like this again."

"I appreciate it, really, I do," his friend replied. "What are you doing with all of that?" he asked as the human headed toward the door, tray in hand.

"You know Leila's been taken for nosing into some of the visla's affairs. Something is about to happen, Tuk, and I think it has to do with his Council of Twenty buddies."

"Shh!" Tuktuk hissed, looking around with fear in his eyes. "Do not mention them, Charlie. Those are *powerful* people."

"I know. And I think they're making a play to become even more so. Why else would they need tens of thousands of weapons? I haven't heard of any war going on."

"Because there isn't one. And what weapons?"

"The ones the visla's manufacturing here. Shit. I wasn't going to tell you that."

"But there is no war, Charlie."

"Precisely. So why the weapons? It looks to me like they're prepping for something. And now Leila is in trouble because I brought it to her attention."

"So the tray?"

"Taking her food. Hopefully they'll let me in to see her, at least for a minute. If I had a proper konus I could take the guards, but I only have this weak-ass trinket with just enough juice to clean the pens and that's it."

"You were a gladiator, Charlie. Of course they're going to be cautious giving you potential weapons."

"I know. And that's why I have to get her out a more traditional way. By subterfuge, and good old-fashioned physical violence, if need be," he said, heading for the door. "But, Tuk, my offer still stands. If my ride out of here pans out, there's a seat for you and Magda. Think about it at least, okay?"

"Okay, Charlie. I'll think about it."

"Great. Oh, and while you're at it, is there any way you could see if Magda has any old warm blankets in storage that won't be missed?"

"Uh, okay. But why?"

"Long story. Let's just say it'll be cold where we're going, at least for a while, and the extra layers will be a lifesaver."

"I'll see what I can do."

"Thanks, Tuk. That's all I can ask."

Charlie gave his friend a little nod and headed out the side door into the night, the vaguest beginnings of a half-formed plan coalescing in his mind. He just hoped it would solidify into something more concrete by the time he reached the men guarding Leila.

CHAPTER TWENTY-NINE

The grounds were eerily quiet as Charlie made his way to the far end of the building beneath which Leila was being held. The hustle and bustle of earlier had ceased abruptly, and an uneasy silence now hung in the air.

"Something's up," he observed as he strained his ears. Far in the distance, he thought he could hear *something*, but in the general vicinity of the estate's sprawling structures, it was quiet. *Too* quiet.

Walking with confidence, hoping it would be sufficient to bluster his way past the guards, Charlie rounded the corner at a full stride, making sure not to look hesitant in the slightest. It was the clipboard and hard hat principle at work. Act as if you belong and most often no one will question you.

Unless that someone happens to be the visla's daughter.

"Malalia," he said, startled at seeing the young woman walking toward him. "I thought you were in bed by now."

"I tried to sleep after you left, Charlie, but what you said about the groundskeeper's daughter concerned me so greatly that I simply had to come see what was going on, and if I could help in any way."

"Really? That's wonderful. Thank you, Malalia. I'm sure Hertzall was thrilled."

"Well, I haven't spoken with him as of yet," she said, looking at the two guards standing near the doors. "Is this for Leila?"

"Yes. I thought she could use some food, seeing as she missed dinner."

"You're such a considerate man, Charlie. Come, leave it with the guards. They'll make sure she receives it. Let us walk a bit. I wish to speak privately."

He hesitated.

"I really should bring it to her personally. I mean, I wouldn't want to trouble Dinuk's men."

"It's no trouble, I assure you."

There really wasn't a way around it.

"Okay, I guess," he said, handing the tray to the nearest guard.

"Excellent. Now, come. Let us talk. I have important things I wish to discuss with you."

The pair quietly padded down a path lined with low shrubbery on either side until they reached a crossroads where several other trails linked. Malalia veered right, and Charlie followed close behind.

"I hope you found the tech-magic items I had brought here for you useful. My men really didn't know what they were looking for, and I worried not all of it would be of value."

"Oh, that. Yeah, I appreciate your having those pieces recovered. I have not really had a chance to see what I can do with them, but I do hope to make myself of greater use around the grounds if I can."

"Well, you know, Charlie," she said, leaning in conspiratorially, "another of my father's ships will be passing that way in a few weeks. I may be able to have another collection of pieces brought back for you. Would you like that?"

"That would be great," he replied. "It would be wonderful to be able to use the science of my world to help the inhabitants of this one."

Turning to look at him, her shoulder brushed against his, contact that was longer than could possibly be unintentional.

"You really are a kind man, you know? It's a rare gift, this spirit of generosity and compassion."

"Uh, thank you," he replied. "And you're a kind woman, Malalia. It must be difficult at times being the daughter of a powerful visla, but you seem very well adjusted."

She laughed brightly, flashing a warm smile his way.

"Thank you, Charlie. That means a lot to me."

"Well, it's true," he said. "And you went out of your way to make sure Leila was all right. It's really kind of you. Speaking of which, what's going on down there, anyway? I can't see any reason they'd hold her like that. She's spent her whole life on these grounds. It's not like she's some random outsider they need to guard."

Malalia looped her arm around his and drew him close as they walked.

"You know, Charlie, from what I gathered, it sounded like she was inquiring about the Zomoki. About its powers and how to tap into them. Naturally, this made Father uncomfortable, and he felt he needed to hold her from the others until he could ascertain her motives. I mean, for his personal animal keeper to mistreat one of her charges, it was quite a shock to him."

"I imagine it would be," he said, careful with his words lest she realize he was on to her ruse. "Still, it might have been innocent curiosity about the animal in her care. She doesn't strike me as the type to exploit a captive creature like that."

"Maybe not, but just the other day, when we went to see the beast, Father mentioned that a long time ago there were people who could actually connect with Zomoki on a primal level. Legend has it that some could even share their power."

"That sounds really dangerous."

"I'm sure it was, but then, you managed to ride atop of one, and came out unscathed! How in the heavens did you ever manage such a thing?"

And there it is, he mused with a little sigh. *Honestly, I'm surprised it took her this long.*

"I told you, I really don't know. In the heat of the bout I wasn't thinking and just scrambled for the safest spot I could, away from the men trying to kill me."

"Atop a Zomoki's back was the safest place?"

"Compared to the men with slaaps and swords trying to kill me, yes, for that moment at least. Like I said, it was just a reflex reaction, but it saved my life."

"But how were you able to stay mounted without being thrown? I hear the beast managed to cast a powerful spell in spite of the control collar on its neck."

Charlie assumed that she didn't know the truth, much like the others at the bout that day. The truth that it wasn't the Zomoki who had cast the spell, but Charlie, drawing from the creature's vast stores of magical power. So long as they thought it was all about Ara, he would remain free to enact their plan. The moment they suspected he knew more than he was letting on, he would be imprisoned just like Leila was.

"I was just holding on for dear life when she took to the air," he said with an amused sigh. "You have no idea how frightening it was when I suddenly found myself airborne."

"But it flew you over to the pole and helped you grab the ring."

Charlie forced a laugh he hoped sounded natural. "Oh, I really don't think it was trying to help me. In fact, I think it was actually trying to throw me off its back and just happened to swerve close enough for me to grab it. Blind luck. And as for the spell, I didn't even know Zomoki possessed that kind of magic."

"Most do not. I mean, from what I've heard. But once in a very long while, a Zomoki is born with great power within. It is akin to the way vislas are born with power far exceeding that of emmiks or mesters. Or how a handful of one race makes up all of the Drooks in the systems, yet the vast majority of their people have no power at all."

"I guess that makes sense. I still haven't figured out why some people in certain systems have different powers and gifts, but I think it has to do with the radiation from their particular suns."

"We have known this for a long time, Charlie."

"Well, it's all new to me, so I'm just figuring it out as I go."

"And the Zomoki's power? What did you make of that, being so close when it used it?"

He turned and looked her square in the eyes.

"To tell the truth, I was zapped unconscious by the collar before I even knew what had happened. I only know now because people have told me about it. It's like learning about your own life secondhand, you know? It's rather disconcerting."

"Yes, it would be," she said, sliding her arm from his. "It was nice talking with you, Charlie, but this time, I really should be off to bed," she said, turning back toward the estate. "I'll be sure to ask my father about Leila when I see him in the morning, but for now, forget about her. Until he knows what she was up to, I feel my father will keep her locked up, for all of our safety."

Charlie bristled inside but kept the dopey smile on his face. He was just a harmless slave. No reason to worry about him at all.

"Thank you, Malalia. I'll just wait to hear what the visla says, then."

She smiled, satisfied, and walked off into the shadows.

Charlie, however, was most definitely *not* satisfied.

"Ara will know what to do."

CHAPTER THIRTY

"Okay, I'm not using my outside voice this time. Are you happy?"
Charlie silently called out as he entered the dragon's enclosure.
"Ara?"

The space was empty, signs of a struggle marring the churned soil near the large, unbolted doors opening from the rear walls. Someone had forced the Zomoki out––against her will, at that––and there was only one person with the power to do so.

"Shit. Maktan," he said, following the tracks to where they suddenly vanished just outside the enclosure.

The dragon had been subdued, then loaded onto a transport of some kind. Whether she was even still on the planet was now up in the air, and despite his desperate desire to race to find answers, Charlie knew there was only one truly reliable source. Not his friends, and certainly not the visla's manipulative daughter.

He would have to rely on the weakest link in the wizard's armor––his guards. Not the trusted ones, though. He needed to find the others. The ones routinely given the shit details. The ones most likely to talk.

But one could not simply approach them empty-handed and strike up a casual conversation about the abduction of a certain house-sized Zomoki. Subterfuge was required. Fortunately, Charlie had one caffeinated card up his sleeve that no one else in the galaxy seemed to possess.

"Hey, fellas, how are you all doing tonight?"

"Hi, Charlie," the men replied, casually.

A pair of the team of security staff lounging in their late shift station had casually sparred with Charlie shortly after he arrived, curious if the gladiator could show them any new moves. Charlie had indeed imparted a few minor tidbits of knowledge to them, while being careful to ensure he never showed his martial superiority.

This feeling of equal footing allowed an easy camaraderie with the men, who enjoyed a boost to their egos as they held their own with this alleged top fighter. Little did they know the degree he was sandbagging to stroke their egos.

"Hey, I couldn't really sleep, so I made some coffee and was going to work on some little projects out at the pens. I made a big pot, and I sure can't drink all of it, so I brought it over in case you guys wanted some."

The men eagerly accepted, their moods perking up even before the caffeine hit their systems.

"Thank you, Charlie."

"Hey, it's my pleasure. So, everything calm tonight?"

"For the most part. You?"

"Yeah, the same," he said, sipping his cup. "Well, actually, there is *one* odd thing. I was fixing some fencing on the bundabist corral, and I noticed the Zomoki is missing. Did the visla sell it?"

The men groaned and looked at one another knowingly.

"Oh, *that,*" one said, obviously less than thrilled. "He had us move the thing a little while ago. I'll tell you, it fought something fierce when the girl tried to subdue it."

"Girl? But I thought Leila was locked up?"

"No, not her. The visla's daughter. She had on her father's slaap and was shocking the beast into submission. I'll tell you, it was a little unsettling, how much she seemed to be enjoying it."

"I bet," Charlie replied, carefully keeping his face neutral. "So, they had you load it on a ship, huh? That must've been a lot of work, even with lifting spells."

"It was a pain, all right, but we only had to get it onto a transport sled, so it wasn't all bad."

"Well, that's good to hear. Where'd you wind up taking it?"

"Hey, you know the visla will have all of our heads if you talk about his private stuff," a guard Charlie didn't recognize interjected. "Best to keep to your own business. You don't want to be on the visla's bad side. Believe me, I've seen what he can do to people who dig around in his private affairs."

"Thanks, I'll remember that. I was just curious, is all," Charlie said.

Truth be told, he didn't need them to tell him where Ara had been taken. In fact, he had a very good idea *exactly* where she was.

"All right, then. I'd better get back to work. No sense being up and awake if I don't get anything done. You all enjoy the coffee, and have a safe night."

"Thanks, Charlie. You too."

He left the men and took off at a quick jog across the grounds. At the crossroad of paths, he took the left fork, heading toward the grove of trees leading to the low wall surrounding the inner layer of the estate.

"This is going to suck," he muttered as he slid his fingers between his collar and his neck and squeezed tight.

Charlie then began running.

Running straight for the low wall a mere handful of meters away.

"*Konus magusi. Konus magusi. Konus magusi. Konus magusi.*"

He repeated the spell over and over in his mind as well as whispered through his lips as he ran, doing all he could to lessen the power of the collar that bound him as his feet raced faster and faster. The burning sensation building against his skin began to spike rapidly, nearly making him lose concentration, but his gladiator training came in handy, and he redoubled his efforts and pushed through the pain. Somehow, he managed to keep his footing even, as he increased his pace to a full sprint in the low light.

The wall was closing fast, and despite the reduced potency of his control collar, Charlie felt like his neck was on fire. His eyes were watering, blurring his vision and screwing up his depth perception, the burning agony threatening to sap his very consciousness.

With a final determined surge, he leapt as high as he could, clearing the wall, a physical blow slapping him as he passed the barrier in midair. His legs were still moving fast when he landed on the other side, his momentum carrying him forward several steps, but Charlie was out of control, unconscious on his feet.

Finally, he crumpled to the loamy soil in a heap, the glowing collar around his neck slowly fading back to its normal golden hue. His prone body heaved with every breath as his respirations slowly returned to normal.

CHAPTER THIRTY-ONE

The shapes of the dark path began to slip back into focus as Charlie struggled to his knees, an itching burn marking his neck where the restraining collar had tried—and failed—to keep him back. Fine lines of cleanliness streaked his cheeks, where his watering eyes washed a pattern in the dirt acquired upon impact with the ground.

Well, that answers that question. The barrier is just the wall and not beyond it, he noted thankfully as he forced himself back to his feet.

A bellow rang out down the glen from the direction of the weapons factory.

Ara.

He took off at as much of a run as he could on his unsteady legs, stopping a moment to grab a knotted branch from a fallen tree. Apparently, Hertzall only cleaned the innermost ring of such detritus. That, or the tree had only recently fallen. Whatever the case, the Earth spaceman turned slave gladiator finally had a weapon he could wield regardless of magical aid, and it felt good in his hands. Solid. Tangible. Ready to do harm, if need be.

Another roar. Someone was hurting the Zomoki.

Harm, it appeared, was on the menu.

Charlie raced to the rear of the building, hiding against its dark shape in the shadow cast by the illuminated clearing to the front. Ara was obviously being held there, the question was, what could he do about it? From the sound of things, there were several guards with her, and all he had was a wooden club, and not a terribly impressive one at that.

As quietly as he could, Charlie snuck along the wall, pausing to peer in a window before continuing his advance. The building was nearly entirely empty, with just a handful of crates and materials remaining, a few slaaps and konuses lying on what appeared to be a designer's work table.

That just might be the edge I need.

He silently slithered in through the window, sticking to the shadows of cover as he made his way to the small table. Five guards and a handful of the green-and-black factory worker things were hauling the last few cases out the front doors.

Ara was there. He could see her massive red shape through the doorway. Judging by the caution with which they exited the building, she wasn't in as much distress as he had feared.

With their attention firmly fixed on the Zomoki their master had bound just outside the building, Charlie seized the opportunity and snatched the slaaps and konuses from the table and retreated back to the shadows, slipping out the window and taking up a hiding place behind a dilapidated storage container.

Okay, let's see what we've got here.

He slipped a slaap onto his hand, lacing his fingers through the familiar holes of the weapon.

No charge. Shit.

He tried another with the same result. Two more were likewise possessing only the faintest trickle of power––just enough to test integrity but no more.

Oh, come on, he grumbled to himself, sliding the last slaap

165

onto his hand. This one, though very weak, at least had enough of a charge to cast a few times. He hoped it would be enough.

He then repeated the process with the konuses. He had grabbed a dozen of the much smaller devices, and every last one of them possessed only a fractional charge.

Twelve of them, he mused, an unconventional idea popping into his head. *Well, it'll either blow my arm off, or it'll work... maybe.*

As quietly as he was able, he slid all of them to his wrists, six per side, taking care to tie them together with a piece of fabric torn from his tunic so they wouldn't jingle against one another as he moved. *It'll have to do.*

Peering around the edge of the building, he counted eight guards and seven of the stocky factory worker creatures. Ara was bound at the far end of the clearing, her golden collar pulsing brightly, holding her firmly in place. She could move, but not much. Regardless, the visla's men stayed well clear of her.

"Fifteen to one. I guess there's no sense strategizing too much," he said with a little sigh. "Probably just going to get myself killed anyway."

Charlie began running through all of the spells in his arsenal in a sing-song rhyme, the mnemonic trick refreshing his memory, as he hadn't been training the spells since he transitioned from gladiator to house slave.

"Well, no time like the present," he said, breaking into a run.

The first two men he fell upon didn't know what hit them.

For the record, it was a big wooden club.

After that, bedlam ensued as the minimally armed gladiator tore into his opponents with reckless abandon, his club swinging in tandem with his fists and feet. He was desperately trying to save the few uses in his slaap, hoping to make them count. The konuses were so weak he doubted they'd do much, even stacked as they were.

The guards, to his benefit, were relying on their conventional weapons, uncomfortable with the situation and reluctant to discharge their slaaps in so dense a group of their own men.

Charlie, however, was used to fighting in such chaotic conditions, and a few carefully aimed spells took down three of the guards in quick succession before his slaap was no more than a powerless chunk of metal on his hand.

He discarded it immediately and tried to pull one from a fallen man, but the relentless onslaught of both guards and workers prevented him from retrieving it, forcing him instead to fall back, swinging his club high and low. The fake-out head attacks opened up the midriffs and knees of the nearest two attackers, but the others were quick to fill the gap left as they fell.

Unlike the old martial arts movies he had enjoyed watching back on Earth, these alien fighters did not wait and take turns attacking. They moved on him as one, and Charlie found his blows met by counterstrikes more often than not.

Nevertheless, he had reduced their numbers significantly. This was a blessing and a curse, in that he had more room to fight now, but so too did they have a clearer shot on him with their slaaps.

Instinctively, Charlie cast defensive spells in quick succession, blocking their attacks while closing the distance enough to wield his club with efficacy. Of the fifteen, only four remained, and of those, only two were guards. The rest lay scattered on the field, battered, broken, and in some cases, dead.

This wasn't a casual bout. This was for keeps.

Another worker fell to Charlie's club, but still another managed to flank him, lunging in with a rather wicked-looking short sword.

The blow should have skewered him, but the attacking guard fell to the soil, the blade barely scratching Charlie's skin. A black-hilted dagger jutted from the side of his head.

He spun to catch glimpse of a cloaked figure rushing into the fight. Whose side he was on, however, Charlie couldn't tell, as the man seemed intent on fighting anyone in his path. The remaining guard and worker both fell to the man in quick succession. He then aimed his assault at Charlie, moving with such speed and power he found himself using every last bit of his training just to keep pace.

Faster and faster their hands moved, punching, blocking, deflecting minor spells.

Charlie feinted a high kick, then threw a stink spell in the hooded man's face. A flash of pale flesh filled Charlie's field of vision, then stars as a fist caught his nose, sending him flying.

Charlie recovered and was back in the fight in an instant, pressing the mysterious attacker with a quick combination of blows. Despite moving the man back, he couldn't help but feel almost as if he were being toyed with.

From the corner of his eye, Charlie saw a stunned guard had recovered and was rushing at them both, a small sword raised high for a killing blow.

"*Effian Zina!*" Charlie thought, casting the bastardized spell with all the force he could pull from the stacked konuses.

They were all barely charged, but somehow, the combined power of them swelled up, driving the improvised spell and blasting the poor man in half.

Charlie didn't have time to marvel at what had just happened. The cloaked attacker moved close and grabbed both of his wrists, uttering a spell he had never heard before.

"*Floxzan horaxia,*" he hissed. Charlie felt the little power remaining in his konuses drain from the devices as if they were popped water balloons.

Rather than allow himself the luxury of being startled by the complication in his situation, Charlie did what any good Earthling would do. He fought dirty, head-butting the hidden face beneath the cloak, following with a hard punch-kick, driving the man backward and very nearly knocking the wind out of him.

His hood had fallen back from the blow, and Charlie finally got a good look at his opponent, just as he drew a dark blade from the scabbard hidden beneath his cloak.

A Wampeh. And one that looked strangely familiar.

CHAPTER THIRTY-TWO

"I wouldn't do that if I were you," a booming voice said, the pale man's long black hair blowing from the force. "Drop it."

In the course of fighting, Charlie had managed to drive his opponent backward, right into Ara's holding space. The Zomoki now loomed directly over him.

"I said, drop it."

The Wampeh looked up at the enormous head––and the sharp teeth her massive jaws sported––and complied, dropping the sword to the dirt. He looked back at Charlie and smiled, his pointed canines somehow bright, even in the dim light.

"You know, I could have killed you a dozen times," he said. "But overall, not a bad showing."

"You're a cocky one, aren't you? And it was *nine* times you could have landed a killing stroke, by my count," Ara corrected him. "And I can't help but wonder why you didn't."

The Wampeh turned his gaze to the golden-eyed dragon. "So it's true. You *do* speak. I'd heard tales that a very few of your kind still possessed this ability, but had long doubted them."

"You'll find my kind can be *quite* surprising," she replied.

"Uh, Ara? What's going on?" Charlie asked.

"Ara?" the Wampeh said, actual shock flashing across his face. "Your name is Ara?"

"I only call her that. Her real name's kind of a bitch to pronounce," Charlie said.

"You're Aranzgrgghmunatharrgle?" the pale man said, his eyes wide with awe.

"How did you––?" Charlie asked.

"Legend said you died hundreds of years ago. None held even the slightest hope you were still alive. All believed you dead."

"A belief I wish to have continue," Ara said.

"Of course, Wise One," the Wampeh replied, bowing his head slightly.

"So, you do not wish to test your mettle against me, then?"

"My fangs would never pierce your scales," he said, meeting her gaze. "And even if they could, I would never try."

Something in the way he spoke to her, that strange, almost reverence in his tone, made Charlie believe the man was telling the truth. He held her in high regard, for some reason, and Charlie suddenly had the sneaking suspicion the strange man was far older than his physical form suggested.

Ara sniffed the air, studying the Wampeh, cloaked in deep gray, a slight shifting pattern to the material.

It must be enchanted, Charlie noted as the man's form shifted, making him hard to focus on despite being right in front of him. The face, however. *That* he saw clearly.

"I know you," he said, realization dawning on him. "You probably don't remember. It was nearly three years ago, back in the bazaar of some small world with a blue sun. You were fighting a group of armed men, and it looked like you were losing. But when a visla appeared you suddenly cast a killing spell out of the blue, taking down all the others, leaving him broken."

171

SCOTT BARON

"He was a mester, actually. A visla would have been far more work," the Wampeh corrected.

"You-you drank his blood. I saw it," Charlie continued.

"Yes, I did. And you, Charlie Gault, saved my life that day when you shouted a warning and distracted the miscreant attempting to skewer me from behind. I owed you my life." He retrieved his dagger from the head of the fallen guard, wiping the blade and tucking it back into its sheath beneath his cloak. "And now we are even."

"How do you know my name?"

"I know many things."

"Wait a minute. Was that you racing toward the estate the other day when the bundabist escaped?"

"You saw me?"

"Only a glimpse."

"Hmm," he said, perplexed. "Most intriguing. But yes, I was infiltrating Visla Maktan's grounds that day and needed a distraction."

The beasts' escape suddenly made far more sense.

"You opened the pens. That's why both of her locking spells failed."

"Again, correct," he said. "I was preparing to take the visla if opportunity presented itself. Sadly, you triggered my trap before I could lure him to it."

"Trap?"

"Yes. Just the other side of the low wall you so valiantly vaulted just now."

"You crossed the visla's perimeter?" Ara asked, leaning in to see the burns on his neck better. "That shouldn't have been possible."

"It was rather impressive, I must admit," the pale man said. "He misused a defensive spell and somehow drained much of the power from his collar. Quite clever. Unfortunately, it was a far different spell he ran into while heading the other direction the other day."

"That's why my neck was untouched. It wasn't the perimeter spell that shocked me during the hunt at all."

"Correct. It was a *very* specialized spell. One designed to disable Yoral Maktan long enough for me to dispose of him while his guards were preoccupied. But then you stumbled into it. An unpowered man in a trap meant for a most dangerous visla. And yet, somehow, you survived. It is most curious."

Charlie hadn't realized just how close he had apparently come to dying. Prior to the most recent near-death experience, that is.

"You said you were here to dispose of him. You're an assassin," he stated plainly.

"Among other things."

"Was it you who brought me to my room, then?"

"Guilty as charged."

"But if subterfuge is so important, why admit all of this to me?"

"Because you are aligned with the Wise One, which says much for your character. And also because we have overlapping interests, as I think you've discovered."

"The enemy of my enemy is my friend," Charlie muttered.

"A wise saying. Did you come up with it?"

"Uh, yes. Yes, I did. Just now, in fact."

"Very catchy. I shall appropriate it—with your permission, of course."

"Knock yourself out. But you've got to help me out here. I mean, I get it that Maktan is not the best man around, but why kill him?"

"Do not be deceived by his niceties. Visla Yoral Maktan is a key member of the Council of Twenty, and that alliance of powerful systems is oppressing the hundreds of others in the galaxy. They have even gone so far as to overthrow peaceful rulers on the most distant of worlds. Those worlds that were content to be as they were, not a part of the Council's rule. It is terrible, yet something few have heard of."

"Because of the distance, of course."

"No. Because they have killed all who voice their discontent. The Council of Twenty intends to control *all* of the systems, taxing them heavily, while providing little benefit for the residents. Their men fight for coin, and if the vislas aim them at a peaceful world, their mercenary forces have no qualms with striking first and asking questions later, if at all."

Charlie looked at the man with a quizzical expression on his face. Here was a stone-cold killer, a man who drank the blood of his powered enemies, and yet he was fighting for what seemed like a noble cause. The dichotomy made his head spin a little.

In any case, the Wampeh was on his side. At least for the time being. And having a vampiric assassin watching your back was the kind of plus that puts your other concerns a bit more at ease.

"You're not what I expected," Charlie said. "But I think I'm glad to know you, um...?"

"I am called Bawb," the Wampeh replied.

"Bob?"

"Yes, Bawb."

Charlie grinned. "You're a deadly vampire space assassin, and your name is Bob?"

"Is there a problem?" Bawb asked, a curious look in his eye.

"No, no problem. It's just, I expected something more, I don't know. More *badass*, I guess."

"You can call him Geist, if you prefer," Ara said.

The Wampeh's eyes flashed at the name.

"Yes, my Wampeh friend, I know who you are," the mighty Zomoki said. "Your reputation precedes you. The deadliest assassin in thirty systems. In, out, and never seen."

"An exaggeration, of course," Bawb said. "And only thirty systems?" he added with a sly grin.

Ara let out a rumbling laugh. "Oh, I like this one. But more talk later. At the moment, I need your help, Charlie."

"That's what I'm here for. But what can I do? It looks like the visla has you pretty well pinned down."

"Yes, the incantation is a strong one, but I believe you can break it. The way you drained its bond before."

"But I don't even have a konus. Mr. Geist here drained the weak ones I salvaged, and all of these guards only have combat slaaps."

"And about that, the use of a dozen konuses like that should have torn your arms clean from your body, yet somehow, you once again remain unscathed. I think there is potential within you, Charlie. But now is not the time to tap into it. Now is the time to help release me."

She turned her gaze to the Wampeh. "Bawb, would you be so kind as to lend Charlie your konus?"

The pale man pulled up his sleeves, revealing ornate, armored armlets running from wrist to elbow. He pulled the konus from his wrist and handed it to Charlie.

"Fully charged," he noted.

"Thanks," Charlie said, slipping it onto his arm. It had been so long since he'd worn a proper konus, he had forgotten how good it felt. Suddenly, channeling his unconventional spells didn't seem too far-fetched.

Ara leaned her massive head low, allowing Charlie to wrap his hands around the glowing band on her neck. Bawb, the Geist, watched with fascination.

"I noted him doing something similar in the bout on Gilea. But what spell is this?"

"It's a *konus magusi* spell," Charlie said, the collar flickering as he said the words before he even began to focus on his casting.

175

"A simple defensive spell? It should not have any effect on that collar. Fascinating."

Charlie turned his attention back to his task at hand. Or *in* his hands, as the case may be. Slowly, he began the spell, channeling it from within, his lips moving silently. Ara refrained from comment. Just this once, she'd not correct the action if it helped him release her sooner.

The collar's glow began to fade, the magic restraint lessening more and more, until the collar finally returned to the dull illumination of its normal resting state.

"That's enough, Charlie," Ara informed him.

He looked up from his task. "Holy shit, it worked!"

"That it did," Geist said, taking the konus Charlie held out to him and sliding it back over his wrist.

"Thanks for that."

"Anything to help Aranzgrgghmunatharrgle," he replied, pleased to have been of assistance to one he so revered. "You should know, there appeared to be an unpowered konus of substantial design near the smelting molds. Perhaps it might be of use to you," Bawb said, then turned toward the darkness.

"Wait, where are you going?"

"I need to find and kill the visla before these men are discovered. He is already very heavily guarded. This incident may make him nearly untouchable."

"Except for the Geist," Ara noted.

"Perhaps. But easier is far preferable to difficult, is it not?"

"Indeed," she agreed.

"But he's always by himself. Why, just the other day he took me for a walk out on the grounds. We were totally alone. Why didn't you just strike then? I know you were already here by then."

Bawb the Geist, deadliest assassin in thirty systems, simply laughed. "Oh, Charlie. He was most certainly *not* alone."

"I was there, Bob. He was."

"No, he was not. Allow me to demonstrate."

The Geist then showed one of the reasons he had earned his reputation when he slid his hood over his head and vanished without a word.

"Where'd he go?"

"I am still here, Charlie," he said, removing the hood. For a moment he looked like a disembodied head floating six feet above the ground, then Charlie made out the slightest hint of his shape, blending with the background almost seamlessly.

"Holy shit, that's active camouflage! Our government was working on something like that, but they never got it functional, from what I heard. But this? This is amazing."

"It is called a shimmer. The spell, in conjunction with some form of enchanted covering, makes the wearer nearly invisible to those not specifically looking for it. And rest assured, I am *always* looking for it. The visla has a dozen guards with him at nearly all times when he is outside the estate's walls."

"And I had no idea."

"No reason for you to have. But now I must return to my task. Be safe, my new friends," he said, walking away.

"He's gone, you know," Ara said. "Left the planet."

"What?" the Geist blurted.

"He was trying to force me to power his weapons––to no avail, I'm proud to say. He even had a pair of claithes among them."

"His personal ones. He drained them putting down a rebellion," Charlie noted.

"Terrible things, those. In any case, I was no use to him, so he had to start the process himself. Something is afoot, and he couldn't wait. He departed aboard one of the larger of the transport ships, focusing his energy into the weapons within, personally delivering them to the other vislas and emmiks involved in their covert war."

The Wampeh's shoulders sagged slightly. "Then it is too late. I have missed him."

Ara sized up the man and made a choice.

"Help us rescue Leila and make our escape, Bawb, and rest assured, Visla Maktan will come to you."

CHAPTER THIRTY-THREE

The Wampeh was disconcertingly efficient in his movement, though Charlie was unsure whether he felt more uncomfortable or envious as he watched the man quickly strip their victims of weapons and the few skrees they might use to call for help.

"You know, you fought quite well," he said, pulling a slaap from a dead guard's hand. "Especially given you'd already fought off nearly a dozen opponents, and underarmed as well. Your errors were more due to fatigue than tactical miscalculation, though there were still plenty of those to exploit."

"Thanks," Charlie replied. "Coming from you, I'll take that as a compliment, I guess."

"I mean no disrespect. And if we make a clean run upon rescuing your friend, I'd even be glad to show you a thing or two."

"You want to train me to be an assassin?"

The Wampeh laughed. "Hardly. You stand out far too much for that, and even with years of training, I feel a shimmer wouldn't keep you entirely out of sight."

Charlie tightened the bonds of the few survivors of their fight.

"You should kill them, you know," Bawb said.

"I agree with the Geist," Ara added.

"I know, but I still don't feel good about killing people, at least not when they're already bound and gagged."

"So untie them," Bawb said.

"You know what I mean."

The Wampeh flashed a wry grin. "It doesn't mean my solution isn't a valid one."

Ultimately, they decided that since the visla was off-world, and the completed weapons had gone with him, the likelihood of anyone happening to come to the building was quite low. Regardless, Charlie and Bawb threw the bound survivors in a storage closet within the building.

Ara disposed of the others. Charlie didn't ask how.

"Come close, Charlie," she said when he exited the building. "Is that the newly designed konus you were speaking of, Geist?" she asked, eyeing the ornate device the human was carrying.

"Yes, that is it," he said. "And it seems quite a good fit for Charlie, wouldn't you agree?"

Her golden eyes scrutinized the magical device. Indeed it appeared to be one of a kind, a prototype of a new design, and one with immense potential if she was right.

"Place it on the ground before me, Charlie."

"What are you going to do?"

"Just do as she says, young one. You are about to witness something few have ever seen," the Wampeh said, stepping back well clear of the area.

Charlie did as he was instructed, laying the konus on the soil at Ara's feet.

"Now, stay back," she said, leaning in, focusing her gaze on the ornate device.

A golden light flowed from her eyes into the konus, and

Charlie could have sworn he felt a rippling of the world around him, a ball of magic pressure swelling out from the now-glowing konus. A moment later, Ara sat back on her haunches, satisfied with her work.

"Put it on, Charlie," she instructed.

"But it's still glowing hot."

"You will not be burned. Trust me."

At this point, he either trusted the dragon or he didn't. The choice was obvious. Wrapping his fingers around the konus, he found the seemingly hot metal actually quite comfortable to his touch, the glow slowly receding into its mass as he slipped it onto his wrist.

"*Whoa,*" he gasped.

He had wielded magical devices before. Konuses, slaaps, even the extremely powerful konus belonging to the Geist. But this was different. The energy felt so much stronger. Deeper. Limitless. And more than that, it felt viscerally right, as if it were already a part of him.

"Interesting," Bawb said, watching Charlie as he began glowing faintly.

"Hey, why is he glowing?"

"He isn't. You are."

Ara was right. Charlie realized the glow was actually coming from *him*, a transfer from the konus that was slowly absorbing back into his body.

"Guys, what's going on here?"

"Something astonishing. The Wise One gifted a fraction of her energy to this device, and somehow, amazingly, you seem to have bonded with it. The konus will most likely only respond to you now. I've never seen anything like it."

Charlie laughed nervously.

"Well, it must be the Zomoki blood in me. It does strange things to a man."

The shock on Bawb's face was clear, as if he'd been slapped.

"Blood, you say? But that's impossible. Zomoki blood is deadly for most who merely touch it. Fatal for all but the strongest of Wampeh to ingest it."

"Well, I'm not a Wampeh, and I didn't ingest it. Some got on a wound and mixed in a few years ago."

"A direct blood-to-blood bond?" he asked, his gaze turning to Ara. "Is this true?"

"It is, it seems. Believe me, I was just as surprised as you at first, but it seems this man from another galaxy somehow survived the process."

"Astonishing," the Wampeh said, an odd look flashing across his eyes.

"Don't even think it," Ara warned.

"I would do no such thing."

"Perhaps, but the temptation for a Wampeh with such skills as yourself might be too much to overcome."

Charlie looked at them both, thoroughly confused.

"Uh, guys? What are we talking about, here?"

Ara shifted her gaze to the human. "We're talking about our Wampeh friend, and the rare ability he possesses."

"Absorbing people's magical energy through their blood. Yeah, I figured as much."

"You already know of this?" she asked with surprise.

"I saw him do it once before. A wiza––a *mester*, actually, as he pointed out. He crippled him in combat, then drank his blood."

The Geist merely shrugged as if it were just another day at the office.

"The point, Charlie, is that while my blood would kill him if he did ever prove so foolish as to attempt to drink from me––"

"I wouldn't. And I told you, your scales are too hard, anyway."

"As I was saying, while my blood would undoubtedly kill him stone dead, yours is now a mixture he might be able to metabolize and assimilate. The temptation of possessing even a fraction of a Zomoki's power would be too much to resist for many."

Charlie assessed the assassin casually leaning against the building. He didn't know why, exactly, but the terrifying man was actually growing on him. More than that, despite his bloody occupation, Charlie detected a deep sense of honor coloring the man's aspect.

"Bob, will you try to drink from me?"

The Wampeh looked at him calmly, betraying no emotion. "No, Charlie, I will not."

"And do you give me your word on that. On your honor?"

He could have sworn the assassin flinched, just a tiny bit, but without hesitation, he replied. "You have my word, Charlie. So long as you live, I will not drink from you."

So long as I live, eh? Nice loophole, he mused. *But it's as good as I'm going to get. For now, anyway.*

"All right, then. I take you at your word, Bob." Charlie slung the small bag containing the captured weapons and turned for the trail back. "I'm going to need to ask a favor of you."

"Oh? Already, you place yourself in my debt?"

"If that's what you want to call it, then fine. I owe you one."

Bawb considered the offer a moment, silently staring at the human who so freely offered a debt of honor. "Very well," he said. "What is it you require?"

"I want you to help me free Leila, the groundskeeper's daughter. She's being held in an underground storage room, but there are a whole bunch of guards there."

"Then we shall slay them together," the Geist said, warming to the idea.

"No, we need to try not to kill them. Many of them are actually okay guys. It isn't their fault the visla stuck them on the shitty overnight detail. If we can, we need to take them out, but without drawing blood."

The Wampeh looked disappointed but reluctantly agreed.

"You know, Charlie. This is looking like less and less of a fun deal we've struck."

"Well, I'm sorry, Bob. It is what it is."

"Very well, then. Let's get on with it."

Charlie turned to Ara. "Will you be okay here?"

"Yes. The collar is back to normal, thanks to you, so while I'm confined to the grounds, I am no longer bound to this spot."

"Excellent. We'll be back as soon as we can. Where will you be?"

"Just call out. I'll hear you. We share the bond, after all."

"Right, forgot about that."

"How do you forget such a thing?" Bawb marveled.

"I'm a little preoccupied, okay? I've already near fried my head off jumping this barrier once, and now I get to do it a second time in the same night."

Bawb the Geist seemed quite amused by that. "Charlie, you have a Zomoki-powered konus. I don't think you'll have much of a problem this time."

"Oh, you're right," he said. "I forgot about that."

"Amazing," Bawb said, shaking his head. "Well, there's no sense waiting around here. Shall we?"

Charlie took off at a jog without another word, the Wampeh assassin close on his heels, his soft boots not making so much as a sound as they ran. Charlie saw the wall approaching and wrapped his fingers around his collar, once again chanting the konus magusi spell. He easily vaulted the wall, landing smoothly on the other side.

"Hey, I don't think the barrier is charged," he said, removing his fingers from the collar.

A jolt of pain surged through his neck as his proximity to the low wall triggered the collar. He quickly scurried away, back toward the estate, rubbing his neck where it had zapped him the worst.

"You were saying?" Bawb said.

Charlie didn't have to turn to look to know the man was smiling a pointed-fang grin.

"Come on," he replied. "And remember, try not to kill anyone."

"You take all the fun out of it," he grumbled.

"So I've been told. By you, in fact," Charlie said with a wry grin. "Now, follow me."

The duo crept toward the holding area together, human and Wampeh working as a team for the first time in known history. An unusual alliance, and one that would prove both a boon and a curse for both men.

CHAPTER THIRTY-FOUR

The restraints holding Leila's wrists were not of magical origin. Of that she was certain as she worked the bindings holding her arms behind her back, fastened to the heavy chair. She'd been in the subterranean room for hours, though with no sun or moon to guide her, she couldn't be entirely sure what time it was.

What she did know was it was getting late. Even without external means, her growling stomach told her quite clearly it was well past her normally late dinner time.

"Hey! Can I at least get something to eat in here?" she called to the closed door across the room.

There was no reply.

In fact, the only visitor she'd had since being brought to this place was the visla's daughter, and that had been an entirely unpleasant experience.

It was interesting how Malalia—once a childhood playmate of Leila's—had evolved into a more feminine—and more cruel—version of her father. When she questioned Leila about precisely what she had seen out at the building in the glen, she had been rather liberal in the application of pain-inducing spells to ensure a truthful answer.

"I'll tell you what you want to know," Leila had said between castings as the spells released their grip. "There's no need to torture me."

Malalia had merely smiled as the glow of her konus faded, her eyes shining, cold and icy. "I know you'll tell me," she had said. "And I know there's no *need*, per se. But there are a few spells I've just been *dying* to try out."

She cast again, the spell's magical grip driving jolts of pain and shock through her captive's restrained body.

By the time she was finished having fun with her test subject, Leila was soaked with sweat.

"I told you, I didn't know *what* was out there. I heard something going on by what had previously been unused land and went to see what was happening."

Malalia studied the exhausted woman impassively, as if examining an insect or tiny animal before deciding whether to squash it with her boot.

"I believe you," she finally said. "Though I think my father will want to have a few words with you as well. You sit tight, now, and I'll be back in a little while to continue our discussion. And, Leila, thank you for your cooperation."

The visla's daughter closed the door behind her on the way out, leaving Leila quite alone. That had been the last person she'd seen, and that was hours ago.

Her wrists were red and raw from her struggles against the rope binding them, but her efforts were finally beginning to pay off, as the slightest bit of slack had been worked into the restraints. It wasn't much, but Leila flexed her muscles, strengthened by a lifetime of work outdoors handling wild animals, and pulled. Miraculously, she felt a flow of circulation restored to her hand as she managed to slip her thumb's lowest knuckle past the bindings.

"Child's play," she said with grim amusement as the rest of her aching hand followed her digit to freedom.

She shook her numb limb, the welcome blood flow and rush of sensation returning to her fingers raising her spirits just a bit. When her hand felt under her control once more, she set to work undoing the other wrist's restraint until, finally, she was free.

Leila quickly set to work searching the room for anything she could use as a weapon. The thought of having to fight her way out of a place she had called home her entire life made her physically ill, but she'd deal with that—and hopefully find a logical solution—once she was out of captivity. Surely, they wouldn't persecute one who had been such a loyal servant all those years. Or so she hoped.

The room, much to her chagrin, was nearly devoid of anything even remotely functional as a weapon. Beyond the rope that had tied her to the chair, she was essentially empty-handed.

"Fine. So long as they're not powered, I should be able to handle them," she grumbled as she moved near the door. "If I can tackle a full-grown bundabist, I should be able to take down a security guard. Especially the ones Maktan puts on night shift."

As quietly as she was able—which for a woman who grew up stalking game around the compound was pretty quiet—Leila eased the door to the room open a crack and peered out into the hallway.

No one there.

It appeared as if the guards had thought her well enough under control to leave the inner area unmanned. That meant only a few of them in the upper hallway at the top of the stairs, and possibly just outside the exterior door.

Leila padded down the short hall, confirming her location in the outermost section of the farthest structure before mounting the stairs and heading toward fresh air. She heard talking at the landing above and crouched low as she reached the uppermost step, making as small a visual signature as possible. Yet another trick learned from years tracking animals that served her well tonight.

The two guards stood on the landing in front of the stairs, their backs facing the approaching woman. It seemed they were concerned only with people trying to break in, not break out.

Their slaaps were in the pouches on each of their hips, and so far as she could tell, only one of them wore a konus, which Leila intended to make her own very shortly. Better yet, facing outward as they were, they'd never see her coming.

If she played her cards right, she might even get clear without them knowing it was she who effected the escape. The odds were slim, and a hasty plan was devised to best disable the two men while providing her a good chance of going unseen. Satisfied it just might work, Leila moved.

She struck the man on the left hard below the ear. She hoped it would knock him out cold, but even if it didn't, it would stun him long enough to take down the other man before returning her attentions to the first one.

Fortunately, her attack produced the desired reaction, the man crumpling to the floor. Before he even knew what was happening, the man on the right found himself in a tight choke hold. Less than ten seconds later, he, too, slipped into unconsciousness, the blood flow to his brain temporarily restricted.

Leila eased him to the ground and quickly trussed him up with his friend, her years of animal work again coming in handy as she repurposed the length of rope that had previously held her prisoner. She then slid the konus off the man's wrist where it lay just beneath the rope. As an afterthought, she took their slaaps as well. She'd never used one before, but figured it would be better to have one and not need it than need one and not have it as she made a run for it.

Unlike other sections of the building, this one only had one way in or out, the other wings being locked off. All she had to do was make it down the corridor, cross through an antechamber, then she'd have a clear shot to the outside.

Leila took off at a jog as she slid the konus onto her wrist. She was glad she had when she rounded the corner to find Malalia sitting on a low couch across the room. The powerful woman seemed as startled to see her as Leila was at her appearance, but quickly recovered her cool demeanor, rising to her feet, konus already aglow.

"So, it seems you broke free. I suppose it figures. Animals escape, after all, and you do rather smell like them."

Leila didn't wait. She knew Malalia would cast any moment, and it would be over. So she did what she had to. She charged at her.

The visla's daughter quickly cast a basic attack spell, but Leila got lucky. Her limited knowledge of defensive spells had equipped her with a few selections from her daily work with occasionally dangerous animals.

Fortunately, one was a general protection from magical assaults spell, typically used when rounding up packs of a small creature that resembled a larger, more canine version of a skunk. Its magical stink spray was horrid and was strong enough to make anyone's eyes water. The protection against that managed to deflect enough of Malalia's spell to let Leila advance farther.

A second spell, however, knocked her feet out from under her, sending her sliding back across the hallway. Malalia was ready for her, a wicked look in her eyes.

"Nice try," she said mockingly. "Now, I think it's time to teach you a *real* lesson."

Something triggered the woman's self-preservation reflexes, and she spun, casting a brutal energy-sucking spell as she did. Bawb raised his konus, casting a quick defense as he wrapped his arms around her.

Malalia shrieked, but he had a firm grip.

"Unhand me!" she yelled, then did the most unexpected thing. Immobilized by his strength, she turned and *bit* the Wampeh. Not something he was expecting at all, and while his grip didn't lessen, his konus faltered just a moment. It was all she needed.

Malalia, Wampeh blood fresh on her lips, quickly cast a vicious spell. She threw herself across the room as it broke his grip with magical force, but Bawb took far more of the impact, the spell sending him flying backward at speed and right through the wall. A wicked, bloody smile blossomed on her lips, and at that moment, Charlie realized she wasn't just bad. She was *Bad.*

Charlie jumped aside as his new ally flew past, hoping he was as tough as he seemed, then he raised his own konus, bringing it to bear on Malalia.

"Charlie," she said sweetly. "Why are you pointing that at me? I thought we were friends?"

"Let her go, Malalia. There's no need to fight."

The false smile slid from her face in a flash. "Oh, please. I've seen you fight, you know. While you may be good with a blade, your magic is no match for mine."

"It doesn't have to be," he shot back. Then, before she could utter a spell, he silently cast the strongest *dipangu* spell he could, directing the full brunt of the stench spell right at her face.

Malalia gagged at the horrid odor, her casting failing, the spell's words choked off as she held back her gag reflex. It was an unconventional attack, but in combat, conventional loses.

Before she could recover, he cast the *yapzi* spell, the sensation of swarming flies around her head making the young woman swat all around her, even though she knew it was just magic.

"Very funny," she finally managed, then cast a powerful *eeflanguley* spell, trying to knock him over with its ramming force.

191

Charlie cast a deflection at the last instant but still found himself slammed back into the wall.

Malalia raised her hand, konus fiercely aglow. She was about to cast something big, he realized. Without thinking about what he was doing, Charlie uttered the first spell that came to mind. *"Eikood pord!"*

A shriek escaped the woman's lips, right before they were sealed by the mountain of poop that materialized on top of her. She scrambled from the pile in a rage.

Bawb crawled through the rubble of the wall he'd been blasted through, his decorative armlets suddenly glowing with embedded runic scrollwork.

Those whole things are konuses, Charlie realized, just as the Wampeh cast a fierce stunning spell, driving Malalia, shrieking, to the ground, where she finally blacked out from the force of it.

The assassin known as the Geist strode to the fallen woman, fangs bared.

"No!" Charlie shouted.

"But she has *power*, Charlie. She is dangerous."

"Maybe, but she's just a kid trying to impress her dad. Don't drain her, Bob."

The Wampeh growled, but did as his new ally asked. He did, however, strip the fallen woman of her konus as he bound her wrists and cast a silence spell. It would fade shortly, but she wouldn't be casting, at least not for a while.

"Such power," he said as his fingers brushed her skin while he stripped her of her weapons and bound and gagged her. "Even without a konus."

"Makes sense. So does her father," Charlie replied. "Now, come on. We have to go."

Leila scrambled to her feet and darted past the downed woman, crinkling her nose as she passed the feces-covered woman.

"Oh, shit."

"Bundabist shit, to be precise," Charlie chuckled. "I'd shifted it earlier but hadn't gotten around to dropping it in the composting pile."

"How convenient."

"Not how the spell was intended to work, but I'll take it," he replied.

"And those other spells?"

"Diversions, really."

"You have got to teach me those," Leila said. From the tone in her voice, compliance would not be optional.

"Okay, but now we have to run."

Bawb handed Leila the fallen woman's konus. "Here, take this. It is still a bit smelly, but it is far more powerful than the one you are currently wearing."

"Uh, thank you," she replied, taking the offered device.

"Oh, this is my new friend," Charlie said. "He's a blood-sucking space vampire assassin. You can call him Bob."

Leila hesitated, the deadly man's vibe putting her on edge. But he had helped save her, and if he was a friend of Charlie's...

"Many thanks for your assistance, Bawb."

"I was assisting Charlie," he replied. "In any case, we must go. Now. Others will arrive soon, and we'd best not be here when they do."

CHAPTER THIRTY-FIVE

"My father will know what to do," Leila said for the umpteenth time.

Charlie and Bawb just grunted what could be construed as an agreement––or mere desire for her to stop saying that––and continued across the grounds, heading for the kitchens.

When they had exited the building Leila had been held in, she was astonished to find a half dozen guards, each of them unconscious and bound.

"We need to put them where they will not be observed by others," Bawb said, hoisting one of the men over his shoulder.

Charlie tried that trick, but found he lacked the Wampeh's inhuman strength, which made sense as the pale man actually *was* inhuman. Leila opted for the more logical choice, grabbing the nearest man by the ankles and dragging him.

"We really need a cart," Charlie grumbled. "I swear, one of these days, I'm going to reinvent the wheel and blow all of your minds."

The trio made quick work of the task, stashing the slumbering assortment of alien staff inside the doors, then headed off at a quick run. All three of them possessed excellent conditioning, and had someone actually seen them and attempted to pursue, they'd have been hard pressed to keep up.

Charlie held up his hand, signaling a silent halt when they neared the kitchen staff's quarters.

"Okay, I'm going to get Tuktuk. You guys keep your eyes peeled and yell if anyone is coming."

"If we yell, *more* of them will come. This is a foolish plan," Bawb said.

"It's a figure of speech. *Tell me* if someone is coming, okay?"

"It shall be done."

"Good. I'll try to be fast."

Charlie darted for the entryway, staying out of the light, despite the seeming absence of any guards. After the shimmer trick Bawb had shown him, he wasn't so sure anymore, despite the Wampeh's assurances they were alone.

He quietly eased the door open and slipped into the building, ears searching for any sound of trouble. With the coast clear, he then tip-toed down the hall until he reached his friend's room.

"Tuktuk? Hey, Tuktuk," he whispered, softly knocking on his door.

No answer.

Charlie eased the door open and peered inside the room. "Tuk, you in here?"

The blue man was nowhere to be seen.

Shit. I bet I know where he is.

Charlie hustled out of the building, back to his waiting comrades.

"He's not in there."

"No?" Leila said, surprised. "But it's late, and the kitchen is dark. Might the visla have taken him?"

"No, don't worry. I know where he is."

Charlie took off toward the housekeeping quarters, the other two following close behind.

"Charlie, what in the Gods' name are you doing here?" Magda demanded from behind a partially opened door.

"Magda, I need to speak with Tuktuk."

"And what makes you think he is here?"

"Really?"

"It's okay, Magda," the blue chef called out as he trundled to the door wearing nothing more than a thin robe. "What's so urgent that it couldn't wait until morning, Charlie?"

"It's happening, Tuk. We have to go."

His friend's eye stalks darted, flashing a quick look back into the room. "Uh, Charlie, I told you, Magda won't leave. And if she won't, then neither will I."

"But this is your chance for freedom."

"I know, and I really appreciate it. But I've found something better than that right here. I know it's a little crazy, but that's the poet in me. I'm in love, and that's just as worthy of a fight as anything."

Charlie hated to admit it, but the hopeless romantic in his heart had no choice but to agree.

"I'm gonna miss you, man," he said, pulling his friend into a tight hug.

"Hey, I only have a robe on, here!"

"Sorry," Charlie said with a chuckle.

"No worries," his friend replied. "And listen, Magda did what you asked. There's a huge pile of old blankets in your room."

"Give her my thanks. And the best of luck to you two. I wish you nothing but happiness."

With that, Charlie closed the door and left his friend, wondering if he'd ever see his smiling blue face again.

Charlie stepped into the shadows where Leila was squatting, waiting for him.

"Where's Bob?" he asked.

"Here," the Wampeh said, appearing out of thin air.

"It was so creepy how he just disappeared," Leila said. "Like, here one second, then gone."

"It is an acquired skill," the pale assassin noted.

"Add that to the list, then. I want you to teach me that too," she replied.

"Should I be successful in my task, then we shall see."

Leila cast a curious look at Charlie. "What's he talking about?"

"We can talk about that later," he covered. "Right now, we need to hurry."

He took off at a run for his room, arriving just a few minutes later, unseen by the lone wandering perimeter guard they'd easily avoided.

"Take all of these," he ordered, pointing to the neatly tied bundles of old blankets.

"What are these for?" Leila asked.

"We'll need them. Trust me."

"I trust you, Charlie, but—"

He was already out the door, racing to the wine cellar beneath the kitchen. By the time the others had joined him, he had already uncovered his stash of Earth tech and was rapidly sorting through the pile, looking for anything he might be able to salvage.

"What is all of this?" Bawb asked as he picked up a broken oscillator.

"Tech from my world."

"It feels *wrong*."

"That's just because you're not used to science and technology," he replied. "Here, look at this."

He activated the medical scanner and waved it over the Wampeh's chest, then showed him a slightly blurred image of his organs.

"It's not calibrated for Wampeh physiology, but you get the

idea. It lets me see what's going on inside without breaking the skin."

"This sorcery is abhorrent," the Wampeh said with disgust. "It *feels* wrong."

"You're just not used to it, is all." Now quiet, I have to concentrate a minute."

Charlie dug through the pile and managed to find a pair of communicators. They were totally drained, of course, but he had hopes of maybe restoring their charge somehow. Over against the wall was a crate he recognized. The one containing the items sold along with him when he had first become enslaved.

"Oh, please still be in there," he murmured as he popped the lid.

A happy smile spread across his face. A few choice items were there, intact and unweathered, safely in storage since day one. Most importantly, the carbine and pistol, along with their small cache of ammunition, were tucked in with the rest of it. A deadly oversight by people who had no idea what they had in their possession.

"My friends, we are in luck," he said, loading the pistol and strapping its holster to his hip.

"What manner of *tech-magic* is that, then?" Bawb asked.

"Oh, this isn't science tech," Charlie replied with a grin. "It's a weapon."

"I sense no power." The device seemed to intrigue the assassin.

"I'll show you how it works later, okay? But now, we have to get out of here. If the visla returns, he'll activate our collars and we'll never be able to flee."

Leila took a step back.

"Wait. What do you mean, 'get out of here?'"

"We're leaving this place," Charlie replied. "It's no longer safe here."

"But this is my home."

"You fought with the visla's daughter. She is currently trussed up and covered in bundabist feces. Do you really think he will let that pass?" Bawb asked. "I know men of his nature. To merely be sold would be an optimistic outcome."

The very notion of being sold brought a surge of emotion flooding back into her mind, the memory of her own mother being ripped from them by armed guards when she was but a child flashing in front of her eyes as if it were yesterday.

"My father will know what to do," she said, yet again, but this time her voice quivered slightly.

"Perhaps we should bring her to her father," Bawb suggested, studying her reaction. "He has seen much. I believe his parental insight may aid our friend, here."

Charlie couldn't help but agree.

They gathered up all of the supplies they could and secured them in a pair of empty crates, the Wampeh using a minor spell to lessen their weight, though not make them levitate entirely.

"So, that decorative armlet is actually concealing konus," Charlie said, noting the faint glow from within the assassin's sleeve.

Bawb smiled a pointed grin. "A misdirection, Charlie. What seems a simple piece of decorative adornment is in fact something far more. Weapons are often seized when entering protected buildings, you see. But this? It passes all but the most detailed inspections."

"Oh, I just thought it was another way to wear your konus."

"It is, but few, if any, can see that. It's impressive you noted its presence. Impressive, and most unusual."

"When will you stop saying that?"

"When you cease to surprise me."

CHAPTER THIRTY-SIX

"But Father, I can't just leave!"

Hertzall may have been seen as an oddity among the visla's staff, but his many decades of quiet service had afforded him the opportunity to observe a great deal of things, some not entirely pleasant. To his knowing eyes, the writing was plain to see.

"Believe me, dearest, I have no desire to see you leave either, but it is the logical thing to do."

Leila was pacing the room. She'd been pacing non-stop ever since they arrived at the groundskeeper's little cottage.

"My friends? My animals?"

"Your friends will understand. And the animals? I'm sure they will be well taken care of. The visla is not one to take his rage out on his trophies."

"But what about you? I can't leave you here." She turned to Charlie. "Take him with us."

"Daughter, I am an old man. Well, relatively old, anyway. But what I'm trying to say is, this is where I belong. You are young and have your entire life ahead of you, and there is still so much you can accomplish. Me? I'm set in my ways, and I'm left to myself in this place, which is how I prefer it to be."

"But I can make it right. I can apologize. Whatever it takes to earn the visla's forgiveness and stay here with you."

Hertzall smiled sadly at his daughter. "You fought Malalia, my dearest. And not like your childhood spats he always overlooked. You're a grown woman now, and from what you saw, the visla is on a war footing and will do anything he has to in order to protect his interests. You're a slave, Leila. Do you think you are not expendable to a man like him?"

"Your father is a wise man," the Geist said. "While you may be willing to risk the visla's mercy, I can tell you from personal experience, he will show none."

"But he's always been a good man."

"To the public eye, perhaps. To the hundreds of systems he has ravished with the other members of the Council of Twenty, he has been an oppressor and tyrant. Here, you see him in his home environment, relaxed and content. Out there? He kills without mercy and leads with an iron fist."

Hertzall walked to the stone chimney of his fireplace and leaned on the mantle, staring at nothing for a time. He then pulled on a seemingly fixed rock, working it free from its home with a series of tugs.

From within the small space behind it, he withdrew an emerald pendant the size of a large almond. The stone was a deep green, and the way it picked up the light as it slowly spun on the end of its chain made it glimmer with an almost enchanted glow as he grew close to his daughter.

As it turned out, that was precisely the case.

"Is that a Magus Stone?" the deadly Wampeh asked as he watched the light sparkle from its facets.

"It was your mother's," Hertzall said. "A dowry she had on her person when she was captured and sold into slavery. She managed to hide it in—well, let's just say she hid it well. The one possession she managed to keep with her as she traded hands until finally arriving here as one of the visla's new acquisitions."

"I've never seen that before," Leila said. "And what is a Magus Stone?"

Her father went silent, lost in memory a moment.

"A Magus Stone is something of a magic power sink. They are exceptionally rare, and only found in the Horahn system on Yudan, the home world of the Alatsavs," Bawb said, eyeing the stone.

"Hertzall, didn't you say Leila's mother was an Alatsav?" Charlie asked.

"What? Oh, her mother. Yes, the most beautiful woman I'd ever seen," he replied. "Such a lovely shade of green, and those eyes..."

The Geist was intrigued by the confirmation. "Properly used, a Magus Stone of high clarity can be slowly fed magical charge indefinitely until it holds enormous power."

"How is that even possible?" Charlie wondered.

"Power-wielding families have been rumored to spend multitudes of lifetimes depositing magical energy into a stone, passing it down from generation to generation, adding to it over the years. It is believed one such stone may have been the key to the eventual destruction of Visla Balamar, destroying not only the man, but his entire domain."

"I've seen the place," Charlie noted, "and I wondered how they had managed such destruction."

"Vislas have coveted the stones ever since the discovery of their existence, going so far as to make the Alatsav people something of a hunted race."

Hertzall walked to his daughter and slipped the chain over her head, the stone coming to rest below her shining, golden collar. "*Alamansa doran nictori Leila.*"

The stone glowed slightly a moment, then fell dark again.

"What did you just do?" she asked, alarmed.

"I had held onto that all these years, hoping one day your mother would return and I could put it around her neck once more. But I'm no fool, and now it passes down her family line to you, Leila. It is now bound to you, and you alone."

She ran her fingers over the emerald. It was slightly warm to the touch, but other than that showed no signs of magical properties.

"Another trait of the Magus Stones is they typically show no outward sign of the power within," Bawb said, noting her expression. "One might just be a rock, while another could be a world-ender. This is why the black market is full of fakes. No one can argue they knew better, because it is impossible for any but the stone's owner to truly gauge the power within."

"But I don't sense anything."

Her father tenderly stroked her cheek with the back of his hand, "You are only *half* Alatsav, Leila. It will take time and effort to become attuned with your stone."

"*My* stone," she repeated.

"Yes, *your* stone."

Tears welled in the young woman's eyes, matching those of her father. He embraced her, then stepped back, holding her at arm's length, taking in the sight of her one final time. Content, he nodded his head.

"You will be fine, daughter. Now do as your father says and go with these men. Leave this place, and don't look back."

It took every ounce of willpower, but she did as he bade her, turning and walking from her childhood home, ready to see the stars.

"Are you following, or coming with us?" Charlie asked. "I assume you have a ship stashed around here somewhere, being an assassin and all."

"A what?" Leila blurted.

"Bob here's an assassin, sent to kill Visla Maktan. Only the visla skipped town, so now he's going to join us, seeing as

Maktan wants Ara so bad. Pretty much guarantees he'll come looking."

"And when he does, I shall complete my task," the Wampeh said.

"Seriously? He's an assassin?"

"It does not make me a bad person. And I can assure you, I mean you no harm."

"Great, I feel so much better now," Leila said sarcastically. "Where are we going, anyway? I don't see any ships."

"No, you wouldn't. We're leaving this place another way. And I think you're going to like it," Charlie said. "But, Bob, what about you? You haven't answered me yet."

The Wampeh slowed his pace slightly as he contemplated the situation.

"I had a small craft standing by. However, it was discovered and is now under a restraining spell. I was going to simply steal another ship and its crew if need be once the task was completed, but your option intrigues me, and I can always steal another ship at a later time."

"Hang on. How did you fly here? From what I've seen, all ships are run by Drooks, but I don't see you having any partners."

"And I do not. Rather, I possess this," he said, pulling a slender metal rod from a mount on his armlet.

Charlie had thought it was an integral part of the armlet's design. Once again, he was proven wrong about something in this strange galaxy.

"So, you have a metal bar. Awesome."

"A metal bar, it seems, but inside is a Drookonus. In layman's terms, it is a very primitive version of a Magus Stone capable of storing a significant amount of Drook power. Enough to power most smaller craft for weeks at a time. It was a costly item to come by, but has proven its value on many occasions."

"So why aren't you stealing a ship?" Leila asked. "And what about this other option intrigues you?"

The Wampeh smiled as they approached the darkened clearing. From the shadows, the waiting, enormous, deep red creature rose to her full height. The movement caught Leila's attention and her eyes went wide as she realized what she was looking at.

Charlie grinned. "You're going to love this."

CHAPTER THIRTY-SEVEN

"She speaks?" Leila was flabbergasted.

"Yes, she speaks. And you really should stop referring to her in the third person," Ara said with an amused sparkle in her golden eyes.

"I--sorry. It's just, I--"

"Yes, I imagine it can be a little bit overwhelming. Are you going to be all right? Charlie, perhaps a beverage for our friend," the dragon suggested.

"No, I'll be fine. It's just unexpected is all." Leila blushed furiously. "Oh, God, I hope I didn't say anything offensive around you."

"Not that I noted," the Zomoki replied with a toothy grin.

Charlie showed the blankets they had lugged with them. "Hey, Ara. Do you think these will be good enough?"

She glanced at the assortment. "Yes, I think for the three of you this should suffice. I will try my best to keep it as comfortable as possible, but it will still be cold."

Leila cocked her head like a confused puppy.

"What will be cold?" she asked.

"That's the surprise," Charlie said. "We're not flying out of here on a stolen ship. We're flying out of here on a Zomoki."

If it weren't for the faint green already present in Leila's skin, she might have looked physically ill. As it was, the plan was certainly not what she'd expected.

"We're going to fly on a Zomoki. *This* Zomoki. And she's going to fly us in *space*? Blankets won't help us, Charlie. I mean, I've never made an interplanetary flight, but even I know there's no air in space. We'll suffocate before we freeze."

The Geist smiled. "And now we arrive at the next part of this discussion," he said, clearly amused at the girl's compounding revelations.

"Ara possesses magic, Leila," Charlie informed her. "Like, a *lot* of magic."

"But I thought that was just silly legend-type stuff. I mean, sure, there's been a little bit of reporting in the animalist community on Zomoki with minor power in them, but nothing of any significance. Only crazies believe that."

Charlie raised his hand. "Crazy guy, here."

"Me as well," Bawb said, raising his hand aloft, throwing Charlie a conspiratorial wink.

"Dude, don't wink at me. It's kinda creepy."

"Apologies. I found it amusing."

"It is, but I've seen you drink people's blood before, so cutesy gestures feel a bit wrong, if you know what I mean."

"I suppose," the pale assassin replied, lowering his hand.

"Excuse me. Let me just clarify for our poor friend before your banter, witty as it may be, only confuses her further," Ara interjected. "You see," she said, lowering her head to Leila's eye level, "I am capable of more than mere flight. I can jump us from planet to planet. Even system to system, given enough preparation time and adequate recovery. But first, I must gain adequate altitude."

Leila eyed the supplies they had gathered with fresh eyes.

"You're saying we wrap ourselves with blankets and hang on for dear life while you magic us to another planet? Is that it?" she said.

"More or less. I'll need Charlie to reduce the efficacy of the visla's restraint collar in order to breach the enclosure fields surrounding his lands."

"You can do that?" Leila asked the human.

"Yes, he can," Ara replied. "But once we are clear of those, the collar should pose no problem, unless, of course, Maktan gets within line of sight of us once more, at which point he could activate it again."

"So keeping him far away is key."

"Ideally, yes. Though our Wampeh friend needs him close to complete his task. But we will address this issue and devise a proper strategy once we are clear of the visla's estate."

"But he can track our collars. Eventually, he'll find us."

"Which is the later part of the plan," Bawb said with a pointy-fanged smile.

Leila stepped back, arms crossed. "I hate to be the bearer of bad news, but this is not a plan. This is running with no goal in mind, and no idea where we're even going."

"Well, that's not exactly true," Charlie chimed in. "We'll have to make a few stops along the way, but ultimately, we will be traveling to the Balamar Wastelands."

The Geist's eyebrows raised in surprised interest, but he remained silent.

Leila did some quick mental calculations. "I know of it. My father told me the stories of what happened there. But that system is incredibly far away."

"Yes, it is. Hence our requiring multiple jumps to get there. It will take some time, but it can be done," Ara said.

"And once we get there, I'll retrieve the plasma cutter from my ship. If it's still functional, I think it may be able to slice through the visla's collars regardless of whatever spells he has on it."

"How is that even possible?" she asked. "No magic, save the caster's release spell, should be able to open a collar."

"But we've seen technology from my galaxy doesn't always seem to be affected by the magical rules of this one. If my guess is right, it should cut the metal without any problem. What the spell will do at that point, however, is anyone's guess."

The Geist removed several lengths of rope from their gear. "Wise One, if I may, it would be best for your passengers if we looped a rope around you so as to provide a more secure means of holding on as we soar. With your permission, of course."

Ara nodded and lowered herself to make the task easier for the nimble assassin. In just a few minutes a suitable rig had been carefully arranged, the knots lying flat, ornamental in their arrangement, like an unexpected bit of dragon shibari.

"Shall we?" the Wampeh asked. "I hate to state the obvious, but the longer we delay, the greater our chance of capture."

Leila tucked her Magus Stone into her tunic and added a scavenged coat from the pile over her attire, then began hauling blankets atop the Zomoki.

"Well? What are you two waiting for?" she asked.

It seemed that once she accepted the situation and made peace with the reality of having to leave her home and family, that old practical efficiency she showed in all aspects of her life kicked back in, and with force.

"Come on, chop-chop. The sooner we go, the better."

"Yes, ma'am," the human replied with a snappy salute.

Charlie and Bawb shared an amused look and began hauling their gear to the rope harness, tying off the small crates to Ara's belly and layering the blankets atop the Zomoki's broad back.

In less than five minutes they were seated and tied in, bodies pressed close and blankets wrapping them snugly. Charlie sat at the front of the trio, with Leila in the middle and Bawb at the rear. The seating arrangement had very practical reasoning behind it.

Charlie wrapped a hand around Ara's collar, gripping it tightly. His other hand wrapped around his own collar.

"I'm sorry, Leila, but I only have two hands, and I need to focus on Ara and my collars. If the restraining spell takes me out before we're clear, it's all for nothing. But you should grab onto my wrist and maybe grab your own collar. If we're lucky, some of the spell will reduce the power of your collar as well. But I have to warn you, it'll probably hurt like hell."

"Pain I can handle," she replied, the slight hitch in her voice betraying her confident act.

"I will not let you fall," Bawb said from behind.

"Thanks, Bawb."

The Wampeh nodded once.

"Okay, then. Let's do this. How high do you think until we hit the boundary of the visla's containment spell?"

"I can't say for sure, Charlie," Ara replied. "He's a particularly cautious man, so I wouldn't be surprised if he has more than one, arranged in layers. Concentrate on your casting and nothing else. Don't stop until I tell you."

"I won't."

Ara flapped her wings once. "Everyone secure? Then let us waste no further time. Charlie, please begin."

The unlikely human wizard loosed the spell in his mind, forming a looping, rhythmic repetition of it as he pulled power from the Zomoki-charged konus. Her collar began to glow as she rose in the air, but Charlie's spell immediately quashed the reaction, driving the restraining power back into the metal. His own collar, likewise, was entirely cold and unreactive.

Leila's began to glow slightly, her connection with Charlie being an indirect one. It burned slightly, and she found herself shifting uncomfortably in the cold air as they rose higher and higher.

Suddenly, the pain stopped entirely. She leaned forward and it returned. Confused, she leaned back again, and once more it ceased. Carefully, she snaked one hand into the layers of her blankets and coat. The collar was cool to the touch. Then her fingers felt something else. A warm stone around her neck that was just barely in contact with the metal band.

Her mother's Magus Stone. It was negating the visla's spell.

The stone did hold power, after all. And Leila, it seemed, was becoming increasingly connected to it.

"Charlie, you may stop. We are above the outer limits of the visla's reach. Now, hold tight everyone," Ara said. "This may feel a little bit... *odd*."

The world shimmered and everything went sideways, then, in a flash, the dragon and her passengers were gone.

CHAPTER THIRTY-EIGHT

It was rare for the visla to lose control. His entire existence, in fact, was focused on maintaining a carefully calculated appearance to all outsiders. But he was not outside, and those facing his wrath would never speak of it. Not because of loyalty or fear, but because they couldn't.

Visla Maktan stepped over the fallen body of the guards he had so brutally dispatched during their interrogation. To fail so completely at their duties, letting not only the Zomoki escape, but also the one man who might be able to control her, had pushed him over the edge.

Normally, torture was left to his underlings to handle. At least in all but the most exceptional cases. In this instance, however, he had personally squeezed every last ounce of truth from his disgraced men. Then he dispatched them in a multitude of violent ways.

If not for the soundproofing spell he had cast on the walls and door to the chamber, those waiting outside for their turn to be questioned would have undoubtedly fled, consequences be damned.

He had been back in his estate barely ten minutes when

word reached him. Dinuk was able to have the life of the messenger spared, and he himself was safe, having been off-world with his master. The others, however, were all fair game, and many would not see morning.

"By hours, you say?"

"Yes, Visla," Dinuk replied, his head hung low. "The men who found Denna Maktan said it could not have been more than four or five hours ago."

"They disarmed her and left her trussed up like an animal?"

"Yes, Visla."

"And they are nowhere on the grounds? You are certain of this?"

"Yes, Visla."

"So, they must be outside the perimeter, somehow. I've cast the stunning spell, but there has been no connection. Send all of my vessels out across these lands. Have them travel in every direction at top speed. Find them, but do not engage. Once we have them located, I shall handle them myself."

"I want a piece of them," Malalia said, staggering into the room.

She was a mess, her clothes filthy from Charlie's attack, and her senses still jumbled from the powerful blast from the Geist. Even so, the fierce determination in her eyes would have scared any man foolish enough to get in her way. As it was, the only men actually in her way lay dead and scattered on the ground in front of her.

Malalia ignored the corpses, stepping over them as if they were no more than an inconvenient pile of debris. "They humiliated me, Father. In my own home. I demand justice."

The visla looked at his daughter with critical eyes.

"You are filthy, Malalia."

"Yes," she grumbled. "It was the human. Little bastard hit me with one of his stupid waste-removal spells. What sort of man does that?"

Maktan couldn't help but appreciate the novel approach. "I can see why he gained a reputation for being a particularly resourceful gladiator. Using spells not meant for combat, and effectively, I must add. Most original."

"Father!"

His eyes hardened. "Do not worry, my dearest. You will exact your revenge once I have the beast back in my possession. But Charlie must live, at least for a short while. The other you may do with as you please."

"There were two others, actually. Leila was not alone," she said.

"Oh? Now this interests me greatly. Who else of my staff would dare raise their hands against my family?"

"He wasn't from here, Father. He was a Wampeh."

The visla blanched slightly, but hid it well. For anyone to have snuck through so many layers of spells meant an assassin, almost certainly. For it to be a Wampeh, however, well, someone with great power wanted him dead.

"I see," he said after a moment's thought, stepping close to his daughter. "What more can you tell me about this––is that blood on your mouth? They dared to strike you?"

"No, Father. I was only stunned and bound. But do not worry, the blood is not my own. When the bastard grabbed me, I bit him," she said with a feral sneer.

Maktan slapped her fiercely then took a disgusted step back.

"If you weren't my daughter––" Fury, but also fear burned in his eyes. "You would dare sully your bloodline with this, this, *contamination*?"

"What? No, Father, it was nothing like––" she blurted with tears of shock in her eyes.

"Get out of my sight! Bathe. Burn those clothes. You are the daughter of Visla Yoral Maktan. Do not forget it. Now go. Make yourself presentable. Then I will have you see the healer at once."

He turned and stormed from the room, muttering as he walked.

"Stupid child. And *Wampeh* blood of all things. She must know the risks," he said, then disappeared out the door, the soundproofing spell cutting off his angry rant.

Malalia watched him go silently. What could she say that wouldn't just make his rage even worse? She looked at the dead men littering the floor and found herself wishing he had left at least a few of them for her to take out her aggressions on.

Dinuk had stood perfectly still for the whole thing, not wanting to anger either his master or his master's child. Now he was stuck, hoping Malalia would forget about him and leave.

No such luck.

She flashed him a look, daring him to say anything. Dinuk, for his part, stared straight ahead, lips firmly sealed.

"So, Dinuk," she said, malice dripping from her tongue, "Father wishes to be informed the instant they are found."

"Yes, Denna Maktan," he said, eyes straight ahead.

"And you wouldn't dare go against my father's wishes."

"No, Denna, I would not."

She studied him a long moment in silence. If he was afraid, he did a fine job of hiding it.

"Very well, then. You do as my father asks. But I, too, am requiring something of you."

"Anything, Denna."

"When you find them, you will tell my father, as ordered. But you will tell me their location as well. That way you will be obeying my father's commands, while also obeying mine. This does not contradict his orders, and therefore, you will do as I require. Is that understood?"

"Yes, Denna," he said, not liking the predicament she'd put him in one bit. Her logic was sound, but that wouldn't lessen the ire of his master if he found out.

"Good. Now, let's keep this to ourselves, shall we?" she said, pressing a filthy finger to his lips, then walking from the room.

Only when she was gone did he allow himself to breathe. And that breath suddenly smelled faintly of bundabist poop.

"One of those days," he grumbled, then set off to launch a search the likes of which the planet had never seen.

But Charlie and the Zomoki were much farther away than that, and no matter how hard they looked, Maktan's men would not find a trace of them on that world.

CHAPTER THIRTY-NINE

Ara's sizable mass lay hidden beneath a grove of large, burgundy-leaved trees beside a small, murky pond, populated by large bottom-dwelling fish the size of a small pony. The thick canopy provided her excellent cover from prying eyes, while the convenient water and food source allowed her to dine at her leisure without expending energy needlessly as she recovered from her first jump in a long time.

The planet they had arrived on only moments after departing Visla Maktan's realm was a small, humid world in a relatively nearby system. It was several light years away, but for the Zomoki, that posed little problem. When they arrived in a flash of magical energy, the sudden shift from the frigid air of the upper reaches of the atmosphere to the near-oppressive heat of their destination was enough to take your breath away.

The important thing was, they were free.

It was a relatively sparsely populated planet, and one with plentiful resources, which was partially why Ara had selected it from the many worlds she had visited over her lifetime. This one would provide a safe haven while she recovered, and it was a place she could likely remain unnoticed.

"Were you successful?" she asked Bawb upon his return to the grove.

He was carrying a large sack over his shoulder, and had clothed himself in a common worker's attire, brought along when they fled Visla Maktan's estate.

"Yes. Quite, in fact," he said, dumping the contents of the bag to the deep azure grass.

"Is that bread?" Charlie asked, snatching up a fresh-baked loaf and inhaling deeply.

"The baker was very amenable to a simple barter," Bawb said, offering a slice of dried meat to go with it. "He also threw in some of his home-cured garoki meat."

"What's a garoki?"

"A large, herbivorous animal," Leila answered. "Not uncommon, but still relatively unusual to use for food stock."

"On this world they are wild game," Bawb noted. "The proprietor showed me the mounted head of the beast. It was a particularly sizable one, even by garoki standards."

"And these greens? Do we cook them, or eat them raw?" Charlie asked of the strange produce piled beside the now-empty sack.

"These may be eaten either way, though I think the tubers are much more palatable when roasted."

"Noted. I'll make us a fire and start putting together a meal, then."

"Anything I can do to help?" Leila asked.

"Yeah, actually. Could you gather up some dry wood?"

"I could, yes. But why?"

"Uh, for the fire. Or you could try your hand at making a wand. Might be an interesting experiment."

Leila and Bawb shared an amused look.

"Charlie, we don't need to burn wood for a fire. It is wasteful, dangerous, and smelly. Every child knows the basic campfire spell from a young age," she said with a smile in her eyes.

"Well, I'm not every child, then. I didn't grow up here, you know."

Leila moved close and selected a small rock, placing it on a clear patch of ground. *"Ogeufne,"* she said.

A small blaze ignited above the rock, spreading heat and warmth but not singeing the grass pressed down around it.

"Fascinating," Charlie said. "And it won't burn anything around it? Then how do we cook with it?"

"It only directs the heat upward," Leila answered. "This way you don't accidentally burn down a forest. It's a really useful spell. *Slovera,*" she said, extinguishing the flame. "Okay, now you try."

"But I don't know it."

"You just learned it, Charlie. Just focus on the rock while saying the words, and a flame should ignite."

"Again, a wand would help."

"What is this *'wand'* you speak of?" Bawb asked.

"A stick. A piece of wood about so long, tapering at the tip. We don't actually have wizards and witches in my world, but the fairy-tales all talk about them using a wand to focus their magic and cast spells."

"A wooden konus? Or slaap? But in the form of a stick?"

"*Wand.* But yeah, basically."

Bawb seemed intrigued by the novel idea. "Wood, charged with power. It has never been done. It simply cannot hold the magic. It would be an interesting stealth weapon, but dry twigs have no capability."

"Well, it's a fairy-tale, okay? And if it weren't, well, maybe magicians just grow them that way or something. It wouldn't be dead then, right? Hell, maybe they could even embed Ootaki hair in a split branch and then bind it so it'd heal with that inside, right?"

"Fascinating," Bawb said, taking the idea seriously. "Imbue a living tree with power. Clever, Charlie."

SCOTT BARON

"Look, I'm just making this shit up as I go. Pure speculation on my part. I don't know if any of that stuff would even work."

"Enough chatter, you two. Try the spell," Leila said.

He grumblingly obliged, focusing his gaze on the stone. It seemed so innocent and simple a thing to do, but for a man who had rather excelled at learning combative magic, starting a fire felt like a whole different type of magic, and one he was unfamiliar with.

"Um, *ogeufne,*" he said, feeling the konus slightly warm as he cast the spell.

A large flame shot up, then quickly receded to a reasonable size.

"Wow, that was really good," Leila said. "Just try to keep it lower next time. We wouldn't want to catch a tree on fire, after all."

"Obviously," he snarked. "Now hand me that pot and I'll whip us up some grub."

"Grub?"

"Food. Sorry, I guess that doesn't translate quite right. Ah, the joys of human slang and alien translation spells." He laughed. "Spells. If you'd told me I'd ever believe in magic, I'd have laughed in your face. And now, here I am, actually casting spells. Crazy."

"I could say the same for your tech-magic," Bawb said. "A magic that does not abide by the rules of our worlds? It was unheard of. Unimaginable. And now?"

"I guess it's been a bit of a shock for all parties," Charlie agreed. *"And I've even befriended a dragon,"* he said, silently.

Ara flicked her golden gaze his way with an amused look in her eye. *"Zomoki, if you please. And though the answer is yes, I would technically consider us something more than friends at this point. We are bonded, Charlie. A connection unbreakable until death."*

"So morbid, Ara."

"Just being factual."

"And how are you feeling?" he said aloud, for the benefit of the others. "That was a pretty big jump you made."

"For me, not terribly big, actually. But it has been quite a long time since I last jumped. Normally I simply cast a protection spell and travel through space at a leisurely pace for short trips. It's quite relaxing. But to answer your query, I am tired, of course, but far less than I anticipated."

"This is good news. How long until you think you'll be ready to jump again?" the Geist asked.

"I should be refreshed by tomorrow, I would think. Being able to move freely, unfettered by the visla's magic, has been quite restorative."

"Excellent," the Wampeh replied, rising back to his feet. "I shall acquire us additional supplies for the next jump."

"But I'm cooking," Charlie griped.

"Yes, but I can obtain sustenance elsewhere while carrying out this chore."

Charlie looked him in the eye. "You're not going to drain anyone's blood, are you?"

The vampiric assassin smiled. "No, Charlie. It would be bad form to do so while we are in a precarious position. And besides, that is only something I do with powered individuals. Otherwise I prefer my nourishment in the form of food, like any other man."

Charlie dug in the nearest crate, pulling a pair of portable comms units from the pile.

"Okay, but hang on a minute, I want to give you one of these––if I can get it working."

The pale man watched him curiously, unsure about the strange tech-magic in his hands.

"What is that, Charlie?"

"It's a comms unit. It's kind of like a skree."

"But it operates without magic?"

"It used to. The batteries are dead, but I think I've found a

SCOTT BARON

way to charge it magically. At least enough to work for a little while."

Charlie dredged up the silent spell from his mind and focused.

"*Yaka illum*," he cast.

Nothing happened.

"Ara, how did you power my konus?"

"It is a Zomoki skill. I opened my power like a faucet until a trickle flowed. Even among my kind, it is a difficult ability to acquire."

"Huh. But I wonder, maybe..."

He took the dragon's words to heart, clearing his mind of everything but the spell he wished to use and the intent behind its casting.

"*Yaka illum*," he silently repeated over and over, a mental picture of a battery charging from a trickle of power filling his mind.

After a moment, he stopped. "Well, I guess that didn't work," he grumbled.

"Charlie?" Leila said. "Are they supposed to have lights on them like that?"

He looked at the comms units. It had taken a minute, but they had somehow assimilated the power and turned on. The battery cells read a quarter charge.

"Awesome!" he exclaimed.

"That shouldn't be possible," Ara mused.

"Your powering the konus must've made it possible."

"But Charlie," she said, "your konus's power has not been drained in the slightest. I would have noticed."

"Huh," he said, confused. "Well, the important thing is, it worked. Bob, take this with you. It'll let us talk if anything comes up."

The Wampeh took the device.

"What is the command to activate it?"

"No, it doesn't work like that. You push this button here, then hold it to your ear."

"Hold it to my ear? How utterly inelegant," he griped.

"Well, you could try the video setting, but that tends to use the battery faster."

He and the pale assassin spoke over the devices a moment to ensure he was comfortable with their operation, then Bawb took off at a jog, leaving the others to their repast.

"Tell me, Charlie. How exactly did you power the tech-magic devices?" Ara asked.

"I just did like you said. I pictured them charging in my mind. A trickle of power filling them up."

"And did you feel anything? Anything at all?"

"Nope. But it was a small charge, so maybe that makes sense, I suppose."

The Zomoki shifted, resting her head on the soft grass. "Yes, that could be it," she said. But she wondered if it wasn't something more. Something far more.

CHAPTER FORTY

The next world was not nearly as pleasant.

"Are you shitting me?" Charlie griped from the shelter of the ice cave Ara had melted for them with a few well-placed bursts of flame. "Why did you choose this place?"

Ara was quite comfortable, easily able to shift her own temperature with the simplest of castings that were second nature to her.

"It was the best option, given our path, as well as the need to remain unobserved by any who could report to Maktan or any of the other members of the Council of Twenty."

"But do you really think they would find us so quickly?" Leila asked. "We've only been gone less than a week, and there are countless worlds separating us from his realm."

"Be that as it may, the Council of Twenty have a long reach, and many spies spread throughout *all* of the systems. You may trust me on this matter, as I have dispatched more than a few of them in my travels," Bawb noted.

Charlie paced back and forth, rubbing his arms to keep the blood flowing. A small fire had been cast, and Leila and Bawb sat before it, warming themselves as best they could. Charlie, however, was a bundle of nerves.

"How long do we have before Maktan is able to get a fix on us by our collars?" he asked.

"Please stop pacing," Leila requested.

"Sorry. It's just we're sitting here kind of exposed, and we really don't know how much time we have."

"Technically, we've been here half as long as the last system," Ara noted. "And I should be capable of making our next jump in one, two days tops. This was a much longer one than previously, and while that requires a longer refractory period, it also puts more distance between us and our pursuers."

"So they're on our trail already? You're sure about that?"

"Oh, most certainly. The thing is, we are much too far away for them to get an accurate location any closer than a very general vicinity. That could be dozens, if not hundreds, of systems. And they do not possess the ability to jump as far as I do. They can travel quickly, yes, but not like a Zomoki."

"Well, I guess all we can do is sit here and wait, then."

Leila rose and walked to him. "There is one other thing we can do to pass the time," she said with a curious look in her eye.

"Oh?"

"Yes."

"Well, I––"

"And I already asked Bawb, and he said he would be willing to participate."

"Wait a minute. What exactly are you talking about?"

A shower of ice and water sprayed Charlie and Bawb, the *klaatu endatha* spell having been applied a bit too forcefully for their particular environment.

"Okay, I guess she has that one memorized," Charlie said

with a grim laugh as he shook the coating of ice from his hair. "You ready to move on to the next one, Bob?"

The Wampeh, likewise, was brushing the layer of ice from himself. "I think we should fine-tune this one a bit first. Control is crucial, even with defensive spells."

Leila looked quite pleased with herself, and Ara was downright amused.

The two men had been drilling her in the art of rapid-fire defensive casting, first spending the entirety of the prior evening having her memorize a very simple list of spells––while not wearing a konus––then progressing to her first stumbling attempts the following morning after breakfast and a piping-hot cup of coffee.

All were grateful that Charlie had the forethought to snag all of the prepared beans available in the kitchen as they frantically loaded up supplies before fleeing the visla's estate. For him it was the soothing flavor and heat in his belly. For the others, the coffee seemed to have a more tangible effect. Namely, the strength of their magic.

"When do I get to learn some offense?" Leila grumbled.

"The infant must crawl before it learns to walk," Bawb said. "And in the event of your coming up against a powered opponent, these defensive spells, while seemingly basic, will protect you from nearly all attacks, at least for a while, so long as you maintain your focus."

"He's right," Charlie added. "When I was fighting in gladiatorial bouts, I would win because of unconventional tactics, which most often consisted of heavy reliance on defensive spells. It frustrated people to no end that they couldn't seem to land a shot. And when that happens, they get careless."

"And careless means vulnerable," Bawb said. "*This* is why we focus on these particular spells. It is not for any lack of ability. Far from it. You have picked up more in a day than many are able in weeks."

Charlie looked at the section of their ice cave she had pulverized with an overly ambitious defensive spell. "Yeah, that's some powerful casting you just managed." He turned to Ara. "Hey, do you think it would be okay to show her my rhythmic combinations?"

"I'm sorry, your what?" Ara said.

"You know. How I join a few spells together in a sing-song casting. Don't you remember? It's what I accidentally did during our bout."

"So that's what it was," the dragon said. "I had wondered about that. It was an abnormally powerful spell, even with you tapping into my power. Especially as you'd never done so before. But you say you combined them?"

"Yeah, I'll show you. Bob, cast a *kika rahm* at me. A good one."

"Are you certain about this? That can deliver a rather solid blow."

"Yeah, you'll see."

"Very well."

The Wampeh set himself, then cast. "*Kika rahm!*"

But Charlie had already begun the rhythmic incantation joining a *yap zina* leg sweep spell and an *eeflanguley* ramming spell. The effect was impressive, utterly negating the assassin's spell while simultaneously taking him off his feet and tossing him backward several steps.

"Fascinating," Bawb said with a wide grin. "This is an application I have never seen. And, Charlie, I have trained with many, *many* masters."

"Well, it's something I just sort of stumbled upon one day. You see, I sing things to myself to help me remember them. A mnemonic device."

"What spell is 'mnemonic'?"

"It's not a spell, it's a mind trick to help you make quick associations to remember things. Only I was doing it with words

I didn't understand. Still don't, actually. And one day, someone will have to actually explain to me why magic words don't translate."

"No one knows," Bawb said. "It is just the way it is."

"Well, anyway, I guess it's a little like German. You combine words to make one longer one."

"But that does not work. Spells do not function that way."

"Normally, no. But some of them apparently do if you sing them just right."

"The evolution of spells in this galaxy," Ara said. "What were mere sounds became spells. And now you've stumbled upon an unusual aspect of them."

"A magical Easter egg."

"A what?" Bawb asked.

"Hidden stuff. Bonus material," he replied.

The Geist regarded Charlie with a newfound respect. Also with a bit of wariness. Charlie noticed the shift in attitude.

"Don't worry, Bob. I'll show you both all I know." *Or at least almost all,* he added to himself.

"So, what say you we get back to work? Leila has a lot of catching up to do."

The group trained all day, well into the night, and by the time the following morning greeted them with a pale brown sun, Ara, though still a bit weak, was ready to jump once more.

CHAPTER FORTY-ONE

The first week or so of their flight from Visla Maktan and his Council of Twenty allies had gone about as smoothly as anyone could have expected. By the end of the second week, the group had become comfortable with one another as Leila's abbreviated training was picking up speed and they made longer jumps, putting more distance between themselves and their pursuers.

By week three, however, tensions began to grow, the stress of the whole thing finally starting to wear on them all. That was how they came to be noted by one of the Council of Twenty's many spies.

The day had begun like all of the others in recent weeks: waking, eating, spell training for Leila, sparring and combat training for all three of them, then a cautious foray into the trading market of their current planet.

Ara had selected a warmer world. One where her companions could not only source food and rest more comfortably, but where the Geist might also find a meal of a more *special* variety.

"I can't believe you're okay with this," Leila said. "You're talking about eating people as if it were no big thing. Like they were no more than livestock."

The Wampeh shared a glance with Ara, the Zomoki holding her tongue this once.

"They are not livestock to me," Bawb said. "It pains me that you would think I perceive them as such after the time we have spent together."

"Well, it pains me too, Bawb. But the way you and Ara have been talking about finding you a power user to feed on hasn't exactly done much to put my mind at ease about the whole thing."

"You misunderstand, Leila. Ara and I were merely strategizing, determining the best possible course of action to help ensure we are as prepared as possible for the eventual conflict with the Council's forces."

"And eating people helps how, exactly?"

"You know the physiology of my kind. The abilities we possess."

Leila blanched.

"You're not serious, are you? I mean, we've all heard rumors, sure, but those are just stories. Tales told to children to make them behave, lest the Wampeh come to get them. But they aren't true."

Bawb smiled, the tips of his fangs poking out between his lips like tiny, shining points of light. It was a mildly unsettling effect he had spent some time developing.

"It is a rare ability, yes. But I can assure you, it most definitely is real."

Charlie trudged back into their campground located several miles outside of the city, pulling a small cart he had constructed. His trading had gone well, and he returned with a good sampling of local baked goods, as well as a few baskets of produce. They would eat well for a few more days, though they hadn't enough coin to procure meats of any sort.

Soon they would be off once more, growing closer to their ultimate goal. In just a few more jumps, they would finally arrive at the Balamar Wastelands. All they had to do was keep their cool until then.

"What's up?" he asked, noting the tension in the air. "Everything okay?"

"No, everything is not okay," Leila replied. "Bawb is going to eat someone."

"Really?"

"No, I'm not going to eat anyone," Bawb replied.

"Good, because––"

"Just drink some of their blood."

"See?" Leila blurted. "It's not right. And––and what the hell is that thing you're pulling?"

"This? Just a little cart I whipped up. I figured it'd be easier than carrying everything. It's a long walk, you know."

Bawb examined the simple conveyance with interest. "Most intriguing. But why didn't you simply use a portage spell?"

"Because I don't know any, and all of the carts already powered by them belong to other people. Folks aren't too appreciative when you take their stuff, you know."

"You could have paid for a casting. It is commonplace."

"But *this* was free. It saved us some coin, and we need every bit we have."

"Yes, I agree, but this *thing* you rigged, it will draw attention." He looked at the parallel lines it had left in its wake. "And it leads others to us."

"What, the tire tracks? That's just what they do when they roll. Don't worry, traffic will wipe out the trail in no time."

"But no one uses this means of portage, Charlie. And those tracks may yet be visible for some time," Bawb said, kneeling to examine the round discs of wood. "Still, I admit, you have created an interesting device. Perhaps at some future time it may even be of use. But for now, we must avoid drawing attention to ourselves."

I guess I finally did *reinvent the wheel.*

Leila stepped between them, a fire in her eye. "You still haven't addressed the whole drinking-people's-blood issue. He actually wants me to believe he can suck up people's power through their blood."

"Oh, he can," Charlie said, casually, as he took a bite out of what passed for an apple-like fruit on this planet. "I saw him do it once, actually. A few years ago, back before we were friends."

Leila turned an even paler shade of green. "So it's true?"

"I told you as much," Bawb said. "And it is something I only do on rare occasions. Contrary to public belief, blood is not the most appealing of things to drink, and of my kind, I have yet to meet anyone who actually enjoys it."

"But you still do it."

"Obviously. The benefits far outweigh the temporary unpleasantness. To incorporate another's power into my arsenal of skills has saved my life on many occasions."

"So why don't you drain me? Or Charlie? Or Ara, even?"

The Geist smiled. "You are nearly entirely unpowered, Leila. The skills to wield a konus are there, no doubt, but to drink from you would be of no benefit. And besides, I consider you a friend, and it would simply be rude."

"And Charlie? Ara?"

A different sort of smile shifted on the assassin's face. "We have an...*agreement.* And, much as you have grown on me these past weeks, they, too, I now consider friends."

The Wampeh scooped up a handful of dried berries and popped a few in his mouth.

"Now, Charlie, what did you see while you were gathering supplies?"

"Not much, actually. There were a few lesser casters in the

marketplace, but no one who stood out as particularly powerful."

The Wampeh's shoulders sagged slightly. "This is disappointing."

"But," Charlie continued with a grin, "I did hear there is a trader at the far end of the marketplace whose employer comes from a black sun system. And *that* person is rumored to be a very powerful one indeed. So much so that they never even have to show their abilities. Others kowtow to them as the defacto overseer of the region on rumor alone."

"Hmm," the pale man mused. "I have seen this behavior before. Far too often men like this are pretenders. Users of hidden magical stores to give the impression of power."

"Well, that may be the case, but not so here."

"How are you so sure?"

"About the power? I'm not. But the rest of your statement? This is no man putting on airs. Of that I'm sure."

"Again, how?"

"Because he is a *she*."

CHAPTER FORTY-TWO

Bawb had only taken one relatively small container with him when they had hastily departed from Visla Maktan's estate several weeks prior. Today was the day the others finally saw what was inside it.

"You packed *fancy* clothes?" Charlie asked, eyeing the finery the Wampeh was unpacking. "Running for our lives, and that's what was important? Not food, or weapons, but clothes?"

"The clothes make the man, Charlie. And these are quite dear to me," he replied, slipping out of his road-worn attire and into the intricately embroidered ensemble. The top was close-fitting, but not in a showy way. The trousers were likewise tailored, designed to enhance the man's assets, while still allowing the assassin freedom of movement.

Charlie had no doubt there were hidden pockets sewn in for him to hide knives or other weapons, but when his pale friend was fully clothed in his new outfit, he had to admit, the guy cut a dashing figure.

"You have your comms unit?" he asked.

"No. I will carry the skree we procured. Your tech-magic would only raise suspicions."

"He has a point," Leila agreed. "Blending in is important."

Charlie looked the Wampeh over. After several years living in the galaxy so far from home, he was finally developing a familiarity with the way things worked, at least most of the time. And Bawb did, in fact, look like he belonged on the strange world, though not as a commoner, for certain.

"So, shall I assume you are planning on a not-so-stealthy assault on this power user?" Charlie asked.

"You assume correctly, my friend," he replied with a particularly cheerful smile. "I shall present myself as a well-off trader, come to discuss potential business."

Leila stepped over and adjusted the fall of his shirt, smoothing a stray fold. "I have to admit, Bawb, you clean up well."

"Thank you, Leila. Now, let us hope this woman agrees with you."

"Are you sure you're her, uh, *type*?" she asked.

"I am hopeful. However, should she prefer the fairer kind, I may return to ask for your assistance."

"I'm sorry, you what, now?"

"Just kidding," he said with a grin. "If that is the case, I will resort to less pleasant tactics."

Charlie and Ara shared an amused look.

"You heard that, right? That's validation. Bob actually made a funny."

"Yes, I heard it as well," Ara agreed with a toothy smile.

"No one will ever believe you," the Wampeh said. "And if they did, they'd never live to tell the tale," he added with a wry grin as he slipped out into the night.

Ara rose to her feet, surprisingly quiet for a creature that size.

"I'm going to forage for something more substantial than fruits and vegetables. I will return shortly. Keep your skree handy. He should be fine, but nevertheless, it is wise to have an ally standing by just in case."

She then turned and, with a flap of her wings, rose into the night sky and quietly blended into the dark.

The walk had been uneventful, and Bawb soon stood at the entrance to the most powerful woman in the region's palatial home. The grounds were lush, and the shrubbery surrounding the estate seemed innocent enough to the casual passerby. To the Geist, however, the dual purpose was easy to see.

Sharp thorns adorned the branches of the low trees, planted not for decoration, but for defense. The outer shrubs were innocuous, but the layer of green on the innermost layer was anything but.

"Imonus vines," he noted, the distinct smell of the poisonous plant woven through the other greenery wafting to his hyper-sensitive nose.

A slight bending of the light from key positions on the roof and building perimeter gave away the shimmer-cloaked guards monitoring from hiding. They should have spent more on their shimmer spells, he mused, but with his keen eyes and years of experience, he doubted any but the absolute finest shimmers would fool his piercing gaze.

Acting as casually as he could, Bawb adopted the slightly inebriated, loose-limbed walk of a trader on shore leave after a long journey. It was something he had used often, as drunks were universally seen as harmless annoyances rather than deadly threats.

He knocked on the door, then leaned on the signaling panel, acting oblivious to the notification tone it was undoubtedly chiming nonstop inside the building. A minute later footsteps could be heard hurrying to the door, which swung hastily open.

"Yes?" demanded an irritated man, whose ornate cloak did

not entirely cover his dual slaaps and heavy-duty konus. "What do you want? The hour is late."

"Is it? I've been in the black so long, time rather loses meaning, if you know what I mean."

The guard looked the Wampeh up and down. He had a muscular build, but his finery and affect suggested one who was fond of the comforts of power rather than the exercise of it. A trader, then, and one with substantial wealth, it appeared.

"What is your business with the emmik? Have you come to seek trade?"

"You are perceptive, my friend. Binsala is my name, and trading is indeed my game. Now, if you'll please take me to see the man of the house, I'd very much like to see if we might engage in some mutually beneficial business."

The guard softened a bit.

"Very well, Binsala. Please, come in," he said, moving aside and granting the assassin entry. "But I should clarify for you," he said as the door clicked shut. "The man of the house is not a man, but rather, Emmik Yanna Sok."

"Oh?" Bawb replied. "I do not know this emmik. Does she trade?" he asked with an innocent smile.

The truth of the matter was he knew of Yanna Sok—*everyone* knew her story—but the Wampeh had never come across her personally. She was a Tslavar, and a particularly brutal one, by all tales. The tall, green, elfin woman commanded a fleet of vessels spanning dozens of systems, including Captain Tür's slave trade ship, which Charlie had once called home.

Decades of hard work had put her atop the bloody heap vying for control of the system, and it was with a notable proclivity for violence that she maintained control.

The heavily armed guard laughed warmly. "Does she trade? Oh yes, friend, she most certainly trades. Come, I shall make introductions."

CHAPTER FORTY-THREE

For such a brutal woman, Bawb had to admit, the emmik had exquisite taste. Carvings of the great masters from a dozen systems adorned pedestals in her great meeting room. The furniture, likewise, had been crafted by artisans of incredible skill. A few of the pieces he recognized, their bloody origins known to but the few who had been present during the conflicts in which they had gone missing.

Yanna Sok was no visla, but her powers placed her at the top tier of emmiks. With her natural abilities, combined with her wealth and access to magically-charged weapons, it was surprising she hadn't made a play for one of the visla-controlled realms. But Bawb respected her decision to lie low––in her own way.

She had tested the bounds of her cage, and rattled the bars fiercely, and now knew with certainty how far she could push before the Council of Twenty would pull on her leash.

The well-dressed Wampeh was shown to a low couch, upon which he was comfortably seated while the emmik was informed of his visit.

"May I offer you a beverage while you wait?"

"I wouldn't turn down a drink," Bawb said, playing the part of a freewheeling trader.

"Preference?" the guard asked, opening a locked liquor cabinet behind the other bottles on display.

"Surprise me."

The heavily armed man chuckled and poured a tall glass of a light blue liquid with a light effervescence. Bawb reached up, accepting the glass graciously. His sleeves slid back slightly, and the guard eyed his ornate armlets with curiosity.

"Ooh, is this *real* Aslaak? I haven't seen a bottle in years. Wherever did the emmik find it?" the assassin asked, gently swirling the contents of the glass and giving it a deep sniff, silently murmuring a detection spell before sipping its unenchanted, undrugged contents.

"The emmik has her ways," the guard said. "Now, if you're settled in, I'll return with the emmik shortly."

"Thank you, I'm quite comfortable. You've been a most excellent host."

"We do as the emmik wishes, and treating her guests well is a top priority. If you'll excuse me." With a little bow, the guard left their guest to his own devices and went to fetch his employer.

Bawb had not noticed any obvious signs of covert surveillance, and his quiet incantations had triggered no reaction, giving him a measure of confidence there were no spells actively monitoring him, though with one as powerful as Yanna Sok, it was always possible she had masked them too thoroughly for his hasty efforts to uncover.

He sipped his beverage, enjoying the rare treat. That it had been offered to a simple trader, even one as well-attired as he, was an indication of the emmik's true wealth. That, or her desire to give the impression of it. In her case, however, he was quite sure she had the resources to back it up.

A few minutes later a tall woman, elegantly dressed in form-fitting trousers and a loose top breezed into the room, followed by a half dozen guards-in-waiting. She had a near-pirate swagger to her stride, and both her confidence and power could be felt as soon as she entered the room.

For a naturally magical being such as she, the use of slaaps, konuses, and other devices, was something she only lowered herself to when outside the walls of her home, where she would need to conserve energy if possible. Within her abode, however, the lithe woman was free of such accoutrements, and radiated power regardless.

"I hear you are interested in trade," she said, taking a seat across from him and comfortably crossing her legs, sturdy leather boots pointed at him as her leg bobbed atop the other.

"Yes. I am Binsala. I have come to seek out new trade in this system, and I was told Emmik Sok was the person to speak to."

"You were told correctly."

"Marvelous!" Bawb said. "Then we have much to discuss."

"Indeed, we do," she replied with a cool smile.

Several pair of hands grabbed the Wampeh and hauled him to his feet, roughly forcing his arms back and stripping his armlets from him.

"What are you doing? What is the meaning of this?"

"What I am doing is disarming a spy in my home," Emmik Sok replied. "You think my men are not trained to recognize disguised weapons? And in my own home, no less," she said, picking up his armlets, lazily tracing the runes with her finger. "An exquisite design, I must admit. I would wager the disguise would fool nearly all. And the way your konuses are so expertly hidden within the decorations. Masterful, truly."

"Thank you," he said. "But I am a mere trader. These were acquired some time ago as a means to protect myself on hostile worlds. I'm not one for carrying weapons, you see, but these afforded me some modicum of security without making me appear, *brutish*."

She looked at his ornate attire. Indeed, he was *dressed* like a carefree trader, but his story didn't sway her initial impression.

"No, I think not," she said. "You are a spy, and a fairly good one at that. Had you not slipped and shown your konuses, my men might have even been fooled. In any case, you are unarmed and unpowered."

"I told you, I'm not a powered man."

"And even if you were, that drink just muted your skills."

"Didn't notice any spell," he said, truthfully.

"Oh, the Aslaak isn't enchanted. No, that's a rather lovely vintage, in fact. But no. What *is* enchanted is the glass itself. Not the rim, where a simple detection spell might notice it, but lower. Where you grabbed it. The spell is temporary, but it effectively blocks a person's magic, for a time."

"That's horrendous! And it's illegal," he protested.

"You forget whom you're dealing with," Emmik Sok cooed in reply.

She was rather enjoying the process. Slowly breaking the man, watching the reality of his situation dawn on him bit by bit. It had been so long since she'd last interrogated anyone worthwhile. And for a spy to be sent all the way into her domicile? Well, that warranted extra attention.

Yanna Sok walked close to her captive, looking him over head to toe. "You have all of his weapons?"

"He only had the two konuses on his forearms, Emmik."

"So brave," she said with a mocking laugh. "And so foolish. I think I'm going to enjoy taking you apart piece by piece until you tell me who sent you."

"Nobody sent me! I'm telling the truth!"

"We'll soon know, won't we?" she said with an evil grin. "Bring him to my play room."

CHAPTER FORTY-FOUR

Yanna Sok's victims typically panicked at the very notion of being in the emmik's clutches, but Bawb didn't have much of a chance to contemplate just what the 'play room' designation entailed as he was forcefully hauled down the corridor and up a flight of stairs. A room sat waiting for him, its door open, walls so thick they would silence her victims' screams.

Two of the guards stood outside the doors, one on either side. They were *inside* the house, so really, it was all just for show. Designed to terrorize her plaything a bit more. Bawb cried out as he was pulled into the chamber, the heavy door closing behind them.

"You may release him," Emmik Sok instructed her men.

The four remaining guards stepped clear, leaving the trembling Wampeh standing in the center of the room. There were shackles on the far wall, and several low tables containing a wide variety of torture devices, but most were for show. Yanna Sok far preferred using her hands and the power they contained.

"You really shouldn't have taken the job," she said, circling the Wampeh. "Whoever your employer is, must not have told you whom you were dealing with."

"I told you, I do not have an employer," Bawb said, his voice shaking.

"Yet here you are. A spy in my home. And a foolish one at that."

She picked up the armlets her men had placed on the nearest table.

"These are quite powerful konuses, I must admit. You might have even given me a good fight using them. But that is your weakness. You rely on the magic of others, whereas I possess magic of my own."

"Is that why you don't wear a konus or slaap?" he asked. "Are you so confident in your strength that you leave yourself unprotected?"

Something about his tone, despite the halting voice, made her slightly uneasy.

"You searched him *everywhere*, correct?" she asked her guard.

"Yes, Emmik. He has nothing but the clothes on his back."

A smile blossomed on the pale Wampeh's lips, the points of his teeth shining merrily in the light.

"What do you find so amusing?" Sok demanded. "*Kika rahm!*"

The spell should have sent the man flying, but he muttered a counter-spell casually and stood his ground.

"Impossible. You have no power. And you have no konus."

"Only the clothes on my back," he said with a wicked grin.

Yanna Sok realized her mistake a moment later, but that was far too late for her to stop his attack, let alone launch a counter-spell.

"Idiots!" was all she managed to say before being hit with a flurry of spells, the complexity and fury of which overwhelmed

243

her instinctive defense barriers, battering her to unconsciousness in an instant.

The guards leapt at the Wampeh, whose intricately woven shirt was now glowing with power. A konus's power, but greater. That of immensely powerful Ootaki hair, carefully stored in every shimmering thread of the seemingly harmless material, the natural dyes hiding its true properties.

They had assumed him disarmed, but his weapons were merely a misdirection. The true weapon was on his body.

Bawb spun and whirled between the four attackers, each of whom was heavily armed, and skilled with their weapons. What they were not prepared for was an opponent so eager to fight all of them at once. The men were accustomed to wielding power from a position of strength, with ample time to select and cast their spells.

The assassin in their midst allowed them no such time, combining magical and physical attacks in a flurry, shifting from one target to another, leaving no man even an instant to gather his wits. It was four-on-one, and the fight was by no means a fair one.

The Geist lay the men out with ease. None were powered beings, however, so he left them as they lay, unconscious and battered, but alive. He then turned his attention to the fallen Emmik.

"*Pah nameni,*" he said, rousing her from the murky depths of unconsciousness.

"You...?" she managed, in a whisper.

"I told you. I was not sent by another." He smiled a fanged grin. "I selected you myself."

Emmik Sok finally realized what was happening. He was one of *them.* The rarest of Wampeh. She'd heard tales, but never actually seen one. At any other time, she'd have been fascinated by the man, perhaps even tried to recruit him. But not now, because at this moment, she suddenly knew that she wasn't being spied on. She was his meal.

"Please," she whimpered.

"Shhh, calm yourself," he soothed. "I will not take your life, Yanna Sok. Believe it or not, I hold you in high regard. It is not an easy thing for a woman to achieve what you have in this backward, male-dominated system, even one as driven and skilled as you."

Her body relaxed slightly at the words.

"*But*, I am going to drain you of your power. For a while, anyway. I suggest you wear your strongest konuses under your garments to keep up appearances until you regain your own strength."

She tried to think of something to say, but oblivion wrapped her in darkness as the Wampeh's lips closed over her neck, sucking deeply as he drained her of her blood and power.

He left her and her men sleeping, casting one of his favorite spells, muddying their thoughts for the next day or two. More than enough time for him and the others to make their escape from this world.

With the power of an emmik flowing in his veins, Bawb easily slipped past the household guards, drawing power from his konus armbands, conserving the recently stolen magic. He didn't know when it would come in handy, but it always did, and Yanna Sok was even more powerful than he'd guessed.

He realized he had gotten lucky to take her so entirely by surprise. Had they engaged in a proper fight, even with his konuses, he might not have prevailed.

Bawb slipped into the emmik's personal storeroom and gathered a few key items he and his comrades could likely use in coming days. A case of odd material caught his eye. Carefully, he opened it. Inside were a handful of odd, ugly devices obviously from Charlie's galaxy. Yanna Sok must have added them to her collection when Captain Tür had taken him as a slave.

He had no idea what they were, or if they had any value or use, but thought perhaps his human associate might find them useful. He tucked them into a small sack, along with the rest of his booty. There was much more he'd have liked to take, but there was simply no time, and lacking a proper ship, he couldn't very well expect the Zomoki to carry the extra cargo.

He did, however, have an idea.

Several trips to a local boarding house later, Bawb had stashed away a small fortune in goods from the emmik's home. He'd paid for a full year's rental up front, plus another year's worth for the proprietor to forget he had ever seen him. Eventually, he would claim his booty.

For now, at least, other things took priority.

The assassin known as the Geist slung his haul over his shoulder and stepped out into the night, melting into the flow of the streets without a trace.

CHAPTER FORTY-FIVE

"We really should be going," Bawb said, strapping his handful of new weapons *'liberated'* from Yanna Sok's abode securely to his travel rig. "While the emmik and her immediate guards will remain befuddled by my spell, I am afraid the same cannot be said for the others in the household."

"So, we're screwed."

"I did not say that, Charlie. Merely that there is still a possibility that one or more of her staff may piece together what occurred. If that happens, we may find ourselves in need of a hasty departure. Therefore, preparing for such an eventuality would be wise."

Charlie scanned the distance. All remained quiet, and Ara was still off hunting for her dinner. But Bawb had made a good point.

"All right, I think if Bob feels we may have company it would be a good idea to prep for it," he said, loading his firearms and laying them beside their gear. "I figure you didn't live this long by having bad instincts, right? Now, what was this you said about finding some of my stuff?"

The Wampeh emptied the remaining contents of his sack

from the emmik's compound onto the ground. Charlie's eyes lit up at the sight of gear from his home world. Then he realized what exactly it was they'd deemed worthy of taking with them.

"*This* is what they chose to keep?" Charlie muttered. "Seriously? Of all the stuff we had, they took *this*?"

He held up a portable electron microscope––the one item that actually *was* interesting, if not particularly useful at the moment––and shook it. The rattling of broken bits tumbling about within its housing made the device sound like a very expensive rain stick.

The rest of the booty was of no use whatsoever, though Leila did find a few components interesting.

"Have at it," Charlie said. "Those things aren't ever going to be working again."

"You cannot restore them with a mending spell?"

"Not likely. Unfortunately, being from my non-magical galaxy, they don't fix quite the same way as things here do."

"Oh well," she said as she shrugged and yanked a shiny energy regulator from its cracked circuit board, adding it to a length of braided wire she was using to make a sort of wrecked Earth tech charm necklace.

Leila had been increasingly morose as their flight from Visla Maktan stretched on. Though she was excelling in her training with the gladiator and assassin, and had proven herself a skilled huntress when need be, leaving her father and everything she'd ever known behind was taking its toll. She was often able to hide it well, but even so, her true feelings were starting to show through.

A wash of air kicked up a small cloud of dust as Ara came swooping in, landing as quietly as a massive dragon could. Leila, and even Bawb, to an extent, were taken rather by surprise. Charlie, of course, *felt* her approaching, their bond seeming to grow stronger the more time they spent together. She had fed, he could sense, and that was a good thing. She would need her energy. Trouble, it seemed, was heading their way.

"I saw a group of what appear to be Tslavar militiamen heading this way," the Zomoki said. "Someone must have gotten wind of our camp."

"We should have set up farther from town," Charlie grumbled, picking up a short sword and a slaap. "Okay, Ara. How many are there?"

"Two dozen, I estimate."

That made Charlie pause. "Shit. Okay, then. We need to load Ara up and get out of here ASAP."

"What is an ASAP?" Bawb asked.

"As soon as possible."

"Ah. Clever," he said. "Then yes, I agree, we must depart ASAP."

With great haste they gathered their things, quickly stowing them in the crates, then securing them to the makeshift harness Ara was becoming proficient in getting into and out of. In no time they had loaded nearly all of their gear.

They were fast, for certain, but not fast enough.

"Over there!" a voice could be heard calling out in the dark.

A series of probing attack spells were cast blindly in the direction of Charlie and his friends. Ara easily swatted away one, but the others, fighting blind at the moment, would have no such luck should one happen their way.

Bawb quickly retaliated, casting a killing spell into the night. By sheer luck, it managed to hit one of their assailants, dropping him in an instant. The sounds of panic around him quickly shifted to those of tactical adjustment. These were no untrained ruffians. These men had experience.

They quickly formed a testudo––a shield wall of overlapping wards, the frontmost of them muttering defensive spells, shielding the rest of their number as they launched offensive spells at the much smaller group of offworlders.

SCOTT BARON

"These appear to be Emmik Sok's forces," Bawb said. "I fear they may have already found her and her men."

"You brought them here?" Leila asked, casting one of the defensive spells they had taught her, and just in time, no less, as a stun spell came dangerously close to knocking her down.

"Not precisely," the Wampeh said. "However, if they put out word, I'm sure locals had spotted our campsite prior to now. They would stay away normally––I layered a discomfort spell at our perimeter––but promise of coin can make men do foolish things."

"And ignore spells," Charlie added.

"It was not a barrier, Charlie. More of a *suggestion* to move along. In any case, we are quite outnumbered, even for me."

It was true. Despite the furious castings Bawb was flinging at the advancing men, their shielding spells were too strong, combined as they were. Charlie did the math and knew in his gut there was no way they could overpower that many konus-wearing soldiers. Not as unprepared as they were.

An idea struck, and Charlie––for lack of a better one–– dashed to the crates already lashed to Ara's frame.

"What are you doing?" Leila called out.

"I have an idea," he said, quickly opening a crate and pulling out his intended prize.

The carbine felt odd in his hands. He hadn't been to a range in years at this point, but some things are drilled into you so many times you don't have to think. All you have to do is trust your training to kick in.

Charlie racked a round into the chamber and took up a position between Bawb and Leila.

"Can you two keep up the defensive spells for a minute longer?"

"Yes," Bawb grunted. "But if you have a plan, I suggest you make haste."

Charlie shouldered the rifle and reached out to Ara. *"Hey, I need you to give me a stream of flames over their heads so I can see what we're fighting."*

"I'm happy to oblige," Ara replied in his head.

"Okay, whenever you're ready."

He pressed his cheek to the weapon's stock, lining up his sights in the general direction of the attacking mass.

"Are you going to utilize *that*?" Bawb asked. "Against strong magic, I fear it will have little––"

Ara sprayed a plume of flames, and Charlie opened fire on the now-illuminated attackers.

The report of the weapon firing startled Bawb and Leila. It was so unlike wielding a spell. Inelegant. Loud. Smokey. But it was something else as well. It was *effective*.

Cries of pain and panic reached out to them as they saw multiple Tslavar troops collapse to the ground as Ara's spray of fire faded. Charlie didn't need it, though. Now that he knew where the attackers were, he continued to fire, knowing at least a few rounds would find their mark.

"Bob. Attack spells, now!" Charlie called to the Wampeh at his side.

Without hesitation, the assassin shifted tactics himself and quickly strafed the collapsing lines of the enemy with a variety of spells, ranging from stun and disarm all the way to kill and maim.

Ara sprayed another burst, and the scene illuminated was one of chaos as the remaining Tslavars still on their feet scrambled frantically to retrieve their comrades and pull clear of the carnage. At least a dozen of the green-skinned men lay dead or dying, their blood soaking the soil, looking like pools of treacle in the fire-lit night.

"Leave now! Take your wounded and go, or there will be no survivors!" Charlie bellowed into the sky, firing a few shots for good measure. A violent punctuation to a bloody sentence. "This is your only warning."

The Tslavar forces didn't hesitate, gathering up their fallen men and scrambling back the way they came. Judging by the disarray of their retreat, Charlie didn't think they'd be regrouping for another attack anytime soon. The magical men simply had no idea how to deal with the weapon from a non-magical galaxy far, far away.

The smell of burnt cordite hung in the air, a pale blue cloud wafting over the bodies of the dead. Ara, Bawb, and Leila all turned to look at Charlie. They'd never seen anything like what he had done. No one possessed such magic.

"That was horrifying," Leila said. "And so loud."

"Sorry," Charlie replied. "I didn't have time to warn you about that."

Bawb eyed the inelegant-looking device in Charlie's hands with newfound curiosity. That, and a healthy dose of respect.

"May I see this weapon?" he asked.

Charlie put the carbine on safe and handed it to the Wampeh assassin. He turned it over in his hands, feeling the head still radiating from the barrel. "It pierced their defenses as if they were not there," he finally said. "Yet I feel no power in this device."

"Because there isn't any," Charlie replied. "That's the reason I thought it might work against them. All of their defenses seemed geared against magically launched attacks. *This* is from *my* galaxy, and we don't have magic, so our people had to devise other ways of killing each other."

Ara's golden eyes flashed with interest. "And you utilized this weapon to negate what was an otherwise nearly-impermeable magical defense. All on a guess?"

"I didn't think it would hurt. And at the very least, it might have distracted them long enough to finish loading so we could flee. Admittedly, the results were far bloodier than I had expected."

The three beings so accustomed to their magical ways

surveyed the raw carnage caused by a lone human and his crude device. The devastation was awful. Awful and awe-inspiring. Word would reach the Council of Twenty, undoubtedly. But though they may still joke about the foreign gladiator slave as people may, from this moment on, they would be forced to take the man from Earth far more seriously.

CHAPTER FORTY-SIX

It was a dump.

Not a literal one, mind you, but the next planet the Zomoki jumped to as she and her friends beat a hasty retreat was a rather shitty little world on the ass-end of a distant system. It was grubby, remote, impoverished, and all around unpleasant.

In other words, a perfect place to hide from the Council of Twenty.

They had learned their lesson after the run-in with Yanna Sok's men, and this time, they set up camp a fair distance from the nearest city, though calling it a city was a disservice to cities everywhere. It was more of a shantytown, all told, and a run-down one at that. A decrepit den of scum and villainy.

Charlie and Leila set out on foot at first light to make the long trek into town, careful to downplay their appearances so as not to stand out among the locals and down-on-their-luck offworlders who traded there. This meant their most ragged clothes, with a healthy amount of dirt rubbed into the fabric for good measure.

Both wore konuses hidden under arm wrappings, and Charlie now carried the recovered pistol tucked away under his clothing as well. Having seen what it could do against an unexacting magic user, he decided it would be a good idea to keep it near at all times, if possible.

Funny, for a guy who never really liked guns, he mused when he grabbed it before heading out.

Of course there would be *some* spells more than capable of stopping projectiles, but it was a tactic the locals had not yet had reason to adapt, and therefore, the firearm still held an advantage. They were finally within just a few jumps of reaching their destination. The Balamar Wastelands.

"Ara said she'd take care of sourcing game for us," Leila noted as they approached the small town. "That leaves breads, dry goods, and perhaps some cured meats, to last the voyage into the desert."

"Agreed. And Bawb said the planet is teeming with life outside the affected area, so we should be able to source other items just beyond the perimeter of the wastelands," Charlie said. "Let's just keep a low profile. Get in, get what we need, and get out."

"The sooner we leave this disgusting place the better," she grumbled.

Her mood had only grown more foul when they arrived on the unpleasant world, and Charlie was beginning to wonder if there was anything he could do to ease the strain of the journey for her. She missed her father and friends, and there was little he could do about that, but if he could just find some way to brighten her day, even for a short time, he hoped her spirits might recover at least somewhat.

The town was, they discovered, even worse than they had been led to imagine.

"What a dump," Charlie said.

"Let's just get this over with," his grumpy companion muttered.

They set out through the small marketplace, leaving the

tents and stalls in search of the source of the warm bread they could smell wafting in the air. He wasn't sure exactly what type of flour they were using, but it seemed on just about every world he had visited, both in captivity as well as during their escape, bread was a dietary staple, much like on Earth.

In fact, a lot of things were very similar, once you got past the various alien species and their use of magic rather than technology. And when he thought about it, even that was similar to home. Just replace blue or green skin with hues found on Earth, and ignore the eye stalks, pointed ears, and occasional tentacle, and you had the same socioeconomic woes found in any civilization.

The magic thing was a bit of a stickier issue, but even that could be considered similar to local tools and work habits of different cultures. While the people of Earth had settled on a basic template for their technological advances, the people of this galaxy had likewise based their lives on a common protocol. It just so happened, theirs was magical.

So much was for sale, vendors hawking their wares and haranguing passersby with offers of goods and services—some of them of the less than-savory variety—it could be almost overwhelming, but Charlie kept his eyes peeled for any suitable goods that might cheer Leila up. Unfortunately, he was having little luck.

"Hey, you. Yes, you, pretty thing," a greasy-haired Tslavar thug said from where his shoulder seemed to be propping up the wall he leaned against. He wore a sleeveless vest that had seen better days but showed off his bulging muscles—the effect he was going for. Lounging nearby were a half dozen similarly clothed friends.

Great, an alien biker gang, Charlie grumbled to himself.

Leila avoided the temptation to voice the retort that crept to her lips, but rather, kept her eyes dead ahead, ignored him, and kept walking.

"Come on, cousin," the man said, referring to her palest of green skin. "You're obviously not from here. Why not spend a little time with me and my friends? We could make your stay more...*pleasurable*."

"No, thank you," she said, hurrying past.

Charlie felt the urge to punch the man, but kept it in check. They had to blend in. To go unnoticed. They couldn't afford a confrontation.

Funny, he mused. *I was almost tempted to break that clown's nose. So much for my pacifist ways.*

The leering man watched her appreciatively as she melted into the crowd but made no further moves. Given his unexpected impulse, Charlie was quite glad. It seemed Leila's mood was rubbing off on him. That, or the grubby planet was already taking its toll on his psyche.

CHAPTER FORTY-SEVEN

"Is that everything?" Leila asked as they tucked several loaves of coarse bread with the other provisions they had procured.

"Looks like it," Charlie replied, double-checking they hadn't overlooked anything. "This should tide us over more than adequately," he said as he sealed up their bulging packs.

A high-pitched whimper was barely audible over the din of the teeming masses, but the animalist's ears picked up the sound immediately, her head whipping around to ascertain the source.

"You hear that?"

"Yeah," he replied. "What is it?"

Leila scanned the crowd, searching for the owner of the tiny voice. No one else in the streets seemed to pay it the slightest of mind, but she moved like a woman on a mission, elbowing through the crowd, eyes alert and scanning as the sound grew closer.

"There," she said.

A young girl sat across the roadway, a box at her feet. Charlie wasn't sure what species she was, precisely, just that she had deep umber skin and thickly dreadlocked hair the color of old bricks. The container in front of her shifted slightly, and another yowling howl sounded from its depths.

Leila rushed to the girl's side and peered down into the box. Tears welled in her eyes, but, to Charlie's relief, they were tears of happiness.

"May I?" she asked the girl.

"Sure."

Gently, Leila reached down and retrieved the squirming animal, hugging the gray-furred pup close to her chest.

"Hey, little one, it's okay," she cooed.

The yowling ceased, and a pair of still-blue eyes focused on her as best they could. Charlie had seen it before. Though she was minimally powered at best, Leila possessed a true connection to animals of all types. Whether it was for that reason she became Visla Maktan's animalist, or if she developed the skill because of her role, he was unsure. Regardless, the pup quickly calmed as she stroked its neck.

It was *very* young, Charlie realized. The little beast was so young, in fact, its eyes hadn't even taken on their adult coloring. It was little wonder it was so upset. The poor thing was crying for its mother.

It possessed enormous paws for such a little animal, he noticed, but Leila was too busy burying her face in the animal's thick fur to notice. Judging by her reaction, he doubted she'd have cared. It looked a lot like a wolf pup, but there was something to its shape that felt otherworldly. Then again, they were on another world, so he supposed that was to be expected.

"How much?" Leila abruptly asked the child.

The young girl's nose was sharp, and the bread in their packs was fresh.

"One loaf. The dark kind," she replied, sniffing the air.

"Pay her," Leila said, then turned and began slowly walking back through the marketplace, cradling the pet without even bothering to ask its origins.

SCOTT BARON

Charlie dug a warm loaf from his pack and handed it to the girl. She immediately tore off a steaming piece and happily jammed it into her mouth. The bread did smell good, he had to admit, and Charlie was glad he had purchased more than one loaf of that particular variety.

"Hey, wait up!" he called as he ran after Leila.

He needn't have worried. She had stopped not far away and was procuring a large container of a thick white paste from a vendor.

"Boramus milk," she said, dabbing a dollop on her finger and letting the sharp-toothed pup suckle it. "It's best when diluted with water, but it's perfectly suitable as-is, and it travels well."

"That's milk?"

"Extremely dense and nutrient-rich milk. And they're native desert creatures, so their milk doesn't spoil easily."

She paid the man and sealed the paste tight, the little wolf pup squirming in her arms.

"No, little one, not now. You'll get more when we get back to camp and I can make you a proper bottle."

Amazingly, the animal quieted down.

"I don't know how you do that," Charlie said.

Leila shrugged. "It's just what I do," was all she replied.

The cloud that had been hovering over her head was not only gone, blown to the winds, but her newly cheerful demeanor made the abrupt transition feel somewhat akin to a rainbow bursting through gray skies. It was a change Charlie was glad to see, and their friends would most certainly be glad of it as well.

"Come on, let's get back. I'm sure the others will want to meet your new friend."

"I'm going to name him Baloo," she declared with a happy smile.

Charlie led the way through the crowd, making a path easily, the confidence in his gait sending a subconscious message to those in his way that while he seemed benign enough, this was not a man to be trifled with. It was quite a change from that couch potato engineer who had arrived all those years prior.

"Hey!" Leila shouted.

Charlie spun to see the Tslavar thug and his friends just as they snatched the pup from her arms.

"Give him back!"

"We just want to talk to you, pretty girl. Why don't you come have a drink with me and my friends and I'll give this thing to you."

The hair on her neck wasn't bristling, but the angry energy flowing through her was channeling to her konus instead. "I said, Give. Him. Back."

The Tslavar tossed the animal to one of his friends. It shrieked in distress at the rough handling.

Oh shit.

A crackling had begun forming around Leila's hands. They had taught her enough to defend herself, and the konus was a fairly powerful one, but this was looking to turn ugly, and fast.

The pup let out another pained yelp, and Leila's eyes flashed with rage. Charlie knew without a doubt that things were about to going to get violent. The only question was how much.

Leila acted on instinct. An angry mama bear protecting her young. She startled the Tslavar with a brutal kick to the groin, followed by a knee to the face as he fell. She didn't stop, driving forward toward her pup.

The fallen man's associates weren't as disorganized as they seemed, and quickly cast repelling spells the moment the surprise wore off. Charlie figured it made sense. Ruffians of that nature were likely used to impromptu fights.

Leila quickly cast a series of defensive spells, barely catching the onslaught from the counterattacking men.

Nice, Charlie admired. *She picked those up really well.* He made sure his pistol was securely fastened—it would be bad, indeed, if he lost that in a brawl—then stepped into the fray, casting a simple series of mild spells to break things up.

"Hey! Just give the lady her dog back, and we'll be on our way," he said.

"Like hell we will, offworlder. I'm going to feed it to my—"

He didn't get to finish the sentence. Leila knocked him stone cold with a *kika rahm* spell.

"Where'd you learn that?"

"Saw you do it," she replied, casting another defensive spell.

The ruffians attacked en masse, leaving Charlie no choice but to cast more forcefully than he wanted. This was not good. They were drawing attention.

"We need to leave," he hissed to Leila. "We can't make a scene."

"Too late," she growled, hurling another spell, though easily deflected by her intended target.

Charlie saw what she was referring to. Five more of what he assumed were the men's friends were rushing to join the fray. Two of them carried short swords, a third carried a club, and the remainder wore slaaps. Things suddenly went from inconvenient to dangerous.

Charlie didn't hesitate. To hesitate facing those odds would be to let the opponent settle into a comfortable attack. His gladiator training kicked in full force without him even thinking.

A whirling series of attack spells bombarded the farthest men, while defensive spells blocked the near ones. To an onlooker it would seem like he had pinned himself into a corner, but Charlie turned the spells, casting the opposite pattern, drawing the overzealous attackers into striking range.

Now we play. He smiled menacingly.

Fierce blows rained down on the men, Muay Thai kicks to the legs dropping them low enough to spin into round kicks to the head. Charlie unleashed his training as if his life depended on it. Given the disparity in numbers, it very well could.

Banduzriha! he cast with his mind. The combination of spells shouldn't have worked, but for some reason it felt *right* to him. The resulting impact sent two men tumbling through the air. They wouldn't be getting up anytime soon.

Charlie dove under a sword, landing a solid punch to the groin of the man holding the pup. He dropped the animal, gasping for air. Charlie caught the scared critter and tossed it through the air.

"Leila! Catch!"

He turned back to the fight, entirely confident she had the reflexes and instincts to reel in the pup unharmed.

With several of their colleagues down, the attackers now launched new assaults in earnest. Gone were the injuring spells, replaced with killing ones. Charlie defended them with counters of his own, but they were too many. He had one option left. He just hoped it would work.

Dipangu! he silently cast, smothering the men with the stench of feces. As expected, they didn't realize it was a spell, but instead, allowed their focus to be broken just for a moment while they looked for the source of the smell. The opening was all Charlie would get. Fortunately, it was all he would need.

He vaulted the fallen men, launching himself into the midst of the remaining attackers, effectively nullifying their spell-casting ability. To cast against him was to risk casting against their friends as well.

Charlie switched tactics, letting his training flow. He disarmed one man, taking his sword and crushing his knee, then literally disarmed another with the captured weapon. He moved like a man possessed. Less than a minute later, a small pile of dead men lay strewn around him.

Charlie breathed hard, forcing himself to slow his respirations. He looked at Leila. She was okay.

She looked at the fallen men, then at Charlie. Their shared look said it all. So much for going unnoticed.

The pair quickly gathered up their things and fled the scene, hopeful their violent encounter would pass as just another brawl in the rough-and-tumble town.

It would not.

CHAPTER FORTY-EIGHT

The charred animal Ara had procured for dinner looked terrible. Bawb, however, didn't seem to mind, making quick work tearing into it, flinging aside the burnt pieces as he filled his belly with proteins and fat.

"It's really not as bad as it looks," he said, noting the expressions on Charlie and Leila's faces.

Ara had been quite successful in her hunt, returning not only sated after a respectable feast, but also bringing back the smoldering remains of some sort of animal, though Charlie had no idea what it actually was.

Bawb wasn't concerned by such trivial details.

"I hope you killed it before roasting it," Leila said, pulling out her handy knife and carving off a steaming piece.

"Of course," Ara replied. "I may be a Zomoki, but I am not some brutal killing machine who takes pleasure in tormenting my food."

"That would be a cat," Charlie joked as he sliced off a piece for himself.

"What is a 'cat'?"

"Small, furry animal about so big. Long tail. Claws. Likes to play with its food before killing it, and even then, they sometimes just do it for fun."

"Ah, much like a domorsk," Ara said. "Nasty creatures, those. Cruel just for the sake of it. *Those* I do not grant a swift demise."

Whether that meant being torched alive or some other terrible fate, Charlie didn't want to know. "It's not bad," he said, chewing slowly. "Though it could use a little something to punch it up a bit. If only Tuktuk had come along."

"I am sorry I did not think to pack a selection of spices for you, Charlie. I hang my head in shame."

"Funny, Ara. But now that you mention it, I will pick some up before we leave––if it's feasible."

Bawb looked at the squirming pup in Leila's lap.

"And tell me again, exactly how many men did you kill?"

"No more than I had to. And besides, it's a rough planet."

"And all for that," the Wampeh said, gesturing toward the little animal as he suckled Leila's makeshift bottle. "It hardly seems worth it."

"Don't listen to him, Baloo," Leila cooed to the pup, scratching its ears.

Baloo stopped drinking the watered-down milk long enough to give a tiny yowl that sounded quite a bit like his name, then tucked back in to finish his meal. The smell of meat intrigued him at first, but the lure of warm milk was far more tempting. "Instincts," the animalist had said when the others noted his interest in meat despite his extremely young age.

The Geist had noted the little beast seemed to be of some off-world species he hadn't encountered before. Given his age, as well as slight malnourishment, he gathered that traders had captured his mother in some other system and taken the youngster from her fairly recently. Leila was inclined to agree.

"I shall keep an ear to the ground when I scout the town this evening," Bawb said. "Perhaps I might even ascertain the animal's planet of origin and species."

"I'm not giving him back," Leila said, holding the warm ball of fur protectively.

"I wouldn't dream of it. Whoever took his mother obviously does not care for the well-being of these creatures. It is inhumane to pry an infant away at such a young age."

Charlie gave him an amused look. "Interesting outlook for an assassin, Geist."

The Wampeh fixed a calm gaze on his human friend.

"Being as intimate with death and its many faces, I think I might be in a better position than most to understand the value of life, as well as the crime of harming those too young to defend themselves."

"No one is going to hurt Baloo," Leila said.

The pup yowled at his name.

"That's right, Baloooo," she howled back at him.

The Wampeh smiled his pointed-tooth grin. "Leila, given the size of that boy's paws, I do not think anyone will be able to hurt him before long."

He licked his fingers clean and rose to his feet and placed the castoffs from his meal into their communal waste bag. He then poured some water into a rag and wiped his hands and lips clean. His camouflaging cloak slid on silently as he turned toward the night.

"I will return in several hours. Ara, I assume you will smell me coming?"

"You're *very* good at hiding your scent, Geist, but yes, I will sense your arrival."

"Good. We are camped far enough from town that none should stumble upon you. If others approach, slay them without hesitation. This is not a friendly planet, and you have drawn attention to yourselves. Exactly how much, I shall soon learn."

With that, Bawb melted into the shadows.

He made good time heading into town, running at a casual pace that let him stretch his legs for a change. Their flight and subsequent hiding had been physically demanding for the man so accustomed to maintaining peak levels of prowess. Unfortunately, not all of their bolt holes afforded the freedom to train as he would have liked.

Wind flowed through his hair as he ran, and his blood sang as it coursed through his veins. *This* was how it was meant to be. To revel in the abilities of his body. So many wasted their lives never seeking their limits. Bawb had sought, found, and exceeded them, and couldn't imagine living any other way.

He slowed his run to a casual walk and steered onto the main road as he grew closer to the commerce area, making himself extremely visible so as to blend in with everyone else all the better. Just another man walking the street. No dodging or skulking, nothing at all sinister in his manner.

The assassin had learned many years prior that one of the best ways to become invisible was by becoming the opposite: something highly visible but also something others would not take note of. Adjusting his gait to mimic that of a less athletic man, he allowed his broad shoulders to round slightly, masking his muscular build. From there, he was just another man on the street, occasionally stopping to buy a trinket or snack from a vendor, laughing at their silly jokes, and generally being a completely average guy.

"The Council knows we are here," he said when he returned to the camp late that night.

"How? We haven't been here long, and skrees don't send beyond the system," Leila said.

"The show you put on in town apparently caught the eye of a Council spy. Not a very good one, either, I might add. The locals all know who he is, and several noted him watching your brawl. He headed straight for his ship after you left town. It will take him a few days, but once he has reached a Council outpost, *they* will be able to skree across far greater distances."

"And you found all of this out, how, exactly?"

The assassin smiled amicably, assuming the guise of a friendly trader in mere seconds. "People talk freely to Binsala the jovial trader. Especially when he is loose with his coin and eager to hear their stories."

"It's scary how well you do that, Bob."

"Thank you," he said, slipping back to his normal demeanor. "In any case, a liberal spreading of coin—courtesy of Yanna Sok—loosened tongues a bit further. We have time before the Council arrives, but not as much as I would hope for."

Charlie groaned. "Great. And just when we were off their radar."

"What is radar?"

"It's a tech thing. It's how you track objects in the sky from great distances."

"Fascinating," the assassin said.

The Zomoki seemed intrigued as well. "That is a tech-magic that could prove most useful, Charlie."

"Only I don't have one," Charlie replied.

"Does your ship? Perhaps we could retrieve it when we reach the wastelands."

"Yeah, it has one, but the unit is built in, and it'd be impractical to try to remove the whole thing."

"Too bad," Ara said. "It might have afforded us a measure of warning when the Council arrives. But if we distance ourselves quickly enough, they may lose our trail. Sadly, there are only so many worlds within reach of this system, and they will know that. By trial and error, they should be able to find us if we stop jumping."

"And only a few worlds until our destination."

"Exactly."

"Well then, we'd best get there and get to work firing up that plasma cutter if we're going to get these collars off before they get close enough to activate them."

Despite the threat looming over their heads, the group slept well that night. Constantly looming danger had left them numbed to all but the worst of it, and unless they were facing an imminent threat, sleep was far more vital than worry.

The following morning they packed up, cleared their campsite of all traces, then vanished into the sky.

CHAPTER FORTY-NINE

A new day and a new world greeted the travelers, and a fresh breeze left a slight chill in the air. They had arrived in the dead of night, though their hiding spot nestled safely between a pair of low hills surrounded by tall trees was located several miles from the nearest town. The odds of anyone stumbling upon them were incredibly slim.

Bawb had left at first light, heading for a distant township to inquire of an old acquaintance of his. They were low on dried goods for the difficult trip into the Balamar Wastelands and would have to source more before making that final jump. The Wampeh hoped the debt owed him would help take care of those needs.

"I'll be back before nightfall," he had said, then pulled up his hood and vanished into the morning mist.

"It's creepy when he does that. Am I the only one?" Charlie asked.

"You're not alone," Leila noted. "But he's on our side, so I'll just look at it as a good thing. Not every day you get a stealthy assassin watching your back. I sleep better with him around."

"And I'm chopped liver?"

"You're not a lunchtime food. Why would you even suggest that?"

"No, it's an Earth saying," he clarified. "Nevermind. We should see what food we can source while Bob's doing his thing. It'll be hours before he's back. Maybe we can scrounge up something tasty in the meantime." He looked up at their resting dragon friend. "And how about you, Ara? You feeling okay after that last jump?"

She shifted on her haunches and sighed. "Fine. Just a little tired, is all. We didn't travel terribly far, and the Balamar Wastelands are an easy trip from here. A little rest and a good meal and we should be able to jump by tomorrow."

"So soon?"

"Like I said, the last one wasn't very far."

"Great. Then you rest up. Leila and me, we're going to see about finding us some food. Any preference?"

"Oh, I'll hunt a bit later. I feel the need for fresh meat, and the flight will do my wings good. Too much lurking around on the ground, not enough flying. It will feel nice to stretch a bit."

"Okay. We'll be back soon. Come on, Leila."

"Hang on. Not yet."

"What? Why?"

"Baloo's hungry."

"You can feed him while we walk."

"I *can*, but then he may get a jostled tummy, and I don't want to be vomited on again. Once was enough. That stream was *cold*." she said, holding the makeshift nipple of the Boramus milk bottle to the pup's eager mouth. "Eat up, little one, then we're going for a walk."

Charlie scratched behind the warm little beast's ears. He really was a cute critter, he had to admit, and Leila's mood had been incredibly boosted by having the new addition to their team.

"You just about ready?" he asked ten minutes later.

"Yeah. He should be fine now. Nice and digested—or at least digested enough to not make a mess on me."

"Great. Away we go, then. Back in a bit, Ara."

"Mm-hmm," the dragon murmured, then lazily closed her golden eyes as she soaked up the sun's warmth.

Charlie and Leila made good time to the nearest marketplace, and while they were unable to source any goods suitable for their trip to the wastelands, they did come across a few other useful items in the course of their excursion.

As an added bonus, their little furry companion was a hit with everyone they traded with, and by the time they made the return trip to their camp, Baloo had amassed quite a collection of toys and treats, all donated with pleasure to the amicable little furball.

"He's going to be better fed than we are," Charlie said as they dropped their loads with the rest of their gear. "Hey, Ara. You seen Bob yet? It's getting kind of late, and he said he'd be back before nightfall."

The Zomoki shifted and opened her eyes.

"He's not back in camp, but I do smell him nearby. I believe he is down near the stream, washing off the blood."

"Blood? Oh, man, did he eat someone again?"

"I couldn't say," she said, an amused look in her giant eyes. "But knowing his skills, I'd think the blood would have wound up *inside* rather than outside if that were his intention, don't you think?"

"Point taken. But he's not hurt, right?"

"Not that I can smell. The blood is definitely not Wampeh."

Charlie breathed a small sigh of relief. Bawb could certainly take care of himself, but that didn't mean unforeseen problems couldn't arise out of the blue. And odd as the Wampeh was, Charlie found himself growing rather attached to the assassin.

"Ah, you're back," Bawb said when he strolled into the camp fifteen minutes later.

"Yeah. Not much luck finding dried goods, but we did get some other supplies. How about you? Any love from your source?"

The Geist hesitated a moment.

"There were, *difficulties.*"

"Difficulties? How so?" Charlie asked, a hint of concern in his tone.

"Nothing I couldn't handle. It just seems my old acquaintance had other ideas as to the nature of his debt to me. He foolishly attempted to attack me."

"But he was a friend, right? Why would he do that? Was he enchanted or something?" Leila asked.

"No. I'd actually have preferred that. In that case, I could have seen fit to let him live. But no, he was not enchanted. Merely paid off."

"All the way out here? But we're so far from the core systems."

"Indeed. That word has reached this far does not bode well for us. Not well at all." He turned to the resting Zomoki. "Wise One, do you think you will have the energy for our final jump tomorrow?"

Ara sat up and stretched her wings one at a time, rolling her neck like a prizefighter readying for a bout. "Yes, Geist. I will be ready. But first I must hunt and replenish my strength. Organize your goods. We will depart in the morning."

With a few powerful strokes of her wings, she lifted into the dusky skies and quickly flew the opposite direction of the nearby town. She'd hunt, but not so close to prying eyes and ears.

Charlie and Bawb set to making a small fire and laying out some of the day's acquisitions for their dinner, while Leila mixed another batch of milk for Baloo. The pup had only taken the smallest of sips when his eyes sharpened and a tiny little growl rumbled from his throat.

"Now that's new," Charlie said, scanning the nearby woods.

Bawb was already on his feet, darting for cover, and Leila had done likewise. Charlie took the hint and joined them.

"There are many attackers," Geist said. "I do not think I can flank them given their formation, and Ara will not be back for some time. We're going to have to fight them head-on."

"Shit. *Again*?" was all Charlie could say.

Then the attackers descended on them.

CHAPTER FIFTY

The trees nearest Charlie's head erupted with concussive blasts as successive layers of carefully cast spells pinned him down. These were no ignorant townsfolk who had followed the newcomers in hopes of robbing them. These were professionals.

"How many, Bob?" Charlie called to the assassin, safely tucked behind a sturdy tree trunk nearby.

"I can't say for sure, but it sounds like about two dozen."

"Two dozen? What the hell did we do to earn that kind of attention?"

Another flurry of spells howled through the air, pulling branches from the trees above.

"You mean besides stealing a notoriously touchy visla's new Zomoki, slaughtering a bunch of his men, and knocking out his daughter?" Bawb asked, a wry grin plastered to his face.

"Well, there is *that*," Charlie conceded. "You're enjoying this, aren't you?"

"It's been a long time since I've seen proper battle, you know. My encounters are typically of a far quieter and more *personal* nature."

"Will you two stop yapping and fight back?" Leila shouted. "We have to do something."

"What would you have us do?" Bawb asked. "At the present time we are rather effectively pinned down by a much larger fighting force. They have us outnumbered, and from what I'm sure you've seen by now, they are not targeting us directly, but are rather, lobbing harassing spells at us."

As if to punctuate his statement, a whirlwind of rocks and sticks whizzed past them with no particular target.

"This is them testing our strength, and as we have not fired back, they do not know our numbers, nor our exact positions. At the moment, it's something of a waiting game, I'm afraid. Now, when they make their move and step out into the open, well, that's another story," he said with joy and perhaps a little bloodlust in his eyes.

"But how did they find us? We've only just arrived on this world last night," Leila noted. "There's no way they tracked us from the last system."

"No," Bawb agreed. "However, given my encounter with my *former* acquaintance, I think it is safe to say word of *someone* out of the ordinary may have trickled through the channels. These aren't the visla's men, that much is obvious, so I assume they are likely men for hire. Every system has them, and we just happened to be in the wrong place at the wrong time and these caught wind of us."

A tree burst into pieces, a hail of bark and leaves raining down on them.

Charlie felt a great annoyance swelling in his chest. "I'm getting pretty damn tired of this clear-cutting spell-casting bullshit," he growled. "*Dipangu!*" he said, casting a spell in their enemy's general direction.

"Did you just cast a novelty spell at them?" Bawb asked.

"Yeah, I did. If they can hector us blowing up trees all

around, then I figure they can deal with an annoying little trick of my own."

Leila looked at them both, confused. "What did you do, Charlie?"

Bawb cracked a toothy grin. "He just bombarded our enemy with a stink spell. Feces, to be exact. Right about now, they will all likely be wondering if they stepped in something on the way to the attack."

She fixed her gaze on the odd human. "You're insane. You do realize this, right?"

"Call it what you will. I was getting pissed off, and casting it felt good."

The spell apparently made an impression on their attackers, as a surge in spells blasted across the field with particular violence, then ceased. The silence after so many minutes of destructive power was deafening.

"You out there. You are outnumbered and outclassed, but you do not have to die this day. We are here to take you back dead or alive, and believe me, I think we would all prefer alive, am I right? Throw out your weapons and step into the open and surrender, and you have my word you will not be harmed."

Hang on a second. I know that voice.

"Marban? Is that you throwing this weak-ass shit at me?"

"Charlie?" a shocked voice replied.

Charlie rose to his feet, hands in the air.

"What are you doing?" Leila hissed.

"It's okay," he said, walking into the clearing.

A large man with a pair of bandoliers strapped across his chest, sporting a nasty scar from his head to his collarbone walked out from behind a tree big enough to provide a man of his size adequate cover.

"Hold your fire, everyone. That's an order," he said, an enormous smile spreading across his face.

"It *is* you!" Charlie said, grinning from ear to ear.

"Little brother, you're alive!" Marban bellowed with joy, scooping Charlie up in an enormous bear hug. "Everyone, stand down. There will be no killing today. We've been misled. This scruffy bastard is one of us."

From behind cover, nearly twenty men came into view. There were a lot of new faces, but also many Charlie recognized from his brief stint fighting alongside them as a space pirate years prior. He greeted each of them with a warm hug and a slap on the back.

"It's okay, guys. We know each other."

Bawb and Leila had already gathered as much and were walking toward their former adversaries, who were apparently now their friends, if not allies.

"Marban, this is Bob, and that's Leila," Charlie said. "Guys, this is Marban. He's a good man, and a dear friend."

"We fought some interesting raids, did we not?" Marban said with a grin.

"That we did."

"You never told me you were a pirate, Charlie," Leila said, eyeing him with newfound curiosity.

"It never came up."

Marban laughed. "Same old Charlie. So I assume you didn't tell them about the time you slipped in that freight hauler's blood and fell into—"

"There's plenty of time for stories later," he interrupted. "But where's Captain Saramin? It's not like him to sit out a fight."

The large man's joviality faltered slightly.

"I'm sad to say that the captain met his end at the hands of a Council ship a little less than a year ago."

"No. What happened?"

"It was a glorious end. Fitting for a man of his caliber. You should have seen it. There he was, leading the charge into a beautiful freighter we'd tracked to the back side of one of the smaller moons of Rodnin, when we ran right into a waiting squad of Council troops."

"You boarded a Council ship? What were you thinking?"

"No, it was an ordinary freighter. Or so we thought. But we soon discovered it was carrying something of great interest to the Council. Something guarded by far more than the usual accompaniment of armed crew."

"Let me guess. Weapons. Magical weapons, and lots of them," Charlie said.

"How did you know?"

"Because the Council of Twenty is preparing for war. Or slaughter, depending how you look at it."

"No, they wouldn't be so foolish."

"Believe me, they are. I saw it with my own eyes on Visla Maktan's estate. Slaaps, thousands of them, all being prepared for their expansion into systems not yet part of the Council's conglomerate. They're going to slaughter whoever they have to in order to consolidate power. They're just working on procuring enough power to see their plan to fruition. That's where the Zomoki came in."

"Ah, yes. Beautiful creature, that one. Amazing how you've managed to tame it. We had to wait for it to leave before attacking."

"Smart move. But tell me, Marban, I'm still confused as to what happened aboard that Council ship. It has to be tied in to what I saw in some way."

"Perhaps, but I didn't see much, I'm afraid. It was all we could do to escape, but the captain sacrificed himself so we could get clear. Oh, Charlie, you should have seen it. The legendary Saramin fighting at full-bore. He single-handedly took out over a dozen heavily armed Council troops before they even landed their first blow on him. It was magnificent."

"But why didn't he run? I know the *Rixana*. She's a fast ship, and well armed––"

"Because another compartment opened, and he saw who else was onboard and coming to join the fight. There was a visla, Charlie. Not one of the truly powerful ones, but strong enough to end the fight in an instant. He knew what was about to happen, and in the seconds he had before capture, he triggered his personal destruct spell."

"The failsafe? I always thought that was just a rumor he spread to make sure no one tried anything stupid."

"We all did, but Captain Saramin cast that spell, and not even the visla could stop it. The men and I barely made it back to the *Rixana* before the other ship burst into pieces. It all happened so fast, the Council never received word of who had attacked the ship, but we run a much lower profile now. No sense tempting fate, after all."

"Yet here you are, chasing down the Council's enemies," Bawb said.

"I don't know anything about that. All I know is there was a bounty posted by Old Grayagg. No names, just a basic description and dead or alive."

"Yes, Old Grayagg will not be paying any bounties ever again," Bawb said.

"Really?" Marban said with interest. "Well, Charlie, it appears your Wampeh friend here is something of a badass, if he managed to take that tough old bastard out. I wonder if he's ever considered a career in piracy."

Bawb laughed. "My friend, you could not afford me."

"Well, in that case, dinner's on you," Marban replied with a jolly laugh. "Come, little brother, tonight we eat, drink, and catch up on old times."

"Indeed. And we will toast Captain Saramin."

"So we shall. We will drink to the captain until we cannot walk straight."

A massive feast was laid out. Charlie's pirate brethren, it seemed, had greatly improved the quality of their food since he was last with them. Roasts and vegetables and breads were all to be had in abundance, as was alcohol of a wide variety. In addition, Marban had the men bring down a case of dried foodstuffs from the ship, a special gift for his friend's journey.

"You really want to go to the Balamar Wastelands?" Marban asked, more than a little drunk.

"We have to. I'm pretty sure it's the only place I'll have a chance of cutting these collars off. They're far stronger than any I've ever seen."

"And then?"

"And then I help Bawb kill Visla Maktan and stop whatever he's got planned. After that, who knows?"

Marban took a deep drink and sized up his friend. "You know, you've changed, Charlie."

"For the worse, I assume?"

"Nah, nothing like that. It's good to see you passionate about something. An actual cause. To be honest, I rather miss those days, myself."

Charlie looked at his friend with inebriated eyes.

"Yeah, you know, Marban, you never did get around to telling me where exactly you came from and how you wound up with Captain Saramin in the first place."

Marban grinned, emptying his cup. "You're right. I didn't."

CHAPTER FIFTY-ONE

The pirate crew who had stayed on the surface, eating and drinking until late with their prey-turned-pals, woke groggily with the morning sun already climbing in the sky. They had feasted well, drank much, laughed, and sung, and generally had a good time the prior night.

Most men would have emptied their bowels in fright to wake with a full-grown Zomoki staring at them, but these were not most men, and Marban's rough-and-tumble pirate crew merely experienced the briefest flash of adrenaline before rising and stumbling off into the woods to relieve themselves.

Ara had been watching them for some time as each one of them performed the same morning ritual.

"At least they could have walked a little farther," she grumbled.

"Sorry, Ara," Charlie said with an apologetic shrug as he stretched. "Pirates, ya know?"

"Indeed, I do."

"Where were you last night, anyway? I can't imagine you had to travel all that far to find a suitable dinner."

"Oh, I ate quite well. There was a herd of rather delicious beasts just over those mountains in the distance. The flight felt wonderful, by *the way. It's really nice stretching your wings like that. But after I ate my fill, I noticed you had company. At first, I was concerned, but the smells were of feasting and the sounds of friendly talk and song, so I decided to stay clear a bit longer so as not to put off your guests. Many are discomfited by a Zomoki in their midst."*

Oglar, a particularly stout man, stumbled out of the woods, still highly inebriated and bleary-eyed. The pirate weaved unsteadily around his waking comrades until he bumped right into Ara's massive flank. He turned his bloodshot gaze higher and higher as he took in her mass.

"Hello, Zomoki," he slurred, patting her side, then staggered off toward the nearby stream.

"Yes. Quite put out, I see," Charlie said with a silent laugh.

The enormous Zomoki chuckled as she watched the man go. *"You certainly do have some interesting friends, Charlie."*

Soon all of the pirates had risen and quickly set to work rustling up a hearty breakfast. The men were nothing if not hearty eaters, and a well-fed crew was a happy crew. Within just a few minutes they were all tucking in to a hangover-curing––or at least hangover-*lessening*––meal. Charlie even broke out one of his precious sealed containers of coffee.

"You realize there is only so much of that in our packs, right?" Leila noted.

"Yeah, but these are friends, and I'm glad to share. Besides, Tsokin berries have to grow on other worlds. They were just used as a decorative shrubbery, after all, so they can't be *that* difficult to find."

"That was more of my father's area of expertise, but I think you're right," she replied.

Charlie brewed up several pots of hot coffee and passed the steaming beverage around to the men who hadn't decided to head back to the *Rixana* early. While none of the pirates possessed powers of their own, the effects of the drink on their hungover heads was immediate.

"Now *this* is amazing," Marban gushed. "We need some of this on the ship. I feel fantastic!"

"Hey now, don't get carried away. It's just caffeine."

"Whatever it is, I like it!"

Bawb let out a little snort of amusement. "We would be happy to provide you some to take back to your ship," he said, giving Charlie a knowing look.

"Yeah, I'll hook you up, Marban. It won't be enough for the whole crew, but I'll tell you how to find and process the beans so you guys can start making your own when it runs out."

"Most kind of you, little brother. Most kind!" He took a swig of the hot, bitter brew and swished it on his tongue, savoring the unusual flavor as much as the effects. "A Zomoki on your side, and this invigorating beverage––I'm beginning to think you might actually stand a chance."

"Thanks for the vote of confidence," Charlie replied with a grin.

Baloo, silent the majority of the evening with all the drunken pirates around, poked his head out of his bundle sack and let out a little howling stretch. Marban spun, his eyes lighting up at the sight of him.

"Oh my. I haven't seen one of those in a long, long time," he said, moving to greet the littlest member of the family. "Hello, little friend. My, aren't you a handsome one."

Baloo gratefully accepted the head rubs and ear scratches the large man so freely gave out. For a tough and intimidating pirate, Marban had quite a soft side for the small animal, it seemed.

"His name is Baloo," Leila informed him.

"Hello, Baloo. Hello, little one."

It was a bit unusual, seeing a burly pirate baby-talking a pup.

"So, you've seen these before?" Leila asked. "It's a new breed to me."

"Yes, I have. But that was a long, long time ago, and quite far

285

away," he said, a distant look in his eye. "How did you acquire him? If I may ask. And where?"

"A few systems back, in a backwater town. From what I could tell, it was probably the lone survivor of a litter from an animal someone trapped on some world then didn't know how to care for."

"So you saved him," Marban said, tenderly petting Baloo as he latched onto the bottle Leila had prepared for him.

"We saved each other," she replied.

The way she looked at the animal, he could tell it was true, in the emotional sense, if not the physical.

"You've done a good thing, Leila. And he will be with you for life."

Charlie had watched the conversation with interest. "Hey, Marban. It seems like you know an awful lot about our little mystery friend. What exactly is he?"

"A Beringian, if I'm not mistaken. A very rare breed used to protect the families of powerful men when they were away from home. Loyal, smart, intuitive—there was a saying once. 'Strike a child guarded by a Beringian with your least-favorite hand, for you will never be seeing it again.'"

"I like this saying," Bawb said with a laugh. "And given the size of our little friend's paws, I think he will grow to formidable size, indeed."

"And possess bone-crushing jaw strength," Marban added.

"You hear that, Baloo? You're going to be big and strong," Leila said, snuggling her nose in the squirming furball's neck and smothering him with kisses.

Marban smiled warmly as he watched his new friend. "Charlie, a word, please," he said, then walked into the woods.

"Back in a minute," Charlie said, then followed.

Marban was waiting for him just out of earshot of the feasting pirates. An odd look was on his face. One Charlie had never seen on his scarred visage before. It was a look of concern.

"You're really going to go to the Balamar Wastelands?"

"Yep."

"You realize nothing lives there."

"I know, but my ship should still be there. At least, what's left of it. But if the inner compartments stayed shut, the gear I need should still be intact, and hopefully salvageable. And if the guidance systems can be accessed, I may even be able to figure out if there's a way home."

"A wise course of action. But tell me, if you do manage to get those collars off without the aid of the visla's spell, do you honestly think you and your Wampeh friend stand a chance against him? Against the Council of Twenty?"

"Well, we'll just have to see about that. If it stops a systems-wide war, it's worth the risk. And besides, I mean, we do have a Zomoki on our side."

"Yes, but she is old, Charlie. Sure, she'll be a great ally, for a time, but her scales are dry and flat. I'm afraid she's simply past her prime."

"I'll take her past her prime any day. She's my friend, and trust me, there's more to her than meets the eye."

Marban's concern did not seem abated.

"Look," Charlie continued, "if things get bad, we'll just jump away. Bob isn't stupid, and he sure as hell isn't suicidal. If we can't win, we'll run."

A long silence hung in the air.

"Very well, little brother," Marban said warmly. "You have grown into quite a fighter, and I admire your spirit. I only hope you survive this quest of yours. I would very much like to hear tales of your adventure as we drink to each other's health in our old age."

"Time will tell, my friend."

"Yes, that it will."

. . .

Marban and his men left a short time later, the pirates leaving no trace of their presence anywhere to be seen. Besides the destroyed trees, that is. But if one of the Council's members were to scout out the location, all they'd find would be a well-trodden campsite and a Zomoki-sized divot in the soil.

"You guys ready?" Charlie asked as they sat atop Ara's back, swaddled in blankets, their meager gear strapped to the mighty dragon.

"As ready as one can be, I suppose," Leila said, holding Baloo tight.

"Okay, then. Ara, take us to the Wastelands."

The Zomoki flapped her great wings and soared high into the sky. Then, in a blink, she was gone.

CHAPTER FIFTY-TWO

The smell of lush, damp forest hit Charlie in the face like a water balloon of aromas as soon as Ara popped into being just above the verdant wild lands of the planet's surface.

"Are you sure this is it?" Leila asked.

"Of course," Ara replied. The jump had been a success, the Zomoki's casting never once in doubt.

She was old, and with age came knowledge. With knowledge came a certain degree of skill. That, and she had been to so many worlds in her many years, that she was quite proficient in traveling between them, though she typically preferred more leisurely––and less draining––means.

She swooped low, flapping her great wings hard as she settled into a small clearing among the trees. Using that much magic always took its toll on her, but for simpler things, like flight and basic magic, she'd recover in under an hour.

"My God," Leila gasped as she slid from her back onto the ground. "It's so green!"

Baloo wiggled from her grip and galloped away, making it several steps before tripping over his own oversize feet.

"Reminds me of a Great Dane," Charlie said.

"Is this a form of royalty where you are from?" Bawb asked.

"No, nothing like that. It's a kind of dog. Enormous goofballs who have absolutely no idea how big they are. When they're puppies, they trip over themselves constantly. A friend used to rescue them, so I've spent a fair bit of time around the silly critters."

"They sound like an amusing, if not terribly logical, breed," Bawb said, taking in their surroundings, ears straining, listening for any sound of danger.

"We are safe here," Ara informed them, sniffing the air deeply. "Our arrival appears to have gone unnoted."

Charlie took in the area around them. Trees loomed overhead, providing them shade and cover, and the general feel to the area was that of a bountiful woodland. He knew Ara would need a brief respite before she could push on.

"Let's see what sort of edibles we can find," he said, slinging an empty bag over his shoulder. "We've got dried goods from Marban, but we should load up on what we are able and save those if we can. Ara, you good here?"

"Yes, Charlie, I'll be fine," she said, curling up in a warm patch of the orange sunlight. "You go on. I'm just going to rest a bit before we continue."

"I'll be quick," he silently told her.

"Take your time. You should enjoy this place while you can. Soon enough we will be in quite a different environment."

Baloo had already been trussed up in a makeshift lead, and Leila was letting the curious pup waddle into the woods, sniffing everything as he went. Despite his diminutive size and youth, the animal was already showing signs of being quite an adventurous critter. It seemed that even just a few meals of the nutritious Boramus milk Leila had procured had given him an enormous boost in strength.

"Come on, Baloo," Leila said in a sing-song voice, gently tugging the lead tied to her furry friend.

"Awoooo," he replied at the sound of his name, trotting to his new mom on unsteady young legs, then flopping down at her feet.

She picked him up and hugged him close to her chest.

"Okay, buddy, let's give you a little break," she said, cradling him as she increased her stride, moving deep into the forest. "See you all back here shortly," she called out behind her, then was gone.

Having been raised by the groundskeeper, and having had all of Visla Maktan's lands to explore as she grew up, Leila was a totally different woman once she was back in nature. Cities she could deal with, but it was in the wild that she was truly at home.

Bawb had already disappeared into the flora, but that didn't surprise Charlie. It was an interesting sensation, realizing that a deadly assassin––one who could likely kill him without much effort, and despite his gladiatorial skills, no less––was out there, silently moving among the trees.

Charlie was just glad the Geist was on his side. At least, he was pretty sure he was. One thing he was sure of was his safety for the time being, anyway. The Wampeh's reverence for Ara, and his sense of honor, would prevent him from doing anything to draw her ire.

Well, I guess that leaves me to my own devices for a bit. Time to wander the woods and try to not pick poisonous mushrooms.

He picked a direction and stepped into the woods, hopeful he'd return with something edible, and maybe even some fresh water if they were lucky. They were well-stocked as it was, but there was an odd taste to the containers they had filled on the last planet, as if the depression and mood somehow worked its way into the water table itself.

The muted red of the dragon's scales looked even more like

dried blood in the orange light of the dual-star system's suns. Her golden eyes, however, shone bright, quick to focus on a seemingly empty patch of air across the clearing.

"Hello, Geist," she said.

A moment of silence. Then the Wampeh lowered his spell, slipping into the visible spectrum.

"Your senses are quite sharp," he commented, pulling several small animals from his carry sack. "I even went so far as to cast a muting spell to hide the smell of myself and my catch."

She let out a low chuckle. "Oh, my dear Wampeh, you do not get to reach my age without learning a few tricks of your own."

Bawb smiled, the genuine amusement reaching all the way to his eyes, for a change. "I thought you might enjoy some nourishment without having to hunt, Wise One," he said. "I hope these are to your liking."

"Why, thank you, Geist. That is most considerate of you."

"You've borne us on your back across many systems. I think this is the very least I can do."

Ara puffed a tiny jet of flame, roasting the carcasses before snatching them up in her enormous jaws in a single bite. "Delicious," she said. "And most appreciated."

"And how are you feeling? Is your energy returning?"

"I feel quite well, actually. The rays of this system's suns have always been particularly restorative."

"Ah, so you've been to this system before?"

"Yes. But that was a long, long time ago," she said, falling quiet, a note of distant sadness in her eyes.

The pale man sat down quietly beside her and picked a handful of berries from a pouch on his hip, eating them silently. Together, the unlikely pair of a Wampeh and a Zomoki breathed the fresh air, soaked up the sun, and listened to the wind.

At least fifteen minutes of tranquil silence had gone by when Leila could be heard drawing near.

"Baloo, come back here!"

Both Ara and Bawb smiled. The antics of the little beast were proving a welcome bit of amusement.

"Leila, how was your expedition?" Ara asked as she entered the small clearing. "Any luck?"

"I found some edibles, but not as much as I'd have liked."

"Here," Bawb said, tossing his pouch to her. "It seems I had better luck than you."

Leila popped a few of the deep purple berries in her mouth, savoring the sweet and tangy explosions of flavor on her tongue. "Mm, thanks, Bawb."

"It is my pleasure."

"You save any for me?" Charlie asked, striding into view from the far thicket.

"Of course," she replied, handing him the pouch.

He took a few berries from the cache and handed the rest back to her. "So, I didn't find much in the way of normal food," he informed them.

"None of us did, though Bawb did forage these for us."

"*But*," he added, "I did find a rather large growth of these."

He removed a modest-sized sack from within his larger collection bag and opened it for the others to see.

"Tsokin berries?" Bawb asked, puzzled. "But these have a notoriously bland flavor, and not much in the way of nutritional value."

Charlie grinned, knowingly. "Perhaps, my pointy-toothed friend. But just wait and see what I do to them."

"You make that sound so nefarious," Ara said. "Just tell him."

"These are what I make the coffee from," he clarified for his Wampeh friend.

Bawb's eyes widened. He had most certainly experienced the benefits of Charlie's bitter brew, his powers crackling with newfound vigor after a few mere sips.

"Well, then. This is a good turn of events," he said. "But it is

293

getting later in the day. Perhaps we should set up camp for the night and push on in the morning."

Ara stretched her wings as the red sun grew lower in the sky. "No, we shall finish our journey before nightfall. Charlie has assured me there is ample shelter for you at the site of his crashed ship. As for me, the night air will do me no harm."

"Then let's get to it," Charlie said, tucking his supplies into the open storage containers and climbing atop Ara's back.

The others joined him, Baloo cozily swaddled in a bundle against Leila's chest. Ara flapped her mighty wings, and they lunged into the sky, quickly leveling out over the treetops as they flew toward the setting suns.

The red one was nearly below the horizon, and the orange color of the land was shifting toward yellow, which would last until the second sun followed its twin into the night.

It felt strange, seeing those first alien suns any human had ever beheld firsthand once more. Three years had passed since his arrival in this galaxy, and Charlie was a completely different man, but the memories of those initial days returned to his mind, fresh and sharp as they flew.

Ahead, the lush greenery abruptly shifted to red and brown soil as far as the eye could see.

The Balamar Wastelands, he noted. *Never thought I'd see this place again.*

The twin suns and their shifting spectrum as the darker of the two set was an unusual, yet familiar sight. Ara swooped low over the treetops and crossed the edge of the wastelands. The air immediately became warm and dry, and it was due to more than just leaving the wooded area. A mighty casting had created the Balamar Wastelands all of those centuries ago, and traces of its magic still lingered to this day.

Little cairns of stone dotted the landscape periodically. Ruins, Charlie now knew, of what had once been a fantastic realm, reduced to rubble in one horrible instant. A little smile tickled the edges of his lips. Beneath one of them, he knew, was something people had killed for. Something thought lost. And something he alone knew the location of.

Hot damn, he thought as they flew deeper into the wasteland. *I'm back.*

CHAPTER FIFTY-THREE

"You flew in *that*?" Bawb asked in disbelief. "In *space*, no less?"

Ara banked low and circled the half-buried wreck of Charlie's ship, the crash landing trench gouged in the soil and scattered debris trail long lost to the sand and winds. Dropping lower, she flapped her wings powerfully, kicking up the long-silent soil as she settled down beside the vessel.

"It didn't always look like that," Charlie replied, sliding from the Zomoki's back. "And remember, we crashed here. This wasn't some picture-perfect landing."

His boots made little puffs of red dust when they hit the soil. *Son of a bitch, I'm really here.*

He walked up to the long-silent remnant of his former life and reached out to touch its wind-buffeted skin. The ship had actually held up quite well, given the environment. Its hull had weathered the elements and seemed no worse for it, aside from a layer of dust covering everything. Charlie wondered if the interior had fared as well.

Leila joined him, Baloo tucked against her chest, blissfully asleep, as puppies are wont to do. Her eyes played across the foreign shapes and materials of the craft, trying to make sense of this tech-magic that was so different from any she had ever known.

"How did you ever survive this landing? And in *this*?"

"It's sturdier than it looks, and the power systems were the most state-of-the-art ever made."

"And you say this was not powered by Drooks," Bawb said, stroking the stored Drook power rod in his armlet.

"No, I told you, we use a fission reactor to create power. And if we're lucky, the core is still functional enough to direct a charge to the plasma cutter. With that bad boy running, it should be relatively short work cutting our collars off."

"Well then, I suppose we should get to work," Bawb said, helping unload their gear from Ara's load-bearing harness.

"Not tonight," Charlie said, eyeing the setting red sun. "The yellow one will drop below the horizon in less than an hour if memory serves, and it could be dark inside. No idea if the emergency lighting I jury-rigged is still functional at all. But with all the little holes in the hull, daylight will at least provide us a bit of ambient light."

"We have spells. We can––"

"Trust me, Bob. You don't want to go wandering around in there with only portable light if you can help it. No, let's set up shelter, have some dinner, and get a good night's rest. There will be plenty to do in the morning."

Charlie began pulling wind-smoothed pieces of the ship free from the wreckage, setting them up to form a shelter as he'd done with Rika in years past. A sad shadow drifted across his spirits at the memory.

He'd been here, in this same place, moving these same pieces of wreckage with his mission leader. His friend. Now she was gone, lobotomized by the Tslavars and sold into servitude like some mindless piece of meat, not the brilliant pilot she once was.

Charlie pulled more of the panels to their makeshift camp,

the bits of hull material effectively blocking the breeze that stirred with the approaching nightfall.

"Charlie!" Leila called out in shock.

He dropped what he was doing and ran to her, Bawb already there, a deadly blade in hand.

"What happened?"

"Baloo," she said, pointing to where the curious little animal had been digging.

Jutting out of the red soil was a bright flash of white. He knew immediately what it was, if not who. A bone. One of his former crew. The pup had somehow found the remains of his dead crewmates.

"It's okay. It's one of mine," Charlie said. "We lost almost twenty people when we crashed. We buried them––I mean, the ones we found enough of. Some of them were no more than pieces. The hull tore to shreds..."

Charlie fell silent. He had fought, he had even killed since he first arrived in this strange galaxy, but the memories of that day hit him in the gut as hard as if it were yesterday.

"It was an honorable thing you did, seeking and burying your friends," Bawb said, studying the burial ground intently. "But there is something odd here. I sense traces of magic. Ara, do you feel it?"

"Of course, Geist. A killing spell was cast." She paused, sniffing the air. "Four of them. There are more bodies under this soil."

The memory of the green slave ship captain brutally murdering those of his crew too injured to be of value to him flashed through Charlie's mind. Captain Tür. The man who had made him a slave. Who had sold him off to become a gladiator. Who indirectly made him what he was today.

"I know what happened," Charlie said quietly. "These four were survivors along with me and Rika. When the Tslavars arrived, we were taken as slaves, but our friends were injured.

They were healing, it just would have taken time, is all, but the Tslavars didn't want to spend the power on them."

"So they killed them?" Leila asked, shocked. "Why not just leave them behind? There was no need to kill them."

"I've often wondered that very same thing," he replied, then fell silent.

"Their claim," Bawb commented.

"Their what?"

"Their claim. Normally stranded are fair game, but you are not from the conglomerated systems. Nor are you from this galaxy. I suspect they killed your friends so there would be no possible witnesses to negate their claim to you and your friend. If they had not done so, though highly unlikely, the potential of a challenge to your enslavement could still have been made, should they be found."

"So they killed my friends to make sure they could keep us as slaves."

"Yes. And as this wreck site proves your extra-galactic lineage, I believe a reasonable argument against your being subject to this realm's rules of bondage could have been made."

Charlie jaw flexed involuntarily. "All over some goddamn slavery," he growled. "You know, we abolished that practice on my world hundreds of years ago. And now, here I am, deep in space and what do I find? A people just as cruel and backwards as the ones we drove from existence back home."

"It is an imperfect system, for certain. But one that is being challenged. Why do you think I was tasked with killing the visla, Charlie? He is one of the key players on the Council of Twenty. With Maktan out of the equation, the rebellion stands a far greater chance of success. They may not be able to free all of the systems, but with pressure applied to the right places, there is a very real possibility of them freeing at least some of them, and that is a start."

Charlie pondered his assassin friend's words as they

carefully re-buried his deceased crewmate while Leila tied Baloo's lead far enough away that he wouldn't go digging up any more bones. Once the pup was secure, she quietly laid out a meal from their perishable supplies.

"I've got it," Charlie said, sitting down and absent mindedly starting their fire.

"Charlie?"

"Yes, Ara?"

"Did you notice what you just did?" she asked, an amused tone to her voice.

"What?"

"You cast the fire spell without even thinking about it. And you did it *silently* as well."

The others took note of her words. They hadn't noticed when it happened, but it was true. He had started the fire without muttering the spell.

"How did you do that, Charlie?" Bawb asked, an eyebrow arched high and curious. "Only the most powerful of vislas can cast without uttering a word."

He thought about it a moment.

I don't feel any different, he mused.

"I can't rightly say, Bob. It just happened," he finally answered.

"Interesting."

It was a statement the Wampeh assassin had made more and more frequently as he spent time with the unusual human. Given what he'd seen in his time accompanying the man from Earth, he had a sneaking suspicion he'd utter the word a great deal more in the future.

CHAPTER FIFTY-FOUR

Light peeked through the myriad holes pockmarking the hull of the *Asbrú*, making the outer compartments feel almost like a disco ball with their glinting multitude. The elements had wreaked merry havoc on the metal shell, the Wastelands' periodic windstorms battering it relentlessly. Fortunately for Charlie and his friends, the innermost reaches of the ship were left unscathed.

That meant the reactor still functioned, and while many of the peripheral systems had failed due to environmental wear, it was looking like a bit of elbow grease and a lot of scavenged cabling might get some systems functional, if not fully online.

"Watch your step in there," he warned Leila as she inched her way down into the ship. "It was unstable back when we crashed here, so I can only guess how things might have broken down over time."

"Seems pretty solid," she replied, testing the floor with her boot. "Maybe whatever was loose before has settled into place."

Bawb surveyed the interior, his sharp senses scanning for any unexpected hazards. "This place is a disaster."

"Duh. We crashed, Bob."

"You know what I mean," the Wampeh shot back. "But I would tend to agree with Leila's assessment. The storms alone would have shaken the most unstable sections into either collapse or a more solid configuration as they moved. I'm hoping for more of the latter."

"Okay, then. So long as you all know to keep your eyes open and walk carefully. And for heaven's sake, don't go flipping switches on anything. It's going to take a while to track down what's active and what isn't, and I don't want any unplanned discharges if we can avoid them."

"Discharges? I thought you said your kind did not use powers," Bawb said, his eyes bright pinpoints as they reflected the sunlight peeking in through the holes in the hull. "I do not sense any magic here."

"I told you, it's not magic. It's tech. Reactors. Electricity."

"I don't like it," the Wampeh said, crinkling his nose with distaste. "This place, this ship. It feels *wrong*."

"Just a different type of power than you're used to, is all. Don't worry, you'll get used to it. I felt the same about magic when I first got here, after all."

"Perhaps. For now, let us be hasty in retrieving the thing you described."

"Plasma cutter. Right. I know the tanks supplying the gasses were intact after the crash, and I saw others we could jury-rig if need be, but the big thing is going to be powering the system up. It still takes a fair amount of juice."

"Juice? This tech-magic from your world runs on beverages?" Leila asked.

Charlie almost laughed aloud, but managed to refrain. This was their first exposure to actual Earth tech, and while he may have told them stories, there was simply so much to learn, and they'd only just arrived.

"No, Leila, it's not powered by actual juice. That's just a slang term for power we use on my world," he said.

"Strange. Even with the translation spell, some of your expressions just don't make sense."

"You should try talking to teenagers sometime," he replied with a grin. "Anyway, the ship seems stable, though some sections appear to have shifted since I was last here. Let's move deeper and see about retrieving the plasma cutter and getting these damned collars off, shall we? I think if we head this way and cross over via the upper levels we can avoid the most extreme damage."

Charlie took the lead, guiding his friends through the dimly lit wreckage of his ship, up higher and higher until they passed the ruined command center, then aft a few compartments before preparing to descend to the jumble of metal that had held the plasma cutter when he was last there.

As they walked, he pointed out systems and explained their functions. It was a crash course––literally––in Earth tech.

"You say you built this vessel?" Bawb asked, eyeing an enormous jumble of wires that had been torn from the bulkhead.

"I didn't actually *build* it. I was one of the lead designers, is all. Most of the fabrication was handled by robots. The welding and all that was done in sections, then assembled into their final configuration. Men and women then came in and worked alongside the machines to install all of these miles of cables and tie in the machinery."

"It lacks style, and is brutish in design, no offense," Bawb said.

"None taken."

"But the sheer scope of the endeavor––I must admit, your people appear capable of great feats, even if the powers behind them are unknown to me. And the ship jumped, like Ara does? Amazing."

"Well, technically we were still in the experimentation stage on the whole jump thing. We call it an Einstein-Rosen Bridge, by the way. Unfortunately, something went horribly wrong, and we were sucked through a wormhole."

"What's a wormhole?" Leila asked as she carefully climbed over a toppled control rack.

"It's like how water drains, you know? Spinning and vanishing down a pipe. Only this happens with space, and no one knows where that pipe leads."

"In your case, it led you to this world," Bawb noted.

"Correct. Or, *more* correct would be to say it led to this *galaxy*. And if we're lucky, the systems I'm pulling may be able to tell me where exactly we are in relation to my home, and hopefully even show me a way home."

"Is that why you are collecting these seemingly useless things as we move through the ship?" Bawb asked.

"Yeah. If I can get them charged, the residual trace of whatever pulled us here may still be in there. And *that* just might guide the way back. Of course, it'd take a helluva lot more power to send a message, and I'd be long dead before they even received it, but at least I could hopefully let someone back home eventually know what happened to me. Us. My crew."

He fell silent a moment, the memories flooding back as he walked the ship he had spent so many years of his life creating.

"Okay, enough of that. We should keep moving. The plasma cutter is about a dozen compartments away, but if we cut through Cargo One we should be able to bypass a few of them."

He turned and headed off down a warped corridor, the metal bent and distorted from many years ago.

Come on, don't be blocked.

Charlie pushed the partially open airlock door blocking his path, and, miraculously, it began to grind open.

"Bob, gimme a hand with this, will ya?"

The two men pushed hard, and despite years of grit making its way into the craft bit by bit, the door gave way to their efforts and slid into the wall. The compartment it exposed took the aliens' breath away.

"What is all of this?" Leila said, her light flashing across the equipment, then falling to rest on the massive machine in their path.

"*That*, my friend, is a *mech*. It's in travel mode at the moment, so you can't really see its normal configuration, but when it's not in here all folded up, it's an enormous metal man used in environments too dangerous for people to go."

"A metal man? But how does it move? I sense no power. No Drooks," Bawb said, running his hand along the enormous machine's cool mass.

"Normally it has power cells that fit in there." Charlie pointed to the sealed compartment. "But that's them over there, and as you can see, they're bent to hell and won't possibly fit. So all it has––or had, last time we checked––was just enough power to run systems tests but not function beyond that."

"Fascinating. And there is no way to power it now?"

"Nope. Those were the only power cells that fit it. I could run a trickle charge from the reactor, but that wouldn't solve the bent housing problem. So this bad boy is stuck, unfortunately."

He looked at the mech, thinking back to the simulations he had run with his friend so many times. Over the years, he had managed to put her fate out of his thoughts, but now, here, in this place, Rika's memory haunted him with every turn.

"Come on, there's no sense lingering in here. The plasma cutter should be up this way, and if we're lucky, it'll still have enough of a charge on board. Once we get it to the surface, these collars should come off."

"Should? We came a long way for *should*, Charlie."

"I know, Leila, but I'm almost positive it's the one thing that this galaxy's magic won't stand up to. But there's only one way to know for sure, so let's get cracking."

CHAPTER FIFTY-FIVE

It had taken several trips and an entire day to finally get the plasma cutter disassembled enough to fit through the damaged sections of the ship and hauled to the surface. The twists and turns inside made even Drook-powered lifting spells difficult to utilize, but eventually, the last of the components reached the first sunlight they'd seen since being installed in the craft many years prior.

Charlie had decided to bring every possible gas they could use on the strange, magically enhanced metal bands around their necks. It had required additional trips, but was well worth the effort in his opinion. If they could find the right combination, he figured they should be able to cut through them, whatever the hell type of metal they were.

Of course, plasma would also cut right through the person on the other side of the collar, so he took Bawb on a scavenging expedition to find the toughest scraps of heat shielding from the hull that they could fit between themselves and the collar. They then trekked through the belly of the ship and recovered a half dozen space suits, all sealed and pristine, waiting for them all those years, safe from the wear of the elements.

"These are a form of armor?" the Geist had asked.

"What? No, this isn't battle stuff, Bob. These are to protect us from the extreme temperature fluctuations in space."

"Wouldn't a basic environmental spell be more——"

"Yes, Bob, it would. But we don't have those where I'm from, remember? So us poor humans have to come up with other ways to survive in space. The good thing is, not only can we use one as a thermal buffer to keep us from burning when the heat shield under the cutter gets hot, but we can also wear them when we fly with Ara from now on. She can take us into space with no problems."

"But without breathing spells——"

"They have their own closed-loop air systems, and with the CO_2 scrubbers built in, we have a day or two of air in each suit. And there are extras, so we can even repurpose one for Baloo. He's small enough to easily fit."

"I do not understand much of what you just said, Charlie, but I am starting to see the wonders of this craft with new eyes. It may not be aesthetically or magically pleasing, but the accomplishment is nonetheless impressive."

"Thanks. Now let's get this stuff back to the camp. I'm gonna have a long night rebuilding that cutter, but if the power cells hold up, I think it just might do the trick with these bits and bobs to shield us."

"And none too soon, I expect. The odds of Maktan and the Council finding us increases the longer we stay still, and if they get close enough, they will be able to track us by those collars."

"I've seen that at work before," Charlie said, recalling his recapture by Captain Tür after being kidnapped by pirates. By his friends.

"There you are," Ara said as Charlie and Bawb emerged from

the ship. "We were beginning to wonder if perhaps Leila should come in and search for you."

"All good, Ara. We were just grabbing a few other useful supplies while we were at it. These suits are all intact. That means we can safely exit the atmosphere next jump."

"Oh? That is excellent. It will make the process so much more efficient, not to mention requiring far less power to jump."

"Yeah, I knew you'd like that."

"And what of the collars? Will your device be able to remove them?"

"I think so. I just need to get the plasma cutter back together, and we'll give it a try. In the meantime, would you mind wearing this little harness of gear I rigged up?" Charlie asked, holding aloft a small addition of cargo netting to clip to the lines she already wore.

"Of course. That seems like a paltry weight for me to carry."

"Oh, it's not the weight I'm wondering about. It's your magic."

"Hmm. Go on," she said, intrigued.

"I've cast an incredibly basic *yaka illum* spell to feed power into them, kind of like I used once before to trickle energy into one of my old devices. The thing is, I have no idea how I made it work at the time, but I was thinking, if it's in proximity to someone of your enormous power, maybe it'll absorb enough by osmosis to function eventually. If you agree to it, of course."

The Zomoki pondered a moment, looking at the strange tech-magic devices.

"An interesting idea," she finally said. "You have my permission."

"Thanks, Ara," he said, then clipped the navs and drive arrays to her harness, hoping they might one day show him the path home.

Charlie looked out across the horizon. The twin stars

illuminating the planet were already dropping low in the sky, and as the red sun set, a small sandstorm was starting to blow across the wasteland. Charlie knew there was simply no way he'd be able to finish rebuilding the cutter before it hit.

"We should cover our gear and move inside to shelter," he said.

"But I thought you said it was best to camp outside," Leila noted as she fed her squirming pup.

"Normally I'd say yeah, that's the safest thing, but it looks like this sandstorm might pick up during the night, and now that we've had a good look around, I think we can pretty safely move into the outer compartments over here," he said, gesturing at a hole torn in the ship's side. "It's not air-tight, but it should protect us in case the wind picks up."

"What of you, Wise One?" Bawb asked the Zomoki. "Will you be safe?"

"Thank you for your concern, Geist, but I have experienced far more uncomfortable nights than this. In fact, the sand might feel good. A bit of exfoliation could be nice."

The Wampeh flashed a pointy-toothed grin. "Very well. We shall cover this salvage against the elements, then retire inside."

Charlie and Bawb made quick work securing coverings for the plasma cutter assembly they had spent so much time and effort hauling out of the ship. Leila tied Baloo's lead firmly inside and helped them carry in any supplies that were not entirely sealed.

Waking to find grit in your foodstuffs was something she'd experienced enough times during their flight to want to avoid, if at all possible.

The yellow sun followed its red sibling below the horizon, the sky turning golden before fading to darkness.

"Good night, Ara."

"Good night, Charlie. Sleep well."

After such a long day's work, even with the winds buffeting the hull of the ship, as soon as Charlie lay his head to rest, he did just that.

CHAPTER FIFTY-SIX

Morning brought with it a brisk chill to the air that none of them had expected. Apparently, whatever weather had triggered the sandstorm the prior night had also dropped the temperature low enough for them to see their breaths.

Give it an hour, Charlie mused as they huddled around a fire spell for warmth as they ate a light breakfast. *Knowing this rock, I wouldn't be surprised if we're sweating balls by afternoon.*

He warmed his hands on a smaller fire spell he cast near the plasma cutter parts. He was getting the hang of that spell, though the Boy Scout in him would always want to pile wood and make a proper one. But for now, this was doing the trick. Namely, keeping his fingers warm enough to have feeling. It would be hard reassembling the complex plasma cutter without it.

Charlie began laying out his components, blowing dust and grit from any remotely sensitive areas before bolting them to their respective assemblies. It seemed that one of the makeshift tarps had blown away in the night, but the bits it covered didn't appear any worse for wear.

It was quick work putting the unit back together. Even taking the time to explain what he was doing to his curious alien friends as he went, Charlie nevertheless found the process almost Zen-like in its doing. He was working with tools, not magic. Using his hands, not spells, and it felt good.

He may have adapted to life in a magical galaxy, but he was an Earthling first and foremost, and he felt more connected to his home than ever as he ran his hands over the reassembled unit.

The tanks were lined up and connected—he was going to try a combination of Argon, Hydrogen/Nitrogen mix to start, that particular setup being recommended for thicker metals. He'd have preferred Oxygen as the slag runoff would be less, but this was faster, and given what he'd already seen of the collars' properties, he figured it was the best choice. Especially as they had no idea what cutting them might do to the magic contained within.

Faster would definitely be better, if they wound up in a hurry for any reason.

The gas flowed perfectly, and the instrumentation lit up crisply at the throw of the switch. The cutting unit and its supply feed seemed in excellent working order. The power cells, however, were another issue. They showed a charge, but something was janky with their output. Whether it was a faulty connection or just a damaged unit, without proper diagnostic equipment, there was just no way to know.

"Okay, I think that about does it," Charlie said, cracking his back as he stood up from his labors. "So, who's first? Ara, you wanna give it a go?"

"While I appreciate the offer, you are the only one who understands this device. Should you become incapacitated by your collar if the Council arrives before you have finished, you would be unable to fix or utilize it. I believe it is in our best interest if you are the first."

Bawb and Leila nodded their agreement.

"Okay, then. Guinea pig Charlie it is," he said as he picked up the scrap of heat shielding from the hull and wadded up space suit material beneath it and wedged the two beneath his collar, creating a flame and molten metal runoff deflector. He slid the protective glasses on, picked up a broken mirror he had salvaged from one of the ship's heads, and positioned the cutting nozzle.

I hope to hell I don't burn a hole through my neck, he grumbled to himself, then took a deep breath and put his finger on the switch. "Okay, here goes nothing."

The plasma cutter activated, and an intense heat assaulted his neck and face. Charlie quickly moved the tip against the collar. A fine spray of molten metal jetted from the collar, the slag solidifying instantly in the air as the magical power of the device fought to maintain its integrity. It was that unintentional safety that wound up keeping him from being burned by the plume.

"Magic seems to be trying to keep the collar together. How does it look from what you can see? I think I'm almost there," he said through gritted teeth.

Leila had turned her eyes away, but Bawb had cast some sort of protective spell, allowing him to gaze at the flames unharmed.

Of course the assassin would have something like that up his sleeve, Charlie mused.

"It appears to be nearly through, Charlie. Though the distant end also seems to be attempting to reconnect."

Shit. Must. Cut. Faster!

Charlie cranked up the cutter and kept going, moving as quickly as the device would allow.

Almost. Almost!

An enormous crack shook the air, and a shockwave of dissipated magic shot out across the wasteland as the collar fell from Charlie's neck, the glowing golden glyphs dark and silent, the band nothing more than inert metal.

"Are you okay?" Leila asked, concern in her eyes.

"Yeah. That actually wasn't so bad," Charlie lied, doing his best to hide the adrenaline shakes threatening to take hold.

He looked at Leila's collar, much slimmer than his. Of course, it made sense. After all, he was a dangerous gladiator who had flown a Zomoki. By comparison, cutting hers off should be a cinch.

"What do you say, Leila? Yours should come off pretty quickly. We should probably get it first. I have a feeling we'll need to rig something special for Ara's band. It's hella thick."

"And let us not forget, the band attempted to reattach itself when cut," Bawb added.

"Right. That too. We'll need something to wedge in there to block it."

Bawb removed what looked like a handkerchief from a hidden pocket. "I believe this might serve the purpose."

"A hanky?"

"Ootaki hair."

"Oh, shit. In that case, yeah, that just might work," he agreed. "But first, let's get Leila's off. This should only take a minute."

Charlie quickly set up the rig and slid the protective gear in place.

"Hang tight. This'll be quick," he said, then powered up the cutter.

As anticipated, Leila's was far easier to remove, and while it did unleash a similar surge of power, the intensity was far less than what Charlie's had let loose. Looking at Ara's massive collar, he shuddered to think what cutting that thing might release.

Charlie and Bawb set to work wedging huge pieces of heat shielding under the collar around Ara's neck. Despite her protests that heat really doesn't harm Zomoki, Charlie insisted.

"It's a plasma cutter from another galaxy, Ara. You're a

magical badass here, but this is from far, far away, so humor me, okay?"

The dragon chuckled warmly at his concern. "Very well, do as you wish."

He did, and a few short minutes later she was protected as well as she could be as the torch began slowly cutting into her collar. The metal was so much thicker than Charlie's, and the magical power contained within must have been enormous because no sooner would he make a cut than the molten metal would attempt to reconnect. Only Bawb's diligent use of magic and Ootaki hair to block it kept the slowly progressing cut open.

The plasma cutter abruptly sputtered out.

"Shit! What the hell? I know we're not out of gas," Charlie said as he rushed to the rig.

The problem was apparent immediately. He was correct, the unit did have an ample supply of gas. The problem was the power cells.

"They drained," he grumbled, tapping the dark display. "Must've had a faulty contact. I can rig something up from the reactor to trickle charge them back to capacity, but I'm afraid it's going to take some time before the cutter's ready to go again."

"Then I suggest you get to it," Ara said. "I sense a great power approaching. Massive. But it is still relatively far off. Unfortunately, I fear they will be able to track my collar fairly soon."

"Shit. Okay, I'm going to get this charge started ASAP."

"Earth slang," Bawb informed the Zomoki. "That means as soon as possible."

"Thank you, Geist."

"My pleasure."

Charlie had a makeshift charging system up and running within twenty minutes, but it would be a few hours before the power cells held enough juice to even dare try the cutter again.

From what he could tell, they had one more shot at it before being joined by some very unwelcome visitors.

"It'll take hours, and there's nothing we can do about that."

"Can we flee?" Leila asked.

"We could, but I don't think they'll leave this equipment intact when they find this place. No, this is our last, best chance at getting her collar off."

"So what do we do now?"

An idea struck him as he pulled the heat shielding from Ara's dull, worn scales.

"For now, I'm taking you water hunting."

CHAPTER FIFTY-SEVEN

Leila wrapped Baloo in his little swaddling harness and strapped him to her chest before climbing aboard the dragon's back. The flight Charlie had proposed wasn't a long one, but with every meal the squirming pup grew stronger. It would only be a matter of time before he managed to wiggle free of her grasp, and Leila wanted to be sure that didn't happen while they were aloft. Fortunately, their flight didn't take long at all.

Ara had only just completed a low-flying loop of the area surrounding the crashed spaceship when Charlie called out excitedly.

"There! That's the one. I'm almost sure of it."

"Almost?"

"Yes, Ara. It was a few years ago, and these piles of ruined rocks do mostly look the same. But even without the crash trail from my ship marking the way, that one looks familiar."

"Very well, then," she silently replied, then glided in for a soft landing beside the cluster of rock cairns that had caught Charlie's eye.

The shifting winds across the red soil had long ago filled the trench that had scarred the wasteland's surface. But the remains

of the stone structures dotting the landscape were far older––
and far more durable––than the humans' ship.

"Yeah, that's the spot. Right over there," Charlie said as they
dismounted. "Grab the digging tools. This should be it."

Bawb and Leila helped unload the gear from Ara's harness
and lugged it to the seemingly innocuous pile of rocks where
Charlie had already begun digging with his hands.

"Thanks," he said, grabbing a shovel and speeding his work.

Leila tied Baloo to a small outcropping and filled a water
dish for him, placing it in the shade. "Here you go, little guy.
Now you stay in the shade. We have some work to do."

The trio dug into the soil that was piled up against the rocks.
Ara seemed slightly agitated, sniffing the air.

"You okay?" Charlie asked.

"Yes. It just seems, *odd* here. Familiar, but not right."

Charlie paused and looked his friend in the eye. *"Are you
saying you were here* before *this happened? When Balamar was still
alive?"*

The look in her eye told him the answer.

"Jeez, Ara. Exactly how old are you?"

"A gentleman never asks."

He was working on a clever reply when Leila's shovel struck
stone.

"Hey, there's something here!" she called out excitedly as she
pulled dark, damp soil from the crack between the rocks. "Look.
It's damp."

"Yeah, I've seen this before. Last time I was here. The waters
we want are past that rock. Bob, what are you doing? We could
use a hand, here."

The fearless Wampeh assassin, however, had taken several
paces back and showed no signs of coming any closer.

"Wise One, are these truly the waters?"

Ara sniffed the air. "It seems that way, Geist."

"Then you know what they will do to me."

"I do." She turned to Charlie. "His kind are rather invulnerable to a great many things, but the Balamar waters are a power that is deadly to his rare variety of Wampeh."

"Oh? Like, even just touching it?"

"Yes, though I've never actually encountered it myself," the assassin said. "But stories of the effects among my people are clear enough. Simply put, a touch will burn my skin on contact, like acid or fire. Any more than that and I will combust."

"Holy shit. It's like some outer space holy water," Charlie said.

"This is not outer space, Charlie. We're on a planet."

"Yes, Bob, I know. But you get the idea," he said with a grin. "I swear, you sound more and more like a vampire every day."

"A what?"

"Tell ya later. An old Earth legend. Actually, given your tastes, you'll probably get a kick out of it."

"Are you two going to stand around talking, or are you going to help me dig?"

"Apologies. Where are my manners?" Charlie said as he began pulling dirt from the stone sealing the hidden cistern as he'd done years before. "But Bob's gonna sit this one out, I'm afraid."

Several minutes of digging later, they had finally uncovered the large rock Charlie had covered up after his previous visit to the wasteland. It was exactly as he left it. Well, exactly, *plus* a few extra feet of sand and red dirt that a recent storm had shifted atop the buried opening.

"Okay, it pivots on the smaller bit. We just need to lever it like this," he said, putting some muscle into the task. Unlike his first encounter, his limbs were more than up to the task after years of hard work and harder training. Moments later, the rock tilted aside.

"I'll grab the water containers," Leila said as Charlie slid into the opening.

"Thanks. Back soon," he told Ara, then vanished into the dark tunnel leading deep underground.

Unlike before, this time he had control of basic magic, and even the moisture in the air felt different as he walked down the carved stone path, rounding the curve and stepping into the vast subterranean cistern.

It was just as he'd left it. A large pool of faintly iridescent water in a strangely illuminated cavern. He didn't think twice as he stepped into the water and slipped into its depths.

The first time had been an innocent accident, a human where no human had ever been, swimming in what seemed to be a refreshing pool. Now he knew the truth about the waters. The power they contained. And with every moment in their depths, he felt his body's aches and pains diminish.

He was still very much carrying the power from his first visit within him, but now, with a tiny bit of Ara's blood flowing in his veins, the effects were amplified. Charlie swam to the rocky shore and sat chest-deep, drinking the waters deeply. He could sense the power spreading throughout his body, as if every cell was being born anew. The water would kill almost any who drank it in this galaxy, but the strange man from far away was not only immune, but also able to assimilate its power.

"What are you doing?" Leila asked from the shore. "We're supposed to be bringing this up to the surface, not going for a swim."

"I know, but it feels *amazing*," he replied. "Here, put your finger in the water. Don't drink any, of course, but let's see how your kind reacts to it. Ara thinks you should suffer no ill effects."

"Or I'll explode, like Bawb."

"Well, yeah. But I really don't think that's likely," Charlie said with a wry grin. "Just a drop, okay?"

Reluctantly, she held out her hand. "Okay. But just a drop."

Charlie took his hand from the water and held it over hers,

allowing a few drops to land on her palm. A faint glow emanated from the contact, then faded into her skin.

"Oh, my."

"Was that a good 'oh, my' or a bad 'oh, my'? I'm a man. Sometimes we don't know the difference."

"Silly. That was good. *Unusual.* The blister forming on my hand from digging is fading, and the irritation is gone."

"Well, that answers that. You're officially invited for a swim, so long as you remember not to drink, of course."

Leila hesitated at the water's edge, then stepped in. A light glow rippled across her skin as she sank in up to her neck.

"Oh my God. All of my aches and pains."

"Gone, right?"

"Yes. I feel *amazing.*"

"I know. It's incredible, right? I just wish Bob could join us. Poor guy could probably use it more than either of us," Charlie said.

"He just needs to drain someone dry and he'll feel fine, I'm sure."

"And Ara could sure as hell use a nice bath in here, I'd wager. But there's no way she's fitting through that tunnel."

"And smashing open the top would expose this to the elements. It would be gone forever."

"Well, technically, it doesn't evaporate like normal water," Charlie noted. "But if the cistern cracked, I imagine it would leach into the soil and disappear."

The pair reluctantly climbed out of the pool, their wet clothes sticking to their bodies. Leila looked at Charlie, and for just a moment, he had the briefest of flashbacks to his time in the pool with Rika. She had imbibed the waters as well, but it wasn't enough to save her from being lobotomized. But knowing what he now did about the water's properties, Charlie couldn't help but wonder how much she had healed over the years.

SCOTT BARON

Unfortunately, she'd been sold off and was long gone. Just another victim of the Tslavar slave trade.

"Come on, let's get back to the surface," he said, picking up the water containers and beginning the trek up to their friends.

"Please stay back," Bawb said when he saw the soaked duo climb from the opening.

"Don't worry, man. I wasn't gonna hug you or anything," Charlie joked. "But *you*, on the other hand," he said, warmly rubbing Ara's flank. "I've got something for you."

He took the larger of the containers and poured a slow stream of water across her scales. They seemed almost to absorb it rather than let it run off into the soil, and despite being dry and dull, Charlie could have sworn he saw a little more color to them.

Ara shuddered at the sensation. "It's been so very long," she said. "Thank you, Charlie. Even this little bit is a wonder I never thought I'd feel again."

A light bulb lit up in Charlie's mind.

"Hey, Leila. Fill up the rest of the containers, will ya?"

"Of course. But what are you going to do?"

"I'm gonna have Ara give me a quick lift back to the ship. There's a couple of pieces of gear I think she'll really appreciate."

With that, Charlie climbed atop the Zomoki and flew back to the crashed *Asbrú* to gather a small power cell and his other components. If things were still functional and he could make his idea work, his giant, scaly friend was going to love this.

CHAPTER FIFTY-EIGHT

"What, exactly, is that thing supposed to do?" Ara asked as Charlie unloaded the salvaged equipment and power cell from her harness.

Most of their gear was already unloaded back at the camp, but they'd all decided it would be wise if she kept the harness system on for the time being to more easily carry any needed supplies while in the wastelands. It was also proving most helpful in Charlie's little experiment.

"It's a cooling system pump," he said, unstrapping the unit from her rig and carrying it to the opening in the rock formation.

"It is not *that* hot out, Charlie. Are you ill?"

"No, not like that," he chuckled. "We used this as a backup should we need to direct coolant fluid to certain systems should they overheat."

"And?"

"And those systems were torn out of the ship, but this baby was spared. So now, with the help of this power cell I scraped up, I'm going to fire it up and get you all the water you need."

"I fail to see how."

Charlie pulled open the duffel bag he'd hastily filled. Lengths of hosing tumbled to the ground.

"With these," he replied. "Just need to apply a dab of silicone to the gaskets and connect them together, then we should have a long enough run to reach the cistern."

Bawb watched with interest––from a few paces back, of course. "This will pull the waters to the surface?"

"Not all of them, but yeah. I'd suggest you stand well upwind when we fire it up. Wouldn't want you accidentally getting splashed."

"I will fly him back to our camp while you work. I do not wish to risk any harm to our Wampeh friend," Ara said. She turned to Bawb. "Are you ready to head out?"

"Of course, Wise One," he replied, nimbly climbing onto her back.

A moment later, she was airborne while Charlie showed Leila how to connect the hoses. By the time Ara returned, they'd run a line all the way to the cistern and were just connecting the final length of hose to the end of the pump.

"This'll be a whole lot easier than carrying up bucket after bucket," Charlie said as he locked the final piece into place. "You ready?"

"Indeed," the mighty Zomoki replied.

"Okay, then. Here goes."

Charlie flipped the switch on the unit, sending power to the impellers. The pump hummed and vibrated as a powerful suction ran the length of the hose into the depths of the hidden cavern system. Then the length in his hands became rigid with pressure.

"In three. Two. One––"

He opened the nozzle and unleashed the stream of water. It was no firehose by any means, but the system was quite adequate for their needs. A stream of water arced through the air, a fine mist wafting as it did, creating a beautiful rainbow in the luminescent droplets.

As soon as the stream hit Ara's massive body, she began steaming under the twin suns. As before, the water seemed to absorb into the dried-out scales rather than running into the soil, though with the quantity being applied, some certainly did.

The Zomoki looked almost like a cat having its sweet spot scratched, her body twitching involuntarily in places.

"Yes!" she exclaimed, blissed out from the healing waters.

"So, this was a good idea, then?"

"You have no idea."

Charlie laughed to himself. *"I think I have an inkling."*

Head to toe he sprayed her down, which, for a beast of her considerable size, took a fair amount of time. He had moved from tail to tip and was just running the water over her head when Baloo slipped his harness and ran into the mist as best his little legs would carry him. The fine droplets swirled around him, creating a sheen on the pup before absorbing through his coat, making him steam a little in the heat.

"No, Baloo. Come back here!" Leila scolded.

Charlie watched, amused, as she scooped him up in her arms and carried him back to the shady spot he'd been tied up in. Turning his attention back to the task at hand, the mist, he noted, seemed to have dissipated. Then he saw why.

Ara had turned unexpectedly and caught the stream in her mouth, drinking deeply while he was watching Leila and Baloo.

"What are you doing?" Charlie shouted, quickly shutting off the stream.

Ara snapped out of her blissful daze. "What? Oh, that. I don't know. I was just thirsty, and feeling so good."

"But you said——"

"I know, but I'm much larger than other creatures," she said, a flash of uncertainty in her eyes. "I should be fine. Now, we should get back to camp. Your device may be ready by now."

"Right," Charlie said, nervously eyeing his friend. "We've got containers filled, so I'm going to bury the cistern again, just in case. Wouldn't want anyone else stumbling upon it."

"No, that we would not, indeed," she replied.

"Leila, load her up, will ya? I'm going to seal things up and bury the entrance."

"Of course," she said, hefting the water containers. "I'll get them strapped in, then I'll give you a hand."

They both worked quickly, then, once everything was buried and hidden, Leila scooped up Baloo and they climbed atop their friend for the relatively short flight back to their camp. Before they did, however, Ara flapped her wings mightily several times, blowing clean any traces of their visiting that particular pile of rocks among the hundreds in the wasteland.

"Ara, what's wrong?" Leila asked as she touched down unsteadily at camp. Then she noticed the giant Zomoki's collar was beginning to glow. It was a tiny bit, but something had triggered the device.

"Charlie, you see this?"

"Yeah. Maktan must be getting closer."

Ara twitched in pain.

"Help me unload these," Leila said, urgently pulling the water containers from their friend's harness. They'd removed nearly all of them when Ara lurched backward unexpectedly, crying out in pain.

"What's happening?" Bawb asked.

Ara seemed not to hear him, her collar glowing a little more brightly as she fell to the ground, curling herself into a ball, her head tucked under one wing, but the collar still visible, the runes pulsing ever so slightly.

Her scales seemed to harden and dry out, quickly losing the little luster they still retained. Whatever was happening to her, Ara was quite unaware of the goings-on around her. She heaved one last time, then fell silent, her hide as cold and hard as stone.

"Ara? Can you hear me?" he asked, silently.

Nothing.

"What the hell just happened?" Charlie said in shock.

"I-I believe we have lost Ara," Bawb said quietly. "And with her, our only way out of here."

The collar glowed clearly now. Something was coming. Someone. And they knew exactly who it would be.

Charlie sank to his knees, his gut twisting in shock. Slowly he rose and gave his friend one last look, then turned to the others, anger and fierce determination in his eye. "We need to set up defenses. They're going to come for us, but we don't have to go easily. And we can take as many of those fuckers with us as we can."

"While we have gathered a fair collection of slaaps and konuses, I am afraid we are at an enormous disadvantage out here. There are no woods to hide in. No town to blend in with the locals. And we are going to be terribly out-powered when they arrive," Bawb said, stating facts but making no move to flee.

An abandoned crate in the pile caught Charlie's eye.

"Yeah, but we do have something they won't expect," he said, opening the container. The gasket hissed as it touched fresh air for the first time in years.

By some great fortune, the Tslavars had sealed it back up before discarding it as junk when they captured him. Charlie picked up one of the machine guns and cycled it once.

Oiled and ready. Just as they'd left them.

"The Tslavars had no idea what they had in their hands," he said, offering one to the Geist. "The mechanism is pretty simple. Just point the open end of the tube at the enemy and squeeze that curved bit shaped to accept your finger."

Charlie then showed him how to swap out magazines and chamber a round.

"I do not like this device. It *feels* wrong. But in our current circumstance, I shall make use of any weapon at our disposal."

"Good," Charlie said. "Here, Leila. Take this. It's a pistol.

327

Smaller and easier to handle, it's the same principle but better for closer range. And a word of warning, it is loud. Why don't you fire off one shot, just to get comfortable with it?"

Leila did, and while the violence of the non-magical device was distressing, she seemed quite in control of it.

"Okay. We don't have a ton of ammo, but they'll be expecting magic and will be casting spells to defend against that, not these. The range isn't great, but we should be able to take some of them by surprise. I doubt any of them have spells to protect against bullets. They may modify defenses for projectiles, but by the time they do, we will have given them something to think about. Maybe buy ourselves a little time."

Time for what, was the question hanging in the air.

Charlie knew full well that recapture would almost certainly mean death. And if not, it would be a life where that would have been a preferable option.

Bawb geared up in his impressive collection of powered equipment, from his Ootaki undershirt to his gauntlet konuses. He filled every pocket and pouch with slaaps and konuses they had taken from the enemy during their flight. Charlie, likewise, carried all he could, and even Leila was sporting a pair of well-charged konuses on her wrists.

They settled in and scanned the horizon, unsure when, or how, the attack would come.

But come, it surely would.

CHAPTER FIFTY-NINE

The first line of Council ships looked like no more than specks of dust in the wind as they approached. Had it not been for the steadily glowing collar around Ara's neck, they might not have noticed their arrival until too late.

"Prepare your defenses. They're here," Bawb said, squinting at the approaching craft.

Charlie and Leila scoured the horizon until they too saw the distinct movement of the nearing vessels. Bawb looked at Ara's collar. It remained the same.

"The visla is not among those ships," he noted. "These are no more than advance scouts, moving in to survey our numbers and defenses. The rest of their fleet is likely just out of range at the far edge of the wasteland."

"Why wouldn't they just attack?" Leila asked.

"Because we have a Zomoki, and a very powerful one at that. Surely they have heard of some of our encounters since fleeing the visla's estate."

"Shit, so that's probably how they stayed on our tail."

"Yes, Charlie, to an extent. However, I believe this has

ultimately worked out to our benefit. They are cautious now. Perhaps too cautious. This, we can leverage to our advantage."

Bawb pulled a pair of exceptionally heavy konuses from his pouch and slid them atop his other devices.

"Shouldn't you be saving those for the main attack?"

"If they realize our weakness, they will be of little use," he replied, looking at Ara's inert form. "We have lost our most powerful weapon. Should they report back, the entirety of their forces will descend upon us. Only their uncertainty buys us time."

He turned and began casting spells the like of which Charlie had never heard. Strange, powerful spells that nevertheless appeared to be doing nothing. Charlie knew better than to interrupt the assassin with questions while he was concentrating. Finally, after long minutes, the casting stopped. Fine beads of sweat evaporated from the Geist's brow in the heat.

"That should get their attention," he said, amused, casting the drained konuses aside into his storage bag.

"You drained them *entirely*?" Charlie asked, amazed.

"Indeed. And well worth the expenditure. I only hope it stops them before they see we are no longer protected by a Zomoki. If they skree back to their leaders that we are without her, all will be lost."

Charlie looked at the bulk of the motionless dragon. His friend. He'd lost others, but this one hurt in a different way. But there was no time for mourning. He had to think quickly. There was simply no way to bury her or otherwise hide her from view. No spell he knew of had that kind of ability.

"What about an *occulo*?" Leila asked. "It might confuse them."

"We do not have the materials to create the substrate needed, unfortunately. A good idea, though. Very creative and unconventional tactics," Bawb said appreciatively.

330

Charlie watched a distant sandstorm off in the distance. Much as they were not fans of the gritty bombardment, they could really use the cover one would provide about now.

Hang on a second. Sand!

Charlie gathered a handful of the red sand and placed it beneath the nozzle of the plasma cutter. *There's a bit of charge*, he noted. And there would definitely not be enough time to fully charge the device. *What the hell.*

He flipped the switch and fired up the plasma cutter, a burst of intense heat instantly turning the sand into a molten mass. He cut the power and used a knife blade to spread the glowing blob into a small disc.

"What are you doing?" Bawb asked. "That device cannot possibly target the approaching vessels."

"No, it can't," he said. "But it can test a theory."

"How so?"

"With this," he said, casting a gentle cooling spell combined with a few drops of the iridescent water they had brought back from the cistern.

The drop spread out to a molecule-thin coating, which then spread evenly across the surface as it cooled, bonding to the material. What resulted was a crude mirror. Bawb looked at his reflection and recoiled.

"I am backward! What manner of magic is this?" he said, quickly checking himself, ensuring he was in fact not altered in any way.

"It's a mirror," Charlie said. "Something from my galaxy. Like an *occulo* spell, only naturally occurring."

"It is in reverse."

"Yes. Like looking into very still water. And if we make a large enough one––or at least enough big pieces––we can use them to break up Ara's shape from the air. It will look like a jumble of angles that can't possibly exist."

Bawb nodded appreciatively. "This is ingenious."

"I can't take credit. Not entirely. It was something I learned about way back in boot camp. An old kind of camouflage used a few centuries ago when men relied on their eyes to find targets. This was well before tracking and targeting systems evolved to where the human eye was obsolete. They called it 'Dazzle' originally. It wouldn't work for a damn to protect against radar scans from my world, but for Council scouts using their eyes, it just might work."

"Then we should begin immediately. What do you require?"

"If you have a smelting spell of some kind, you need to melt big sheets of sand like I did with the plasma cutter. You can't touch the waters, but Leila can apply a tiny bit to each, then use a general spreading spell. The water doesn't evaporate like normal water would, and it seems to bond to the glass of its own accord."

"Clever. And dangerous. But I shall do as you request," Bawb said, gathering a lesser konus so as to not drain his main devices while carrying out the task.

They moved quickly, and in less than ten minutes had many improvised mirrors laid out across Ara's body. They piled sand and debris against her as well, further adding to the camouflage. They couldn't tell exactly how it would look from the air, but Charlie felt it was good enough. If it wasn't, they'd find out soon enough.

The Council ships sped their approach as they neared, having apparently assessed the situation enough to realize there was no major defensive position to hinder their flight. Bawb began casting narrowly targeted force spells while the ships were still far out. There were only a half dozen, but an additional several larger ships were following in their wake a few minutes behind.

"What are you doing? Don't waste your power," Charlie urged.

"Trust me."

The ships easily deflected the spells, their casters having no trouble with the Geist's seemingly-desperate attempts. Charlie was about to make a crack along the lines of 'told you so,' when a great, shuddering flash blasted out above. Three of the ships exploded and plummeted from the sky. Two of them banked sharply into each other and spun to the ground, where they broke apart on impact. One of them, however, dropped like a rock.

Bawb uttered what sounded a lot like a Drook spell, targeting the plummeting craft. A faint hover spell latched onto the hull, and while it hit the ground hard, it remained intact.

"What the hell did you do?" Charlie asked, amazed. "I didn't know you had spells that could smash through their defensive shields."

"I don't," Bawb said with a satisfied grin as he surveyed the destruction. "But I do know quite a few powerful stun spells."

Realization dawned on his human friend. "Holy shit. You weren't attacking them with those long shots. You were making them focus on force shield defenses."

"Precisely."

"And those spells you cast earlier. The ones that drained those big-ass konuses. You left a bunch of stun fields hanging up there in the sky, didn't you?"

"Very perceptive."

Leila looked at the wreckage, confused. "But they should have been able to deflect those."

"Normally, yes. But with my barrage of direct force assaults, they shifted all of their attention to stopping that type of attack. With no other spells being cast and thrown in their direction, that would have been a tactically sound decision, normally."

"Only you left booby traps in the sky," she realized. "And they didn't see them cast because you did it a while ago. But the amount of power needed for them to stay in place that long with nothing solid to anchor them——"

"Would be extreme, yes. Possibly enough to drain a konus, even," he said with a smile. "And the sand in the air provided a small––but effective––aid to the process."

"You knocked out the Drooks."

"And the ships fell from the sky. Yes. Five of six are destroyed. As for the final one, those not killed outright by the deceleration will certainly be immobilized for a little while."

The larger ships behind the scout craft circled the area, holding a perimeter as they tested the defensive spells. Unsure how to proceed, several dropped to the surface a ways away and unloaded their ground forces.

"It seems we will have a more conventional fight on our hands soon, and it's only a matter of time before they figure out the aerial traps," Bawb said as he fired off a series of diversionary attacks. "I fear that while they fell for the first series, these other craft will clear them once their men close in on the perimeter. They will assault us full-on shortly."

As predicted, a ground battle commenced, with magic flying as the Council troops swarmed toward the crashed Earth ship. The wreck provided decent cover, and Bawb and Charlie used it to their advantage to fling spells back at the attackers from relative safety. Bawb's were deadly, while Charlie opted for diversionary ones until his foes were closer.

The charging men were out in the open, but with the threat of the wrath of their Council leaders should they turn back, they ran headlong into the blender of defensive spells. Better to die in battle than at the dissatisfied hands of their masters.

Bawb cast quickly, switching from slaap to konus as easily as breathing. Charlie had forgotten that he had topped up on Yanna Sok's blood––and therefore her power––not long ago. The boost made him a far more formidable enemy than the Council had anticipated.

Also shocking the assaulting troops were the occasional projectiles that pierced their shields and thinned their ranks from quite a distance. Charlie was never the top gun marksman in his brief stint in the military, but he had achieved high enough rankings, and today he made every shot count.

Side by side the men fought while Leila cast the defensive spells they had taught her, keeping stray attacks from landing a lucky hit.

A roar sounded above as one of the large ships sped past them, quickly banking around for another pass.

"The ships have figured a way around my traps, it seems," Bawb said, resigned to his fate. "It has been an honor fighting beside you both."

He did not stop casting, but he also made no attempt to seek additional cover in retreat. The legendary assassin was not going to be captured, that much was certain. Given the forces about to assail them, Charlie didn't think that would be an option anyway.

CHAPTER SIXTY

Once the Council ships had found the means to pass the Geist's clever aerial spell shields, it was just a matter of minutes before all of them were through, carefully lining up their attacks, while their ground troops continued their assault.

"We're cooked," Charlie said, reluctantly accepting the situation. "I might be able to overload the ship's reactor. The blast would be rather impressive."

The others looked at him and nodded. At least they would take a lot of those bastards with them.

A massive explosion rocked the air, followed by another, then another. Chunks of flaming wreckage dropped from the sky as the Council ships were torn to pieces by spell blasts far beyond their capacity to defend. The destruction lasted only a few moments. Then all was still in the air.

For a moment, anyway.

The massive shape of a familiar ship rocketed through the smoke and floating debris, its weapons now targeting the hordes of troops on the ground. The destruction was brutally efficient, and those not killed outright turned tail and ran, willing to face the wrath of their vislas rather than the certain and violent fate that had just swooped in on them.

The *Rixana* made another pass, strafing the survivors for good measure before dropping her cargo shuttle then quickly pulling up to a safe position in low orbit.

The shuttle dove in hard, avoiding the few shots from the survivors on the ground. Its doors opened, and two dozen men spilled out, strapped to the teeth with weaponry, their bandoliers bulging with tools of destruction. The few holdouts on the ground didn't stand a chance. Within minutes, the pirate horde had wiped them out to a man, stripping them of all weapons, then double-timing it to the cover of Charlie's crashed ship.

"Marban?" Charlie said in disbelief as the men swarmed into the shadow of the wrecked craft.

"Hello, little brother! Excellent day for a hunt, wouldn't you say?"

The men embraced there and then in the middle of a battlefield. Charlie would say it was just dust in his eyes that had made them damp, had anyone asked.

"How did you––?"

"Oh, we did some asking around after we last met," Marban said. "You've really started something, it would seem."

"What do you mean? And why the hell would you risk yourselves like this? You're pirates, not rebels. This isn't your cause, and now you've put yourselves at risk."

"Not that we don't appreciate it," Leila interjected.

"Of course. We're grateful, no doubt. But still," Charlie continued.

Bawb walked over to the scarred pirate and took his hand in greeting. "It is good to see you, Pirate."

"And you, Assassin."

Bawb laughed. "Ah, so you know my calling?"

"And your reputation, *Geist*," he said. "From one of the brotherhood of violent men to another, it is an honor to fight alongside you."

"Is that even a thing?" Charlie asked.

"No. But it sounds rather badass, don't you think?" Marban replied with a hearty laugh.

"I do, actually. Maybe we should start a club and make T-shirts if we somehow survive this. But you haven't answered my question. Why risk yourselves, the *Rixana*, for us?"

A look crossed Marban's face. One Charlie had seen once or twice in the past. Whatever he'd been before his pirating days, his sense of honor ran true and deep.

"Because the systems are aflame with rebellion, and you were the spell that ignited the fire. The Council ships at the edge of the battlefield are rumored to contain the Council's secret weapon. A terrible weapon they've had in the works for many, many years."

"The doomsday device?" Bawb asked, his eyebrow arched high.

"According to the Council turncoat who joined our cause, yes. Something only a handful know of, housed and protected within a ship at the rear of their formation. We hope he will obtain its exact position for us shortly. Once we know which it is, we will blast it from the sky before the Council can utilize it."

"Solid plan."

"Yes. And knowing that weapon is here, the rebels in the other systems are free to fight without fear of it being unleashed upon them. So there it is. We either stop this now, or never."

"What do you mean?"

"There is no going back to a life of anonymity, dodging the Council and working at the periphery of their sphere of influence. Because of you, word of the Council's plans has leaked out. Their plans for war. Rebellion is spreading, and rapidly. It didn't need much, to be honest, but you provided the reason for *all* of the oppressed systems to stand up to the Council. There's even a slave uprising."

"Seriously?"

"Yes. When word that the impetus for all of this was not just a former gladiator, but also a *slave*, well, the discussions of slave labor versus paid labor gained momentum. It's something many have advocated for a long time, arguing men would gladly work harder and more efficiently for safety, lodging, and a decent wage. When you factor in all the power costs of maintaining restraint collars and overall living costs, it actually comes out about the same. I notice you no longer wear a collar, by the way. Leading by example, I see."

"Alien emancipation. Who'd have thought?"

"It's early days, and that's a whole other discussion, but slaves and rebels are fighting together, and the Council has found itself spread thin with so many fires to extinguish. They never expected to be this spread out, and as a result, even with superior weaponry, they no longer have the advantage of sheer force."

"Twenty brutes against several hundred? I bet they're having their power tested at every turn," Bawb noted. "A most intriguing development. This means the assault force hounding us would be led by Visla Maktan himself."

The pirate nodded.

Charlie picked up a container of water, then locked eyes with Bawb a moment. The Geist nodded.

"Hey, Marban, come with me a minute. I want to show you something."

"Lead the way, little brother," he said, following Charlie into the ship's hull. When they emerged a few minutes later, he seemed to have a distinct spring in his step, and to those looking more closely, his hair appeared to steam slightly in the sun's rays, almost as if he'd recently been wet.

"I have to admit, Charlie, you do not cease to amaze,"

Marban said with a chuckle. "This craft of yours, I'd have liked to see it when it was intact. The design and tech-magic are confounding, but fascinating all the same. And I recall you once said that you actually helped design it."

"That was a lifetime ago."

"Nevertheless, I can appreciate the effort, despite its current condition."

"But it's no *Rixana*."

"Well, no. But she's a special ship, and one I've grown very attached to over the years," Marban said. He glanced over at the hulking shape camouflaged by mirrors and debris. "I'm truly sorry to see you've lost your Zomoki friend, Charlie. She seemed a good sort and would have proven a useful ally."

Charlie nodded his somber agreement.

Marban turned and surveyed the destruction of the battlefield with sharp, clear eyes, then spoke to his assembled men. "Okay, you lot. It's going to get ugly pretty soon. Eat and rest. There is a good chance many of us will not see tomorrow, so let us all make a damn good showing of it!"

A little cheer of agreement rippled through the pirates, and Charlie couldn't help but feel a swelling of pride in his chest. His former crew of pillaging lunatics were backing a cause. And if Marban was right about the momentum the nascent rebellion had gained, there was actually a possibility they might win.

"Hey Bob, what do you think about—" He looked around, but the Wampeh was nowhere to be seen. "Bob? Hey, has anyone seen a pale, bloodthirsty vampire dude?" he joked.

No one had.

"Leila, where'd he go off to?" he asked, concern growing.

"I don't know, Charlie. He must've slipped away while we were digging in with Marban's men."

Charlie scanned the wasteland, looking for his friend. There was no sign of him.

"Hang on," he said, his eyes widening slightly. "Where'd that downed Council ship go?"

CHAPTER SIXTY-ONE

The surviving crew of the lone Council craft to escape destruction were astounded at their good luck when they abruptly woke and came to their senses. The pilots had survived, though one had broken her leg during the crash. Two of the three Drooks powering the craft were also unharmed, though the third would require serious healing to ever power a craft again.

A contingent of troops had been aboard as well, all of them anxiously awaiting the opportunity to prove their worth in the assault. Unfortunately for them, all appeared to have broken their necks on impact. It was highly unusual for so many to die in that manner, but the pilots saw the flaming wreckage of the large vessels and decided it was high time to flee back to the others to regroup. They could figure out what happened to the troops later.

"Craft *Arvanus Three* requesting passage," the injured pilot said as they approached the waiting ships, all nestled safely on the ground at the very far edge of the wastelands.

"You were to complete your assault, *Arvanus Three*."

"We tried, but all the other ships were destroyed. We lost one of our Drooks, and the troops aboard were all killed in our crash."

A long silence hung in the air, then her skree crackled to life. "Very well. Passphrase?"

"Magnanus oralian," she replied.

"You are clear to pass, *Arvanus Three*. Your presence has been requested aboard the command vessel for debriefing when you arrive."

"Understood," she replied.

Sitting in plain view among the dead soldiers, safely camouflaged by his shimmer, Bawb was glad he let the pilots live. The passphrase would have been the end of his little venture. He was even more pleased with his choice when three more different phrases were requested as they flew deeper into the ranks of the waiting forces.

The ship landed at the rear of the parked ships, safely behind the much larger vessels. The injured pilot and her associate stumbled from the craft, while a small team of slaves removed the bodies of the dead soldiers. The Drooks were left in place, their injured friend assessed and determined to be salvageable. He was no sooner removed from his seat than a replacement was sent to take his place. The ship would fly again, and soon, it seemed.

Bawb, however, had other plans.

When the slaves had cleared the craft, the Wampeh assassin cast a very light sleep spell, knocking the Drooks out without obvious signs of attack. Shedding the hood of his shimmer cloak, he bent their necks to the side, drinking deep from them one by one, until barely any power remained in their slumbering bodies. He then cast a healing spell, erasing the puncture marks on their necks.

The Council commanders would be confused, but they would not know what had befallen their Drooks until it was too late.

Bawb exposed his armlets and focused the Drook energy swimming inside of him, sending it into the power rod lodged in the decorative metal. Soon, the full power of three Drooks was safely stored away, ready for use at a later time.

Silently, he snuck from the craft, his shimmer protecting him from prying eyes, his assassin skills silencing his every footstep.

His plan was simple. Sneak onto the main command ship and slaughter as many as he could. Cutting the head off the beast was their best bet to stop the doomsday weapon from ever being triggered, and if that meant he took out Visla Maktan in the process, all the better.

He had quietly dispatched a pair of guards and hidden their bodies when a startling roar filled the sky. Defensive spells were all cast toward the front of the fleet in the direction of the battle, but this was coming from behind. Behind, and above.

The *Rixana* dove hard, all of her substantial destructive spells aimed at a single ship. The craft was positioned between two larger vessels, but the attack avoided those, singling out the slightly smaller craft, which promptly burst into flames and broke in half from the sheer ferocity of the barrage.

"The doomsday ship," Bawb muttered as he realized their inside man had come through. The *Rixana* had managed to down the craft with a single, audacious attack. But what if the contents could be salvaged? Bawb could not allow that to happen.

With great haste, the Wampeh skirted the flaming debris and plunged headlong into the wreckage of the craft. If any of the doomsday weapon was still intact, he would be sure to destroy it before it could be retrieved. Much as he wanted Maktan's life, this was simply more important to the greater cause of the rebellion.

Judging by the distress in the faces of the men who had exited the nearby ships and were now racing toward the wreck, he would have to move fast. Whatever was in there, they all seemed greatly concerned for its recovery.

With a disregard for safety, the assassin sped through the flaming wreckage. The front of the ship seemed to have taken the brunt of the attack. Nothing could have survived, he surmised. So, the back it was.

Bawb raced through the shattered corridors, scanning everywhere for this weapon of ultimate destruction. He found a particularly thick door—rent partially open from the explosions. The very nature of its construction told him this was what he was looking for. Whatever was inside was the deadliest weapon ever seen, and he had to get in there and destroy it before the Council's lackeys arrived.

With a focused blast from his slaap, Bawb bent the door back farther on its ruined track until enough of an opening presented itself for him to force his way in. The lights were still functioning on a standby spell that stayed active even when the ship was demolished.

In the flickering glow, what he saw took his breath away. Something entirely unexpected.

CHAPTER SIXTY-TWO

Dozens of dead Ootaki were strapped to their seats, shining gold collars pale in comparison to their brilliant hair. And the hair, the length was extraordinary. It must have taken decades to grow, the power within increasing every single day as the Council––a group of the most powerful magic users in the galaxy––poured additional power into the Ootaki over the years.

It seemed obvious, and horrible. They must have been taken as infants, kept as slaves their entire lives, raised for this one terrible purpose. They had never been shorn, and as such, held an even greater amount of power than would have been expected. These poor, peaceful beings were to have their hair harvested, the power behind a most terrible weapon.

But they were dead. And with their demise, all power in their uncut locks was lost forever, instantly dissipated into the ether. There had been a fortune great enough to buy a small planet aboard that one ship, and with one well-placed attack, the pirate rebels had robbed the Council of not only a vast amount of wealth, but of the power source for their weapon as well.

Bawb quickly scanned the chamber. Most of the Ootaki had

died from concussive impact, but others seemed to have lost their lives from the shower of shrapnel sent flying when the ship broke apart and crashed.

Something was off. Not all of the berths were filled. *Some* of the Ootaki had not been aboard the ship. A great amount of power was still present somewhere on the battlefield. Enough to wipe out thousands, if his guess was correct. He had to warn the others.

His enchanted blade flew into his hand at the sound of metal scraping behind him. Bawb dove on instinct, rebounding from a crumpled wall, lunging blade-first toward his adversary.

Only the reflexes of one of the greatest assassins alive kept his knife from sinking home in the chest of the Ootaki who had miraculously survived, her bloodshot, concussed eyes trying desperately to focus as she attempted to free herself from the debris fallen atop her.

She was the lone survivor. A freak bit of luck had collapsed a portion of hull around her in just the right way to deflect the bulk of the barrage. She was still obviously knocked senseless by the explosions, but she was alive. Bawb assessed the young woman.

Mid-twenties, by his guess, with arm-thick braids of golden hair wrapped in loops around her body. He wondered if its magical power, combined with such a density of golden locks, had protected her as well, forming a sort of magical shell around her body. It was possible, but unlikely. The others hadn't survived, after all. No, she was just lucky.

He moved the large piece of metal from atop her, then began working at the enchanted straps holding her in her seat. The young woman's senses started to return, and at the sight of the battle-dirty Wampeh, she started to scream, thrashing violently in her restraints as panic set in.

Bawb quickly silenced her with a firm hand over her mouth. The look of pure terror in her eyes triggered something in him.

An unusual sensation for a man of his profession. But odd as it was, he felt empathy for her.

Perhaps it had been all that time spent with Charlie and his friends. Their do-good ways were starting to rub off on him, perhaps. Whatever the reason, Bawb the assassin did something unexpected. He released his grip.

"Do not scream. I am not going to hurt you," he said as soothingly as he could, locking his gaze with hers with as kind a look as he could manage. "I am not with the Council. I am going to set you free."

He removed his hand entirely and waited.

For a moment it appeared the panicked woman would begin shrieking again, and that would bring the Council guards in no time, but to his pleasant surprise, she seemed to calm down as she stared into his eyes. A little twist of something in his chest almost made Bawb wince, but he maintained his stoic expression.

"I am Bawb," he said, slowly moving his blade so as not to alarm her. "I am going to cut you free now. What is your name?" he asked as he began slicing her restraints.

"Hunze," she replied in a weak voice.

"Did you say Hunze?"

The young woman nodded.

"Okay, Hunze, here's what's going to happen. I am going to get you out of here and back to my friends, but before we do, I need to do something about that collar."

He dug in his pouch, producing a fine handkerchief of golden thread. Hunze's eyes went wide as she realized what it was made of.

"I assure you, none of your kin were harmed in the acquisition of this," he said soothingly as he wrapped the collar tightly. "There. That should block it, at least for a short while. Now come with me."

She sat motionless, paralyzed with fear.

"Hunze, I want you to listen to me," he said, gently taking her hands in his. "I swear to you on my honor, no harm will befall you so long as I am by your side. But if we do not move quickly, I fear this will be for naught."

Slowly, she rose to her feet, and Bawb could see the full extent of the hair wrapped around her body. The braids were simply massive, and at her age, the amount of power the great lengths held was enormous. She caught him examining her hair and flinched.

"No, you do not have to fear me. I have no interest in your locks. I will not take them from you, nor will I allow any of my brethren to touch a single hair on your head."

It was odd, but for some reason the assassin known as the Geist knew what he was saying was true. He would defend this unknown innocent to his last breath.

"They really must be rubbing off on me," he muttered as he took her hand and led her from the chamber.

There were Council forces approaching, he realized, and if they saw her, it would be over before it began. Bawb searched the wreckage for anything that might be of use, something to protect her with. Then he saw it.

"Yes. That will do perfectly."

He ushered the Ootaki woman into the charred cargo conveyance. It was a simple thing, essentially a minorly Drook-powered crate that floated where the operator wished. For their purposes, it was perfect. Perfect, and left his hands free for dirtier work.

Bawb silently dispatched a half dozen men as he led the floating box from the ship, donning the long, protective coat of one of the fallen troops along the way.

"They need reinforcements in the cargo hold," he called to the men jogging toward the ship. "You'd better hurry!"

The attack had been from above, and they were surrounded by the most powerful forces for a dozen systems, so none of the troops even thought to question the man walking *away* from the wreckage. A few minutes later, Bawb secured the crate in the abandoned transport he had arrived in. The Drooks would be of no use to him, but he had all the Drook power he needed in his armlet.

Carefully, he directed the power to the ship and took off. Unlike his entry to the most secure areas, his departure did not require pass-phrases. And it was a good thing. While the ship was certainly airworthy, he didn't think it could withstand a heated pursuit.

Clear of the fleet, he flew low and slow, taking a wide loop around his friends to approach from the far side, where the automated defenses would not shoot him down. He just hoped the skree message he had sent had reached the *Rixana*. He had no desire of being shot out of the sky.

CHAPTER SIXTY-THREE

"I do not see why your friend finds this so distasteful," Marban said, hefting the small carbine with the appreciative hands of a man who had seen much combat. "I mean, yes, it is a foreign weapon, powered by a strange tech-magic I do not quite understand––though the concept of combustion you have described makes basic sense. Regardless, it is elegant in its inelegance."

Charlie handed him his pistol.

"Here, try this. It's a hand-held variant. Smaller, less power, but more portable and, of course, concealable."

Marban handed him the long gun and took the pistol in his hand. After only an initial discussion on the subject, his trigger discipline was already exemplary.

"So I just point and squeeze, like the other?"

"Yes. But don't lock your elbow when you do. The kick can be uncomfortable until you get used to it."

"And I line up these glowing dots on what I wish to harm, yes?"

"You're a natural, Marban."

"Why, thank you, little brother," the pirate said with a jovial grin.

When the Geist had disappeared from camp, taking the downed Council craft with him, he had left behind the strange weapons from Charlie's world. But it wasn't because he disliked them. Far from it, actually.

He hadn't achieved his reputation and stayed alive so long by shying away from new methods of killing. However, given the speed with which he would be moving, and the fluidity of the situation, he deemed it unwise to rely on any weapon—however effective—that he was not entirely familiar with.

His enchanted blades, slaaps, and konuses, however, were as much a part of him as his body and could be wielded without conscious thought. Those, along with his very customized shimmer, were all he wore as he raced to one of the most dangerous targets of his career, the firearms left behind where he was certain Charlie would see them.

The result was an additional tool now in Marban's hands as they prepared for the next wave of violence, however it may present itself. There were only a few guns, but Jamal Quick, the long-dead security and emergency response team leader from his crashed ship, had packed a fair amount of ammunition.

It seemed odd to Charlie at the time. They were making a simple test flight, not preparing for battle, but Jamal had his routines, it seemed, and one of them was a certain degree of basic preparation, regardless of the situation's needs.

And the current needs made Charlie quite grateful for Jamal's seeming overpacking.

Better to have it and not need it, than need it and not have it, he thought with a smile as he watched Marban take a few more practice shots to familiarize himself with the weapons.

"You feeling comfortable with those?" Charlie asked.

"Yes. Once you get the hang of them, it's actually rather refreshing not having to cast a spell. Something relaxing about doling out destruction with your hands while your mind can focus on other things. I see the appeal."

"Good. Because it looks like you're going to get a chance to use them for real," he said, staring off into the distance at the rapidly approaching low cloud of sand.

Marban pulled out his skree and contacted the *Rixana*, quickly confirming Charlie's assessment.

"They say there is a sizable ground force approaching. It seems they landed just outside the targeting capability of long-range spells and were deposited by transports. The larger ships are hanging back, while the ground-skimming ones are making an assault approach."

"That's not good."

"No, it's not. The way they've configured themselves puts the *Rixana* at a disadvantage if she attempts to engage them before they reach our location. The larger ships' positioning would expose her flanks while she attacked."

"Meaning we have to handle the ground forces ourselves. Shit. This lets their ground skimmers leverage their position and speed capabilities as a checking piece against us. The *Rixana* is out of the fight."

"Yes. At least until they gird their loins and attack like men," Marban said with disgust. "Though in that regard, we are fortunate the Council is so unaccustomed to actual resistance. They are not used to a target who fights back, and fiercely at that."

"A degree of cowardice from the mighty Council, eh?"

"Yes, but also consider that Visla Maktan almost certainly wants to recapture your Zomoki. He'd direct them to use only smaller forces until she is under his control once more. Obviously, his men have not seen what befell her, thanks to your rather ingenious camouflage."

A commotion arose among the men as they noticed a lone transport rapidly approaching from their rear flank. Somehow

SCOTT BARON

one had slipped by the defenses, it seemed. That, or it had actually taken the long way around the wasteland, traveling solo to avoid drawing the attention a larger force would.

"Target that ship!" Charlie called out, calculating the lone craft would arrive well before the main attack group.

The pirate defenders quickly shifted a portion of their ranks into position and began casting spells. Their aim was true, but the craft's pilot was skilled, and nimbly dodged the attacks.

"Belay that! Hold your fire!" Marban bellowed.

"What are you doing?" Leila shouted.

"It's one of ours."

"It's a Council ship," she replied.

"No, that's not what I mean," he said, waving his skree. "Message from the *Rixana*. That transport is carrying one of ours. Your assassin friend, in fact."

"Bob?" Charlie said with a bit of confusion. "What the hell is he doing?"

"They reported spotting some rather frantic activity at the rear positions after their last aerial attack. I think something big may have gone down, and we'll be able to ask him in person in a minute."

Blasts rocked the far side of the wrecked ship, sending everyone diving for cover.

"Shit, they've got some projectile casters," Marban noted. "Clever. We'll have to divert defensive spells to counter the barrage, and that will give their ground forces a window to get within striking range."

The rebels cast fast and furious, deflecting the balls of crackling energy lobbed their way.

"What are they?" Charlie asked. "I've never seen anything like that."

"Could be a number of things. Maybe even Ootaki hair woven into the material. Whatever it is, there's enough charge in them to cause some pretty significant damage if they hit."

Their little band of defenders continued to cast, trying to pick off individuals at a distance between defensive spells. They were holding their own for the moment, but Charlie could clearly see it was a losing battle.

The stolen transport pulled to a stop behind them, and Charlie briefly nodded his greeting to the Wampeh as he disembarked. He would have asked him about the container he was hauling with him, but he had more pressing matters at hand, stopping the attack first and foremost. He raced back to a firing position along the hull of his ship.

Bawb quickly pulled the floating cargo box to the silent plasma cutter. He didn't know exactly how to gauge the amount of power the tech-magic device contained, and he didn't have time to learn. He would make his attempt, and would either succeed or fail.

"Come," he said as he opened the container. "I must remove that collar from your neck."

Hunze looked at the battle raging around her, terror in her eyes.

"I will protect you," Bawb reassured her. "But we must hurry."

She had lived a life of relative comfort, always pampered––as much as a slave would be––while being raised for her valuable hair. And now she was in such a foreign and hostile environment, her mind could barely comprehend the violence she was seeing. But the pale man had something in his eyes. There was power and death there, in abundance, but there was also something else. Something that made her trust him.

Shaky legs slid down to the ground.

"Good. Come," Bawb said, taking her hand and leading her to the cutter.

He quickly wedged the protective bits in place as they had done for Charlie and Leila, then he pulled back the protective wrapping and, without a moment's hesitation, activated the strange device and began cutting. The plasma burned hot, and the collar around her neck began to part, but the tech-magic device sputtered irregularly.

"Work, you cursed thing," he growled.

The band was nearly cut through, it was so close. He simply could not allow it to fail now. Ignoring the heat, he grabbed the hot ends of the collar and pulled fiercely as the cutter sputtered its last then fell silent. The sound of his sizzling flesh was horrible to Hunze's ears, but the pale, powerful man merely ignored what must have been excruciating pain.

He pulled with all his might, some of the magic taken from Emmik Yanna Sok flowing through him as he battled the last dregs of damaged magic holding the collar in place. Then, finally, the band snapped free. If not for the battle raging around them, the others might have noted the magical release, but given the circumstances, it went unnoticed.

Hunze looked at the band now lying on the red soil with disbelief, then timidly raised her fingers to her neck. For the first time she could remember, the familiar weight was gone.

Bawb assessed her and smiled.

"You are free," he said, satisfied. "Now you must hide. There is a battle to fight."

He reached into a pocket and retrieved a slaap, gingerly sliding it over his terribly burnt fingers.

"Wait," the Ootaki said, taking his hands in hers.

The assassin paused, unsure, as she reached up to her head and plucked a single hair from her head, then pressed his hands together, wrapping them with the long, golden strand. A strange sensation flooded the Wampeh's limbs, almost as if a swarm of insects was racing across his forearms and hands. Then, as quickly as it started, the feeling ceased.

The hair, he noted, had lost its golden glow, turning to dust as he separated his palms. Shock filled him, which for a deadly assassin was really saying something. But there it was. His hands were whole. Healed. What would have surely been a debilitating injury for the rest of his days was gone, and with only a single strand of hair.

"Freely given," he muttered under his breath in awe, realizing why so much power had been contained in a lone hair. "But why?"

Hunze took his hands in hers. "You freed me. You are a good man."

"Really, I'm not."

"You are," she repeated, and the way she looked at him when she said it made him almost want to believe her.

Bawb the Geist shook his head, clearing his mind. A battle was afoot, and he needed all of his wits and considerable skills if he expected to survive.

"The fighting is near. Come, you must hide."

The young Ootaki woman took his hand and followed him back to her container. Bawb carefully sealed her inside, then moved it behind their other supply boxes for better protection. Then he ran to join the fight.

CHAPTER SIXTY-FOUR

Charlie felt a flood of relief when he saw the pale assassin race up to join the battle.

"Where were you?"

"Busy," the Wampeh replied, quickly casting a flurry of spells at the rapidly approaching Council troops.

"Not cool, running off like that."

"I had things to do," he replied. "And you should know, the Council's doomsday weapon is no more. Well done, Pirate. Your comrades struck true. I merely finished the task."

Marban ceased firing a moment to slap him on the back. "Well done, my pointy-toothed friend!" he said with glee, then resumed firing both human and magical weapons.

Bawb assessed the forces growing near. They were falling in great numbers, but they had the men to spare and would eventually overrun their position.

"We are in an untenable position. Perhaps a hasty retreat is in order. I have procured a transport," he said.

"Not an option," Charlie replied. "The Council ships are positioned in a way that blocks any attempts at flight. It just doesn't move fast enough."

"Then it is only a matter of time," the assassin said plainly.

Charlie racked his mind. They couldn't flee, but they were so limited in fighting resources. If only the ship had power, maybe they could come up with something, anything, to sway the tide. Suddenly, a light bulb flashed on in his mind.

"Bob, do you still have that Drook power thing? The Drookonus, I think you called it?"

"I do," he replied, pulling the freshly recharged Drook-powered rod from his armlet.

"I need to borrow it."

Without a second thought, Bawb handed the invaluable tool to his human friend. Charlie had proven himself repeatedly. He hoped whatever he had in mind this time would prove worth the expenditure. In any case, they'd all be dead soon enough, and it was far better to use the power and die than leave a fully charged Drookonus for the Council to capture.

Charlie pocketed the magical device and handed Bawb his machine gun.

"Okay, you guys. Hold them as long as you can," he said, then took off at a run––right into the gaping hole in the wrecked ship's hull.

"Where in the world is he going?" Marban asked. "The fight's out here."

"I have no idea," Bawb replied.

The battle raged on for a solid half hour, Marban and the Geist fighting side by side, both using a combination of weapons in tandem. The Council forces had moved far closer and were chipping away at the pirate defenders, using their downed ground-level transports for cover as they bombarded their opponents.

One of the stronger casters leapt from cover, a major attack spell already on his lips as his slaap powered up. His head exploded in a mist of blood and bone.

"I must admit, these *are* rather effective devices," Bawb said, admiring his handiwork.

Marban laughed merrily. Even in the face of certain death, he seemed to revel in the fight.

"You've adapted to these weapons well, my friend. And so quickly."

"Necessity is a powerful motivator," Bawb replied with a toothy grin.

Soil filled the air as an enormous explosion rocked the far side of the ship.

"Looks like they have reinforcements," Marban noted with a sigh. "It is only a matter of time."

"Agreed. But we will meet a glorious end, will we not?"

"Indeed," he agreed with a strangely satisfied smile. "If we have to go, this is quite a way to—"

The ship shuddered violently. So violently that the surviving defenders and the wounded were forced to scramble back from the hull.

"What in the worlds are they doing now? What kind of attack is this?" Marban wondered aloud.

He got an answer when the topmost portion of the ruined ship burst outward, sending a shower of debris flying.

"Oops, sorry about that. Watch your heads down there," Charlie's voice boomed out.

All eyes turned upward, and despite their years of hard fighting and familiarity with the many faces of death and destruction, even the most hardened soul felt a primal reaction at the sight before them.

The giant mech climbed quickly out of the ruined ship's hull, jumping to the surface with a thundering boom as its enormous feet shook the ground. It was incomprehensible to the men of both sides, and, for a moment, everyone stopped their fighting, staring at the towering metal man in awe.

Then it turned toward the attacking Council forces and

charged straight at them, its mighty legs pistoning, driving it forward like a rumbling juggernaut, ready to demolish anything in its path. The terrified men scattered, utterly unsure what to do in the face of a giant, metal man.

Charlie nimbly maneuvered through their fleeing ranks, smashing their ground transports to bits, kicking and stomping all who tried to cast a spell against him. This was so much different from his time in the simulator. He was always a mediocre pilot, but this was something new. The mech felt faster. Stronger. Better. Connected to him on a visceral level. And better yet, the Drookonus now powering the mech did far more than simply activate its systems. He had access to *power*. Charlie felt almost a part of the machine.

Once he had managed to cast the right spells to tie the device in to the mech's systems, Charlie found he could redirect a fraction of the stored Drook energy to bolster his own spells as well, channeling them through the ship's exoskeleton, even though the Earth-born craft was never designed for such a purpose.

Laughing merrily while strapped securely in the pilot's seat, Charlie went on a cathartic rampage, smashing the enemy's forces like a playing child on a sugar high. It was *awesome*, and in mere minutes, the entirety of the remaining members of the Council ground forces had scattered, fleeing back toward the relative safety of their ships. Ships where Visla Maktan and his associates were monitoring the unfolding events with great displeasure.

The men ran, and ran, moving as fast as their legs would take them. Being on foot, it would take some time to reach them, but Charlie––despite the adrenaline high of his victory––knew far better than to pursue them. Instead, he turned back to join his friends and allies.

The mech settled onto the ground and powered down. Charlie popped the hatch and climbed to the ground, only to be met with an enormous embrace from his scarred pirate friend.

"A moving statue! An actual *moving statue!*" Marban roared with an enormous laugh. "You surprise me yet again, little brother!"

"Yes, even for you, that was, *impressive*," the Geist agreed.

"You didn't say it could do *that*," Leila added. "All you said was it was a tool of sorts."

Charlie grinned. "Well, it wasn't designed for that, but necessity is the mother of invention."

"I like the sound of that," Marban said. "Did you just come up with it?"

Charlie paused.

"Why, yes. Yes, I did," he said with an amused grin. "Now come on, I think we earned a little respite. We'd best use it to plan our next course of action."

Far across the wasteland, a furious Visla Maktan paced the deck of his personal cruiser. This was not how things were supposed to go. The Council had never suffered such a humiliating defeat, and at the hands of a mere handful of pirates and slaves at that. The fury building inside him grew, even as he forced himself to affect the image of a calm leader.

The human slave was proving far more resourceful than expected. Overwhelming force wasn't an option. Not if he hoped to recapture his Zomoki. And with a rebellion now fully underway, spreading Council forces thin across dozens of systems, they needed its power even more than ever.

No, this would require different tactics than the Council's standard fare, and he had an idea that just might work.

CHAPTER SIXTY-FIVE

The Council had taken hours to come up with a new plan of attack, and the rebels, though pinned down, were beginning to feel a glimmer of hope. They had lost the Zomoki, but in its place had a monstrous, moving statue. One that fought well, they were pleased to note.

How Charlie had managed to merge the powers of both galaxies was something of a mystery to Bawb, as well as the others.

"You say the Drookonus powered your 'mech'?"

"Yeah. It took some doing to get it to link to my systems, but once I figured out the basics, the rest sort of fell in place."

"But it should not be capable of such a thing," Bawb said, perplexed.

"Well, there's a saying on my planet. 'Don't look a gift horse in the mouth.'"

"Why would I look a gift in its mouth?"

"To check the teeth."

"But why would I not check the teeth?"

"Because it's a gift."

"How does this relate to the dental condition of this 'horse' of which you speak? Your people have some truly strange customs, Charlie."

The human was working on a clever retort when a barrage of incoming spells and enchanted projectiles began raining down upon them.

"Take cover!" Marban yelled as they ducked under the protective shell of the wrecked ship.

"You mind?" Charlie asked.

"Please," Bawb replied, handing him the Drookonus once again.

Charlie darted to the mech and climbed in, silently casting the web of spells that tied the magical power device into the giant machine. Moments later, it lurched to its feet, a faint shimmer to its exterior where Charlie had figured out a way to direct even more magical power to defensive spells.

"Let's get some!" Charlie shouted over the external speakers, then ran out to meet the oncoming assault.

It was a mixed bag attack. Some aerial, but mostly terrestrial once again. It seemed a great deal of effort was being placed at one specific point, as if their attackers hoped to pierce the defenses by sheer force and numbers.

Charlie and the rebel pirates stepped up to the task, pushing them back, while the *Rixana* dropped sporadic magic-dampening payloads from high altitude, their dispersal being unnoticed until they were just above the Council ships and too late to counter. It wouldn't stop the powerful wizards from casting, but it would diminish the harm they could do to their friends on the ground.

The battle raged, but seemed almost evenly matched. It was looking like the fight could go on for hours.

Just as Visla Maktan had anticipated.

A sleek shimmer ship darted around the perimeter, going wide before slowly approaching from the rear. By their very design, the vessels were unable to do much damage, being used solely for reconnaissance due to their inability to carry much weight while maintaining their shimmer camouflage. But it was enough.

The ship pulled next to the downed Zomoki, its hatch silently opening and discharging its lone passenger.

Malalia Maktan had come with orders to charm the human and stun him, then signal her father on his skree for reinforcements. She would then kill as many of the others as she could before the main forces arrived. It was her opportunity to redeem herself for what he had deemed her epic failure in letting him escape with the Zomoki in the first place.

"Dead, and cold," she said quietly, running her hands along the inert dragon's form. "Father, the Zomoki is no more," she said into her skree.

"What?" he said in shock. "What happened to it? I need that power."

"I do not know, but it is cold and hard as stone. What do you wish me to do?"

"Complete your task. The moving statue must be controlled by a powerful caster. Once you disable the human slave, find the one responsible for its motions and end them as well."

"As you wish, Father," she said, then set off to finish her mission.

All eyes were on the fighting going on between the two sides, leaving the visla's daughter relatively free to approach from the rear. If she could find Charlie and disable him, the rest would fall easily from her vantage point.

A shrill barking erupted to her left.

"What in the worlds––?"

Baloo, tied up far away from the hostilities had taken note of the intruder, and did not like her one bit, from his reaction.

"Silence, animal," she hissed, raising her slaap and casting a killing spell.

"*Klaatu endatha!*" a woman's voice said from nearby,

dispersing the spell and redirecting its energy harmlessly back at Malalia.

Leila stepped into view, one of Bawb's large konuses on her wrist. "Stay away from Baloo, you bitch!"

Malalia laughed.

"The groundskeeper's daughter, of all people. Oh, how delightful. "*Binari pa!*"

Nothing happened.

"*Binari pa!*"

Leila pulled aside her lapel and grinned.

"So, the slave managed to rid herself of her collar, I see. No matter," Malalia said, then began casting a flurry of attacks.

Leila was limited in her knowledge of fighting spells, and Bawb and Charlie had been primarily focusing on teaching her defensive spells, telling her you must learn to survive before you learn to strike back. At the moment, it was something she was very grateful for.

Malalia saw her tactic and laughed. "You are wearing a powerful konus, yet you can't even cast a proper offensive spell. Oh, my dear, how pathetic. This is going to be fun."

Leila continued casting as fast as she could. It was the same series of defenses over and over, the words and intent flowing from her lips easier with each repetition. Malalia didn't seem perturbed at all, toying with her, letting her block the spells, looking forward to eventually landing a killing blow.

Then something unexpected happened. Leila added a counterattack spell into the mix. An unusual one. Charlie's favorite.

"*Dipangu!*" she shouted, flinging a foul fecal smell into Malalia's face.

The visla's daughter was taken by surprise, and Leila used that window to draw within reach. Malalia instinctively cast a protective spell, aimed at stopping any magical attack.

That's when Leila punched her in the face. Hard.

The powerful denna saw stars, though she wasn't looking up into space. Then the former slave punched her again, a bloody gush springing from her nose. She tried to cast but couldn't enunciate through the gagging blood in her mouth. Leila didn't relent, proceeding to beat the ever-loving shit out of her former tormentor.

"And that's for trying to hurt Baloo!" she said, landing a ferocious kick to Malalia's jaw, knocking her soundly unconscious.

Meanwhile, Visla Maktan and his supporting Council emmiks and mesters moved forward, pressing the assault now that they had word the Zomoki was no more.

Charlie's mech was making a good showing of it, but it was definitely taking a beating. Soon it simply wouldn't be able to hold up to the abuse any longer. The defensive spells, however, were strong, somehow reinforced and amplified by the metal of the ship. Perhaps it was an element from Earth's foundries that reacted with the Drookonus so strongly. He wasn't sure, but if they survived this, he was quite curious to discover why.

The battlefield was littered with bodies, the fighting men spread out in battle. Bawb was a dervish of violence, darting through the enemy ranks, appearing, killing, and vanishing, living up to his deadly nickname.

A massive blow struck the mech's left leg. A small conveyance had been smashed into him like a battering ram, and like it or not, he was going down. Charlie greatly amplified the spells protecting the metal man as he fell, and in so doing, unintentionally saved his own life.

"*Azuro namana verata,*" Visla Maktan and the other magic-wielders in the fleet simultaneously cast as one. It was a spell not meant for combat, but the visla had learned a thing or two about asymmetrical warfare in his days. The spell was designed to freeze livestock for later use. With a slight alteration of the spell, the Council wizards had frozen nearly half of the rebel pirates, along with a few of their own men.

But that wasn't the end of it. They followed up with another mighty spell, one that turned the ground into quicksand, slowly swallowing the frozen men one by one.

Charlie grabbed the Drookonus, punched out of his harness, and jumped from the mech, diving hard for safety. And he almost made it, landing just shy of solid ground. Behind him the mech was already sinking into the soil, and to his horror, Charlie felt his legs pulling down as well, as his hands scraped desperately at the solid edge.

Not like this. I can't go like this.

A pain shot through his wrist. Marban had seen him go down and raced to his side, diving and grabbing him at the last moment. With a mighty heave, he pulled Charlie free.

"Can't have you dying on me, little brother. The ship's on its way, and there's still plenty of fighting to—"

The pirate fell silent, frozen in place.

Charlie looked around him and realized another spell had frozen still more men. The Drookonus in his hand was still powered up, the protective spell from the sinking mech keeping him safe in its final seconds of activity. Then the spell failed, and Charlie felt his legs go weak. Massive explosions of destructive magic erupted into the visla's defensive spells, shaking the ground violently.

Marban toppled over into the shifting ground, following the others to their sandy doom, but Charlie was suddenly airborne, carried above invisible shoulders in a dead run toward the safety of the *Asbrú*'s hull. Bawb dumped him to the ground, flinging his shimmer cloak aside.

"Are you all right?"

"I-I think so," Charlie stammered. "Shit. Marban—"

"I saw. But there is no time to mourn. The *Rixana* delivered a massive assault and bought us some time, but we must come up with a new plan."

"Right. A plan," Charlie said, climbing to his feet.

He looked around. More than half of their number were gone, either killed outright, or frozen and buried alive. Magic was low, ammunition was low, and the mech was gone. The human and Wampeh walked to see if there was anything in their supplies they might have overlooked. Anything to help their cause. What they found surprised them.

Leila sat atop a crate, feeding Baloo a bottle of milk. At her feet, Malalia Maktan lay trussed up and gagged, and very much worse for wear, both eyes swollen, her nose caked with dried blood.

Leila shrugged. "She tried to hurt Baloo," she said, matter-of-factly.

Exhausted as they were, and despite the dire situation they faced, Charlie and Bawb couldn't help but laugh.

It was short-lived, however. Friends had been lost, and more would follow. Now, above all else, they had to prepare.

CHAPTER SIXTY-SIX

"Still no word, Visla," Dinuk said, eyes averted.

"Then she failed," the furious wizard said after a moment's silent reflection. "Very well. Enough. We attack now, and I will lead the assault."

"But, sir, we don't know what—"

"The Zomoki is dead, Dinuk. That means we can focus all of our energies against the pirate ship above, should it be foolish enough to attempt to intervene once more. This time, we put an end to these rebels."

He stormed out of the chamber to prepare for battle. His claithes were still drained from assisting Mester Norkal. They would take time to recharge. Time he did not have.

"Had I known I would need them again so soon, I'd have left her to her fate," he growled as he surveyed the weapons at his disposal.

A pair of powerful slaaps would have to do. Fortunately, he had more than enough power of his own even without the artificially powered devices.

Bawb saw the attackers coming in the distance. "This is it. The visla's personal ship is leading the attack."

As if to punctuate his words, massive spells began erupting around them, only the ruined Earth ship's bulk protecting them from the onslaught. They would be overrun soon enough, but that wasn't enough for Maktan. He wanted them to suffer.

"How many of the pirates still wear collars?" he asked the Council intelligence liaison.

"It would appear at least a half dozen, Visla."

"Good."

"Without support from above, or that moving statue, we should be able to overrun them quite easily," Dinuk pointed out.

"Not good enough. They will pay for their folly," he said. "Make sure your slaves are secure."

"They are."

"Very well," he said, then uttered a spell. "*Amassula binari verata pa!*"

It was no ordinary spell. It was the closely held, *secret* Council spell that would trigger *any* collars in the area. A brutal back door in case of uprising, only known to a select few of the Council elders. The spell wouldn't last long enough to stop an entire rebellion, but in this particular instance, it would leave his prey in tormented agony while he landed and slew them with his bare hands.

The collar-wearing pirates fell to the ground, writhing in pain, clutching their glowing collars.

"What's happening?"

"It appears to be a Council trick," Bawb replied. "I will try to stop them."

He quickly slipped an additional pair of thick konuses onto his arms and began casting a secret spell known only to his assassin's sect. The glowing collars dimmed a moment.

"No you don't," Visla Maktan growled when he felt the disturbance in his spell, redoubling his casting efforts.

Bawb threw the konuses to the ground, hot from the

SCOTT BARON

engagement, then turning cold as ice, all of their stored magic used up.

"It is no use, the visla's magic is far too strong. Without support, we will be overrun."

Moments later, the visla's craft appeared above, hovering just the other side of Charlie's crashed ship. Despite the heat of battle, the powerful man couldn't help but be a little amazed at the unlikely craft from another galaxy. Then he turned his attentions to the men below and increased the force of his spell.

One of the pirates died convulsing from the power surging through his body, while the others foamed at the mouth. Visla Maktan smiled, his bloodlust high, when an unlikely shifting of an unnatural jumble of reflections caught his attention. He spotted the large, glowing collar of the Zomoki hidden beneath them.

"Clever," he said. "An unusual camouflage. But it is of no interest. The Zomoki is dea––"

The mirrors shifted and slid aside, falling to the ground, shattering to pieces. From beneath them, a dark and brittle form moved. Ara, her collar glowing bright, slowly rose to her feet.

"No. It was supposed to be dead!" he said in shock.

His terrified troops fired spells at her, but they had no effect as the Zomoki slowly rolled her neck, then took a deep breath, the dark and dull scales of her body cracking and falling away as she did. Ara took another enormous breath in, then let out a fierce roar that shook the very air the Council ships floated on.

With a flex of her mighty muscles, the dried scales burst from her body, sending the fragments flying like shrapnel. She shook vigorously as the dust around her settled, her body now glowing a bright, deep red, shining in the twin suns' light.

"Cursed creature!" Maktan yelled. "*Binari pa!*"

The stun spell hit hard, making her stumble backward a step. But that was as far as she went. Ara cast a fierce glare, her golden eyes fixed on the visla and his fleet. Then, quite to

Maktan's surprise, she *cast back* with a roar and a burst of flame from her mouth, dropping all of his men within range, while igniting half of his ships with magical Zomoki fire. The collar on her neck glowed even brighter as he fought with all of his power.

Charlie caught Ara's attention for a moment, and an enormous golden eye winked at him. Then she locked her gaze on Maktan and smiled. Moments later, the unbreakable collar around her neck exploded into tiny pieces, the shockwave knocking the smaller ships from the sky. Maktan's vessel shook, then sank to the ground, his Drooks immobilized by the impact.

"Impossible!" Maktan said in shock.

All around him the Council's fleet were turning tail and fleeing, the ground forces scattering while there was still hope of drawing another breath. The surviving rebels were few, but they were invigorated, charging at the downed ships across the field of death and destruction.

"Visla, we must go!" Dinuk said with more than a hint of urgency in his voice. "I have your emergency craft ready."

"What?" the visla said, still in shock. "Oh, yes. Load my essentials. I am right behind you."

Maktan looked at the dragon one last time. "Not today, but someday, you will be mine again."

With that, Visla Yoral Maktan did something he had never done before. He turned to flee.

The sight of his trusty head of security bleeding out on the ground, his neck sliced nearly all the way through, caught him off guard, as did the dagger plunged into his side. The blade was enchanted, and he found himself quite immobilized.

The Geist slid back his shimmer hood, standing close to his target. "It has taken a lot of effort to reach you, Visla Maktan. Many good men have died trying to stop your and the Council's plans. And all of that power, for what? To die without a whimper."

He gently slid the knife free and placed it back in its sheath. "Magic is a tool to do the job," he said, eyes sparkling with anticipation. "But not the *best* way for someone like you."

The visla saw his assassin's pointed smile, and Yoral Maktan experienced another new sensation at that moment. He knew fear.

The assault had left many of the rebel forces incapacitated, and Leila had done her best to aid them in their agony. Unfortunately, this left Malalia unattended, and while she was beaten and trussed up, she was most certainly not lacking in fight.

With great effort she sliced her bonds against a piece of jagged metal, opening her forearms in the process. But that was of no concern to her, knowing full well she could heal them later. For now, escape was all that mattered. Escape back to the safety of her father's fleet.

She saw his ship sitting on the red soil when she cleared the side of the *Asbrú* and took off running as fast as her feet would take her. Fortunately, the rebels were taking a moment to regain their senses after the Zomoki's display, which gave her enough time to reach his ship unnoticed.

Malalia raced to her father's quarters and stopped in her tracks. Dinuk, his head of security, lay in a pool of blood, his lifeless eyes staring at her, unblinking. Malalia didn't know what to do. Then she saw his slaaps, which she quickly stripped from his dead body and slid onto her trembling hands.

Carefully, she pushed the door open.

Crouched over her father was a partially invisible form. She moved around the edge of the room, both fascination and horror rising in her as she realized what was happening.

The pale man. The Wampeh. He was drinking her father's

blood, draining him dry. He pulled his red lips from the fallen man's neck and smiled.

"You again. My, my, you are resilient, aren't yo——"

He didn't get another word out before a full-force blast from the scavenged slaaps hit him, sending him flying out the large window, its force field deactivated when the ship went down. Again and again she fired, knocking him back until the assassin tumbled over the side, landing in the red soil below.

Bawb climbed to his feet, anger rising.

"Bob, we have to go!" Charlie said, reaching his friend's side.

"No! I must finish my task!"

"You can't finish it if you're dead. They're regrouping and coming back. And the *Rixana* sent word, reinforcements are jumping in from other systems. More than even Ara can handle. We have to go!"

Reluctantly, Bawb turned and ran with his human friend, looking back at the bloody woman standing on the visla's crashed vessel's deck. He had a feeling he'd be seeing her again. And when he did, he intended to finish her once and for all.

"What happened?" Leila asked when she saw Bawb's bloody face.

"I was interrupted. Malalia——"

"Yeah, the bitch got away during the fighting."

"She somehow acquired a slaap," Bawb added.

"Oh? With her power, how are you not dead?" Leila wondered.

"I should thank you for that," he said with a wry grin. "It seems broken teeth and a swollen tongue make it hard to properly cast a killing spell."

"I'm sorry, my friends, but could we possibly continue this discussion *after* departing this world?" Ara said. "A great many Council vessels are on their way, and if we don't make it to the upper atmosphere before they do, jumping will be impossible."

"She's right. We have a *lot* to talk about, but this isn't the time. Grab the essentials and let's get the hell out of here. The *Rixana* will grab her men and boogie out of here while we distract the fleet."

They quickly gathered up their gear, strapping the nearest cargo containers and supplies to Ara's harness, making sure the EVA suits were accounted for.

"There's no more time. We must go. Now."

With great haste they scrambled up her back and settled in atop her glistening scales. Ara flapped her mighty wings just once and shot into the air, quickly soaring to altitude for their jump. Like a phoenix reborn, Ara radiated power, and though it was something she'd done many times before, this time it felt easy. She cast without effort, and in an instant, they were gone.

CHAPTER SIXTY-SEVEN

The Zomoki flashed into being low in the atmosphere of a small planet orbiting a deep blue sun. The air was warm, at least compared to prior jumps, their arrival being far lower than in the past. The array of Charlie's Earth guidance system glowed faintly where it hung on Ara's harness. Her supercharged magic apparently continued to trickle feed the device during and even after her miraculous rebirth.

"This is awfully low for you to jump in, Ara. You okay?"

"Fine, Charlie. Better than fine, actually."

"I noticed. You care to tell me what's going on? We thought you were dead."

The dragon laughed gently in his mind. *"Why don't we land first, then I'll explain to everyone."*

Ara circled lower, casually gliding over a densely populated city and its surrounding industrial and farming areas. The planet, it seemed, was teeming with a rather modern group of inhabitants. This was not some backwater planet in an undeveloped system. This was a hub world.

After making her passes across the region, Ara settled atop a hill outside the city. Charlie and his friends climbed down from her back and took in the view. Despite the powerful sun's rays casting the world in that azure light, the view was breathtaking.

"What is this place?" Leila gasped. "I've never seen anything like it."

"Tolemac," Bawb said. "A planet of art and power. One of the few independent worlds in the Conglomerate, as well. They trade freely, though they do partner with the Council on most things. They did, however, retain their autonomy."

"Too valuable a society to subjugate?" Charlie asked.

"That, and beloved by those they deal with. I have not been here for many, many years. That my talents would not once be required on a world with such riches speaks volumes, wouldn't you agree, Wise One?"

Ara gazed over the sprawling society tranquilly. "It has been far too long since I visited this place, though this was an impromptu jump. In the heat of our escape, I latched on to the *feeling* of somewhere comfortable. Not home, per se, but close enough."

"So that's how it works," Charlie said. "I wondered how you were so accurate in your jumps. But now that we're safe on the ground, what the hell happened back there? And look at you. You're gorgeous. And a little bigger, too, if I'm not mistaken."

A fine plume of smoke wafted from the dragon's nostrils as she shook with gentle laughter. "Yes, Charlie, I *am* a little larger, though you would do well to remember––with other species at least––that females tend not to appreciate having that pointed out."

Leila laughed. "She has a good point, Charlie."

"Yes, even I know this," Bawb added.

"Guys, I know. Don't ask a woman's age or weight. That's, like, dude rule number one. But this is different," he said, looking Ara in her golden eyes. "You were dead. We saw it. Turned to stone, no less."

"Ah, yes. About that. I suppose I should have warned you, but the change took hold faster than I anticipated."

"So it was intentional?"

"In a manner," Ara replied. "As you well know, the waters have restorative, healing properties. They contain great magic, stored over centuries, and in years long ago, my kind would occasionally visit the great Balamar in friendship and bathe in his waters. But then they were thought lost. A belief you have disproven, I might add. With no one using their power, the waters grew so much stronger. As soon as I felt it wash over my scales I thought it just might be possible."

"What might be?" Leila asked.

"Possible for me to survive."

It dawned on Charlie. "You drank the waters not knowing what they would do to you."

"It was rumored to be possible, but none of my kind had ever dared attempt it. We are not a power-hungry race, and are quite content growing older and wiser, rather than risking it all in a grab for more power."

"You are a unique species in that regard," Bawb said. "I have seen many men and women throw their lives away in the quest for power. *Especially* those with the Council."

"Yes. But unable to be freed from the collar and with the Council's ships rapidly closing in on us, a drastic measure was called for. I figured I just might be old enough and powerful enough to survive. Survive, and be reborn, in a way. Apparently, I was correct."

The similarity to certain creatures on Earth struck Charlie. Dragons. Zomoki, they were called here, but the legends of dragons back home always described them as some variant of lizard. Creatures that shed their scales when they grow.

"You forced a rapid regrowth, didn't you? You made yourself shed your old skin by drinking the waters."

Ara grinned. "Very good, Charlie. Though the process was far more violent than I had feared."

"A hibernation. Like when you're in a cave, right? Only this time you shed far more than a few scales. You shed years of wear and tear. I've experienced the waters. We all know what they can do."

"Yes, they will make me combust," Bawb said with a grim laugh.

"You, maybe. But *us?* We were renewed. In Ara's case, kind of like a phoenix from its own ashes."

"A what?"

Charlie smiled. "I'll tell you the legend. I think you'll like it."

In another system, not terribly far away, Malalia Maktan cradled her gravely injured father's head in her lap. He lay still, so very weak. She had driven off the Wampeh, but the legends of their power seemed to be true. Yoral Maktan, one of the most powerful visla's in the Council of Twenty, had been drained of much of his magic.

The sound of rapidly approaching ships rumbled through in the corridors of the ship. Representatives of the Council, no doubt. Arrived to help in the fight, but too late.

"The Council, they cannot know," he whispered.

"I know, Father. I shall hold your position while you convalesce."

"You will do no such thing. Tell them to go, then fetch me a pair of konuses. I will heal myself while we pursue the Zomoki."

"But I can do this, Father. I––"

"Idiot child. You have disappointed me repeatedly. First you taint yourself with Wampeh blood, then you fail even the simple task of bringing down a mere slave rebel. Were you not my daughter––"

"Yes, you've said."

"Now get me my konuses before the others arrive."

Malalia remained in place, gears turning in her mind.

"Do as I say!"

"Father, you have said the Maktan line has been a cornerstone of the Council's power for generations." Her eyes sharpened. "I will do my part to continue our family's legacy."

Visla Yoral Maktan gasped as he felt the small blade slide between his ribs. Blood flowed onto Malalia's hands. It was so warm, she realized, as a strange thought entered her mind. She raised a bloody finger and proceeded to lick it clean, not knowing what to expect.

A slight tingle of power tickled her tongue, but was quickly replaced by the salty, copper taste of the dying man's vital essence. But there had been a little something. Perhaps the Wampeh truly had tainted her blood.

The doors burst open, and Mester Norkal and Emmik Urzan strode in, followed by their retinue of guards. Malalia quickly put on her best grieving face.

"My father has been gravely wounded," she said. "He may not survive. Quickly! The Zomoki and rebels that did this, we must find them. Find them and kill them before they escape."

"We tracked them when they jumped," Mester Norkal said. "They are not far from here. But what of the weapon. Our investment?"

Malalia sighed. "It was lost. Only the recently acquired Ootaki that had not yet joined the others have survived. They are with you?"

"Yes, a dozen of them, all told."

"It will have to be enough," she said. "We go after them. Now!"

"You are not in a position to give orders, Malalia," Emmik Urzan said.

Malalia glanced at her father as he breathed his last, then stood, calmly.

"*Hokta!*" The spell ripped through her bloody slaap, dropping Emmik Urzan dead to the ground.

"I am Malalia Maktan. *Visla* Malalia Maktan. Those who dare defy me shall face the same fate."

Mester Norkal thought a moment, then decided the odds were not in her favor. "Of course, *Visla*. What would you have of us?"

CHAPTER SIXTY-EIGHT

"What's that?" Leila shouted to the others as a dozen bright lights burned into the atmosphere.

"Council ships," Bawb said. "Has to be."

"But what are they doing?"

Her question was answered by the barrage of spells blasting the surface from great height. The accuracy was terrible, but whoever was in command of the attack didn't care about pinpoint precision. They were carpet bombing the surface, willing to wipe out anything in their pursuit of the escapees

"Quickly, we must depart," Ara said.

"But you just jumped. Can you do another so soon?" Charlie asked, climbing atop her back.

"I have the strength for a jump, yes. Though my accuracy may be a bit off. I suggest you don the protective suits from Charlie's craft, just in case we arrive off-target. Can you assist the others?"

"On it," Charlie said, quickly laying out the space suits and helping his friends put them on as fast as possible. Imminent death was a great motivator, and in under two minutes they were suited up, including little Baloo, safe in his own suit, clipped to Leila's own.

The attack that had been laying waste to the outlying areas was now toppling the shining towers of Tolemac in its indiscriminate destruction.

"They are killing innocents by the thousands," Ara said, horrified. "I cannot stand by and allow this. Hold tight."

With a powerful flap of her wings, she took to the air, flying toward the Council ships, casting defensive spells to protect the planet below, bellowing fire at the smaller craft attempting to target them.

Swarming up from the ground, citizens were fleeing in their own ships, a stream of frantically escaping vessels darting toward outer space, their passengers and crew watching the mighty Zomoki defend their world as the Council ships lay waste to their home.

Aboard her command ship, Malalia observed the battle with increasing fury.

"Why aren't you targeting them?" she raged.

"We are, Denna, I mean *Visla* Maktan. But the Zomoki is exceptionally difficult to hit. And she is *so* powerful. I fear our spells will be ineffective against her."

Malalia mulled over the situation a split second, then made a choice.

"Very well, then. Harvest the Ootaki."

"You wish to shear some of the Ootaki?" Mester Norkal said, trepidation in her voice.

"No. Not *some* of them. *All* of them. Do it now."

The already-deadly slaaps on her hands were glowing dangerously with her nearly uncontrolled rage, and Norkal knew very well that if she was even half as powerful as her father, Malalia Maktan could very well kill them all in her fury.

"Yes, Visla. Of course," she said, meekly lowering her eyes as she hurried off to relay the command.

Ara was doing her best to protect the city below, and while she was perhaps a bit weak for a jump, her power was more than adequate to cast defensive spells. In addition, though their spells were far less powerful, Charlie, Bawb, and Leila were casting right alongside her.

The fighting raged, and magic was flying haphazardly, the blue star's powerful magic radiation making spells go awry as often as not. Without careful preparation, it could be difficult to cast in such an environment, and the heat of battle was anything but ideal.

A small ship, surrounded by defensive craft, dropped from the belly of Maktan's main command vessel and began speeding toward them. The entire fleet quickly reversed direction, heading to space, then flying away at top speed.

"What the hell are they doing, Ara?" Charlie asked. *"Is this some sort of last-ditch kamikaze suicide run? Did we just win?"*

The dragon spun and dodged a flurry of spells, then fixed her gaze on the cluster of craft.

"They appear to be using smaller craft as a deflective shield, protecting the rear one. But this is not a surrender. There's something odd about this. What in the worlds are they—?" Ara fell silent as a deeply unnerving sensation flashed across her senses. *"We must jump. Now!"*

"Wait, but we're not in the upper atmosphere. And you're still wea—"

The Ootaki-powered device was far weaker than intended, the destruction of the majority of the Ootaki who were to provide its magic drastically reducing its yield. Nevertheless, the power was massive. It would not destroy an entire system, but a single world would be turned to dust.

And as it detonated, that was exactly what befell the hundreds of millions of citizens of Tolemac, its horrible magic blasting out and amplifying with the blue sun's powerful rays.

Ara didn't have time to prepare. She was in full-on panic

mode, latching on to the first habitable planet's signature that fixed in her senses. It was an odd and unfamiliar one, but she didn't have the luxury of even seconds to select another. Adrenaline-fueled, full of the charged waters of the Balamar Wastelands, and awash in the rays of the mighty blue star system, Ara jumped just as the magic of a dozen of the most powerful Ootaki on record hit.

There was a massive flash and a swirl of light, then a gut-wrenching pull as the Zomoki and her passengers were thrown violently through a disorienting void, before falling through the atmosphere of the lush planet they had miraculously arrived above.

"Bob, Ara's hurt. We need to slow the fall! Can you reach your Drookonus?" Charlie shouted through the space suit's comms.

"I hear you, Charlie," he replied, confused by the strange communications unit speaking in his ear but not caring at the moment. Not with their violent end at hand. "I can activate it, yes. But I need help arresting this fall. She is simply too large."

"I'm with you," Charlie said, desperately racing through the sing-song list of spells he had memorized over the years.

Come on, Charlie. Drook spells. Come on!

"Got one! Use this. '*Invario floromar necctu!*'" he shouted.

"Are you sure?"

"Just do it!"

Together, the human and Wampeh cast with all of their joined might, drawing power from the Drookonus. It was designed to power a ship, to direct inanimate objects, but given Ara's unconscious state, Charlie thought she rather fit the bill.

They were rapidly approaching a lush, misty bog, when the spell took hold, arresting the fall just before impact. Their gear shook free, tumbling to the ground, as did the Zomoki's passengers, a giant spray of muck and vegetation spraying through the air, covering them from head to toe.

Charlie popped off his helmet and staggered to his friends, helping them shed their gear. "You guys okay?" he asked.

"I think so," Leila said.

Bawb was clearly fine, though not at all pleased with their current location. It seemed they had crashed at the edge of a wooded glen, the murky bog cushioning their impact along with their spells.

Baloo, for his part, was thrilled to have a whole new world of smells to explore. Charlie, however, was at a loss as he squinted at the foggy terrain, trying to make out what sort of fresh hell they had arrived in. Night was falling, but they appeared to be alone.

At least the Council isn't here, he consoled himself.

Far, far away, Malalia Maktan stood on the bridge of her command ship, shocked at what had transpired.

"Play it again," she ordered.

The sight-capturing spell flashed to life on the wall.

"There," she said, eyes wide with amazement. "Just as it hit. Do you see?"

The others saw, indeed. The dangerous woman had just destroyed Tolemac in a fit of rage without consulting the other vislas in the Council, unleashing a huge amount of power they had built and saved for decades. This was bad. But even in the face of what would likely result in their punishment, if not death, they couldn't deny what they saw.

It was unlike any magic they had ever seen. At the moment of impact with the Ootaki-powered spell, the Zomoki had jumped, and there, locked in a frozen image, was her strange escape. A swirling hole of unknown power, and through it, a strange world.

CHAPTER SIXTY-NINE

The survivors had shed their muck-covered space suits and pulled their salvageable supplies to the bog's shore. Charlie and Leila were quite surprised when the Wampeh recovered a container they hadn't recalled seeing before. Even more so when he unsealed it, revealing a shaken, but otherwise unharmed Ootaki woman.

"This is Hunze," he informed them. "She is a survivor of the Council's slavery, and is under my protection."

This was an unexpected turn of events, but compared to what they'd just been through, it wasn't that big of a surprise, all things considered, so Charlie and Leila just smiled and went with the flow.

"Nice to meet you, Hunze. Any friend of Bob's is a friend of ours," Charlie said.

Bawb gathered up a cloak from a container and wrapped it around the girl's shoulders. "You must be cold after that," he apologized. "We had not planned on venturing so close to space."

"My hair keeps me warm," she said quietly.

That was when Charlie realized what he had thought was

merely a strange sort of clothing was in fact a great mass of hair, braided and woven around her body.

"That's a *lot* of hair," he said with a little grin.

Hunze's eyes went wide with fear.

"No, he does not mean it like that," Bawb said. "You can trust these people. They are my...*friends.*" He said the word strangely, almost as if speaking it in that context for the first time in a very great many years.

Baloo had no fear of the new addition to their little unit, and a radiant smile flashed across Hunze's face as he plunged his damp nose into her leg, seeking out scratches.

"There is no way the Council can hide what they did, you know," Bawb said. "The slaughter of so many. It will not bode well for them."

"No, I'd think not," Charlie said, a bit nauseated at the thought of just how many had perished. "The rebellion will definitely grow because of it. The question is whether they will—"

A metallic rumbling echoed through the foggy air, rapidly drawing closer.

"Circle up," Bawb said, adopting what appeared to be a casual stance in front of Hunze. Charlie, however, saw the tension in his jaw. The Geist was on edge and ready to strike if need be.

"What the hell?" Charlie murmured.

Twenty men clad in what looked an awful lot like armor, sitting atop what looked like horses, rode toward them through the lifting fog, another fifty men wearing leathers of some sort, carrying torches and long pikes marching alongside them.

Bawb didn't know this race and instinctively cast a translation spell, fixing it to himself and his companions, ensuring all nearby would be able to understand one another. Too many conflicts had occurred due to poor communication throughout history. He didn't intend for this to be another one.

SCOTT BARON

"Who art thou?" the man riding atop the foremost beast said.

"Uh, we're strangers here, just passing through. We mean no harm."

"Harm? Only invaders would attempt to sneak into my kingdom through the marshes in the dark."

"What? Oh, that. Right. Well, we crashed here, you see. It was totally unintentional. Our Drooks had a problem and lost power, so down we came. Really, we'll be out of your hair in no time."

"You, woman," the man said to Hunze. "Come here. I would see you better."

Bawb stepped forward a pace. "She is under my protection."

"Your protection?" The armored man laughed. "Who the hell do you think you are?"

"I am Bawb, of the Wampeh Ghalian. The Geist. And you shall not touch a single hair on her head."

The metal-clad man laughed, sliding the helmet from his head. "*You* will not allow it? Do you know who I am, *boy*?"

"No. Nor do I care."

"I am king of this realm," he replied, bloodthirst in his voice. "And I shall have your heads atop these pikes."

Bawb sighed. "I have done that in the past to make a point, and I must warn you, it is far messier than you think, and rarely worth the effort."

A look of disbelief passed over the king's face at the sheer gall of the man. Charlie, on the other hand, couldn't help but laugh.

"Dude, we really should start calling you Vlad instead of Bob."

"Vlad? I actually rather like the sound of that name."

"You jest?" the king roared. "I shall behead you all!"

"Really, we don't want to fight. Just leave us alone and we'll be on our way as soon as our friend feels up to it."

The king was enraged. "Kill them!" he bellowed.

Two of his faithful knights dismounted and drew their swords, quickly striding toward Charlie and his friends.

"Fuck it," he said with a sigh, exhausted and not feeling like dealing with yet another magical battle.

Instead, he pulled his pistol from its holster and shot both of the knights dead, the bullets easily piercing their armor. The roar of the gun echoed in the night.

"What magic is this? Men, kill them all!"

"May I?" her welcome voice asked in Charlie's mind.

"If need be. Give me one more try, okay?" he replied, turning to face the king.

"I'll say it again. We have no quarrel with you, and I am sorry for what happened to your men. But as a leader, you should know better than to threaten strangers in your land. Especially those not looking for a fight. Now, please, lead by example and just walk away."

"Away? Fool, it is a fight you have found. Kill them!"

Charlie sighed. "Fine. This foolishness ends now. Ara, if you'd please."

The massive dragon reared up from the mud, what had appeared to be a simple hillside shedding the mud and peat from her back, revealing her true form, golden eyes bright even in the darkness.

A flurry of arrows rained down on them, but Charlie had expected it, easily batting them aside with a simple spell, though with her thick scales, Ara was in no need of his protection. He had even cast without moving his lips, as his friend constantly chided him to do.

The king flew into a rage, then drew his sword and charged. Ara sized him up, then incinerated him with a single breath, then ate both the king and his horse whole.

"Not bad, actually. I could grow to like this type of beast. Though the metal the man was wearing is a bit too tangy for my taste."

391

"Gross, Ara."

The remaining men launched another volley of arrows, which bounced harmlessly off of her hide.

"You know, you'll just make her angry," Charlie said. "You really should stop it."

"What is this creature?" a terrified knight asked. Charlie couldn't tell for sure, but he suspected the man had soiled his armor.

"She's a Zomo—I mean, she's a *dragon*. A fearsome beast, capable of great destruction," Charlie replied. "And she is my *friend*. Now, are you quite finished? Because I think she's still hungry."

The formerly fierce armored men and their retinue of archers and pikemen looked at one another, hesitant and unsure.

"I suggest you play nice and say you're sorry. Unless you want to meet the same fate, that is," Charlie said, tired, irritated, and not having patience for any more of this nonsense.

The knights looked at one another, pale and in shock. A murmur passed through the ranks, stopping when the man who appeared to be their leader held up his hand for silence. He climbed down from his horse, his men doing likewise, dismounting as one. Following his lead, they all slowly drew their swords, then planted them in the damp soil as they knelt before the angry spaceman.

"Our apologies, Sire. I am Captain Sheeran, of the king's guard. Please, spare these men from your mighty dragon."

"Dragon?" Ara asked, silently.

"Just go with it, okay?"

"Fine."

"Apology accepted," Charlie replied. "Her name is Ara, by the way. And she is the mightiest dragon you'll ever see."

"And what is your name?" Captain Sheeran managed to ask in a steady voice.

Impressive. He got over the sheer terror pretty quickly, Charlie noted.

"I am Charlie," he replied, then paused in thought. "*King* Charlie. Now, take me to *my* castle."

"*Wait. Did you just make yourself king?*"

"*Why not? You ate the old one.*"

"*By that logic, shouldn't I be king?*"

"*I doubt they could make a crown that big.*"

Charlie and his friends were provided with horses, the men eager to please their new ruler. The floating boxes that carried their supplies were a marvel, though not as much as the dragon that escorted them, flying low overhead as she surveyed the countryside.

King Charlie. I like it. But where the hell did we wind up this time? Charlie wondered as they rode.

The fog thinned the further they went, dissipating entirely as they rounded a pair of hills. Charlie looked at the sky, marveling at the stars.

Crazy. Some of the constellations even look like—

Adrenaline flooded his veins, his magic spiking involuntarily from shock.

"*What is it, Charlie?*" Ara asked, sensing his flash of distress. "*Are you okay?*"

"*Yeah, I am. But, Ara, I recognize these stars. And I know that moon.*"

"*You do?*"

"Yes," he replied, the reality of his situation setting in. "*Looked at it my whole life. I have no idea how it happened, and it looks like we're a few thousand years early, but I'm home, Ara. This is Earth.*"

"*Your world? Your galaxy?*"

"*Yep. Some way, somehow, I'm finally home. And I'm a king.*"

BUT WAIT, THERE'S MORE!

Follow Charlie on his continuing adventures in the second book of the Dragon Mage series: Dragon King Charlie

THANK YOU

Reader word of mouth is an independent author's lifeblood. So if you enjoyed this book and have a moment to spare, please consider leaving a rating or review on Amazon or on Goodreads, or even sharing it with a friend or two. Your support is greatly appreciated.

Thank you!

~ Scott ~

ALSO BY SCOTT BARON

Novels

Living the Good Death

The Clockwork Chimera Series

Daisy's Run

Pushing Daisy

Daisy's Gambit

Chasing Daisy

Daisy's War

The Dragon Mage Series

Bad Luck Charlie

Space Pirate Charlie

Dragon King Charlie

Odd and Unusual Short Stories:

The Best Laid Plans of Mice: An Anthology

Snow White's Walk of Shame

The Tin Foil Hat Club

Lawyers vs. Demons

The Queen of the Nutters

Lost & Found

ABOUT THE AUTHOR

A native Californian, Scott Baron was born in Hollywood, which he claims may be the reason for his rather off-kilter sense of humor.

Before taking up residence in Venice Beach, Scott first spent a few years abroad in Florence, Italy before returning home to Los Angeles and settling into the film and television industry, where he has worked as an on-set medic for many years.

Aside from mending boo-boos and owies, and penning books and screenplays, Scott is also involved in indie film and theater scene both in the U.S. and abroad.

Made in United States
North Haven, CT
23 September 2024

57784081R00243